QUEEN OF NOWHERE

JAINE FENN

GOLLANCZ

LONDON

Copyright © Jaine Fenn 2013
All rights reserved

The right of Jaine Fenn to be identified as the author
of this work has been asserted by her in accordance with
the Copyright, Designs and Patents Act 1988.

First published in Great Britain in 2013 by Gollancz
An imprint of the Orion Publishing Group
Orion House, 5 Upper St Martin's Lane,
London wc2h 9ea
An Hachette UK Company

A CIP catalogue record for this book
is available from the British Library.

isbn 978 0 575 09699 8

1 3 5 7 9 10 8 6 4 2

Typeset by Deltatype Ltd, Birkenhead, Merseyside

Printed by CPI Group (UK) Ltd, Croydon cr0 4yy

The Orion Publishing Group's policy is to use papers
that are natural, renewable and recyclable products and
made from wood grown in sustainable forests. The logging
and manufacturing processes are expected to conform to
the environmental regulations of the country of origin.

www.jainefenn.com
www.orionbooks.co.uk

For the geeks, who may well inherit the Earth

Intelligence errors are factual inaccuracies in analysis
resulting from poor or missing data.

Analytic Culture in the U.S. Intelligence Community, CIA website

Eat freely with glad heart; fear here no dearth:
But of the tree whose operation brings
Knowledge of good and ill, which I have set
The pledge of thy obedience and thy faith,
Amid the garden by the Tree of Life,
Remember what I warn thee, shun to taste,
And shun the bitter consequence: for know,
The day thou eat'st thereof, my sole command
Transgressed, inevitably thou shalt die

Paradise Lost, John Milton

PART ONE

A WILFUL GHOST

If you're listening to this, I'm dead.

    You've had some dealings with me; you might even recognise the name 'Orzabet'. That doesn't matter. I don't matter. What matters is the information you're getting now, and what you choose to do with it.

<file under: Preface>

After three weeks of luxurious indolence, Bez was ready to become someone else. She had, however, intended to make the change on her own terms. Not like this.

The cops were waiting when she came out of customs, a man and a woman in silver-grey uniforms, looking faintly uncomfortable. The female officer said, 'Are you Medame Oloria Estrante?'

It was a doubly pointless question. For a start, the station authorities would not accost disembarking tourists randomly: they knew, or thought they knew, whom they were addressing. Secondly, Oloria Estrante did not exist. But the fact that the cops used the name, and sounded convinced by it, went some way to allay Bez's initial alarm. 'I am,' she said, in the tone of perplexed irritation hub-law expected from the leisured classes. 'What can I do for you, officers?'

The starliner's other passengers were filing past, some of them looking back curiously. Bez made herself ignore the unwanted attention, at the same time clamping down on the urge to start analysing possible causes of, and ways to deal with, this unexpected and unwelcome development. First priority: stay cool.

The female officer said, apologetically, 'We'd like you to come with us.'

Bez had fired up her basic headware – the legal suite, as she thought of it – the moment she spotted the law. Her overlays confirmed the pair were what they appeared to be; or, at least, their uniforms had genuine tags. That reduced, but did not eliminate, the chance of this being Enemy action. Bez favoured the two officers with a put-upon frown. 'Where to? I was hoping to get some shopping in during the stopover.' She needed to keep conforming to their expectations.

'Just to our offices, to answer a few questions.'

She sniffed. 'Do I have a choice?'

'I'm afraid not.'

'Then you had best lead on.' She kept her tone faintly incredulous, like someone with nothing to fear, but the moisture had left her mouth and breathing evenly took some effort. At times like this she wished she had mood-mods. Fortunately there weren't many times like this.

As the cops fell into step either side of her she asked, 'Can you at least give me some idea what this is about? I'm assuming there's some mistake, which I'm happy to help you clear up.'

'I'm not sure it would be appropriate to say,' said the male officer.

The female cop said, 'I believe Medame Estrante has a right to know what the matter pertains to.' The woman was one of those people who treated the conspicuously rich with deference, regardless of how unpleasant they were in return. Bez had noticed such behaviour before when in this persona. 'We're investigating certain financial irregularities,' the cop explained.

Trying for an air of indignant confusion, Bez asked, 'What sort of financial irregularities?'

'The theft of a significant sum from a semi-dormant account.'

'Theft?' That kind of accusation warranted outright indignation. In some ways interstellar tourists were the easiest cultural group to impersonate; their disdain for those without the excessive wealth required to travel the stars made them imperious and unreasonable, like holodrama caricatures of themselves. 'Ridiculous.'

'The account in question belongs to a Frer Yolson. Does that name mean anything to you?'

Yolson? Ah, of course. Not the Enemy after all, thank the void.
'Medame Estrante?'

She started at the sudden interjection of the male cop, who had just laid a hand on her arm. She flinched, shaking him off. How long was it since anyone had deliberately touched her? 'As I thought, a simple mistake,' she said, fighting the colour rising to her cheeks.

The female cop was staring at her. 'Are you sure, medame?'

'Yes,' she said firmly. She needed more data, but she doubted these two knew much and she was far from confident of her ability to get info from them without arousing their suspicions. 'Shall we carry on and get this foolishness sorted out?'

'As you wish.' The female cop started walking again. Bez fell back into step and concentrated on controlling her physical reactions.

They came out on to the dockside proper.

Tarset was the least glamorous hub-point in human-space, and for most tourists it was no more than a brief stopover between more interesting destinations. The station's dockside district provided the usual services – bars, brothels and basic supplies – but the main concourse was a no-frills, three-storey strip-mall. The only concession to aesthetics was the faux starry sky projected across the ceiling, barely visible through the holo-ads.

The irony was that she had not needed to disembark here at all. She could have checked her datadrop from her cabin on the starliner. But should anyone be taking an interest in her, they might wonder why, when most of the other passengers made at least a cursory visit to the station, Medame Estrante did not; and yet, at the same time, she accessed a secure messaging service. Besides, while genuine tourists were sniffy about the place, Bez had a certain fondness for Tarset. The station had originated as a mash-up of ancient colony ships, and the resulting state of constant renovation left it full of usefully untended spaces, physical and virtual.

Should she access the drop now? It might contain intel indicating why the law were so eager to talk to her. No: her escort would notice if she tuned out, and Oloria Estrante was meant to be a good little Salvatine, eschewing ungodly implants. Going virtual would blow her cover.

It was early evening so the mall was moderately crowded. She weighed up her chances if she made a run for it. Given how co-operative she had been so far, the law might not expect that. If she could get into the service tunnels, it would just be a case of holing up for a while then re-emerging with a new identity. But first she would have to physically evade her escort, who outnumbered her, were combat-trained and carried weapons. Far better to think her way out.

Their progress through the evening crowds was making heads turn. For someone who lived her life as a wilful ghost, such scrutiny was intensely uncomfortable. Bez read the current time-stamp from the chrono display in the top left of her visual cortex, taking it as a single integer and computing its square root. When she had regained her equilibrium, she began to consider how the current predicament could have arisen.

The good news was that whatever the problem was, it did not appear to be related to the Estrante persona itself, merely to the associated funding. The underlying cause would probably be human fallibility. It usually was.

The rich and reclusive 'Frer Yolson' was maintained by the agent she designated as Beta16, one of her oldest and most reliable financial agents. His databreaking skills were sound, and he had no reason to betray her. At least, not willingly ...

This situation could have been initiated by the Enemy after all. Why else would anyone in the hubs care about the financial affairs of a religious recluse in a distant spur-system? Even if these were genuine cops acting on genuine orders, there was still no guarantee this really was just about the funding of a single persona. And once she was in custody, she would no longer be in control of the situation. Should the real question be: from where did the orders to arrest her originate?

No. Bez applied what she thought of as 'best-case principle' to kill that line of reasoning. When paranoia became a way of life, the ability to selectively ignore negative outcomes became a vital skill.

It was either that or constantly be paralysed by fear and indecision. Once she knew more, she would re-assess.

The two officers stopped, so Bez did too. They had arrived at a bank of elevators.

The door opened to reveal a half-full car. At the very front, a young woman and young man were kissing passionately. Everyone paused, united in mild, indulgent embarrassment, waiting for the pair to register that they were causing an obstruction.

If she had been by herself, Bez would have turned and strode off without looking back. But stuck between the two cops, she was no longer an observer but a participant, complicit in this minor emotional drama. The lovers were so rapturous in their oblivion. So very happy. Her heart started to race with an emotion more complex than the fear she was already suppressing, and moisture tickled the corners of her eyes.

The girl noticed what was happening first and broke away from the boy with a shy giggle.

Once upon a time, that was me. Then the Enemy forced my lover to walk into the sun, and everything fell apart.

The boy blushed and looked at his feet. The pair shuffled back to let Bez and her escort enter.

A barely audible sound whispered round the dozen others already in the car, somewhere between an approving sigh and stifled laughter. Events like this brightened a dull day for normal people. Not for Bez. Already tense from maintaining the façade of the Estrante persona under close inspection, the sight of people experiencing the ordinary joy she'd had torn from her opened up a hollow in her soul. She blinked hard but one stupid, weak tear still escaped down her cheek.

She stared at her chrono again, eyes unfocused from her surroundings. She must take this incident as a reminder of her resolve. People would always love and hate and hurt each other but if – when – she succeeded in bringing down the Enemy, then such pain would occur on purely *human* terms.

By the time they reached their stop she had her emotional

7

responses locked down. If the cops had noticed the stray tear, they gave no sign.

They exited the lift at one of the station's admin floors. Tarset's corridors ranged from the plain through the highly customised to the barely serviceable; in this section the décor was well maintained if utilitarian. Bez called up a public map on a soft overlay and used it to track their progress, confirming that they were heading for Tarset's main Legal Enforcement offices.

Any residual thoughts of finding out more from her escort had been blown away by the sight of the lovers, which had left the shell between appearance and true self worn dangerously thin. Instead she found herself recalling the two other times she'd had brushes with the law. The most recent, three years ago on Mercanth station, had been as a victim of crime: hers had been one of a dozen rooms in a mid-level hotel targeted by thieves who had (inexpertly, in her opinion) hacked the locks. The cops had been mildly perplexed by her lack of possessions. The earlier and more alarming occasion had been on Indri, when her illegal headware was newly installed and she had yet to hone her databreaking skills. It was nineteen years ago, but the memory still made her uncomfortable. Her first ever attempt to ride a trickle-down, and she had screwed up. She got dumped and tagged trying to break through the firewall of a local banking node. Because the alert had been raised before she had penetrated the bank's system, she had got away with a fine.

As they rounded the final corner she shut down her headware. Police offices, like customs posts, had active scanners.

She held her head high as she walked through the open door into the hub-law offices, but she could not shake the feeling that she was walking into a trap that was about to snap shut behind her.

PURE PROGRESSIONS

You're receiving this databurst because I need you to act on
what it contains. I'd say, 'Don't let me down' but my feelings
and expectations are of no relevance. You've almost certainly
never even met me.

Instead I'll say this: Don't let humanity down.

<file under: Preface>

The doorway gave into a public reception area with seating provided for those who had business with the law. It was currently
empty, save for a surly-looking pair of youths who might equally
well be victims or suspects. Beyond a half-frosted partition, police
work was proceeding in an orderly fashion at desks and screens.

Bez hesitated for a moment in the lobby but her escort carried
on, sweeping her forward with them. The female officer explained,
'We'll take you straight through and get you booked in.'

'Booked in?' Although she had expected this, Bez did not have
to fake her concern at the prospect.

'It's standard procedure. And if there *is* a misunderstanding,
then the quicker we deal with it, the quicker you can get back to
your ship.'

Bez could only agree with that sentiment.

Once on the far side of the partition, a man in a slightly different uniform approached them, carrying a slate. He addressed Bez
with awkward deference. 'Right, medame, if you would kindly
read the text and acknowledge just here—' He turned the slate
around for Bez to see.

Bez read the display carefully. It was a relatively straight-
forward statement of her rights and current status. She was being
asked to agree to a short initial interview, after which hub-law

9

could, at their discretion, hold her for another eight hours without charge. They could ask further questions during this time, aided by lie-detection technology, in which case she was entitled to a defence advocate. She remembered something similar from her first brush with the law, though in that case they had charged her at the first interview, then released her promptly once she paid the fine. Not seeing any other choice, she thumbed the base of the screen, tensing slightly as she did so, even though the Estrante ID itself was sound.

When she handed back the slate, the booking officer murmured, 'If you'll follow me, someone will see you now,' almost as though this was an appointment she had made for herself.

They left the original escort behind and went up a side corridor to a plain door, which opened automatically.

Bez tried not to be dismayed at the grim-looking room beyond, which contained only a thick-topped desk and two chairs. The woman standing by the chair on the far side had a uniform featuring more silver than any Bez had seen so far today. However, she smiled and greeted Bez politely. 'Come in, Medame Estrante.'

Bez made herself walk over to the table. 'Thank you,' she said, with as much dignity as she could muster. 'And you are?'

'First Detective Hylam. Do sit down.'

As Bez seated herself she saw one piece of silver that did not denote rank: the detective wore a discreet lapel pin in the shape of a loop-headed cross. That could explain what was happening here. The hub authorities got hundreds of requests from planetary law-enforcement agencies seeking fugitives who had fled their jurisdiction, but the hubs were only obliged to act on the most serious; other cases were at the discretion of the local ranking officers. If Hylam was a Horusi, this could be simple religious solidarity. Salvatines were the exception on the hubs, and this particular believer might be taking an interest because the alleged crime involved a follower of her own subsect. Plus, from the look of the office outside, the law was having a slow day. Bez tried not to let her relief show.

Detective Hylam sat down. 'I won't waste any more of your

time than absolutely necessary. Could you confirm that Frer Yolson of the Eagle's Retreat Preceptory House on Sestine-Beta is your second cousin three times removed?'

Bez smiled at the detective. 'Actually, he's my third cousin twice removed.'

'Yet he sends you an allowance. Quite a big one.'

Bez dropped her gaze, reminding herself that this woman thought they held shared religious beliefs. 'I know, and I bless Mother Isis for his generosity.'

'I'm sure you do. I'm still a little unclear on why Frer Yolson, who appears to have access to considerable funds, does this.'

'He won the planetary lottery, which prompted him to take his final vows. So my late father told me anyway.' *Treat this as a test you know the answers to; give those answers clearly and firmly.* 'As for his generous donations ... as I'm sure you know, an accident left me without immediate family.'

The detective nodded, a little impatiently.

'Although I've never met Frer Yolson, I think there may have been some unresolved family issues for which he is now making amends. Also, I get the impression he hopes I will use his gifts to live a good life.' She shrugged in what she hoped was a self-deprecating fashion. 'I suspect my choices disappoint him, may Osiris forgive me.'

'I doubt that, on both counts.' The detective leaned forward and looked Bez full in the face. 'Given Frer Yolson doesn't exist.'

Surprise was an allowable reaction. Even so Bez felt her face fall, the careful mask slipping. 'I'm shocked to hear that,' she managed to croak.

Detective Hylam narrowed her eyes. 'Are you?'

Bez said nothing. This was no mere game of data; the woman across the table from her was used to dealing with liars. Despite giving all the right answers, Bez had aroused her suspicions. The detective continued, 'I appreciate your cooperation so far, however, I'd like to keep you in for further questioning.'

'But my starliner leaves in less than four hours!'

'In that case, perhaps you would prefer we institute full

interrogation protocols and conduct a more thorough interview immediately?' With one finger she gave the table, with its hidden tech, a meaningful tap.

Bez saw the trap now it was too late. Agree, and even if she managed to spin a convincing lie – which she doubted she could – the detection equipment would reveal her attempts at deception. Refuse, and she was admitting she had something to hide. All she could think of was to play for time. 'I believe I have the right to legal representation during a full interview?'

Hylam looked nonplussed. 'You do.'

'And I can choose my lawyer from anyone currently on the law-office roster?'

'My, you did read your waiver carefully,' the First Detective said frostily.

'Then I would like the chance to make my selection before we proceed.' This was much worse than the first time she had fallen foul of the law all those years ago. Back then, she had just begun her life's work, and had had relatively little to lose. Now she sat at the heart of a vast hyperweb. If the authorities pulled on this one loose thread, everything could start to unravel. Nearly two decades of building up contacts, gathering evidence, preparing to strike: to fail now, when she was finally getting close, was unthinkable.

As the detective muttered into her wrist-com, Bez thought, *If only you knew why I'm doing all this* ... But she didn't know. No one did. And they mustn't, not yet.

A few moments later the door opened to admit the booking officer. 'Follow me please, medame.' The man looked disappointed, as though he had expected better from someone of her status.

'Where to?' Bez said, fighting the sensation that events were slipping beyond her control.

Detective Hylam said, 'Somewhere you can make your selection in peace. I'll be seeing you later, Medame Estrante.'

The booking officer led her down another similar corridor, though these doors had numbers on. He stopped outside the third door on the right, numbered '6', and passed Bez a spare slate. Bez took the proffered device and went through the door. It closed promptly behind her. She found herself in a room with a bed, table, chair and sanitary unit, plus a drinks dispenser and basic ents unit built into one wall. No exits, unsurprisingly. Perhaps the station had other less comfortable holding cells for the sort of criminals unlikely to sue for wrongful arrest.

She sat on the edge of the bed and ran a hand over the slate to wake it. As well as the list of duty lawyers, the simple menu included an option to access the cell's ents unit. Bez dialled up some plainsong, choosing a recording by Elarn Reen. The late Medame Reen was not Bez's favourite but she thought the choice apt.

For the benefit of any surveillance, she began to scroll casually through the info on the slate. At the same time, her mind raced.

She had to get out of here before this went any further and that would require hacking the law. Her mission rarely pitted her directly against law-enforcement organisations' virtual security, which tended to be as tight as that of banks, and a lot more dangerous. At least she was inside their firewall. She activated her headware, initiating her full hacking suite.

While the tech came online she queried the availability of the duty lawyers. Most of them were free now, or would be within the hour. When she found one whose current availability was listed as '3 hours+' she selected him. Three hours was before the starliner's departure, so when the law opened the door to an empty cell the cops would most likely look for her on the liner. The standard shift change was in just over two hours, and ideally she would prefer different front-office personnel when she left. So, two to three hours was her window of opportunity. She could work with that.

She put down the slate, sat back and closed her eyes, watching her chrono count out two minutes while she let the pure progressions of the music centre her. Then she brought her deep overlays online.

The ents unit glowed in her enhanced vision, but nothing else changed. She counted out another thirty seconds just in case, then tuned fully into the local virtuality. The room faded to grey obscurity.

The stats associated with the ents unit confirmed her assumption that it hid a camera. Just basic vid with minimal shielding, by the look of it. The camera might have hidden defences, in which case any attempt to hack the device could trigger an alarm. But that was a lot of trouble to go to unless Detective Hylam already knew about her headware and was waiting for her to actively condemn herself by using it. This was unlikely: as well as the legal issues surrounding entrapment, Salvatines weren't renowned for being tech-savvy. If they suspected she was a databreaker, someone would have put an inhibitor cap on her before they allowed her inside their firewall.

She moved her virtual presence across the room, waiting for the subliminal connection as her headware engaged with the camera. The link was weak but that was a good sign: she would expect nothing more from a dumb remote.

Beyond the camera she sensed the local virtuality, the salt-sweet taste of the world of logic and data, a world that made more sense than the real ever did. From the safety of the camera she accessed the stats associated with her cell. She made sure she understood the immediate set-up then moved out cautiously, initially only as far as the camera in the next cell. The occupant was a local man in for possible assault. The cell beside that was empty. The one beyond held a woman, but she was too old, in on extended detention for drugs-related charges. In the fourth cell she found another man. The fifth was empty. The person in the sixth was the right gender and age, and the timing was suitable, but when Bez tapped into the camera's vid feed for that cell, she saw that the woman was too fat. She might suffice if there was no one else. The seventh and eighth cells were empty. The ninth held another man.

She accessed the local registry, which confirmed that there were only twelve cells in this block. Had she known this beforehand, she might not have been so confident of her plan. Still, there was no going back now.

Ten was empty. Eleven, however, was as near perfect as she was going to get. Arrested for unlicensed sexual commerce, and ten years younger than Bez, but there was a good match on height and build. Only twenty-three minutes until this woman was due to be released, though, which was before the shift change. Was it worth the risk? When a peek into the final cell showed it to be empty, Bez decided it was; with only twelve cells to choose from and no guarantee of any new occupants arriving in time, she might not get another chance. Bez still took care to alter the readouts on the unfortunate prostitute's cell. She could not risk failure – and further incrimination – at this stage. Then she drew her awareness back along the line of grey boxes with their clusters of near-identical glowing camera icons.

Reaching the camera on her own cell, she accessed the device's buffer, where she employed one of the standard tricks in any databreaker's repertoire. For the next three hours, the footage the camera relayed would bear a remarkable resemblance to the period Bez had spent sitting quietly on the bed before going virtual.

She paused, checked the stats on her own cell, and then blinked herself back into the real.

Sixteen minutes to go. This was going to be tight.

The first five minutes involved more sitting still while she triggered, and then endured, the sensations of crawling skin and itchy scalp that accompanied any physical transformation. She picked the pre-programmed setting closest to the prostitute's colouration (pale skin; straight auburn hair; blue eyes), adjusting the hair's length and adding the copper and crimson highlights on the fly.

She opened her eyes, blinking repeatedly to clear them. They would water for a while yet. Raising her hand, she saw her skin was already several shades lighter. She ran her fingers through her hair, pulling out the tight curls Madame Estrante had worn; the action also served to lengthen the synthetic strands. The prostitute wore her hair up, so Bez needed to consider that too. But first she had to do something about her clothes.

She unpinned the pointless half-circle hat her tourist disguise had demanded, and shrugged out of the equally flamboyant embroidered coat. She turned the coat inside out then rubbed it, and the hat, across the seat and along the floor by the bed. She wrapped the hat in the coat and stuffed the bundle behind the pillow on the bed. When the items were found, it would be possible to extract samples of her genetic material from among the others she had just picked up, but even if someone went to such trouble, they wouldn't get a positive trace. Only criminals were subject to detailed genetic profiling and Bez had no criminal record in any of her incarnations.

Now for the blouse. She pulled it over her head and used the hatpin to rip the fabric of one sleeve. *If this were a holodrama*, she thought, *then I would be using that pin as a weapon, or have some hidden gadget in it.* The blouse tore easily, as befitted expensive and delicate fabric. She didn't have time to hack the blouse's tag so she used the pin to rip it out of the collar.

One of the detached blouse sleeves made a passable hairband, once she'd teased the final kinks out of her hair. Nothing she could do about the lack of cosmetics. She put the blouse back on, knotting it high under her bust to expose her stomach. Her trousers were too smart, but once she had torn out the tag, she tucked the ruined waistband inside to expose a bit more belly, which went some way towards the right image. The shoes were fine: she avoided tagged footwear, to allow for situations requiring a quick change without full props.

All done, with one minute and thirty-four seconds to spare. She shut down her headware.

If the original booking officer was the one that came for her, she was lost; but she had noticed a number of administrators in the front office, and in her admittedly limited experience of such places, roles were strictly demarcated: the booker-in did not also book out.

Time was up but the door remained closed. She counted out a minute. Two. Three. At times like this she almost wished there were a deity to pray to. Finally, what felt like twenty but was less than six minutes after she had assumed her disguise, the door opened.

The man who stood there was a stranger. Bez exhaled and gave him a genuine smile. The admin officer smiled back, his gaze flicking down to her bare midriff.

Bez forced herself to ignore his expression, reminding herself she was meant to be a sassy streetwalker. 'About time!' she said, starting across the cell.

The man was looking at her face now. He appeared puzzled. Was it the lack of makeup?

'You all right there, "Toni"?' He glanced at his slate as he spoke. Toni was the girl's work-name.

Bez put a hand to her wet cheek. Damn: thanks to the tears from the eye-colour change, she looked like she had been crying. Was he sympathetic? He sounded like he was mocking her. She settled on saying, not untruthfully, 'I've had better days.'

'Yeah, well, perhaps you should think about getting licensed? The law's here for your protection too, you know.' He held out his slate. She thumbed it to acknowledge her release. She had only changed the ID, charge sheet and timer on her cell, not the associated biometrics. Nothing beeped. He stepped back and said, 'I'll show you out.'

A few people looked up as she walked through the office, trying, not altogether successfully, to keep a provocative swing in her step. When Detective Hylam emerged from a side corridor, Bez's heart skipped, but she kept walking. She could feel Hylam's eyes on her. The woman started to walk briskly through the work-stations, heading her way. *Keep walking, keep walking, don't look at her.* Any moment now she would shout out, or an alarm would sound—

Out of the corner of her eye Bez saw Hylam stop and raise her wrist to take a call. Bez resisted the urge to break into a run.

When they reached the lobby the admin officer gestured to the door. 'Now don't take this the wrong way,' he said, 'but I'm hoping I won't see you here again.'

'Me too,' said Bez fervently, and walked out.

A POSSIBLE LOOPHOLE

You think we live in an age of freedom after millennia of
tyranny. You think the Sidhe Protectorate is gone and that
we've seen the last of those evil aliens who masqueraded as
beautiful women.

You're wrong.

Perhaps you'll stop this recording now because anyone
who claims the Sidhe are still around has to be crazy, right?

At the risk of stating the obvious, that's precisely what they
want you to think.

<file under: Core Data>

Her heart was still racing when she turned the corner at the far end
of the corridor. Even though no alarms rang out and she could see
no signs of pursuit, she strode through the admin sector as quickly
as possible, even more unwilling than usual to make eye contact. As
she got further from the law offices, a modicum of calm returned.

Back in the bustle of the main mall she found an empty public
convenience, and unhinged the false top on her left little finger.
From inside this she fished out a pair of spotcams, sticking them
to the two walls flanking the furthest cubicle from the door, which
she then locked herself into. She had already brought the relevant
headware online so she checked the local infoscape to ensure she
was not on any cameras apart from her own. Only when she was
certain she was unobserved did she dive fully into the station's
public virtuality. Here she activated a previously hidden dataegg,
releasing and synchronising various minor changes around
Tarset's infoscape. Now she was Kenid Sari, a casual worker with
a solid Tarset ID and a cashstick containing barely enough credit
to buy one good meal on a starliner.

Once her consciousness returned to the cubicle, she initiated the programmed appearance change for the new persona. Two transformations in one day hurt, but the specialist who had installed her adaptive mods claimed the tech was good for up to three complete changes of dermal and follicular colouration in a given twenty-five-hour period. The eyes took longer to recover so they would have to remain blue for now.

After retrieving her cameras she collected the physical components of her new identity from an automated self-storage unit. In another washroom elsewhere on the concourse, she changed into a threadbare tunic, thin slacks and worn deck shoes, all untagged as befitted this persona's lowly status. A cheap slap-com – the default for anyone whose finances or religion proscribed implants – completed the disguise.

She purchased some strong analgesics and booked into the Salvatine mission house on the dockside. A church hostel was the last place a god-fearing cop would look for a high-living, spiritually lapsed fraudster. She had to endure a half-hour recorded sermon on the godless ways of her fellow hubbers before she could check into her coffin-sized accommodation, but that gave the painkillers time to work.

Once she was both calm and free of pain she accessed her datadrop from the physical safety of her tiny room. The mission house's virtual security was laughable, so it took little effort to spoof her signal off the bordello on the level above.

She had no strong expectation of finding a message waiting; her permanent datadrops existed to field unscheduled transmissions from her most trusted agents – the Alphas and Betas. Most of her beevee messaging protocols changed constantly, and for the day-to-day administration of her huge web of contacts and agents she avoided beevee altogether. But the fact that the permanent datadrops were intended for urgent matters only made it more important to check them regularly.

On finding a datapacket to download, her initial assumption was that it came from Beta16 and contained a warning that the Yolson cover ID had been blown. But the tag was not his. The message originated from a world called Gracen. Up until a year ago, Bez had barely heard of the place. Then she had come into possession of a fabulous trove of information: the memory-core of an Enemy ship. Along with other gems, the files from the *Setting Sun* listed the cover identity of every Sidhe in human-space, intel she had been striving to piece together for years. As a result, Bez had surmised that the insular religious democracy of Gracen was essential to the Enemy's ability to hide amongst humanity. She had recruited an agent there, but up until now Alpha83 had had little to report.

Bez methodically applied the relevant decryption to the message. She knew better than anyone that codes were made for breaking, and that beevee communications could be compromised; but having a key known only to the sender and receiver, a key that had been physically despatched on a timed-to-erase dataspike, was as close as you could get to unbreakable encryption. Quantum effects might allow secure in-systems communication, but for interstellar transmissions the oldest and simplest techniques were still the most reliable.

When she finally read the resulting plaintext, she sat up so quickly that she banged her head on the cube's low ceiling.

Dolls definitely made here. Estimate: one-fifty to two hundred over the last thirty years. Artisan is solo but v. careful. Have located a possible loophole, which may require data skills. Details can follow: please advise protocol.

About a third of the Enemy used names in the same format. The same format implied the same source. Her research had revealed Gracen to be the most likely source. This message confirmed it. 'Dolls' was Bez and Alpha83's pre-agreed codeword for top quality false IDs. Someone on Gracen was procuring watertight identities that allowed the Enemy to impersonate humans. Bez could guess how: 'reviving the dead' was the ideal way to create a persona for long-term use; it was one she used on occasion – 'Oloria Estrante' was a resurrectee – although given the time and effort required to seed such a persona, most of her identities were more transient. But the scale of the Gracen operation was breathtaking. If Bez could prove a mismatch between the original biometrics and those of the almost-human aliens now using the identities, she would have the evidence to unmask a third of the Sidhe in human-space.

Despite her excitement at this potential breakthrough, Bez made herself get a full night's sleep before responding to the message. The next morning she sent a manifoldly spoofed and deeply encrypted beevee message to Alpha83, requesting full details of her findings on a dataspike. The 'spike would go to an interim address, which would initiate a blind pick-up by a secure shipping company, then another dead-drop via a human agent, then a second journey by courier, to eventually end up in a physical drop-box at Kotane.

Kotane was two transits away in the direction of the Gracen system, and though it was not a hub she visited much, she had a watertight and well-funded local persona there. Bez's peripatetic lifestyle came from a need to be in the right place at the right time to pick up and despatch the myriad messages and dataspikes required to run her network, while never staying in one place long enough for potential pursuers to catch up with her. Being dumped on Tarset had already blown her original schedule, and Kotane was a suitable next stop should the Gracen lead not pan out. It would be at least a week before Alpha83's reply reached Kotane, so she could make a brief stopover at the intermediate hub-point to take advantage of the upcoming beevee trickle-down. Where possible, Bez preferred to leave a hub after any serious databreaking, and given there had already been trouble here she was loathe to ride the trickle-down whilst on Tarset.

Priority messages like the one from Alpha83 would propagate across all her permanent datadrops throughout the hub network, but she needed to initiate rerouting protocols from her transient datadrops at Gerault, the hub she had originally been travelling to.

First, she pinged Beta16. Given 'Frer Yolson' was a fiction he maintained, the problem most likely originated with Beta16 himself. A ping held no significant content and required only a simple coded acknowledgement; it was as secure as beevee messaging got.

Although she accepted the need to rely on compromised communications and human agents, Bez sometimes fantasised about a universe with no such restrictions, where the sum total of information that defined and shaped – no that *was* – reality was freely accessible and fully comprehensible. After all, the universe itself was just data, albeit data that self-organised in unexpected ways.

Before getting down to detailed rerouting and re-planning, she looked into onwards transport. By now the authorities would know that 'Oloria Estrante' had not left Tarset on the starliner, so they might still be taking an interest in lone female travellers. The Kenid Sari persona was limited on funds; Bez had a couple of more affluent secondaries here, but none of her Tarset personae held credit sufficient for starliner travel, so she would need to buy passage with a freetrader. But there was one way of making an exit that would not require pre-booking, and would cost her nothing. It was time to call in a long-standing favour from one of her most valued Alpha agents, one of the few she thought of by name. In some ways, Captain Reen was the closest thing she had to an ally.

Her ride was currently in a distant system and would take a while to arrive, and beevee charges were already eating into Kenid Sari's minimal resources, so after she had completed her virtual housekeeping Bez got herself a job. According to the local labour exchange, a chandlers' shop in the mall needed restocking after a refurbishment. In this case, programming bots would have been more expensive than employing menial human labour. The four ten-hour shifts provided Bez with a bit of ready cash, and took her mind off the wait. It was also good cover, given interstellar criminals rarely stacked shelves. Not that Bez thought of herself as a criminal. Any laws she broke were a means to the end that ruled her existence: to take down the hidden alien menace that had destroyed her life and was secretly manipulating countless billions of other lives. Occasional victimless financial hacking was an acceptable price to pay.

The job turned out to be physically demanding, and one of the permanent staff took a dislike to her on the logical if incorrect assumption that she was a hab-rat trying to make good. She did her best to keep up with the work and reacted as she always had to bullies, with cowed incomprehension.

After two days she received an acknowledgement from Captain Reen that he was on his way. However, there was still no word from Beta16. She had sent the original ping on a low priority channel in order to avoid attracting attention, so the problem could just be the limited capacity and scheduling issues inherent in the beevee network outside the hubs. Or he could have suffered a mishap. One of Bez's greatest fears was that the Enemy would find one of her agents, read everything they knew from them, then take their place in her network. That was why every Alpha and Beta had their own unique codes, which changed regularly, and why no one who worked for her, with the exception of Captain Reen, had ever knowingly met her face-to-face. In some ways, Beta16's continued silence was encouraging, because if the Sidhe had subverted or replaced him, she would expect them to be actively using him against her. However, until she knew what had happened she had to cut all ties to Beta16, which meant putting the Estrante persona, with its considerable resources, on ice.

She was not sorry when the contract at the chandlers came to an end. She spent some of her earnings on a beevee connection to check a few of the forums she followed. The expensive and time-consuming beevee-board interactions she had originally pencilled in for Oloria Estrante's visit to Gerault hub would have to wait.

As there was still no word from Beta16 she decided to ask for a datapacket summarising recent news from Sestine, his home system. The beevee charges would seriously deplete Kenid Sari's remaining funds, but she had to know the reason for her recent near miss before she acted on the Gracen data. Only when she was sure the two events were unconnected would she truly believe that the break from Gracen was not too good to be true.

STANDARD NEON-GRID ARCHITECTURE

There are 571 Sidhe living among us, pretending to be human.
Not much in a population of trillions spread over hundreds
of systems, you say. You're right: most of their dirty work is
done by the human collaborators, agents and patsies they've
dominated, blackmailed, bribed or simply fooled into acting on
their behalf.

<file under: Core Data>

Discovering that Captain Reen was running late, Bez tried to be patient. His revised ETA meant she would still be on Tarset for the trickle-down. This synchronisation sweep was a big one, the quarterly update that re-aligned massive volumes of non-essential information across human-space; and, notwithstanding the Gracen lead, she wanted to keep her options open. The trickle-down contained intel she needed, as well as being an ideal opportunity to move around some funds. She would just have to take what precautions she could and hack it from here.

She started by changing both her hotel and her ID, deactivating the Sari identity and taking on that of a freelance engineering specialist. Her new, somewhat smarter accommodation was within the means of this new persona.

She had already checked all her physical drop-points; the dataspikes they contained were scheduled updates from Beta and Delta agents. She spent the remaining day on Tarset cutting a couple of new one-time codesets and starting the resulting dataspikes on their long and circuitous journeys.

When the day of the trickle-down arrived, she found herself unexpectedly nervous. The timing would be close: the beevee update was due to begin at midnight, and Captain Reen should arrive eight hours later. She got some sleep in the afternoon then took a late meal in a dockside diner, after which she ambled round the mall.

She slipped away from the carousers and late shoppers and up to a service door, which opened at her approach. Her current tags gave her access to areas off-limits to the sort of low-life she had recently been impersonating; specifically, to sections of the station currently under refurbishment, which on Tarset meant a lot of empty real estate.

Once in the darkened service corridors, she called up an overlay to guide her to a gutted commercial unit that backed on to the main mall. She accessed the unit's virtual stats to check the projected rebuild schedule and current asking rent. A later completion date and lower rent than the last time she'd looked; they must still be having problems with the ducts.

She walked past the door, turned a corner then retraced her steps. Not that she had seen anyone besides a late-shift maintenance tech since leaving the mall. He had clocked her tags and smart coveralls, giving her a vague nod. But it did no harm to check for a tail. She also slipped into the local virtuality. Equally empty. Back in the real she positioned her spotcams, one beside the door and one on the wall opposite.

She had already brought the relevant headware online so the lock was easily defeated. When the door opened she dialled up her visual acuity to offset the lack of light and saw, as she expected, a large bare room with partitioning and duct segments stacked against the side walls. Bez looked at the ceiling. She hardly needed to have fooled the lock: she could have just climbed in through one of the holes up there. The room was unpleasantly cold and permeated with a smell like over-ripe cheese. She stood in the doorway for a few moments, memorising obstacles, then stepped inside.

The door closed behind her, leaving her in darkness. She navigated carefully across the room to the far wall and sat down. She had a few minutes yet. She calmed herself physically, performing breathing exercises to get her body into a low trance, putting aside the discomfort of the chill, smelly room and the darkness pressing on her eyes. Mentally she was as sharp and ready as she ever was, the prospect of the upcoming trip into the infoscape enough to focus her mind.

Her chrono flashed: time to go. She leaned back against the wall and tuned in to the virtual.

She floated above a plane of light. All around her a network of straight white lines defined countless cubes reaching off into infinity; different cubes glowed in subtly different colours and with different degrees of opacity. Overhead, the artificial structures were bright against the simulated darkness. The cube nearest her – that representing the Freetraders' Alliance office, which her physical location backed on to – was a bright emerald green. As well as the visual simulation, she could hear faint buzzing in several different keys and frequencies. The more distracting sensual analogues that marked the flow of information – taste, touch, smell – she relegated to the back of her awareness.

This was the standard neon-grid architecture, the default virtual schematic for a compact infoscape such as that of a large space habitat. Some station sysadmins tailored their virtualities, but most didn't bother. People who spent a lot of time in virtualities tended to impose their own filters, converting their perceptions of the virtual landscape around them into an analogue of their home, or their favourite vacation spot, or a scene from a game or holo. Bez never bothered: what was the point of having to open lockers, conjure whirlwinds or impale monsters to get what you wanted?

Her entry point was carefully chosen. She knew of several physical hideaways in the station that brought her out into the correct part of Tarset's virtuality. She had considered entering near one of the station's deep consolidation nodes, but getting access to the correct realworld space would have required a more serious hack. Besides, she planned to focus on freetrader data this time, something she had missed out on during the last major trickledown. If there was time, she would scope out the financial updates afterwards.

She spent a while – a whole second in the real – not interfacing with anything, just watching.

When she was sure her presence remained undetected, she turned her viewpoint upwards to the 'sky' of coloured boxes connected by glowing streams. The view was dimmer than it would be during the day: as though concepts like 'day' and 'night' mattered here. Even out in the real, night – like Universal Time itself – was a human construct, but thanks to the shiftspace beacons it was a consensual and constant illusion that held across all hub-points. Planets might be constrained by the vagaries of their physical environments, but hubs, Bez liked to think, ran on a grander and more objective schedule.

She sensed the arrival of the trickle-down at the same moment she got visual confirmation. A resinous, tingling sweetness on the air, and suddenly the architecture brightened as though coming alive. White light flashed through the grid, the notification to local systems to make ready to accept incoming data. The glow faded, and a green-blue wave started to rush along selected data-lines.

Seen from within a virtuality, the synchronising beevee update was not a trickle; it was more like a tsunami.

Like water, its force diminished as it divided. By the time the flow reached the Alliance's cube, it was no longer a wave but a roiling stream impossibly constrained inside an invisible tube.

The volume of data was still impressive. The Freetraders' Alliance administered interstellar trade, and even though travel between the stars was rare, people always wanted to purchase – or make a profit on – commodities they did not have.

She propelled herself gently upwards to meet the datastream, at the same time raising her 'arms'. She paused, waiting until the stream touched the cube behind her, then closed the distance. The virtual analogues of her hands uncurled into the stream.

A jolt ran through her. The power of the interface might take a less experienced databreaker's breath away and eject them back to the real. But she expected this, anticipated it even.

What was actually happening, at speeds too fast for her consciousness to register even in this artificially accelerated frame of reference, was a complex interaction between the programmes in her head and the software that maintained this virtuality.

She forced her hands further into the datastream. She was sinking into the base virtuality now, her visual awareness gone, the maelstrom of data feeding back as a jumble of smells, sounds, tastes and sensual pummellings across her palms and fingers. Ignoring the distractions, she opened her hands wide. Information started to flow into her, through her.

She remained like that, conscious thought processes suspended, for some time. Even after her search-and-sift agents had completed their work and ghosted copies of the relevant information into her internal storage, part of her wanted to stay as she was, in this state of perfect grace.

She had experienced the temptation, and resisted it, before. Besides, there was work to do. She withdrew her hands.

As the visual simulation of the virtuality began to re-assert itself, she sensed that something was wrong. Not here: there was an intrusion from the real. Reluctantly, she pulled her consciousness back, patching her overlays into the feeds from her spotcams just in time to see a figure step up to the door leading into the room where her body was lying.

CHANDIN
(Cyalt Hub)

Everyone has secrets.

Commissioner Phal Chandin only had one secret of any note, but it could ruin his life. Today, newly installed in an executive office on the penthouse level of Cyalt station, he was thinking about families, and The Mistake (as he referred to it when he thought about it at all) was lurking at the back of his mind.

With his recent promotion came reward: a second child licence. Most people who attained his rank gifted the licence to their own offspring. But Commissioners were usually of an age when raising a family was no longer practical or desirable; Chandin, however, had worked hard to become the youngest Commissioner to serve the Pan-Human Treaty Commission for nearly a century. And Gerys was still willing to become a mother again – assuming, she said, that he wanted to be a father again. He was well aware how uneven the burden of rearing their son had been, thanks to having a father married primarily to his work. And his workload was only going to increase. If Milos had shown any interest in starting a family, he would have passed on the licence, but there was no point. Chandin had no problem either with his son's sexuality or his avowed dislike of children, but he would have liked a grandchild, or even better, two. The alternative, to donate the licence to the lottery, was not one he felt comfortable with—

A soft chime disturbed his reverie.

He acknowledged the arrival of his visitor – precisely on time, as expected – and smiled when the door opened to admit Tanlia Crene, his oldest friend and most dangerous enemy. Tanlia advanced smoothly across the carpeted expanse of his office, her gaze sliding past him. 'I have to see,' she said breathlessly by way of a greeting.

He knew that playful tone: always the games, with her. He stood up. 'Be my guest,' he said, gesturing to the picture window curving up and over the outermost quarter of his office.

Tanlia strode right up to the edge, stopped, and said, 'Well, that is something!' as though coming across the view for the first time. Although they were both hubbers by birth, and had seen the crater of Cyalt station from most angles, it was only up here near the rim that the enclosed world of three million souls could be fully appreciated.

Chandin, coming up to stand beside her, had to agree the view was spectacular. They were almost, but not quite, close enough to the curved, blue-tinted roof to make out details of its construction. The sculpted terraces lining the gently sloping walls were arrayed before them. The lowermost buildings, down on the crater floor, were largely covered over – constantly seeing richer, luckier people looking down on you was somewhat oppressive for those who had to live down there, as Chandin well knew – but most of the homes, bars and offices in Floorville still boasted brightly coloured or holo-decorated roofs, which from this height blurred together into a seething dish of colour and flash. Further up the side wall, block housing gave way to the terraces proper, and gaudy holos were replaced by more tasteful foliage. In some of the residential districts the living covering of greens, golds and reds almost obscured the homes it grew across. The plants became more restrained up in the administrative levels but they were still present, along with sculptures and other tasteful ornamentation. Occasional changes in use broke the pattern up here, from the glass-panelled reception area backing on to the docks on the planetoid's surface to the rainbow-traced water gardens, a masterful example of grav-based trickery that was in itself reason enough for tourist liners to stop at Cyalt.

Busy though he was, Chandin waited for Tanlia to turn away from the window. Finally, her voice heavy with apparent regret, she said, 'I suppose we should get to work.'

'We'd better, hadn't we?' he concurred in a similar tone.

The inevitable barb came as she turned away, and was delivered barely loud enough for him to hear. 'It's a shame the angle doesn't give you a better view of the water gardens.'

Chandin repressed a smile. Once, a comment like that might have riled him. Although such sniping had no effect these days, they were both too old and set in their ways to change the rules of their relationship, even if that relationship had moved on immeasurably in the decades since they had, with the naivety of youth, thought they might be lovers for life. He said, 'And how's your new office?' She had also got a promotion, even if it was not the one she had wanted.

'It's perfect,' she said warmly. He half expected her to invite him to come and see for himself, and was almost disappointed when she didn't.

Tanlia waited for him to sit, and to tell her whether she should position herself beside him, like an equal, or across the desk, like a subordinate – which, for the first time in their joint rise through the ranks of the Commission, she was.

Chandin said, 'Shall we sit at the conference table?' The floor space of this office significantly exceeded that of his and Gerys's first apartment. He gestured for Tanlia to take the seat at the head of the long glass-topped table, then sat down at right angles to her and called up an overview of the agenda they had both agreed on. It included everything Chandin's predecessor had been responsible for, along with the areas Chandin and Tanlia had worked on together previously; effectively, she now had his old job, albeit with increased responsibility and status.

Today was merely the opening of negotiations. Chandin both dreaded and anticipated the coming weeks, as the lines of responsibility and power were redrawn. But whatever else was between them, they understood each other's strengths and weaknesses, and cared about their work. Contrary to the two conflicting holodrama representations of the Pan-Human Treaty Commission, it was neither staffed by power-hungry despots exercising undue influence over hapless worlds, nor by faceless bureaucrats mindlessly obsessed with the minutiae of shiftship licensing and interstellar import laws. The power the Commission wielded was executive and had no direct impact on the day-to-day lives of the vast majority of humanity; the function of the Treaties was to ease and police the interfaces between the 933 independent states – hubs, worlds and multi-planet systems – comprising human-space. He and Tanlia would never have risen as high as they had without the ability to see the bigger picture and leave the details to trusted subordinates.

By mutual agreement they began with relatively straight-forward matters that only tangentially impacted their division. The Treaties the Commission enforced had been drawn up soon after the Protectorate fell, when humans were reconstructing their culture after millennia of oppression; though comprehensive, they were also a thousand years old. Times changed, and Legal's primary role was to use modern precedents to reinterpret documents written in another age. It was important work, ideal for those who enjoyed doing a thorough job, but theirs was one of the smaller divisions in the Commission. If he and Tanlia had followed similar career paths in Financial or Trade, they would have been unlikely to end up in direct competition for the same, top position.

The first item on the slate was *Recruitment and Training*. Chandin was grateful for the Commission's policy of recruiting bright students from poor backgrounds, but was happy to have responsibility for the entry-level interstellar law programme revert to Tanlia's office.

The second item was *Historical Documentation*. Another one for Tanlia, whose role made her less of a figurehead than Chandin. Tanlia gave him a rueful smile and said, 'I know you'll miss this job.' She had always held Chandin's interest in obscure documents from Protectorate times to be an affectation, irrelevant to the Commission's current role.

She had a point, but Chandin relished such irrelevancy; he enjoyed tracing the course of decisions made long ago for which he bore no responsibility and whose eventual outcomes he knew.

'I can always take up archive-surfing as a hobby in my new-found spare time,' he said heartily.

Tanlia raised an eyebrow at that.

Next came *Hub Liaison*, which, after some discussion, Chandin acknowledged was one for him.

Chandin glanced up at the change in the quality of light; the view outside had faded to twilight and the office lights had brightened to compensate. He straightened up and rubbed his aching neck. 'Do you want to call it a day – well, evening – yet?' he asked. Given what the item after next was, he would prefer to stop soon. 'Or I can order refreshments, and we can plough on,' he added, before she could disagree on principle.

'How about a drink and we'll carry on for a while … unless you need to get back to your family.'

He ignored the implied slight – Tanlia knew it would be several hours before he could justify going home – and called for a jug of caf. The drinks arrived with commendable efficiency – another testament to his new status.

Sorting out the basics of the internal audit process took longer than expected, and when they sat back Tanlia said, 'I don't know about you, but I reckon IDOB's going to need a session all to itself.'

'You're not wrong there,' he said, letting only the expected level of relief show in his voice. The Identity Oversight Bureau, with its absurd acronym and far-reaching powers, had been Chandin's main responsibility for the last nine years. Sometimes it had felt like the main focus of his life. Now that he was the face at the top of his division, it made sense to hand over most of that responsibility, and Tanlia was the obvious person to take it on. That did not mean he was comfortable with letting it go.

They stood up. 'Same time tomorrow?' he said.

'The sooner we get these initial decisions made, the sooner I can get down to some real work,' she said.

He accompanied her to the door, where they said goodnight, with Tanlia adding, 'Do give my best to Gerys, won't you?'

His wife and his ex-lover got on surprisingly well. Once, after a rather boozy dinner, when he was clearing up in the kitchen and Tanlia's latest ornamental boy was in the bathroom, Chandin had overheard Gerys and Tanlia laughing raucously together. Afterwards, Gerys had admitted with a smile that, yes, they were talking about him and no, he did not want to know the details.

Tanlia was as important to him, in her way, as Gerys was. She was his foil: predictably annoying, relentlessly stubborn, but ultimately competent and with a high degree of professional integrity. But he must never forget that her frivolous and sometimes disconcertingly intimate manner disguised an iron will and a razor-sharp mind.

That was why he wanted to be at his best when they discussed the changes in IDOB. He knew his fears were not entirely rational: The Mistake was a detail, hidden far below the notice of anyone at his – or Tanlia's – rank. But if she, or anyone else, uncovered it … he was finished.

OTHER BEVERAGES ARE AVAILABLE

Designation: Target136
Human alias: Irivera Kendine
Position: Freetrader Captain
Location: The Missed Symphony
Vulnerabilities: Although Target136 has no criminal record,
she and her first officer have been accused of flouting spacer
regulations by the Starliner Guild, specifically regarding staff
rotation; however, the accusations may stem in part from
the usual jealousy the Guild feels towards rival, cut-price
operators.

<file under: Target List>

Bez blinked furiously, the shock of her sudden exit from the virtuality still resonating through her.

She smelled old cheese and shivered at the touch of freezing, dust-laden air. The world swum into partial focus, revealing two figures silhouetted in the light from the open door. One held a small flashlight in its hand. They were both advancing towards her.

If she had any doubts that she was fully back in the real, they were dispelled by this unwelcome sight.

'Can you hear us, medame?'

The one that spoke was a man. He sounded polite enough but Bez's stupid, weak body was currently going through the full gamut of fight/flight responses, and speech was beyond her.

'Tags say she's Peralene Carshay, freelance environmental tech.' That was a man too, and there was something wrong with the shape of his head.

'Perhaps she's had an accident,' said normal-head, playing his light over her.

She squeezed her eyes shut and turned her head away. As the beam moved on she made herself look properly at the men. Her vision was already adjusting and she recognised the uniforms. Hub-law. Again. She reminded herself that she had a solid ID and was authorised to be here.

'Perhaps she was in virtual,' said helmet-head.

Uh-oh.

His companion opined, 'Yeah, looks like dumpshock to me.'

This could be as serious as the Estrante debacle. She had to think of something to say, fast. Assuming she could speak at all. 'I ...' she managed. Now her vision had cleared she could see that funny-head was actually wearing a tactical heads-up helmet. *Ah good*, said some dumb, animal part of her, *it's not a monster after all.*

'Sorry?' said normal-head. 'What was that?'

She managed to whisper, 'Had a bit too much.'

'Too much what?'

'T'drink.' She had no trouble slurring her words.

'You had a bit too much to drink,' repeated helmet-head. He didn't sound convinced.

'Yes!' Her vision kept flicking towards the open door behind the men. 'Had a bit too much to drink and couldn't find my way back to my hotel. Must've fallen asleep here.'

'Right. I don't want to imply anything, but we've just had a tip-off about an attempted databreak at the offices of the Freetraders' Alliance.'

Which explained why they were here. *Shit.*

Normal-head said, 'Did you know anything about that, medame? Or are your reactions, reminiscent of someone recently dumped from virtual, plus your physical proximity to that location, merely a coincidence?'

In situations like this, thought Bez, Sidhe powers would come in really useful. She could have said something like, *It is a coincidence, and you will now forget I was ever here,* then simply walked out.

'We're waiting,' said helmet-head.

For what? A bribe? Perhaps. Tarset beat-cops were not incorruptible.

Normal-head said, 'Are you contracted with anyone right now?'

It took her a moment to work out what he meant. 'No. I was looking for work.' She managed a sickly grin. 'Not much luck. That's why I was, er, drowning my sorrows.'

Normal-head said, 'We would prefer to give you the benefit of the doubt. The station needs technicians, and you've no record.'

'Thank you. Listen, if you *could* overlook this, I'd be really grateful.' How should she phrase it? 'I'm sorry to have inconvenienced you, so if you, er ...'

'Before we decide whether or not we've been inconvenienced,' said helmet-head, 'why don't you let us check you lack the appropriate headware to be the alleged databreaker?'

The alleged databreaker. With Estrante she had at least had a decent deception in her favour, not to mention time to work out what to do. This was happening too fast. She initiated an emergency shutdown on her hacking suite, but it would take a while. She had to buy herself time, or better still, buy off the cops.

'I have credit,' she said.

'I thought you were out of work?' said normal-head, a little coldly.

'No, I've got some. Enough to compensate you for any trouble I've caused.'

'I don't know about my colleague here,' said normal-head, 'but I want to know why you're suddenly sounding so sober, and so spooked.'

Bez stared at them, out of useful responses.

Helmet-head crouched down. 'Right. I'm going to run a scan now. Kindly look straight at me, focusing on the helmet's eyepatch. It won't take a moment, and it won't hurt. If it comes up negative then we can all be on our way, can't we?'

She closed her eyes. This was not how it was meant to end. It was too mundane, too avoidable, too *random*.

'Medame, please! Open your eyes.'

'Hello?'

She felt the guards shift at the sound of the new voice. She opened one eye to a slit and peered past them. Someone was standing in the doorway.

'Yes, sirrah?' said normal-head to the newcomer.

'I noticed a light on in the Alliance offices,' said the newcomer. 'I commed Control and they said you two were in the vicinity and would check it out.' It was a man, and he spoke with an air of authority, like he expected the guards to jump.

To Bez's surprise, helmet-head did. Or at least stood up and said crisply, 'Of course, sirrah. Happy to help. Actually, we have the possible culprit right here.'

Bez risked a soft overlay. The newcomer's tags claimed he was a resident of Tarset, but provided no name or occupation.

'Ah. Did he – sorry, she,' the man corrected himself as he looked more closely at Bez, 'walk through the wall, then?'

'I'm sorry, sirrah, I'm not sure I—'

'I think there was, and possibly still is, someone in the Alliance offices. That's "in" as in physically inside.'

'We'll look into that right now,' said normal-head. He made to leave, but helmet-head wasn't going to let it go. 'Our concern with Medame Carshay here was as a possible databreaker. We were informed of an incursion on the Alliance system.'

'Were you now?' said the man. 'And might that message about a databreak have come from an inexperienced clerk on the night-shift who misread the incident code and gave you incorrect information? Databreak and break-in: easy mistake to make.'

'Er, yes, that's possible, sirrah.'

'More than possible, I'd say, given Control *told me* they'd informed you of the potential *break-in*.' The man shook his head as if disappointed at finding himself surrounded by idiots.

The guards appeared to reach a decision. 'Right, sirrah,' said helmet-head, 'we'll go and check it out.'

'You do that.'

The man moved aside to let the guards pass. Bez hoped he would follow them out but he stayed in the doorway, leaning against the frame with his arms crossed. Bez got the impression he was smiling.

'So,' she said to break the awkward silence, 'is it all right if I go now?' She didn't want to be here when hub-law came back after finding there was no break-in.

'If you like.'

'Right.'

As she was standing up carefully he said, 'Unless you want to come for a caf?'

'A caf?'

'That's right: hot drink made from fermented and flash-frozen beans, containing a mild stimulant. You know the stuff.'

Bez wished she could see his expression.

'So, do you?' he persisted. 'Unless you don't like caf. Other beverages are available.'

'Yes. I mean no. I mean ... with you?'

'With me, yes.'

He sounded amused; was he mocking her? She remembered adolescent situations not entirely unlike this. Those memories still made her cheeks burn. 'Why?' she asked.

'Why not?'

'Because ...' *Because that's what normal people do.* She could hardly say that. 'I have to go now. Get an early night,' she said in a rush. Then, realising how that could be taken, she added, even more hurriedly, 'I need to be up early in the morning. To look for work.'

Was he disappointed? Annoyed? All he said was, 'Of course. If you're sure.'

'I'm sure,' she said firmly.

He moved back, though not entirely out of the way. Bez ended up banging her shoulder on the doorframe in order to keep her distance. Possibly thanks to her screwed-up senses she caught a whiff of him as she passed; a disconcertingly pleasant scent, slightly musky.

She wondered if she should thank him for his offer, but that might imply she wanted to accept it. Instead she muttered, 'Good night,' and hurried away.

He called after her: 'Good night, then, Medame, um, Carshay.' He spoke the name like he knew it wasn't hers.

DATA BONANZA

Obviously, there are more than a few hundred Sidhe in total.
I don't think there are billions, maybe not even millions. They
always were a minority, even during the Protectorate when
they had us firmly under their heel.

I believe the residual population of Sidhe lives outside
human-space, although they take a keen interest in what goes
on here. But even there, we might still be able to hurt them.

<file under: Unqualified Data>

Her instinct was to ditch her current ID and hide out until Captain
Reen arrived, then take on a transient persona long enough to
board his ship. But provided she did not act suspiciously, hub-law
had no reason to come after her, and if someone was watching
the infoscape, then accessing one of her dataeggs was risky. For
the moment, she should stick with this persona, but monitor the
situation.

However, she needed to rethink her departure plans. The
encounter in the service passages had rung too many alarm bells;
when she did leave Tarset she wanted to disappear comprehen-
sively and untraceably. There was only one way to do that.

Once she was sure no one was physically following her, she
stopped off at an independent freight company with a rep for
cutting corners. She made a verbal booking with the bored night-
shift clerk, requesting the 'pay on despatch' option and adding a
discretionary 'service charge' to avoid the transaction going into
the system too quickly.

She then returned to her hotel where she used the room's com,
spoofed to a room on a different floor of the hotel, to set ongoing
searches on the local news, sprinkling dummy keywords in with

the relevant search parameters. She would have expected the authorities to know there had been no physical break-in by now. However, her initial results implied this wasn't the case.

Having been forced to abandon her spotcams, she had to rely on hacked surveillance feeds. She had booked a room with a private emergency exit; if the corridor cam piped anything suspicious to the part of her visual cortex devoted to keeping watch, she would be using it.

One hour and thirty-one minutes after the incident, the search turned up a minor piece about a break-in at the offices of the Freetraders' Alliance. The report claimed the culprit or culprits had crudely sabotaged the surveillance by spraying paint over the pick-ups, then stolen some slates and other office equipment, as well as raiding the office kitchen. The authorities suspected hab-rat youths, probably on drugs. There was no mention of any virtual activity.

So, there had been a burglary at exactly the moment she was hacking the freetraders. This was too convenient, and hence highly unlikely. Then someone, who held considerable power on Tarset station, had happened to turn up when she was about to be rumbled. That went beyond unlikely and into implausible.

She set up a new search on public com footage, looking for a match on the image her eyewear had snapped of the apparently friendly stranger. This she spoofed through a different hotel entirely.

Unwilling though she was to trust intuition, this evening's events felt different from the few other times she had been careless enough to draw attention to herself. At least he was not one of *their* agents: if he had been, he wouldn't have let her go so easily. Unless he was confident she would go back to her hotel, from where he could pick her up at his leisure … She hastily applied the best-case principle.

When her search on the mysterious stranger came back negative, she was neither surprised nor reassured.

She decided that, until proved otherwise, she would regard the incident as unrelated to the problem with the Estrante ID. But it was more serious. While she had safely ditched the only persona that linked her to the still incommunicado Beta16, this incident involved a stranger taking a direct, *personal* interest in her. He had set her up. Or rather *un*-set her up. And then there was his ridiculous attempt to flirt with her. Why show an interest like that? Was he trying to win her trust? To disconcert her? If it was the latter, he had succeeded.

She decided to carry out an initial examination of the data she had acquired before being so unpleasantly interrupted. It needed doing, and it would help her stay centred and calm.

The bulk of the update was ship movements and cargo manifests: what freetraders had visited what systems when, carrying what, over the last three months.

There had been a time when she had believed the Sidhe freetraders were the key to her plan. She had refocused her strategy in the light of the *Setting Sun* data, which was why she had not picked up any freetrader data during the last major update. But the Enemy freetraders were still loose cannons, and she wanted as complete a picture as possible of their movements.

She hoped this trickle-down might solve the mystery of a missing ship. Or possibly two ships. According to the *Setting Sun*'s files, the Enemy owned thirty-two tradebirds, most of them large vessels with a human crew in the thrall of a rarely seen Sidhe captain, an arrangement that chilled Bez to the core. Recent Alliance updates had included data on thirty or fewer Sidhe tradebirds. One of the missing ships was the *Setting Sun* itself, now disabled and abandoned in an uncharted system. But another ship, the *Missed Symphony*, had also been absent last time. She ran a basic search on tonight's data and found no sign of it this time.

She had a couple of theories as to why the *Missed Symphony* was not present in the freetraders' data. The first, less likely one, was that the Sidhe had sold it. The ship was an ex-starliner so the Starliner Guild would probably buy it back. But why would the Enemy sell their largest ship? They had not one but two Sidhe on board, so even if – say – the captain had met with some accident, her first officer would step in. The *Missed Symphony* was a vital asset.

During the last trickle-down, Bez had delved into Guild records, just to be sure, and found no ship purchases in the relevant period. It was possible the ship had been sold to a private individual – a very wealthy private individual – but that did nothing to change the fact that this was not logical behaviour. The Enemy had few enough ships as it was; to sell one of their best would be stupid.

Another possibility was that the ship was being refitted. But given the rarity of shiftships, the yards that serviced them had to be efficient and competitive. Keeping a tradebird off the shipping lanes for more than a few months was not something any shipyard could afford to do. The *Missed Symphony*'s absence from this latest update meant it had not been operational for at least a year. So a refit was unlikely.

Then there was the *Steel Breeze*. This was a Protectorate-era, in-system military vessel that had been fitted with a transit-kernel when humanity wrested the power of interstellar flight from their erstwhile rulers. According to the *Setting Sun* files, the *Steel Breeze* still retained some of its armaments. The ship had appeared in earlier updates, but not the one six months ago, and it was missing from this one too.

Of course, transit-kernels did eventually fail – she tried not to think of the word 'die' in this context – but for two shiftships to go out of service in one year was highly improbable.

Having confirmed her suspicions but come up with no further insights, she moved on to her second area of interest.

The information in the *Setting Sun*'s files had been a veritable data bonanza. One of the most intriguing items was a schedule showing where certain Sidhe freetraders were due to be on particular dates. The dates were regular – once every two to three weeks. The locations were all over human-space. Bez believed this schedule indicated that Enemy freetraders were periodically leaving human-space. She set to work checking the schedule against actual ship movements.

Given the data came from beacons, which recorded details of any ship that used them to enter shiftspace, if the Enemy *were* going off the map, they weren't making standard transits. The received wisdom was that the beacon network had only been installed a thousand years ago, after the Sidhe Protectorate fell and humanity (thought they had) regained their freedom. Bez had not yet come across anything to contradict this. It was logical to assume that the Sidhe, who had travelled freely while humans remained planet-bound during the Protectorate, could enter and leave shiftspace without the use of beacons.

Picking a ship at random, she found that it had indeed gone to the spur-world listed on the date given, as per the *Setting Sun*'s schedule. The freetrader spent two days there, during which, according to the Alliance records, it travelled to a point out-system where it apparently remained, doing nothing and, as far as local Traffic Control knew, going nowhere. It then came back in-system and left via the beacon.

Three more ships matched up to the schedule, having travelled to insular one-world systems far off the shipping lanes, where they apparently loitered beyond the purview of local surveillance before leaving again.

The next ship didn't fit the pattern, but Bez had an idea why. She would need the full picture before she could confirm her hypothesis.

She set data-agents to work completing the job and took a shower.

If she was right, the Sidhe freetraders took regular trips away from human-space in order to meet up with the rest of their people. The thought of a whole society of Sidhe lurking in dark uncharted space beyond the limits of human expansion sometimes kept her awake at night. She consoled herself with the logical addendum to this possibility: however many there were, and wherever they were, their continued absence implied they were not in a position to return en masse and challenge humanity. After a thousand years she would have expected them to have made their move.

Yet they still took an interest. Without beacons to transmit beevee, then unless the Enemy had another, unknown method of interstellar communication, they relied on the freetraders to bring them news. Bez got the impression the Sidhe in human-space

44

operated with a massive degree of autonomy; certainly the *Setting Sun*'s files had provided almost no intel on their activities outside human-space. Yet the Sidhe freetraders made frequent trips off the map; with so few ships at their disposal, and the Sidhe agents in human-space doing such a good job, why did the Enemy in the great beyond need updates every couple of weeks?

She had a theory. While she waited for the evidence to support it, she uploaded the pictures she had taken of the 'helpful' stranger to a transient datadrop, encrypting a short accompanying message, and setting the timed release for four hours after she was due to leave Tarset.

A couple of minutes later she got a com call from hotel reception; acting on the standing instructions she had left with them, an item had been put into storage for her. Checking the security cam in the luggage store, she confirmed that all was as expected.

She considered having a drink but decided against it; thirst would be a lot less inconvenient than having to urinate in the next couple of hours.

She left the room, turning off the lights and locking the door. When she reached the luggage store she checked the corridor feeds to make sure no one was coming then switched her attention to the luggage room's lock and internal cam. Only when the cam was safely looping its low-light image of a dark and empty room did she open the door and slip inside.

A sturdy grey box, measuring approximately one metre by two, stood among the items left by other hotel guests. Bez opened it to confirm that it had been configured correctly.

Just in case anyone was paying attention to her plans, she made a provisional booking for another, cheaper, hotel. Then she commed reception and checked out, leaving a generous-but-not-excessive tip.

Finally she performed a few breathing exercises to induce physical calm, climbed inside the box and, after securing herself in the internal webbing, pulled the lid shut.

AN INTERNAL PROBLEM

The Sidhe in human-space are well entrenched. They've got excellent cover and they don't take risks. Plus, if you are unlucky enough to come face-to-face with them, they'll probably make you forget you ever met them, or force you to do what they want you to do while believing it was your own idea.

<file under: Core Data>

For the second time in a week, Bez found herself regretting her lack of mood-mods. She reminded herself that there were concealed ventilation holes in the side of the box and an internal release on the lid. She was not trapped, and she was not going to suffocate. And she had done this before, when an ultra-secure exit was called for. No matter how good the disguise, if someone was specifically watching the port for a solo traveller of a certain height, build and gender, then her departure could be noticed. Cargo, however, would not be. The ruse was never pleasant, but neither was it dangerous.

She shouldn't need neurotransmitter regulators and adrenalin suppressors; they were the stuff of adventure holodramas, the fabled tools of spies and soldiers. Such gross physical tampering resulted in erroneous feedback, leading to bad judgement and risk-taking. Far better to avoid stressful situations. Which she did, most of the time.

Of course, in a properly ordered universe the human will alone would be enough to override these inconvenient bodily responses. Such control was said to have been practised by the Enemy—

She curled her hands into fists, digging her fingertips into her palms hard enough that, had she any nails, she would have broken

46

the skin. Then she released her fingers slowly while listening to her breathing and watching her chrono.

Once the unpleasantness had passed, she blinked her overlays online and retreated into the comforting world of data.

Examining the results of her search, she quickly concluded that her theory was correct: the movements of two Sidhe freetraders did not conform to the *Setting Sun*'s schedule because these ships were covering for the *Missed Symphony* and *Steel Breeze*. So, the Enemy was adjusting to their loss. But she was still no nearer to knowing the fate of the missing ships.

She had just started a new search, contingent on the results of the first, when a noise outside made her jump. Muffled voices, sounding unconcerned; bored, even. That should be the shipping company's employees, transporting the box to the port. Unless they were taking her somewhere else ... *No*: best-case principle.

The box jolted. Another tug then a lifting sensation. She could still hear the voices, a man and a woman, griping about something, from the sound of it. She made herself breathe evenly and quietly.

The movement became smoother; they must have loaded her onto a trolley. She tried to get back to the data, but the box's motion was too distracting. She retreated into her oldest and deepest mantra, reciting digits of pi.

Her mental routine was interrupted when the box was shoved sideways hard enough to make her swing in the webbing. Sweat broke out all over her body. After that, blessed stillness.

If everything was going to plan, this would only be a temporary stop.

Someone spoke nearby. Bez started then calmed herself as the voice was answered by another, further away.

The box began moving again. This felt like a customs conveyor. A full scan at this point would reveal her. Fortunately the authorities were far less concerned about what left a hub station than what came in. According to the manifest, this box contained cured meats, and no one had any reason to think otherwise. She had paid the export duty on the consignment – which the hub authorities did care about – legitimately. After her near miss in the Alliance system, she had decided against hacking the customs' virtuality to fake the payment.

Of course, there was nothing to stop a bored customs officer doing a spotcheck.

If they did, how would she know, until it happened? That was the worst thing about this method of travel: being not only powerless but also ignorant of what was happening around her. On previous occasions, she had concealed a spotcam on the outside of her box, which gave some idea of her surroundings, but she was all out of cams.

More voices, sounding relaxed. The box lurched to one side. Bez snapped her mouth shut to stop herself making any noise. The voices receded. She let herself exhale.

It was noticeably colder now, but mercifully silent. Bez waited for one minute then went back to her data, checking her latest search, which collated the manifests of the freetraders who had left human-space. As she scanned the results a smile broke out on her face. She was right! The freetraders didn't just take news to their sisters out in the void. They took *supplies*. Not weapons or hi-tech gear, but mundane, basic items like slates, tools, polymer sheets – even clothing and foodstuffs. If the Sidhe had a large and stable planet-based culture, they would have developed the manufacturing capacity to provide such items for themselves. The logical conclusion was that the Enemy operated out of *ships,* probably large ex-colony ships. They would be self-sufficient in basics like food and water but would have to rely on humans for anything that could not be either recycled or manufactured using their limited means. There was no seething mass of aliens out there in the dark, merely the last dregs of a dying race.

If she could curtail the activities of the Sidhe freetraders, she would cut off this supply-line. She dared hope that, should she succeed, eventually the distant Sidhe exiles, isolated from human-space, would wither and die.

The box moved again, without any accompanying voices this time. Bez barely noticed: she was too deep in the data.

Bang BANG.

Bez twitched, suddenly back in the real.

The knock came again. She froze, suspended in the webbing—

'Bez? You in there?'

Although she knew the voice, part of her wanted to stay in the box, safe in her own head. Rather than give in to the foolish temptation, she snatched at the handle above her. She misjudged it in the darkness, stubbing her fingers. She ignored the pain and tried again, grasping the release handle and pulling smoothly. As soon as the lid clicked, she pushed it up with all her strength.

Light flooded in, along with a mix of homely, human smells.

'Christos, watch it!'

Bez grabbed the sides of the box and pulled herself upright. She was in a large, semi-circular ship's cabin. The only other person in sight was the one she was expecting, although he had just recoiled from the box's rapidly opening lid. He gave a wry smile. She remembered that smile, at once friendly and roguish. 'At least it *was* you in the box, not some random piece of cargo,' he said.

'Yes. Sorry. I didn't have a chance to inform you of my change of plan.'

'Was there a problem?'

'Nothing you need worry about, Captain Reen.'

'Right. I thought we agreed you'd call me Jarek?'

They had, after Bez had told him her real name – the name no one else had spoken out loud for nearly two decades. She suddenly felt massively self-conscious. 'Er, yes ...'

'Did you want a hand?'

'No. I'm fine.' Bez pushed herself to her feet. Stepping over the box's high side was trickier than it had been earlier, thanks to legs gone rubbery and numb.

'I'll make us a caf,' said Captain Reen – Jarek – as she straightened up.

'Shouldn't we be leaving?' Looking around, she saw that the ship's living area – the 'rec-room' – was as untidy as she remembered.

'Taro's got that covered.'

Ah yes: one of the two allies he had asked her to procure false

IDs for the last time they met. She hadn't realised he was currently travelling with them; assuming the other one – Nual, that was her name – was here too.

'So, did you want one?'

She focused on Jarek. 'One what?'

'A caf?'

What was it with men offering her drinks? But after an hour and a half in that damn box, she could really use one. 'Yes. Please.'

She followed him over to the galley area (*How hard would it be to put those plates away?*), and, after locating a debris-free seat, sat down at the table. Her time in the box had left her desperate for another shower, but first she needed to speak to the freetrader captain. 'I don't think the memory-core is accurate anymore,' she said. One advantage of deciding to trust Captain Jarek Reen was that there was no need for all those tedious social niceties with him.

Jarek paused, caf jug in hand. 'You mean the *Setting Sun*'s memory-core?' He was the one who had originally procured the data for her – or rather, the physical memory-core of the Sidhe ship, which Bez had decrypted.

'Yes,' she said, a little impatiently.

'In what way? I've found the intel on it pretty sound so far.'

'One, possibly two, of the S— Sidhe freetraders are no longer operating.' How long since she had actually named the Enemy out loud?

'Well,' said Jarek, putting down the jug, 'I might have an explanation for that. What were the ship names?'

'The first one is the *Missed Symphony*.'

'Was that the converted starliner?'

'Yes.'

'It's been destroyed.'

'Destroyed? How?'

'Sabotage. A splinter faction within the Sidhe tried to get hold of it. The others objected. I believe the military term is "asset denial".'

'But they don't have factions. They're a unified force!'

'Apparently not always.' Jarek scooped some caf into the jug and set it to heat.

Bez digested this news. 'Do you have more details? If this is something we can use against them—'

'I believe this was an internal problem which has now been resolved.'

'And you didn't think to tell me about it?'

'You're not an easy woman to get hold of. I thought I'd wait until you called on my services again – after all, I owe you. I didn't expect it to be so long ...'

'I've been busy. What about the *Steel Breeze*? Do you know what happened to that?'

'If it's the ship I think it is then it's also been trashed. Remember I told you how Serenein had defences installed by the Sidhe?' Bez nodded. 'Well, the locals managed to turn them on their erstwhile rulers.'

'Good for them. So that world is definitely out from under their control?' Serenein was one of the Enemy's nastiest little secrets, though the isolated theocracy was not in itself vital to her plans.

'Yep.' Jarek stirred the jug. 'No more transit-kernels.'

That had implications in the long term; Bez wondered if Jarek had considered them. Or if he had uncovered any more Sidhe secret locations. 'What do you know about their other activities outside human-space?' she asked.

'Not a lot; Serenein's the only lost world I've found.'

'But the Sidhe living in human-space have to come from somewhere, don't they? There must be hidden cloning labs.'

'Labs, anyway. I told you they use sperm from Serenein's Consorts to keep their bloodlines strong, didn't I?' He began pouring the drinks.

'You did.' Those sorry youths were all that was left of the Sidhe males. 'But however they reproduce, they have to do it somewhere. What about colony ships? Or perhaps, ah, motherships?'

'Damn!'

'What is it?'

'Just spilt a bit of caf. Wait, I'll wipe it up.' He did so. Bez waited. He looked over at her and said, 'Some sort of mothership arrangement does seem likely, yes. Here you go.' He handed her a mug across the table.

Bez took the drink and said, 'If you find out more about that – about anything relevant – you will tell me, won't you?'

'We're on the same side, Bez.' He took a pull from his mug, but remained standing. 'I should probably check on Taro; he's still getting used to flying on implants,' he said, and made to move away from the counter.

'Wait!' Bez was sure Jarek had more answers; she certainly had more questions. And part of her relished having an honest human interaction she didn't have to fake.

'Don't you want to get cleaned up? You did last time you arrived that way.' He nodded towards the box sitting in the centre of the rec-room.

'I do. I just … can I ask you a couple more things first?'

'Sure.'

'Your sister, Elarn.'

'What about her?'

'The first time we met I asked you why you were fighting the— them. You said vengeance. Was that for Elarn Reen? They killed her, didn't they?'

'Not directly, no, but the Sidhe certainly … caused her death.'

'She only died a couple of years ago. I first got in contact with you five years ago.'

'That's true. Before that I was less focused. With Elarn, the Sidhe made it personal.'

'But how did you find out about them in the first place?'

'That's … complicated. Now might not be the best time.'

'I need to know, Jarek.'

'Fair enough. The short answer is, by accident. I had a run-in with the Sidhe and barely got out alive. Kind of changed my worldview.'

Bez could relate to that. She would ask for full details later, when she was less wiped. 'What about your ship?'

'What about my ship?

'You sold it some months back, didn't you?'

'Yes, I did. But I retain full control.'

'The new owner is very secretive.' So secretive Bez had yet to penetrate their many shells to unearth their identity. 'Is it someone you can trust?'

'Yes,' said Jarek emphatically.

'Even so, involving a third party is a risk—'

'No offence, Bez, but this really isn't anything to do with you. Not everyone can swan through human space hacking themselves new funds as and when they need to. I'm a freetrader: I run a business. Combining my business with chasing after a hidden enemy wasn't working out. I got into debt so I accepted an offer that solved the problem. It has no impact on our fight against the Sidhe.'

'I see,' said Bez. She hadn't expected him to be so touchy. 'I think I'll go have that shower.'

'Good idea.'

As she stood up, Bez had one last thought. To Jarek's departing back, she called out, 'Why didn't you put my box in your ship's cargo hold?'

He paused and half turned. 'Because the hold's full.'

'Full?'

'Yes. Of cargo.'

Bez hadn't had time to check the Alliance data on this ship, but she had been taking an interest in the activities of the *Heart of Glass* for some time, and she knew that it rarely had a full cargo hold.

DISTINCTLY RETICENT

Designation: Target136
Correction to previous data: Deceased.
Designation: Target398
Correction to previous data: Deceased.
Designation: Target437
Correction to previous data: Deceased.

<apply as update to: Target List>

Standing beneath the tepid jets of water, Bez considered her conversation with Jarek Reen. She wanted to trust him. He had provided intel vital to her mission and was the only one of her agents who knew who the Enemy really were. It appeared he had even met them once – and lived. Bez had met a Sidhe herself, although at the time she had had no idea … She dropped that line of thought, and dialled up the shower temperature.

If only she could banish her niggling doubts. Although Jarek had answered her questions, he had been distinctly reticent. Perhaps she had stirred up bad memories, or maybe there was something else going on unrelated to the current situation.

People were so difficult. With a comp, you knew where you were. With a person, there was always the chance they would say one thing and mean something else, and if you challenged them on it, they stopped cooperating at all. Data never lied, or sulked, or dissembled.

She switched from water to air. As she dried, it occurred to her that personal feelings might be affecting her judgement. Since losing Tand she had kept everyone at a distance, operating under the cover of her many false identities, always playing a part. With Jarek Reen, she risked revealing her true self every time she opened her mouth.

She dressed in the spare set of coveralls she had brought with her. As she emerged she found the galley occupied by an unfeasibly tall youth. He looked up and gave her a friendly grin. 'You must be Bez. I'm Taro.'

She nodded. 'Ah. Yes. And, uh, Nual?'

His grin faded. 'She ain't here,' he said shortly. 'Want a drink? We got real juice.'

Her hosts appeared determined to be hospitable. Bez picked her way across the room and took the proffered mug from the boy's hand, careful not to touch his long fingers. He looked so young, yet he must be about the same age Tand had been when he died. And she knew what this youth really was. She struggled for something appropriate to say and settled on, 'You've had headware installed recently, haven't you?'

'Sure have.'

'I thought your captain didn't approve of implants.'

'My captain ...' He looked amused. 'Jarek don't hold with implants for himself, no. Religious upbringing and all that shit. But he's happy enough for me to have 'em. Makes the piloting easier, y'know?'

'Where's Jarek now?'

'On the bridge, chatting to Traffic Control. He said you might want to crash out? I've tidied o— my cabin so you can.' The boy gestured at one of the doors off the rec-room. 'Changed the sheets and everything.'

Bez wasn't sure about sleeping in a strange boy's bed – clean sheets or not – but now she had started to relax, everything was catching up with her. And if she stayed in the rec-room, he might expect her to make conversation. Although she did need to talk to this boy, she wanted to check the state of play with Jarek first. 'Er, yes. I'd like to rest.'

'Room's all yours.'

'How far out from the beacon are we?'

'Four and a bit hours.'

'I'll be up again in three.'

*

Given the state of the cabin, Bez hated to think what it had looked like before the boy tidied it.

She sat on the bed and drank the juice – it tasted like one of the berry blends from Tarset's hydroponics farms – then lay down and closed her eyes.

She had intended to use the time to think, but the next thing she knew, her alarm was waking her. She sat up slowly then paused. Something about that pile of clothes in the corner. Not that she wanted to focus on the mess in here, but her half-asleep gaze had spotted an anomaly. On closer inspection it turned out to be a piece of female underwear.

Either the boy had an unusual social life or he and the absent female crew member were lovers. Presumably she was only away temporarily, given that she had left some of her clothes here. Bez wondered what she was up to. Perhaps she should ask Jarek. After all, his crew were the only other people taking an active interest in bringing down the Enemy. Then again, he hadn't exactly been forthcoming earlier. All that mattered was that he could be relied on when she needed his assistance in her mission.

Out in the rec-room, Jarek was cooking something that smelled appetising, while the boy, Taro, was making an attempt to clear enough of the table to eat off.

'Good, you're up!' called Jarek as Bez wandered over. 'Dinner's almost ready; we need to leave enough time for it to settle before we make the transit.'

'Shiftspace indigestion,' said Taro, shaking his head. 'Not pretty.'

'Ah,' said Bez, 'I was hoping I could use your comabox for the transit.'

'I'm afraid it's broken,' said Jarek.

'Oh.'

'We don't usually use the 'box ourselves. I've been meaning to find the time – and the money – to fix it, and if you'd given me a bit more notice perhaps I would've, but as it was we had to rush here to meet you.' He smiled. The boy smiled too, and shrugged.

'So I'll be conscious in shiftspace?'

'We got good drugs,' said Taro. 'They'll sort you.'

'I— I guess I don't have much choice.'

'Yes: sorry,' said Jarek. 'Let's eat, shall we?'

The food was good – fresh greens and pasta, with no tang of re-cycled sludge – but the thought of having to make a transit while conscious ruined Bez's appetite. Going into stasis carried a tiny but calculable risk of waking up brain-damaged, or not at all, but Bez would take that chance rather than endure the uncontrolled chaos of the void – especially given what Jarek had previously told her about how shiftships really worked.

She couldn't remember the last time she had eaten in company; she had no idea what, if anything, to say. As the other two didn't appear inclined to make conversation either, the meal passed in silence.

Afterwards, while Taro cleared away the dishes, Jarek asked, 'Where are we taking you, then?'

'Eklir station, initially. I'll be there about a day. Then I might need you again, for an onward transit.' Jarek owed her a lot of favours; Bez hoped he was going to be reasonable about having some of them called in now.

'I guess that'll be all right. How's the good fight going, anyway?'

'Everything's coming together.'

'As in, you expect to make your move in the foreseeable future?'

'Yes. I do.' She did not add that this was largely thanks to the data he had provided; he knew how grateful she was.

'That's great, Bez. Obviously, when the time comes, if there's anything you need me – us – to do, then just say.'

'Actually, there is something you can help with.' Bez smiled, relieved the matter had come up naturally. 'Some of our enemies, including the most powerful ones, are going to be hard to bring down, even with the intel you provided. In the end it may come down to assassination.'

Jarek raised an eyebrow. 'I'm not averse to killing Sidhe, though given we're talking about nearly six hundred of them spread across human-space, that might not be practical.'

'This would be for a few special cases only. And I wouldn't ask *you* to do it.' She turned slightly, addressing his young crewmate. 'You're an Angel, aren't you? You and your companion.' Not that the boy had the demeanour of a semi-legendary assassin.

'Yeah, how'd—?'

'Remember,' interrupted Jarek, 'Bez got you those spare IDs? So she knows what's on your original one.'

'Oh, yeah. Sure, I got the mods.'

'And the gun? The x-laser?' asked Bez.

'Yeah,' he said, 'I got that too.'

'Good, because a weapon that can kill someone cleanly from a considerable distance might be what we need.'

'It ain't something I make a habit of,' said Taro. 'But if we're talking about Sidhe, I'll do it.'

Jarek added, 'We're with you, Bez. Just let us know what you need us to do.'

She nodded. 'I will.' She knew exactly whom she wanted at the end of the Angel's laser. 'I need access to your ship's comp now.'

'What?' Jarek looked taken aback.

'Given how I arrived on board, I have to insert my current ID into your records as a passenger, otherwise the authorities at Eklir might ask some awkward questions.'

'Oh, I see. No problem. Did you want to do it before we shift?'

'Yes, I'd rather get this sorted now.' She didn't expect to be good for much after the transit.

'Will it take long? I need to start the power-down soon.'

'I'll only be a couple of minutes.'

'Right.' He got up. 'Follow me, then.'

Although Bez knew where to find the comp, she let Jarek lead her up the ladder to the ship's small, circular bridge. The shutters on the dome were open and the glory of space extended above them; off to one side, the ember-star that Tarset station orbited glowed like a distant red eye. They were too far away to see the jumbled structure of the hab itself.

Jarek lurked at the back of the bridge while Bez slipped into the ship's limited infoscape and made the relevant changes. He then stood aside while she went down the ladder.

Back in the rec-room, Taro was sitting on one of the room's two generously proportioned couches. As she started towards the cabin he called out, 'We thought you'd be better off in here with me.'

'Why?'

'I've done a fair few shifts out of the box: I'll keep an eye on you, be there in case things get too freaky.'

Bez was not sure how she felt about that. 'What about Jarek?'

'He'll stay on the bridge.'

'So he takes the ship in and out of the transit?'

'Yep.'

'But aren't you his pilot?'

The boy laughed. 'Only when he lets me.'

At that moment, the lights dimmed. Under normal circumstances she would be sinking into technologically induced oblivion by now. 'All right. I'll stay with you.'

'You wanna come over here? You'll be more comfy on one of the couches.'

'I'm fine at the table.' She took a couple of steps towards the galley area.

'Suit yourself. I'm gonna get horizontal soon as I've had my medicine.' Taro held up something small.

'And what is that?' she asked.

'Inhaler. You know, for … wait there, I'll bring it over an' you can have a snort too.' She sat down at the table while he came over. 'Right,' he said. 'Here's how it works.' With an exaggerated mime he raised the small device to his face, leaned his head back slightly, and pressed something on the gadget. There was a faint hiss, and his head tilted back further, eyes starting to close. He made a noise somewhere between a cough and a hiccup, then opened his eyes and lowered the inhaler. 'Now that's *much* better,' he said.

He blinked and looked down at Bez with wide eyes. 'I'll leave this for you, then.'

'I'll be fine.'

'No, really. It'll help with shiftspace. Helps with most things, really.' He seemed to find that last comment funny. He put the inhaler on the table then turned carefully, paused, and turned back, wobbling slightly. 'Nearly forgot,' he said, 'Jarek's gonna shout out a countdown to the shift for you, so you know when we're going in.'

Bez nodded. 'Good.' Anything to impose structure on the coming chaos.

He turned again and staggered off, calling, 'See ya on the other side!'

Ignoring the inhaler, Bez went virtual. She took her headware through a complete shutdown, right down to her chrono. Most technology failed in shiftspace … yet the ship would still have gravity and light and heat and air. And human bodies, themselves no more than machines, would continue to function, after a fashion. It was illogical. Or possibly not, given what drove the translation through shiftspace. But that in itself was the stuff of nightmares.

'Five minutes!'

Bez jumped at Jarek's shout. She stared at the inhaler. Should she use it? The only other time she had made a transit while conscious, she had not resorted to drugs. But that was before she had found out about transit-kernels. She grabbed the inhaler and held it to her nose.

Her throat tingled and her eyes watered. Immediately after that, someone removed the top of her head and started pumping her cranium full of foam. Then all at once the foam set, and the initial, alarming rush subsided. She felt all right. Better than all right, in fact.

'One minute.'

Jarek's voice seemed to come from a long way off. She attempted a breathing exercise, but it made her nose itch. She sneezed.

'Ten seconds!'

Bez tried to count down the last few moments, but between the drugs and lack of tech she misjudged it. She had just murmured *four* to herself when the universe went crazy.

DERN
(Olympus Orbital, Ylonis System)

Everyone has secrets.

Dern Morvil had very few, and they tended to be small, awkward ones, like that time he accidentally saw his mother naked when he was twelve. Ten years on, the memory still made his ears burn.

Today was his birthday, and his inbox was full of greetings from friends. There was also mail from Starscape Academy, but initially he ignored that, checking his other messages first. Several of the birthday links were from his old terceball comrades, which cheered him up; even two years after he had acknowledged he was never going to play in the AWL, the team still kept in touch.

He hesitated; he wanted to fire up the beevee link to see what the universe at large had to say, but he still hadn't opened that message from the Academy. He couldn't keep putting it off.

The news was no surprise: he had failed his third and final retake of the entrance exams. The Academy didn't want him. He tried not to be angry, not to think how if he had known an injury was going to end his career as a professional terceball player before it had properly begun, he would have devoted himself to science, not sport. There was, he told himself, no point railing against the universe.

As a boy, Dern had got it into his head that Starscape was short for 'Star Escape' – escape to the stars. He had thought terceball would let him do that: the top players in the All Worlds League actually lived on starliners. A lifestyle that combined his two great loves – sport and space – had been a dream worth sacrificing everything else for. And even when a disastrous tackle shattered his shoulder and ended one dream, there was still Starscape itself, the company that made Ylonis famous.

Except, he hadn't made the grade.

He should look on the bright side. There were other jobs at Starscape. The Academy-trained engineers who created the shift-ships were at the top of the pile, but the corporation still needed support staff: administrators and fitters, accountants and cleaners. He would never represent his system as a sporting hero, and it looked like he wouldn't be following his mother into the Starscape elite, but he could still work for one of only two companies that allowed humanity to fulfil their potential as starfarers.

Or he could get his father to find him a nice, safe job in facilities management. After all, as Da said, 'The shipyards might be the reason the orbitals are here, but without functional habitats for the workers to live in, there wouldn't be any yards.'

No. Better a janitor at Starscape than a manager in the hab offices.

But first he had to tell his parents the bad news.

Before facing that unpleasant task, he decided to indulge in his daily contact with the rest of human-space.

He opened the connection and downloaded the compressed datapacket. Not many birthday greetings here; the messages came from his fellow 'concerned galactic citizens' – as the like-minded souls he communicated with called themselves, using the term with knowing irony. Nothing from 'Orzabet', though; he hadn't heard from him for a while. Assuming Orzabet was a 'him'. Given the kind of data Orzabet sent his way, Dern suspected the name was used by a small, tight-knit group. If Orzabet was one person, he would love to meet him, or her; if it was a group, he'd love to join them. His other out-of-system friends passed on interesting titbits of news that never made the holonets, and indulged in speculation about how human-space really worked, but Orzabet was in a class of his/her/their own.

He swept a hand across his slate and exhaled, looking around his bedroom with its posters of the terceball greats and his carefully shelved collection of vintage animatronic miniatures. No more excuses: time to face the parents.

He still dawdled in the long, carpeted hall, for once actually paying attention to the spun-glass vases in their display niches. Each one was a unique artwork brought up the well from the homeworld. The homeworld set the tone for fashion, for entertainment, for corporate policy. Mother returned from her periodic trips down to Starscape's head offices railing at the dirtsiders' attitude: happy to enjoy the profits and kudos of the orbital yards, but with an irritating sense of superiority springing from nothing more than living in a place where they didn't have to pay for gravity and air.

The last niche was empty. Dern thought his mother had ordered a new vase, but it must have been delayed.

He could hear agitated voices through the door ahead. His parents had always argued. Dern knew the various tones of their arguments, and had even categorised some of them: the 'Ma venting' row; the 'Da nit-picking' argument; the 'work it out by shouting' discussion. Though he couldn't hear the actual words, the tone of this row sounded different. Perhaps now wasn't the best time to interrupt. He was about to turn around when the door opened and his mother strode out. She pulled up short when she saw him. 'Good morning, Dern,' she said, her expression softening into a smile. 'And happy birthday.'

'Thanks. I, er, thought I'd have breakfast with you today.' A stupid thing to say, given he rarely ate breakfast.

'We've just finished, actually,' said his mother, turning slightly. Da stood by the long pseudo-wood table, arms rigid by his sides.

Now Dern had told the lie, he had to follow it up, so he walked into the airy day-room. His mother followed him back inside. As he poured himself some juice from the spread on the table it occurred to him that he might have been the subject of their argument. Certainly they were both watching him like they expected him to say something. The morning soundtrack of recorded birdsong had been muted to near inaudibility. He took a drink to fortify himself then said, 'You know I failed, then?'

'Failed?' his mother barked.

'The exam. For the Academy. I mean, I thought you were … that was what …' His gazed flicked to each of them in turn. 'That wasn't what you were talking about just now, was it?'

'No,' said his father, looking confused.

'You've failed your retake.' His mother's tone was reasonable, but he knew that look. She was angry.

He stared at the table as he answered her. 'Yes. I'm sorry.'

'Adonis' sakes!' snapped Ma.

His father made a small sound, like he had been punched in the stomach.

'I was about to tell you but I thought when I heard you a– arguing that you—'

His mother interrupted him. 'We weren't talking about you, Dern.'

'Your mother's been laid off,' said Da quietly.

'What?' He looked at her, incredulous. An engineering job at Starscape was a job for life.

'As I said, that's not technically true,' said his mother. She turned to Dern, lowering her chin in that way she did when she expected a fight. 'Starscape are putting a number of their staff on "extended mandatory leave".'

'Indefinite and with a decreasing pay scale,' added his father. 'Which amounts to being laid off by increments.'

Dern knew his parents could quibble for hours over definitions, but this was serious. Somewhat to his shame, his main thought was about the money. He looked around the expensive garden apartment.

His mother, knowing him well, said, 'To be frank, the Academy bursary would have been useful.'

'You'll have to get another job, son,' added his father sympathetically. 'A proper one.'

Though Dern had been studying for his retakes for the last few months, he had also worked on and off since recovering from his injury, trying out various posts around the station on short-term contracts. His mother's status gave him a wide range of options, and he had explored a number of them, from accountancy to zoo assistant. He had been open to the possibility that one of the try-outs might reveal his future career, but up until today he had still believed that, having been denied his original destiny, the universe would allow him the next best option and he would end up at Starscape. 'Er, yes,' he said, 'of course. I'll try to find something.' He looked at his mother. 'I know you said I'd be limiting my career prospects if I took a low-pay job at Starscape and then went into the Academy, but given I'm not—'

'There are no jobs at Starscape, Dern,' said his mother bluntly.

His father added, 'This isn't just about your mother. The company is laying people off across the board.'

'They are?'

'Yes, although they're going to a lot of effort to make sure the media don't overplay the story, so we would appreciate you not spreading this around.' Dern recognised the dig at his contacts beyond the Ylonis system.

'Especially,' said his mother, 'as it's only a temporary measure.'

'Why are they doing it at all?' asked Dern. Building shiftships was massively lucrative: demand always outstripped supply.

'There's a component crisis,' said Ma.

'Which component?'

'The transit-kernels.'

'The kernels?' Whenever he made a new friend outside Ylonis, they always wanted to know about the transit-kernels. Was it true they were old Sidhe tech? How come they were so rare? Where did they really come from? Aside from confirming that, yes, they arrived from out-of-system via a supplier who operated under conditions of extreme secrecy, Dern didn't have answers to those questions. 'What's the problem?'

'Apparently there was a serious incident at the plant where they are produced. The supply has been temporarily suspended.'

'What sort of incident? Was there a shiftspace rift?'

His father snorted. '"Shiftspace rift". It's always the dramatic explanation with you, isn't it?'

'It's the kind of thing his out-of-system weirdo friends would say.'

Dern hated it when his parents talked about him as though he wasn't in the room. 'My "out-of-system weirdo friends" might have a point. I mean, everyone just accepts that these mysterious black boxes arrive and we turn them into shiftships. No one asks for details. As long as the credit keeps rolling in, we don't care. You've told me yourself how powerful transit-kernels are, how careful you have to be when integrating them into a ship. Doesn't anyone ever ask why?' Dern quaked inside as he spoke; he never cheeked his parents like this.

His mother stared at him, her expression dark. After a glance at his wife, Da said, 'I'll look into vacancies in the hab offices for you today, Dern.'

Normally it riled him when Da defused Mother's anger rather than face up to it. But today, he was grateful. 'Sure. Thanks, Da.' His mother grunted, but made no other comment. He said, 'I'll be in my room,' and left them to it.

He had a beevee call to make. Back when they had first started exchanging messages eighteen months ago, Orzabet had asked him to report anything unusual at Starscape, and he had promised he would. This certainly qualified.

THE CURSES OF WITCHES

I'd like nothing more than to reveal the aliens living among us, along with the human traitors in their pay, and then have people turn on the bastards and rip them apart.

Obviously, that isn't going to happen.

Even if I – we – could gather enough convincing evidence to expose our enemies and then orchestrate simultaneous, widespread release of that information, most people still won't believe the truth. The Sidhe are dead: long live humanity. We need to out-think them, take a lateral approach. And we need to pick our targets.

<file under: Core Data>

Shiftspace was every bit as bad as Bez remembered.

She felt deeply nauseous and mildly aroused. She retained enough self-awareness to be embarrassed about the latter, although she was also experiencing a degree of dissociation from her body.

Everything she looked at sparkled and traced. That at least could be the drugs. *Yes*, she decided after an indeterminate period of time – linear time being another dubious construct – most of what was happening was *down to drugs*. Her current state was the result of an experiment on herself using a known substance with quantifiable effects. Once the drugs wore off, everything would be fine. Everything *would* be *fine*.

The aural hallucinations were a side-effect of the drugs too. Those voices at the edge of hearing, and the laughter, distant then suddenly close enough that she turned in her seat to see who was there. Just an illusion.

She put her hands flat on the table, pressing her palms into the solid surface, concentrating on that connection. Hands on table, gaze on hands. This will pass. *It will, it will, it will.*

A particularly fulsome giggle made her look up. The boy on the far side of the room was laughing to himself, head thrown back. She had forgotten she was not alone. That made everything worse.

As she focused on him, suddenly he was no longer a gawky stranger. Instead, Tand, the love of her life, was right there, alive and laughing. Not dead. She made to stand up, flooded with relief and desire. But Tand *was* dead; this was another illusion. She made herself sit down again.

The next time she looked up from her hands, the boy appeared to have passed out. Her gaze lit on a box. She remembered that box. She had arrived here, wherever *here* was, in it. Perhaps if she climbed back inside, she could escape the grinding weirdness. She got up slowly, gratified that her body still obeyed her, even if her limbs felt too long.

The box loomed large, and she approached it with trepidation. What was inside? She made herself look, tensing as she did so. Just a mess of webbing. Nothing to be afraid of.

Why had she come over here anyway?

She stood stock-still, hands curled around the lip of the box, trying to remember why. And what. And where. Then, distracted by a fleeting illusory flash in the corner of one eye, she glanced over at the drive column. Oh, yes, that. That she *did* remember. The last, enfeebled males of the Sidhe race, not in unity with their machines like the old legends claimed, but imprisoned within them.

For a moment she was sure she could see the stripped-down nervous system embedded in tech; the mad, silently screaming mind inside the ship, inside *every* ship.

She turned, pushed off from the box, and ran. Or tried to: it was more of a stumbling shuffle through too-thick air, moving forward by virtue of not quite falling over.

There was a corridor ahead. She went down it. The far end throbbed and receded, tempting her onwards. That door – perhaps it was the way out, the route back into sanity?

No. That door was the *airlock*. Going through it would be a terminally bad idea.

She saw another door, off to one side. It was open so she went through it.

Beyond was an odd-shaped room: a torus, with a high ceiling. There were fixings, anchor-points and loose straps, all around the walls. And there was a box, lying on the floor.

She had been looking for a box earlier ...

Approaching slowly, she heard Tand's laugh again. The box had a high, curved top. She leaned over it, and was surprised to find a window in the grey surface. She was even more surprised when she looked through it.

Tand was lying there, asleep in the box. He had been here all along, and no one had told her! She had to get him out.

She ran her hands over the box, looking for some catch or hinge. There was a control panel at one end, but it was dark and inactive. There had to be a way to save him! She had failed her lover once but now she had a second chance. Perhaps there was something else in here, something that would help? She stared around wildly.

There was another box, of a slightly different design. Maybe that box would give her a clue as to how to open Tand's.

She lurched over and looked into the second box.

This one had a woman inside. She was asleep too, and there was something in her cold and perfect beauty that put Bez in mind of childhood fairy tales, of sleeping princesses and the curses of witches.

A noise that was not a laugh made Bez look up.

Someone else was here.

'L– leave ...' The boy stood beside Tand's box. One hand rested on it, supporting him; the other was pointed shakily at Bez. He spoke again, his words oozing through the thick air. 'Leave ... her ... alone.'

Bez looked at the sleeping princess, then back at the boy. 'You lied,' she said. Her voice sounded hollow and unreal.

'Had to—'

'You lied!'

'Yes—'

'No!' Bez launched herself at him, because she had to rescue her

69

lover from this stranger, even though – or perhaps *because* – nothing else made sense.

He stepped to one side, and she fell. She scrambled to her feet. The boy was speaking. She didn't care. She went for him again. He caught her wrist. She lashed out and up, snagging something. Clothing? Hair? The grasp on her wrist tightened. He shouted, 'Don't!' She ignored him.

He threw her across the room, surprisingly easily. The sudden pain of landing inspired a brief moment of sense – *This is a really bad idea!* – but her mind had taken a back seat. She got her legs under her and went for him again. There was something silver in his hand, and he had crouched down into a fighter's pose. She didn't care. She had to save Tand. Nothing else mattered.

Reality returned with a lurch.

Bez checked her charge, veering off to one side. Amazingly, she didn't fall, but instead came to a shuddering halt, bent double. She stared at the floor, the ordinary, non-shimmering floor of the cargo hold.

'Fuck!'

She looked up at the boy's snarl. He stood straight, one arm held up in front of his face. A thin silver blade was slowly disappearing into the sheaf implanted in his forearm. Bez felt a chill rush of horror. She had tried to attack an Angel!

He shook his head, incredulous. 'I could've fucking killed you.' Then he barked, 'Don't touch anything!' and strode away.

Bez sat heavily and put her head in her hands. When the pounding behind her eyes eased, she crawled over to the nearest comabox. Despite Taro's warning, she had to know. She used the box to pull herself up, and looked inside.

An adolescent boy lay there, in the peaceful oblivion of stasis. She had never seen him before in her life.

She pushed off from the comabox, and nearly stumbled. She had forgotten how damnably *tired* shiftspace left you.

She refused to look at the second comabox as she shuffled out of the cargo hold.

As she expected, the other two were waiting for her. Taro was perched on a stool, facing the corridor. He had a tranq-pistol on his lap and a wary expression on his face. Jarek was clattering around the galley, but stopped as soon as Bez came in.

For several seconds they stared at her, and she at them.

Given she had no idea what to say, she decided to start with an obvious but relatively harmless question. 'Who is he?'

Jarek answered, 'He's a Consort. From Serenein.'

'One of the boys they put into …' Bez looked meaningfully at the bulge of the drive column on the far side of the living area.

'Yes.'

'What's he doing in your hold?'

'We brought him from Serenein. They can negate Sidhe powers, to an extent.'

He hadn't mentioned *that* when he had explained about the world where the Enemy bred shift-minds. 'So you plan to, what, usc him as, as a *weapon*, if you meet them?'

'That's the theory. Unfortunately, Consorts are rather … difficult. When we woke him up fully, he wasn't exactly cooperative.'

'But you've kept him with you.'

'Yes. If we can find a way to use the boy – ideally without putting him at risk – we will. So far we haven't.'

Another silence fell. Bez did not want to break it, though she knew she had to. Taro saved her the trouble. 'In case you're wondering,' he said, 'the other one's Nual.' Jarek gave him a sharp look. Taro returned it, saying, 'Come on, Jarek, she must've worked it out. She'll've seen Nual's picture when she sorted our IDs!'

The boy was right: Bez had come to that very conclusion. Which begged the question she didn't want to ask. Rather than come straight out with it, she commented, 'She's very beautiful, isn't she?' Bez had thought this at the time Jarek had given her the holopix for the false IDs: how the woman had an odd, almost unearthly beauty about her. Especially her eyes.

'Yes,' said Taro, 'she is.' He looked down at the gun. 'D'you want to know why she's in a comabox?'

'Taro—!'

The boy ignored Jarek's interjection and stared intently at Bez.

Although Bez had never been good with lies, she tried for one now, because the truth was unthinkable. 'Is she ... hurt?'

Taro pressed his lips together and shook his head slowly.

'Look, Bez,' said Jarek, 'I know how much you value information, but there are some things—'

'She's one of *them*, isn't she?'

'Yes,' said Taro shortly. Jarek gave him another look.

'So, just to be clear,' she continued, 'the ally you travel with, and your lover' – She jabbed a finger at Taro – 'is a, a ...'

'Sidhe, yes, all right,' said Jarek. 'She is Sidhe, but she isn't like the rest of them. Nual's a rebel. She's fighting the others. Meeting her is what started me on this whole mission—'

Bez swallowed hard, at the same time holding up a hand. 'I'm very tired. I'd like to rest now.'

'What?'

'I want to sleep.'

'Bez, I know this is a shock, but you have to understand—'

'Tell me later. I need to get some rest first.'

'If you're sure ...' Jarek looked confused.

'Totally.'

Bez made herself put one foot in front of the other, walking towards the cabin she had used earlier. Any moment now, Taro would raise the gun and shoot her—

But he didn't: he and Jarek just watched her pass in silence.

As soon as the cabin door shut behind her, she exhaled. With the breath came the urge to vomit. *She was trapped on a ship with one of the Enemy ...*

She gulped back acid and made herself turn and examine the door. There was a small raised bump; the lock was com-activated and – surprise, surprise – her hosts hadn't linked her com into the ship's system. She might hack the lock – though in her current state that was not a forgone conclusion – but if she did, Jarek or Taro could still override it.

Forcing herself to ignore her nauseous and dysfunctional state, she began rummaging through the cabin's contents.

Objectively speaking, her next move should be suicide. That

was what it came down to. She needed to take her own life before the Sidhe viper that had seduced her erstwhile ally woke up and came for her. The war against the Sidhe could carry on if she were dead, *but only if the information in her head never fell into their hands.* She had tried to get hold of a suicide implant, but while she had managed to find morally grey medics willing to install the finger-tip compartment for her spotcams and carry out the metamorphic surgery that allowed her to alter her appearance, she had never made the right contacts to acquire implanted suicide technology.

There was nothing useful here: no weapons, no drugs, nothing that could inflict lethal damage. Could she force a heart attack? Certainly her heart was beating fast enough. How about battering her head on the wall?

Realising she had lost the ability to reason, she paused. She dragged over a seat – not looking at the clothes she had to brush off it – and jammed it up against the door. It would not actually stop anyone who was determined to get in, but it might slow them down.

She sat on the bed, facing the door. She was so tired. Tired and scared. If she just closed her eyes for a moment and got focused, she might be able to think of some solution—

She started, and came to. She was lying down. As she pushed herself upright, the full horror of the situation came flooding back. She went from unconscious to wide-awake in two stumbling heartbeats.

The sound that had woken her came again. Someone was knocking on the door. She made herself call out, 'What is it?'

'We're here,' said Jarek, sounding calm. Of course he sounded calm. He had nothing to be afraid of.

'Where?' she called back.

'Eklir hub. We've just docked at the station.'

She had slept all the way in from the beacon! Had the Enemy come into the cabin while she was unconscious and insinuated herself into her mind? Bez swallowed rising bile. The seat in front of the door appeared to be where she had left it. She decided to apply the best-case principle. It was either that or hide under the bed, put her fingers in her ears and start screaming.

She stood up. Currently she appeared to be alive and in possession of free will. She took a deep breath then made herself walk over to the door.

NEWS FROM ELSEWHERE

There's no doubt that the Sidhe are still subtly manipulating human history. I don't claim to know their exact agenda, though I have some theories. Then again, when did we ever understand what they were up to?

<file under: Unqualified Data>

Jarek was waiting for her. Bez looked past him but he was alone.

'Listen, Bez,' he said as soon as she stepped out of the cabin, 'I've been an idiot. I should have told you about Nual earlier, but I was afraid you'd ... To be honest, I was worried you'd react like this.'

'Like what?' she muttered, scanning the room. Where was the damn Sidhe? Why was she prolonging the agony? All part of her unspeakable, inhuman games, no doubt. Oddly, Bez no longer felt fear. She just wanted to get it over with.

'Negatively.'

Bez looked back at Jarek and gave a strangled laugh. 'How in the void's name did you *expect* me to react?'

'I hoped you might listen, because I can explain—'

'I'm sure you can. I'm not interested.' Bez took a step, then another, though she couldn't stop staring, searching for the Enemy. Perhaps the Sidhe was still unconscious: Bez suspected, given the nature of shiftspace travel, that they didn't enjoy transits. But then why hadn't Jarek just kept Bez in the cabin until his mistress woke up?

'She isn't here, you know.'

Bez paused then said, 'Then you had better call her, hadn't you? Because we both know how this has to end.'

'Fuck's sakes, Bez! Nual's still in stasis.'

'Really? Then I imagine she's going to be very angry when she wakes up and finds you've let me get away.'

'No she *isn't*, because as I keep trying to tell you, Nual is *on our side*.'

'No, Jarek, she's on *her* side, regardless of what you might think. That's how they work.' But hope had crept back. If the Sidhe really was unconscious then Bez had some chance of getting off the ship before she awoke.

Jarek spread his hands. 'Is there anything I can say at this point to persuade you I'm still your ally?'

Rather than answer, Bez began walking again. It was only a few steps to the exit from the rec-room. 'I'll be leaving now. There's no need to take me any further,' she said as she entered the short corridor. Jarek called after her, but she ignored him.

Reaching the airlock, she expected it to be locked, or else to reveal the Enemy, grinning evilly and poised to violate her mind, but the door opened at her touch and the 'lock itself was empty.

Bez stepped inside and slapped the panel. When the inner door slid shut, cutting off Jarek Reen's continued protests, she let herself breathe. She checked the readouts, because this could still be a trap. When she was sure she was not about to space herself, she opened the outer door. Ahead was a short docking corridor. She strode down it to the closed door at the far end, where she listened impatiently to the standard disembarkation message. She scanned her com, with its current ID, as soon as the panel lit.

She found herself in a customs clearing area. At this late hour it was empty. The bored immigration officials barely spared this nondescript budget traveller a second glance. Even so, by the time Bez exited on to the station's main concourse she was quaking, her breath coming in gasps. Her first priority was to change persona. If – when – Captain Reen and his traitorous crew came after her, she needed to be untraceable. Though the routine was second nature – unlock dataegg; change appearance; collect props – it left her strung out.

She used her new ID to buy a complete set of replacement clothes, including underwear, dumping everything she had been wearing into a donation hopper. Then she paid a private medical service for a full body-scan. She had been unconscious on Captain Reen's ship, in an unlocked cabin, for several hours. If the Sidhe had got in during that time, there was nothing Bez could do about it; but a physical bug was something else, and right now the only reason she could think of for Reen letting her go was that he had planted, or implanted, some sort of tracking device on her. When the med-scan didn't find anything, she decided she had taken enough precautions to let herself rest.

She booked into a cube hostel and, once locked in the coffin-like space, curled up into a foetal ball and slept.

Another rude awakening. She sat up, her mind in overdrive. The sound came again: it wasn't an internal alarm, but, half-asleep as she was, it took a moment to trace the beeping to a flashing wall panel. It appeared she had slept beyond the allocated check-out time. If she wanted to stay any longer, the hostel's system informed her, she would need to pay. She did so gladly, making an additional payment for use of the washroom. She hesitated before opening the door; her lack of spotcam coverage was an uncomfortable hole in her defences, and the thought of having been so close to one of the Enemy still made her gorge rise. Despite the negative scan and change of clothing, she could not shake the fear that her every move was being watched, that she was merely being allowed the *illusion* of freedom. Soon they would strike, and everything would be over. But the crawlspace outside her cube was empty, and when she ventured into the washroom, she had it to herself.

Back in Eklir's dockside mall, the smell from a fast-food outlet stopped her in her tracks. She went in and bought a meal. As she ate, watching the life of the hub pass by outside the window, she conceded that some of her recent behaviour might not have been entirely rational.

Her initial reaction on discovering the truth about Jarek Reen's companion was to reject everything to do with the freetrader captain. However, he had previously been extremely helpful, not least by providing the memory-core from the *Setting Sun*. It appeared that some time between then and now he had fallen under the sway of the Enemy. The timing was odd – he had met 'Nual' before he gave Bez the Sidhe data – but there were a number of possible explanations. The Sidhe could have convinced her travelling companions she was human when she first met them. Or perhaps she had assumed the identity of a human crew member. Both possibilities had flaws, and there were other anomalies. For example, if the Consort really could negate her powers, why did the Sidhe let Jarek Reen keep him on board? But the alternative, that Reen had been in league with the Enemy from the start, was even less likely: it would invalidate the data Bez had got from him previously and she had had enough independent verification of the *Setting Sun* intel to know it was good.

She decided to continue to trust the memory-core data, though she would be even more careful in corroborating it. Captain Reen, however, was no longer an ally. At least she was safe from him now, as he had no way of tracing the ID she was currently using; nor any of her others, given he was a freetrader not a databreaker.

For the sake of her sanity she decided to look upon this as another near miss rather than assume there was some greater, as yet hidden, conspiracy at work.

By the time she left the eatery, she had decided on her immediate course of action.

She started by looking into onward passage. If Captain Reen had alerted the Enemy, it was possible they would be watching departures from this hub; but given how thinly the Sidhe's resources were spread, and their lack of influence in the hubs, she doubted it. Thank the void she had not told Captain Reen where she was going next. The Gracen lead was not directly related to the intel he had provided, which made following it up more attractive than ever. She needed to get to Kotane to collect Alpha83's dataspike.

She spent a while wandering about the station, stopping here for a caf, there for a sit-down. She bought replacement spotcams, such items being legal here. Eklir was big on gambling, so she dropped in on a public gaming hall where terceball matches and other top sporting events were beeveed in live to allow punters to bet on them. She never gambled but she found places like gaming halls and bars useful, given the large number of distracted people – and hence hackable coms. Such establishments focused their security on protecting credit transfers, and paid comparatively little attention to actual communications. By the time she returned to her room, she had discreetly checked both her permanent and transient datadrops.

The news from elsewhere was largely positive. She noted with interest that the Ylonis shipyards were laying people off due to a shortage of transit-kernels. This supported Captain Reen's claim that he had cut off the supply of those particular items at source. Or someone had, anyway.

She also received the expected datapacket from Sestine. On sifting through the news digest, she discovered why Beta16 had failed to answer her ping. Buried among police statistics she found a report of an aircar accident. Only one vehicle was involved, and foul play was suspected. The aircar's only passenger was in a coma from which he was unlikely to recover.

Bez's first thought was to blame the Enemy, but this was not their style: why arrange a suspicious accident when you can induce an apparently natural heart attack or aneurysm?

No, she had a good idea who was behind her agent's 'accident'. She was not the only person paying Beta16 to carry out shady activities. She had some evidence (held in reserve as blackmail material) that he was involved with one of the criminal cartels that operated in the Sestine system. Arranging an aircar accident *was* their style. Back when she first set out on her mission of righteous vengeance, Bez had contemplated dealing with such organisations herself, although they tended to be single-system and have little influence in the hubs. They would, however, pay well for false IDs and had access to the kind of people she might need to hunt down and kill the Enemy. On balance, she had decided that getting entangled with such blatant criminality was too risky.

She dug a little deeper into the news digest and managed to piece together the likely series of events: Beta16 had fallen foul of his dubious associates; they had responded predictably; as a result of the botched assassination-disguised-as-accident, the authorities took an interest in Beta16's activities; thus, his role maintaining the Yolson identity, and laundering the associated funds, had come to light. The Yolson ID was a resurrectee, and the Church, who were powerful in that system – they often were on lawless worlds – had taken exception to a dead holy man being impersonated in the cause of criminal behaviour. They had gone after the only lead – 'Oloria Estrante'.

The end result was that the Estrante persona was defunct, and all associated funds were inaccessible.

Working out this chain of events took most of a day. The next morning she was awoken by a com message from a freetrader offering a reasonably priced ride to Kotane. After checking out her intel on his outfit, she accepted. To her relief, his ship did have a spare comabox.

CONTRADICTORY INPUT

Beevee is a problem. The Sidhe use beevee, just like everyone else. In fact, it's one of the areas where they have most influence. It's even possible they have secret channels, although experience leads me to doubt this. Still: be careful. Encrypt, encode, and, if possible, distribute your data via dataspikes transported by trusted carriers. Some of you will soon be receiving additional information to this databurst via that very route.

<file under: Core Data>

Kotane was built into a crater on a small planetoid, a fairly common configuration for hub stations; however, unlike most stations, the builders had used clear roofing material. They had also neglected to fit ceilings in most public areas, including dockside. The Kotane system's dim, phase-locked sun shone down perpetually on gently sloping artificial chasms walled with shops and bars, bathing every space not filled by holos or artificial lighting in a red glow. The locals appeared to like the subdued ambience, but Bez thought the combination of long-wavelength light and open vistas gave the station a disquieting atmosphere, making it low on her list of preferred stopovers.

After assuming her new persona, she booked appropriate accommodation and then went for a walk. She stopped outside a homeware store, sitting on one of the benches provided for tired shoppers. She closed her eyes and tuned into Kotane's public com system, spoofing off the shop's signal. She queried a certain shipping company to find out if they had received a delivery for her. They hadn't, which was worrying: Alpha83's dataspike should have been here several days ago.

She made a non-spoofed call to the station's labour exchange, during which she turned down a job in a bar but accepted a week of poorly paid eight-hour shifts in the kitchen of a family restaurant off the main drag. It was credit and it was cover, and it distracted her from fretting.

The work consisted of loading and unloading dishwashing machines and involved almost no human contact. Bez had had worse jobs.

She barely considered the irony of regularly taking on such menial labour when, should all the resources she had used over the last twenty years be taken into account, she was one of the wealthiest individuals in human-space. She was stuck with whatever funds a given persona had at a given time; and as long as she had a safe place to sleep and enough food to eat, she was loathe to waste credit that might be useful to her mission. Having said that, since getting hold of the *Setting Sun* data, she had considered in passing the sort of life she might have when – if – her mission succeeded. Perhaps she would consolidate any remaining funds into a stable persona, and live out her life as that one person. An odd thought, and not one she felt inclined to dwell on at this stage.

She checked for the dataspike again after her first shift. Still nothing. She spent her free time concentrating on other leads, and on the housekeeping necessary to maintain her hyperweb, using some of her earnings to cultivate a couple of new contacts via ongoing beevee discussions.

By the fourth day she was worried enough to ping Alpha83. She considered informing the agent that she, Bez, had decided to remain in the agreed datadrop location, but dismissed the idea of transmitting such information, even with multiple encodings, as too risky.

Another day passed. Bez found herself checking for a ping-back every few hours. It would be a single word, the second half a two-word phrase both Bez and Alpha83 knew. There were several correct responses: the exact word Alpha83 chose would indicate her situation.

The silence from Gracen dragged on. Bez's casual contract

finished. She almost missed the comfortable monotony of imposing order and cleanliness on other people's dirt. The labour exchange had nothing else appropriate but said they would keep her on their books.

The next day she received, along with her expected messages, one from Tarset. The agent she had engaged to search for images of the helpful stranger had got a match. His name was Imbarin Tierce, and he was a troubleshooter for the station's Board of Directors; he was not publically acknowledged or listed, but was rumoured to deal with situations where the Board could not be seen to act. He was, for example, said to be the person who negotiated with a hab-rat gang whose petty pilfering was endangering property and possibly life; if the Board had sent in the law, things could have got nasty, but Sirrah Tierce had met with representatives from the station's underclass. Not long after that, the thefts had stopped – although only after a shipment of the kind of building materials ideal for use in Tarset's dead spaces had mysteriously gone missing.

So, he was someone important, if shadowy, on Tarset hub. That did not explain his interest in her, and raised all sorts of other questions.

Bez slept on the news. In the morning, the labour exchange commed her, offering more work. She told them, politely, that she had made other arrangements.

Actually finalising those arrangements turned out to be harder than expected. Although freetraders travelling between hubs often carried paying passengers, getting a lift to a planetary system was far harder. And a planetary system belonging to a society that eschewed excess material wealth would be lucky if it saw three tradebirds in a year. Fortunately Gracen, thanks to one particular aspect of its culture, was on the standard tourist trail. But that meant using a starliner to get there.

She could have paid one of her secondary agents in the sector to travel to Gracen on her behalf, but that would have taken time; with the intel Alpha83 had unearthed looking increasingly like the best option for bringing the Enemy down, Bez wanted to act swiftly and deal with this personally. Besides, Alpha83's message had implied that databreaking skills might be required to get hold of hard evidence of the Sidhe ID fraud. She herself was the logical person to follow this up.

All these rationalisations would not have mattered one bit if, somewhere deep inside, she had not wanted to make an uncharacteristic move out of the hubs. The last few weeks had brought too many close calls and nasty shocks, and though her natural inclination was to worry at their significance and possible interconnectedness, sometimes the best way to make sense of an excess of contradictory input was to let it lie.

She activated a little-used tourist ID and shunted around sufficient locally stored funds to pay for a return trip to Gracen. When she got back into the hubs, she would need to do some serious databreaking to restore the credit lost in the Beta16 fiasco. She arranged forwarding for her permanent datadrop, and informed those of her agents who needed to know that there might be a slight delay in normal communications.

The journey to Gracen included one change of liner and three stopovers.

Tourists tended to assume that being rich enough to travel the stars made them members of the same exclusive club, which arguably it did, but it was not a club to which Bez belonged, and once she had made it clear she was not looking for sex or companionship, she was actively snubbed by her fellow passengers. This was fine by her. She spent most of her time on the liner in her cabin, researching her eventual destination. She left the liner only long enough to check her datadrops at each stopover, in order to head off any issues that looked like they might arise while she was outside the hub network.

She had to acknowledge the possibility, however remote, that she was walking into a trap. If the Enemy had captured Alpha83 and read the agent's mind, they would know that she had been investigating ID fraud on behalf of a third party. But the name by which Alpha83 knew Bez had no connection to the one she was currently travelling under, and there was no active Sidhe presence in the Gracen system. Those involved in the ID fraud would be human, and most likely have no idea whom they really worked for. Besides, there was *always* the possibility that any new situation was a set-up. Hence the need for the best-case principle.

The system's one inhabited world was painted in muddled shades of brown and hazed with the thin veil of atmosphere. As she watched it on final approach, Bez marvelled at how *big* the planet was. All that mass, most of it wasted.

A soft-spoken announcement over the ship's com suggested that any passengers who had not already done so might wish to change into local attire. Bez was already wearing one of the ubiquitous robes, which, once on-planet, would not only protect against the environment but also declare the wearer's place in the world, though not with anything as subtle as tags. While the holos she had viewed showed Graceni natives swathed in colours apparently denoting everything from a person's age to their favourite style of food, tourist robes were primarily black, with a thin line of decoration down the central fastening and around the bottom hem. The main message a tourist's robes conveyed was the wearer's sexual preferences. Given why people came to Gracen, Bez knew she would not find a robe whose patterning broadcast the silent message, *No thanks*. She ended up settling for clothes that labelled her as *Hetero, single partner, do not initiate contact*.

She unwrapped the second part of the 'local attire', a set of photo-reactive glasses, which the guidebooks referred to as comshades. Outdoors on Gracen such eye coverings were a necessity; indoors they were a social convention. The glasses gave access to Gracen's infoscape: although the locals avoided implants on religious grounds, Gracen had a sophisticated information culture. The shades were oddly retro compared to the contacts or flip-monocles other info-savvy religious cultures employed, but Bez was happy to have her eyes hidden from strangers.

She put on the glasses, adjusting the mic stub to sit snugly on her cheek. The shades flashed up a message asking if she wished them to be initialised to her ID. She sub-vocced 'Yes' and waited.

After about ten seconds she got a message saying she was now fully connected. She shut down the glasses and blinked her headware online. Her tech took less than a second to interface with the local comnet. Good: both methods worked. She would need to be careful, though: the guidebooks warned against tuning in fully; Gracen's infoscape manifested largely as overlays, with few coherent virtualities.

The next announcement stated that landing was imminent, and passengers should proceed to the departure lounge. Starliners usually sent shuttles down to planets, but although Gracen only had one attraction it was an eternally popular one and the ship would be landing to allow everyone to sample it.

Disembarkation occurred with the unctuous efficiency typical of starliner service. As she stepped into the egress tube, Bez experienced the first incontrovertible evidence of landing on an alien world: the air was too dry and smelled wrong. It also made her mildly light-headed. She knew this was no illusion; the guidebooks stated there was a slightly above average O_2 level in Gracen's arid atmosphere, inducing a feeling of (they claimed) mild wellbeing. Bez only hoped the addendum, that one adjusted to the rich atmosphere within a few hours, was true.

The customs hall was full but the formalities were simple and well handled. Bez was quickly reunited with her minimal luggage and directed to her appointed guide, one of about a dozen who waited, hoods modestly raised, just beyond the barrier. Aside from the guides and the tourists, the room beyond was empty, the adverts playing on the walls subdued and relatively tasteful. No broadcasts tried to insinuate themselves into her eyewear; another contrast to the hubs, where anyone not running the latest ad-blockers was liable to get a visual cortex full of unwanted product placement.

In an hour or so the starport would be full of people travelling the other way, mainly tourists returning sated from their trip, but perhaps also some locals. Graceni were free to leave their world, but those that did so were considered apostate, and not permitted to return. Several thousand people – mainly women – chose to leave every year, cutting all ties to their former home. This emi-gration policy made this world ideal as a source of long-term false identities.

She raised her hood before leaving customs; chill air puffed across the nape of her neck as the robe's cooling unit activated. Her allocated guide already had nine people with her; Bez knew the guide was female because of social conventions rather than appearance, for the peak of her hood combined with her shades to hide most of her face. She braced herself for the local greet-ing, holding her breath when the woman kissed her lightly on the lips, with a murmured, 'Welcome, sister.' Fighting the waft of pheromone-laden perfume, she muttered the correct response, 'I greet thee sister,' and pulled back hastily.

While they waited for the last few women to join the party, their guide passed around *cigrenes*, another local vice. The aromatic smoking sticks were a social lubricant rather than an intoxicant, and Bez had already spent time in the starliner's smoking lounge getting used to this dirtborn vice. She found it distasteful but, thanks to her earlier practice, was able to smoke successfully with-out having a coughing fit or setting fire to herself. She took the pale yellow tube and let her guide lean across to set fire to the end with a stick lighter. While her charges enveloped themselves in sweet smoke, the woman pointed out the kiosks where the visitors could buy *cigrenes* for themselves.

As the wait for the last few tourists stretched and the hubbub grew, Bez found herself becoming increasingly uneasy. On the starliner she had enjoyed an impressive level of social exclusion, but down here, with everyone crowded together and eager to sample the local entertainments, the atmosphere had changed. Conversations were breaking out all over, and it was only a matter of time before someone tried to include her in one.

Bez edged up to the guide and said, 'Excuse me, but I just want to get to my hotel. Is it all right if I leave?'

The guide turned to her, shades flickering, 'Oh, aye, Medame Shiqua. Thy accommodation, 'tis done for thee.'

It took Bez a moment to identify the response as a question. 'Er, yes, I've pre-booked. I just need a cab. I believe I can pick one up from outside?'

'Thou surely may. Thy choice is a *tanyen* hotel. Thou art familiar with *tanyen*.'

Tanyen was the term for lone women who were visiting family or working in the city. 'I understand it is acceptable for female offworld visitors who want to experience the real Gracen to stay in *tanyen* establishments.' Her choice made her conspicuous, but it was a risk worth taking when balanced against the kind of attention she would receive in mainstream tourist accommodation.

'Aye, 'tis so, sister. I merely desired certainty that thy choice was with forethought.'

'It was.'

'Thy visit is not for the purifying congress.'

'No,' said Bez shortly. 'It's not. I'm an anthropologist.' People did occasionally come to Gracen for reasons other than sex.

'Then make thy way as thou wilt, sister.' The guide turned to greet another arrival.

Bez pressed through the crowd, heading for the exit. As the doors opened she winced at the blast of heat on her face, then walked forward into the thick, hot air. Her robes ramped up their cooling but they could do nothing for the burning sensation on her cheeks, chin and the backs of her hands: *A naked star is radiating directly onto my skin!*

She felt a crippling sense of cultural vertigo. Although each hub had a distinctive flavour, they belonged to the same, space-bound society. Yet here she was, on a *planet,* for the first time in two decades.

EXPECTED OBEISANCE

Some systems – spur theocracies, anarch worlds and the like – have little or no Sidhe contamination.

Even where the Sidhe have a presence, it's not generally in system governments. There are a few, in locations that are strategically important to them, but not many.

What they do have is people in the trans-system companies, especially those involved with technology or communication. They concentrate their efforts on stifling the development of new tech, controlling our access to existing tech – especially shiftships – and maintaining a position from which they can subtly influence large-scale decisions.

<file under: Core Data>

She made herself step out into the light, keeping her gaze focused on the pale grey paving while her comshades guided her to a row of boxlike white groundcars. She got into one, put her case on the seat, put the *cigrene* she was still holding in the tray provided, and used her shades to tell the cab where she wanted to go. Then she leaned back into the comfortable upholstery – for all of about a second. The cab accelerated away quickly enough to make Bez reach for the handle recessed into the door. Her *cigrene* went flying. She grabbed it then ground out the lit end in the tray.

The cab swung on to a wide highway, where sparse but equally speedy traffic kept pace. After the initial hair-raising manoeuvre, the ride became smoother.

The highway was enclosed by a high, wire fence; Bez was unsure why, given the surrounding red-brown landscape was empty except for odd outbreaks of sun-bleached vegetation clustering around brightly painted truncated pyramids. These structures were the entrances to extensive underground complexes of shops, offices and housing. This city, Meneske, was home to nearly two million people, and though she could not see anyone above ground aside from travellers in other vehicles, there were thousands of people within a few hundred metres of her right now. Even as she had that thought, she spotted a robed figure bent double on one of the spots of cultivated ground. The cab whisked her past before she could get a proper look.

It occurred to her that, with skin paler than the human norm, the locals might be particularly susceptible to their world's harmful solar radiation. When the Sidhe had first transported humanity off their dying homeworld and distributed them throughout this part of the galaxy, they had taken a perverse delight in setting up colonies of a given human culture in a place that was unsuitable, or in settling two or more cultural groups with a strong antipathy in the same system, or even on the same world.

She focused on the structures she was passing, while her shades informed her what she was seeing using cursive lettering and terse phraseology: that large pyramid was the entrance to a men's college (*education: adult, post-pubescent, (male)*); the smaller one just along from it was an extensive complex of high-priced apartments for mixed-sex married couples and sets (*accommodation (30 units): private, high rent, hetero-bonded*); the slightly asymmetrical pyramid next to that was an office shared by a trio of companies (*businesses, non-industrial: Karsene Publications (fem); Element Private Transport (mixed); Sana's Dye Emporium (fem)*). She drilled down for more data on one of the listed companies, getting results that were less comprehensive, not to mention comprehensible, than she would expect in the hubs. Even the local infoscape was alien.

Her destination was coming up. The cab made an abrupt turn into a side road before decelerating to stop at a gate in the fence. Bez paid from the local account set up by the travel company then got out, moving slowly to give her clothing time to adjust to the heat.

When she reached the gate, it slid open for her. Beyond was a path of the same grey stone she had seen outside the starport; on one side the reddish ground was swept clean and covered by an intricate pattern of round stones coloured black, grey and white; on the other side a yellowish lawn of grass-analogue stretched away to another fence.

Bez walked up the path slowly, eyes down. She would have to look at the limitless turquoise sky at some point but she would get acclimatised to the other environmental differences first. She did spare a glance for the multicoloured décor of the building ahead, which included the sensual squiggle of the Aesir, the Salvatine subsect the Graceni followed.

The door, although barely visible among the murals and inlaid coloured stones, opened at her approach to reveal a lobby decorated relatively tastefully in pale yellow and soothing green. They probably painted their pyramids in those garish colours to make them show up in that awful burning sunlight. There was one outbreak of tastelessness, in the form of a larger-than-life-sized metal arm, encrusted with jewels in shades from citrine to emerald. This peculiar item sat upright in a well-lit alcove near the door, one finger pointing to the ceiling and the others loosely curled.

The woman standing in the lobby had her hood down – no men here to see her thick blonde hair – and she smiled as Bez came in. Bez, who had been hoping for an automated check-in, lowered her own hood.

The woman's gaze flicked towards the metal arm. Bez went over to the item – the ulna of Saint Tana, according to her comshades – then leaned forward with pursed lips to kiss the reliquary's open palm. In preparation for such rituals, she had liberally applied lipseal before disembarking, one of a number of prophylactic measures sold on the starliner.

The woman's smile widened at the sight of an outsider carrying out the expected obeisance, after which she came forward for her own kiss and greeting. Bez forced herself to go through the motions with a smile of her own.

'Thou art welcome in my house,' said the woman, stepping back.

Bez gave the correct response, 'Thy hospitality honours me,' then added, 'You're Dena,' trying to mimic the local non-questioning intonation. Interest from curious locals was one of the risks of venturing off the beaten track; Bez was determined to behave correctly without being patronising.

'I am. Kindly follow me.'

The woman led her to a door in the far wall, which opened onto a shallow spiral staircase. The stairway circled a great open space. Bez had read about the atria at the heart of every Graceni building – if building was an accurate term for a structure that existed almost entirely below ground. Graceni architecture was largely subterranean, due to some obscure but deeply held religious belief that amounted to the easy option being ungodly.

A framework, half sculpture and half hanging garden, reached down from the roof, filling the central void. It emitted reflected sunlight and a faint musical tinkle. It was surrounded by swirling flights of winged motes that, Bez realised with a jolt, were living creatures. When she recoiled, her host said, 'Worry thee not: the flutterflies are harmless; besides, they are contained.'

Now that she looked, Bez could see the near-invisible mesh hanging between her and the sculpture. She also noticed how, rather unnervingly, the stairway spiralled *outwards* as it went down, each subsequent rotation increasing in diameter to define a widening cone of empty space below. She let curiosity overcome caution and peered briefly over the guard-rail. The central sculpture extended down for five floors; a couple of floors below that was the ground, which had been transformed into a verdant garden growing up to meet the sculpture. She started when someone walked across the distant, vegetation-covered floor, then stepped back quickly, her stomach fluttering in counterpoint to the vortices of flying bugs.

Dena made two circuits of the spiral staircase before leading Bez through an archway into an ordinary and mercifully bug-free corridor. With the woman's hood down, Bez could clearly see the line of hooped earrings she wore along the outside of each ear. As Dena turned her head she also glimpsed the top of an abstract pattern peeping above her neckline. Apparently, piercings and tattoos were as voluble as robes, and came into their own when people shed their clothing to get down to the 'purifying congress' – or, as one of the tourists on the liner had jokingly referred to it, 'screwing in the name of the Lord'. Bez couldn't help thinking how, if the activities that went on in Gracen's Temples of the Flesh were half as athletic and creative as she had been led to believe, dangling jewellery attached to body parts could be a serious liability.

Her room was larger than a comparably priced one on a hab, and housed a miniature shrine, though no reliquary. The green and yellow walls and furnishings were offset by what appeared to be real plants in pots on small shelves. After Dena had gone, Bez touched one of the squat green succulents to check her assumption, and felt firm yet yielding plant flesh. A fresh menthol scent filled the air, presumably from the plant, temporarily masking the ever-present aroma of old *cigrene* smoke.

She tried to initiate a low-level interface with the local comnet from her headware, and was alarmed when she failed to get a connection. She activated her shades and got the same result. Her eye fell on what she had initially taken to be a peculiar ornament in a niche by the door. It looked like a primitive handset, something she only recognised thanks to the retro holodramas her mother had inflicted on her during childhood. She snatched up the handset and said, 'Hello?'

A few moments later a voice responded, 'Greetings, sister: thy requirement is?'

'I don't seem to be able to access the comnet.'

'No, thou cannot,' said the voice. The line was crackly and faint, and Bez was not sure whether she was speaking to her host; presumably not, unless the woman had sprinted back to her office. 'Thou must step into the stairwell. The rock is thy comfort within thy room.' Then, faintly disapproving, 'Perhaps thou would be more at ease in an establishment accustomed to outsiders.'

Bez was beginning to think the woman had a point, but she just said, 'I'm fine, thanks. I don't want to be any trouble.'

She walked to the end of the corridor, from where she reconnected to the local comnet using the shades. When she tried her headware, the link was solid.

Having reassured herself, she returned to her room and got cleaned up. She began to unwind a little. Despite the uncertainty and possible danger, at some deep level she relished the challenge she had taken on by coming here in person. Or perhaps the heady air was getting to her.

She would start with some datasearches to get accustomed to the local infoscape. The guidebooks claimed the Graceni were meticulous in their record-keeping, and freely shared non-confidential data; an excellent combination, as far as Bez was concerned. The only issue was what they considered 'non-confidential'.

She returned to the stairwell and connected to the local net. However, once she moved beyond asking basic questions about the function of adjacent buildings, or overall population demographics, she ran into difficulties. Neither the organisation of the data nor the paths for accessing it followed the conventions used in the hubs. Gracen's infoscape relied heavily on unexplained shorthand codes and symbols, the virtual equivalent of the visual cues given by colour and pattern. Bez had already worked out some of the local semiotics – for example, exclusively feminine objects and areas of interest had a more rounded and organic design, and favoured mid-spectrum colours – but the nuances were beyond her. It didn't help that most non-statistical data came in the form of journals or discussion threads.

Getting to grips with the alien infoscape would take time, and working in a space like this was not ideal. It was public, but not busy enough to provide heavy com traffic as cover for her activities. She had no intention of visiting any bars or clubs; without a full understanding of the local customs, she risked finding herself in the wrong sort of establishment. The guidebooks said there were places women met merely to socialise, rather than as precursors to visiting the Temple, but those guidebooks also suggested engaging a local if you wanted to venture outside the normal tourist stamping grounds. Hiring such help would attract attention in a way private datasearches would not.

REMILLA
(New Salem, Quondat, Quondat System)

Everyone has secrets.

Except from God, of course.

Remilla finished her prayers and reached for the bottle. Unstoppering it without looking, she breathed deeply, retaining just enough sense to replace the cap before falling back on to the narrow bed.

Her next rational thought, some time later, was to remember what the Community Pastor had said about such intoxicants: an invitation to the Devil, he'd called them. Remilla found this highly amusing and started to giggle, until the girl in the next cubicle banged on the partition to tell her to shut up. With that, the last of the Fume dispersed from her brain and her giggles turned to quiet sobs. It was remembering the Community that did it, because that reminded her she was damned.

It had all started when her sister left to be married. She had missed Armina so much. She had barely been able to wait until Holy Day each week, when they could meet and talk.

Then her first bleed had come, and she too had left her father's house. She was married to Pol, a man respected for his scholarly knowledge. He had read every source of the Book still extant, and was fluent in the lost languages, Lacune and Ederlische. Pol was very smart, and hardly ever beat her, even when she deserved it.

Unfortunately, his studies meant he neglected their farm, so Remilla had to work harder than most women, but such was her duty. She also maintained the weapons they needed to defend themselves against the Heretics – the ploughshares that could become swords; the household chemicals that could be combined to make bombs or poison gas. She performed her more feminine duties too, though that was hard in its own way. Knowing what she did now, she suspected Pol had little interest in sex. But he knew the Community needed to increase their numbers. This was the covenant that defined them: they had been granted marginal land and given licence to procreate freely. A double blessing, the elders called it, because the authorities had given the faithful the chance to show their mettle and the freedom to expand across new territory. Of course, the government had said the same to the damned Mithrai, with their heretical beliefs, and for years now her Community and the Heretics had been in a state of unofficial conflict, a low-key war ignored by the rest of the world provided it stayed in the unwanted northern lands.

Her husband had come to her every month, but after two years of marriage she had failed to conceive. Tongues began to wag, and she found it increasingly hard to meet the eyes of the other women on Holy Day.

Then Armina died. Pol said it was an accident, but would give her no details. There were whisperings in church among the older women who sat near the screen; they claimed there had been another man involved. And it was said that a man in the next valley had been cast out of the Community.

Remilla was torn: she mourned her sister, yet at the same time she was desperate to prove herself more worthy than Armina, to free herself from the shame that fell upon her by association. She heard the term 'red-haired harlot' bandied about; she shared her sister's distinctive colouring and, like Armina, was not always scrupulous in tying her headscarf. She told herself that if only she could give Pol a son, everything would be all right.

When her husband said they should seek external help for her barrenness, Remilla had been as shocked as everyone else. Prayer should be enough. But Pol had some status in the south, and the ability to argue others in the Community around to his cause. So they had travelled to New Salem, taking a roundabout route to avoid Heretic lands, in search of a medical miracle to help manifest God's will.

Remilla's tears flowed more freely now, because having started to recall the past, she had no choice but to remember what happened next, after they arrived in the city.

Perhaps if her husband had invested in technology to stop them getting lost, or if he hadn't tried to reason with the men who had cornered them in that rain-soaked alley; or if she had not stupidly fought back, once Pol had been knocked to the ground and she realised what the men intended. They had not expected a God-fearing little woman to know how to defend herself, but the injury she had inflicted on one of them had made the men treat her with extra brutality. Any pain she had caused was repaid many times over in the following hours. Pol they simply killed.

In some ways her life had ended then. Certainly her old life was gone; her husband was dead, her body abused. The doctors at the charity hospital where she woke up told her she *had* died, briefly. Since then, she had had plenty of cause to wish she had stayed dead.

The hospital discharged her with a week's supply of medicine and a clean if worn set of clothes, courtesy of a church donation network. And that was it. Even if she had managed to find her way back to the Community, they would never have let her in again, not after what had been done to her. One of the charity medics had told her about the internal injuries; she would certainly never bear a child now.

Given she was already ruined, it was not such a large step to start selling herself. Not that she'd intended to fall to harlotry. She had meant to kill herself. She decided to jump from the Skylon tower, favoured spot of lovers and suicides. But as she'd squeezed through the worn fencing and out onto the ledge, a woman's voice had called out from the shadows behind her, offering Remilla something for the pain: 'If you're gonna go anyway, leastways go happy, girl,' she'd said. Remilla, having nothing left to lose, had agreed, and had discovered the glorious Fume, and since then other intoxicants, all of them capable of granting temporary oblivion while putting off the inevitable confrontation with her maker. In return, she worked. A very different sort of work to that on the farm, but all she was good for now.

Somehow, through it all, she kept her faith. A twisted version of it, perhaps, because where once she'd believed she was saved, now she knew she was damned. But even the damned might be redeemed. Perhaps her suffering was a test. A test she had failed so far, but the Manifest Son had died for everyone, saint and sinner alike. There was hope.

Even so, the despair sometimes hit hard enough to make her devour every form of chemical oblivion available in the hope of never returning from where the drugs sent her. When she did come back – sometimes after another stint on the city's charity – she'd get grief from the mamas at the bawdy house. But within a few days she'd be back working the streets. There was no other option.

She was, by standard reckoning, coming up to eighteen years old. She was not sure she would, or wanted to, reach twenty.

She kept her sobs quiet, but even so she failed to hear the mama's approach. She looked up as the curtain was pulled aside, and received a loud *tut* from the older woman standing there. Remilla sniffed and sat up.

'Wash your face and get dressed, girl,' the mama said. 'You got work to do.'

'I thought I was done for the night,' said Remilla meekly.

'You was, but Issa's sick. Can't have her puking over a special client.'

A special client. Remilla tried not to let her dismay show.

The mama clapped her hands, 'Chop chop, girl!'

Remilla jumped to her feet, looking round for her dress and makeup.

The good news was, the special client didn't have extreme tastes. He was an offworlder, half as tall again as Remilla, and he'd apparently ordered, *One normal and wonaya local midgets.* The 'normal' was a girl Remilla had seen around, probably part native and part offworlder, given she was somewhat shorter than the average freetrader or tourist. The bad news was that the john wanted to watch the two of them while he played with himself. This was the worst sort of work. Being used like an object Remilla could accept, because that was what she was, a damned-to-hell broken piece of flesh. Having to feign lust for a stranger to titillate another stranger was far harder.

Fortunately, the other girl led the way and they fell into a low-key dom-sub routine that the john liked enough to jerk himself clean to while he watched, after which he passed out in the stirrup chair. The two of them stayed put until he began to snore, then the taller girl got off the bed. She eyed up the unconscious offworlder then turned and unshackled Remilla. Remilla thanked her with a nod, and scooted across the bed. There was a bottle of Fume on the cabinet, which the john had paid for but barely touched, having already got tanked on alcohol. They were, by Remilla's reckoning, paid up for another half hour, and with the john unconscious it seemed a shame to waste the Fume.

As Remilla's hand closed around the bottle she realised the other girl was watching her. She held the bottle out. 'You want first breath?' she whispered.

The girl shook her head. 'You go ahead,' she whispered back.

'You prefer dust? Or booze?'

'Nah. I don't.'

Remilla looked at her hard. In her two years working the streets of New Salem, she'd never met a whore who didn't need something, and this girl was older then her, mid-twenties at least. 'What ... nothing at all?'

'Nope.'

'So, how'd you deal with it?' Remilla's gaze flicked round the room, taking in the unconscious john. Something about the other girl encouraged frankness.

'You'd laugh if I told you.'

'Try me.'

The john stirred. Both girls tensed, but he just snorted, scratched his balls, and started snoring again.

'You want to talk outside?' asked the girl, nodding at the door.

'Sure.'

'I'm Frej,' she said, as they gathered their clothes and gear. Not her street moniker, which Remilla knew: Frej was her real name.

'I'm Remilla,' she offered in return. It had been a long time since she had told anyone her given name; a long time since anyone had cared enough to ask.

Remilla picked up the bottle, and they crept into an adjacent empty bedroom. Remilla had intended to breathe deep but she felt awkward in front of Frej. 'So, what's your secret?' she asked the other girl, grinning to show she wasn't mocking her.

Frej shrugged like she expected to get insulted. 'I got religion.'

Remilla nearly dropped the bottle. She felt exposed in a way she hadn't when she had been physically naked at the end of Frej's whip. She managed a strangled, 'Oh.'

'Remilla? You all right?'

Hearing her name like that warmed her heart. 'I … I had religion. Once. Maybe I still do, if God'll have me.'

'The Divine is always accessible. Even here.'

Not God: the Divine. 'You're …' Remilla struggled for the right word. She'd heard countless sermons at the Community warning of the many misguided sects pretending to preach the True Faith. Which one of them used the term 'Divine'? She couldn't remember, and finished, a little apologetically, '… a heretic.'

To her surprise, Frej laughed. 'Well, I ain't one of your lot, that's true. You're from that northern patriarchal commune, right? The ones trying to farm the wastes?' She shook her head ruefully.

Remilla nodded, though she wasn't sure what 'patriarchal' meant. She wondered if she should try to defend the Community, but didn't feel much inclined.

'You're still a cut above the godless, in my book,' said Frej.

'Thanks.'

'And if you ever want to come outside and pray with me, I'd welcome the company.'

'Pray with you?' Since entering the living hell of New Salem, Remilla had never shared the act of worship. Sometimes she lurked outside churches on Holy Day, and murmured along with the prayers and chants, but she never dared enter. She was fallen; such places were not for her. Then Frej's exact words registered.

'What do you mean, "come outside" and pray? Surely we'd have to go to church. Or we can pray anywhere – provided we don't disturb anyone.' Remilla had been beaten up by one of the other girls for praying too loudly, and had learned to keep the volume down.

'Church? Nah. I know that where you come from the men say you can only get with the Divine if you follow their rules, but it don't have to be like that. You want to find something bigger than us shitty humans and our shitty lives, you don't need a church. Being outside's good, though, puts you in touch with the Universe.'

Remilla had never heard anyone talk like that. Frej obviously believed, but it was a very different faith from the sort she knew. 'Can you … tell me more?'

Frej laughed. 'Surely can.'

AN ABSTEMIOUS LOT

This has been building for years, but I'm – we're – finally getting close. When we strike, it has to be perfectly coordinated. If the Sidhe get wind of what's happening, they'll take precautions, perhaps just disappear then surface again later.

It'll all come together on R-Day – a single day, twenty-five hours that will change human-space for ever.

You probably want to know what 'R' stands for. Well, 'revelation', or perhaps 'retaking'. Or maybe 'revenge'.

<file under: Core Data>

Bez's musings were interrupted by an incoming com call. For a moment she paused, alarmed – *Who even knew she was here?* – but it was just her host, asking if Bez wished to join the other guests for dinner. She said she would love to: she wanted to make the effort to fit in, and her body needed food. She had used the journey from Tarset to get into synch with local time, but the adjustment had left her more sensitive to physical requirements such as eating and sleeping at regular times. 'Where's the restaurant?' she asked.

'The garden is our dining area. Follow thou the path all the way.'

'With the flutterflies?'

'Sonics are employed to keep the smallest of the All-Father's creatures at bay while we take our repast.' Dena sounded amused.

Bez followed the instructions and went down to the garden, which was wild in the centre but became more formal near the edges, ending in well-trimmed lawn. The tables, which were arrayed in a half-circle against the outside wall, sat on yellow and green paving slabs. About half the seats were occupied, some by single women like her, some by larger groups. Other women milled around, talking and smoking, standing way too close to each other even when they were not obviously lovers. Given how empty this world was, Bez found the Graceni's lack of respect for personal space perplexing. With her darker-than-average skin she drew a few curious glances, but no one approached.

Bez spotted an empty two-person table and sat down. After a while a woman approached her; Bez tensed, wondering if she wanted the other seat. The woman stopped and said with the flat local tonality, 'Evening blessings, sister. Anything more than water to drink.'

There was a carafe on the table, but Bez had noticed other diners with tall glasses or steaming mugs. 'Evening blessings. Do you have caf?'

The woman shook her head ruefully. 'No caf. If thou so desires, we have pear-cactus syrup or mint matte.'

'Water will be fine, thanks.' Though Bez had not paid much attention to the sections on food and drink, she did remember the guidebooks warning potential hedonists that they would find few intoxicants here. Aside from the sex and the *cigrenes*, the Graceni were an abstemious lot. Even caf was a stimulant too far.

The meal itself was self-service: women were going over to an open servery further round the wall and returning with bowls. Bez waited until the crowd died down before fetching hers. The food smelled great, though the unappetising meat-stew-with-white-lumps would have got a starliner chef fired on the spot. She took the bowl back to her place and picked up the linked pair of sticks the Graceni used instead of normal cutlery. She hadn't had the opportunity to practise with these, and her first few attempts resulted in a lot of dropped food, some of which she barely caught in the bowl. Eventually she managed to get the hang of lifting the food to her mouth and snatching it off the sticks before it fell, although she did resort to surreptitiously spearing some of the larger lumps. Despite being lukewarm due to her ineptitude with the sticks, the meal was delicious: the meat was succulent and tender, the white lumps some sort of vegetable that was crisp on the outside and fluffy inside, providing a perfect counterpoint to the stew's richness. Taking her cue from the other women, she lifted the bowl to drink the last of the rich gravy.

Some women were going back for slabs of syrup-drenched honeycomb cake, but Bez decided against this; her antics with the bowl of stew had resulted in quiet amusement on adjacent tables, and she did not fancy providing entertainment during the next course as well. She was about to activate her comshades when she saw Dena coming over.

'Thou art satisfied in body and soul,' said her host.

Dena was looking at her empty bowl, so Bez responded, 'Yes, thank you, the food was excellent.'

'In truth, such bounty is not for the common day.'

Bez said, 'Of course: today's a Holy Day, isn't it?'

Dena's smiled broadened. 'Aye. Thou art a believer?' She actually exaggerated the question, which Bez took to mean she was surprised.

'I'm afraid not.'

'Even so, the Lord All-Father extends his love to thee, sister,' said Dena. 'And thy voice is welcome to join ours.'

Bez had noticed some of the women gathering on the far side of the room; she had been mildly concerned this might be the precursor to some sort of sexual activity, although the guidebooks had been clear that sex was culturally inappropriate outside Temples or private rooms. 'No, it's all right. I'm not a good singer.'

'As thou desires.'

Bez did not think Dena was offended, though it was hard to tell, so she asked, 'Is it all right if I stay here anyway?'

'Thou may treat my house as thy home, sister.'

'Thank you.'

Dena took Bez's bowl and moved off.

After a quick glance round to check no one was paying undue attention, Bez activated her comshades. Over dinner she had been considering the best way to interface with Gracen's quirky infoscape. For a start she needed to declare her gender: actively identifying herself as a woman increased her chances of getting access to detailed data about another woman. It was an interesting reflection on Graceni culture that datasearches did not automatically link back to a person's ID. Information, like sex, was freely available – provided you followed the rules.

Once she had informed the comnet she was female, her view of the infoscape opened up. For the first time she was able to access specific names and addresses.

As was the case with many of her agents, Bez had originally found Alpha83 through the beevee boards – what the trashier news services referred to as the 'interstellar chat network'. That nickname was not only derogatory, it was inaccurate: beevee costs and routing delays didn't allow for anything as frivolous and instantaneous as 'chat'. In recruiting agents for her network, especially the Alphas, Bez looked for intelligent people who had both the material means and the level of commitment to follow a cause she could legitimately claim to share; what she thought of as their 'button'. She never hinted at her real motivation, any more than she included genuine info in her profile. People who would easily believe she was fighting the Sidhe were not the sort of agents she wanted. Once R-Day was imminent, she would have to tell her strategically important Alphas the truth, but she would be very careful in presenting it.

Alpha83 was a recent recruit and her 'button' was religion; even by Graceni standards she was devoutly Salvatine. But she was no hermit: she worked in the records office of the planetary government, and that was what made her useful.

It was possible Alpha83 herself was the Sidhe agent who was procuring the false IDs. But the chances were minimal. If the Enemy knew anything about her, they knew how unlikely it was that Bez would follow up a lead outside the hubs in person. There were more efficient ways to entrap her.

She tried not to panic when she failed to get a match on Alpha83's address. Bez was not the only beevee-board user to post an inaccurate profile. She liked to corroborate names and addresses where possible via independent research, but she hadn't had time to do this for Alpha83. It was not as though she had expected to be visiting her in person.

She did know Alpha83's real name – Khea Foelin – and department – birth registration, Meneske ward. The fact that the woman worked in Meneske implied she lived in the city; when it came to dirtborn agents, Bez had found that people living near a planet's contact point with the rest of human-space were most likely to take an interest in matters beyond their world.

The Holy Day service had begun with prayers, but now the women had moved onto a weird overtonal chanting. It distracted Bez, both because of the unusual structure, which she found attractive, and because of the small imperfections in pitch, which she did not. She exited from her current search. As her attention returned to the real she was startled to find a bug with orange-and-green-veined translucent wings sucking at a spill on the table, its long black feeder flicking out across the liquid. Presumably the sonics had been turned off. Bez changed tables and pulled up her hood, minimising the amount of flesh available as a landing site for curious insects. She activated her headware, dampened her aural feeds to block the noise, then returned to the infoscape.

Her initial search listed fifteen Khea Foelins in Meneske ward. She cross-referenced with another service and confirmed that number.

Next, she checked the publicly available information on these women. Basic data on age, sexuality and marital status was held on all citizens; they themselves chose what additional information they presented to outsiders. As Bez quickly came to realise, this data had less to do with their place in the world than their insights about it, and about the nature of reality, God, virtue and assorted spiritual and philosophical matters. Each individual also tailored her profile, adding holos and music, not to mention voice recordings, idiosyncratic layouts and a plethora of culture-specific words and terms Bez had to look up. The info was there, but not at the forefront; for example, the first subject Bez researched worked as a carer in a crèche, but this datum was only available in a semi-poetic spoken piece on the miraculous innocence of young minds.

By the time she was halfway through her list, Bez began to see basic patterns in the data Graceni women presented; as a result she started to home in more quickly on the relevant info. She had already discarded those she had researched so far, for reasons of age, career choice and, in one case, a diatribe warning against having any truck with the sin-washed universe beyond Gracen.

She carried on, vaguely aware that the chanting had died away. The tenth Khea Foelin was a government worker, and Bez's pulse quickened. But the woman was too poor to indulge in beevee communication, as well as being something of an isolationist.

When she reached the final candidate without getting a hit, she raised her shades to run a hand across her tired eyes. The garden was dim and utterly silent. Checking the time she realised why: everyone had gone to bed. As should she.

Although she planned to recheck her findings once she had got some rest, she had to acknowledge that she might not be able to trace her agent. Quite aside from the annoyance of a wasted journey, the apparent disappearance of Alpha83 had worrying implications, given the Graceni were so open with most of their information.

On impulse, Bez made a call, using comshades rather than headware. The response was automated, but it gave her the answer she needed: although the starliner she had arrived on was already gone, there was another due in the day after tomorrow. She would not give up easily, but it was good to know that if she needed to get away, she could.

DATA NEXUS

Designation: Target93
Human alias: Fera Yasmie
Position: Division Chief for Procurement, Starscape
Location: Ylonis
Vulnerabilities: There are rumours of corporate malfeasance in Target93's background, but not enough evidence to damn her.

<file under: Target List>

Bez preferred not to remember her dreams. Dreams were chaotic and illogical, with a disturbing ability to play on the emotions. But there was one recurring dream she had come to grudgingly accept, despite the conflicting feelings it triggered in her.

She thought of it as her 'data nexus' dream. In it she fulfilled her deepest wish, becoming a focus of information, able to assimilate and order data as efficiently as the most sophisticated comp, yet also capable of understanding all she processed. A miraculous fusion of logical machine and intuitive human; all knowledge was hers to use and comprehend.

She experienced the dream in two apparently contradictory ways. Firstly, as sensation and immanent knowledge: she felt the flow of data through her as physical pleasure. At the same time, her mind's eye visualised the data nexus her/his/itself as a more-than-human figure. But the figure had a human face: Tand's face. The point at which his familiar, for-ever-lost-to-her features became fully realised was also the point at which the dream climaxed. Literally. The data nexus dream usually ended in an involuntary orgasm powerful enough to wake her.

The dream had visited her every few months since Tand had

died, and she remained uncertain how she felt about it. On the one hand, the loss of control scared and embarrassed her. On the other, it was her last link to the only person she had ever loved, the person whose loss had shaped her life. And there was a part of her that wondered whether, should she manage to ride out the uncalled for physical release without being dumped back into the real, she might somehow attain the state of grace the dream initially promised.

This morning when she awoke gasping, she struggled free of the sweaty sheets and lurched into the shower, running the water hot and long and not giving the visitation any more consideration than it deserved. At least she felt more clear-headed today: perhaps the dream was the last attempt of the local atmosphere to affect her brain.

But when she checked the time, she found this alien world had fooled her. Its days were three hours too short and her body had failed to adjust fully. She had slept late and missed breakfast. She picked up the handset and asked her host what she should do about food.

'Thou art free to help thyself.'

'Is the servery still open, then?'

'No, but all the fruits of the garden are for eating.'

Trying not to draw parallels with accepted Salvatine dogma in Dena's suggestion, Bez went downstairs to find newly wiped tables with carafes of water on them. Retrieving a clean plate from the empty servery, she approached the central clump of trees while keeping a lookout for bugs. She found a bush bearing plump crimson fruits and picked one, then took it back to her table where she nibbled at it. The pink inner flesh was sweet yet refreshing, although she missed her morning caf.

She used water from the carafe to wash the juice off her hands, took the remains of her meal over to the servery hatch, then returned to her table. Today, she intended to mine the popular media for intel. The guidebooks had been scathing about Gracen's entertainments industry, and she soon found out why: spiritual debate was valued above storytelling, and Graceni cultural icons were mainly prominent philosophers and musicians, usually men. It was possible to access tailored news services (and porn – they had lots of that) but these required a registered subscription and she wanted to preserve her anonymity for as long as possible. She scanned the publicly accessible reports for any reference to Khea Foelin, but was unsurprised when she drew a blank.

Bez could think of two reasons for Alpha83 having no presence in Gracen's infoscape.

Firstly, she did not exist and Bez had been deceived. In this case, she was in trouble. However, such a deception implied concerted Enemy action, and her previous conclusion – that the Sidhe would not expect her to come to Gracen in person – still held.

The second, less paranoid, assumption was that Alpha83 existed – or had existed – but was not to be found in the information Bez had accessed so far. This implied three further possibilities.

Alpha83 might have moved away, in which case Bez would need to widen her search beyond the Meneske area.

Or she could have pulled her own profile data, although that should still leave basic facts in the public listings.

The most logical, and disturbing, reason for her absence was that she was dead, and all record of her had been deleted.

A targeted search of recent female death certificates turned up one for a Khea Foelin. It was a minimal document, giving only an age, a date and a cause of death. Bez translated the woman's age into standard reckoning, and it sounded about right. The date of death stopped Bez in her tracks: it was four days after Bez had received Alpha83's databurst. While accidents or incidents un-related to Bez's mission did occur – take Beta16's fate – the timing was highly suspicious. The cause of death was given as 'natural', with subcodes Bez had to look up. When she discovered that Khea Foelin had apparently had a stroke, her alarm deepened. It was possible that the woman had a pre-existing medical condition, but that sort of death was a trademark of the Enemy.

Bez wondered if she should run now.

She blinked her overlays away, for once seeking reassurance in the real. She had been peripherally aware of people around her, and now she paid them more attention. It was lunchtime, although the place was only about a quarter full, presumably because most of the women were at work. She turned unseeing eyes on the other guests while performing complex calculations in her head, trying to still the unfocused paranoia gnawing at her. So far, she hadn't left any traces or attracted any attention, and even if she wanted to leave she was stuck on-planet until the next starliner departed. Although her instinctive reaction to any whiff of direct Sidhe involvement was to run, she had no firm evidence, and was not in immediate danger.

Once she felt calm enough, she went up to the servery and got a bowl of thick, slightly sweet, soup. It occurred to her as she ate that something vital was missing from her findings. In her earlier searches, Bez had come across tributes to the recently dead: formal obituaries, personal recollections and lengthy 'death poems'; she had also found accounts of elaborate funerary rites. Graceni culture was almost as obsessed with death as it was with sex. 'Khea Foelin', although apparently dead, had not inspired any such activity. This was an anomaly.

During Bez's initial vetting of Alpha83, her new agent had responded to a comment on a beevee board by a male Christos-sect Salvatine with a typically narrow interpretation of the Book. His original comment had been along the lines of God wanting sexual relationships to be limited to marriage between one man and one woman. Alpha83, with typical passion, had said she refused to believe she was damned for loving her wife. A spouse was a potential security risk, but Bez had needed an agent on Gracen badly enough to accept that risk, and now it gave her a new avenue of investigation.

There was a reasonable chance that the last name Bez had for Alpha83 would be shared by the woman's hypothetical wife: despite, or perhaps because of, the strict sexual segregation that defined their society outside of religious observances, Graceni marriage conventions included changes of name.

The surname 'Foelin' was not common, but Bez still got several hundred hits. She discarded the men – Alpha83 had definitely referred to a wife, not a husband – then began checking profiles. Those that had no mention of a spouse she put aside as 'possible'. Those that mentioned a wife became 'potential'. The eighteenth 'potential' worked in the government records office. Further investigation revealed that Cusa Foelin's department was located in the same building as Alpha83's. It could be coincidence, but Bez found herself believing, or perhaps wanting to believe, that this was Alpha83's wife. She checked Cusa Foelin's profile. Her age and income fitted. Her address was not the one Bez had for Alpha83, but that wasn't conclusive. And she was running out of leads. Before she could think better of it, she placed a com call.

'The blessings of the day on you, caller. If you wish to leave a message for Cusa or Khea, please sp—'

Bez killed the call and sat back, heart pounding. Acts like that – doing dangerous things on impulse – made her head spin. She still did them; like her data nexus dream, it was a kind of unconscious release. And sometimes it paid off.

She double-checked some of her earlier findings and carried out further research. Then she went out, comming for a cab as she walked up to the surface.

Outside, the world burned as bright as ever. She found her eye drawn to a patch of shadow off to one side; about a hundred metres along the highway, there was an underpass – surely redundant given no one walked anywhere. Her cab was still en route so she paused and blinked for data on the odd arrangement. The glasses failed to identify the feature, but a moment later she saw movement. Something was coming out of the underpass. Or rather, many things: her overlays went wild, and it took her a moment to realise she was seeing the same thing, over and over: large quadrupeds, dozens of them, pouring out of the tunnel. She had read up on these: *sika*, semi-wild indigenous animals that the guidebooks said were harmless. Every animal had a separate reference tag, and these unformatted alphanumeric strings were clogging her overlays. The rush of creatures ended and a robed figure on a ground-trike emerged, riding at the back of the herd. Bez could hear his ululating shout from here. The creatures wheeled in response to his cries, veering towards the squat pyramid of the next building, kicking up clouds of dust as they turned.

Bez's cab pulled up outside the gate. As she walked towards it she tried to make sense of what she had just seen. She had encountered animals during her childhood, and many hub stations had biome areas with a selection of fauna, but these *sika* were so big, so wild. Except, they weren't really wild: each animal had a serial number. The animals were all owned, kept for a purpose. They were *farmed*. Bez remembered how good last night's stew had tasted. Why maintain expensive meat vats when you have the space to grow your own in the open air? The guidebooks had said something about being able to get 'real food' here. She swallowed uneasily. Although starliners served non-vat meat for those tourists whose tastes ran that way, she had never felt comfortable about eating food with a fully formed nervous system.

The gate opened at her approach, and she climbed into the cab. As she settled back in the seat and braced herself for the ride, the true strangeness of the arrangement with the *sika* struck her: two worlds juxtaposed, animal and human, each independent and largely oblivious of the other. Like on a station, with hab-rats and citizens – except those two groups were well aware of each other's existence. No, a better analogy was human and Sidhe, where the humans were the dumb creatures, happily going about their business oblivious of their role as victim, unaware of how the universe really worked.

Bez decided to drop that line of thought. Instead she stared out the window at the flat red landscape, picking out the few annotated landmarks.

She reached her destination and got out. This building had a smaller surface presence than her hotel. She endured the automated ID scan at the door. The apartment block had a unit to rent, and in theory any woman who was interested could request a look around. Why an offworld visitor would want to was a question Bez had to hope no one would ask; if they did, she would play up the anthropologist angle, claiming she was interested in a short-term rental so she could continue her studies.

The door opened and Bez stepped inside.

According to her comshades, this building's reliquary was a vial of Saint Jera's blood; Jera was one of the Protectorate-era saints, venerated for having actually fought the Sidhe rather than for merely being holy. Bez took this as a positive sign, before catching herself: all this superstitious rubbish was getting to her.

The lobby had two elevators on opposite walls. Bez picked one, requesting the (minus) third floor. Her overlays didn't reveal any cameras: the Graceni weren't big on surveillance. After a short ride she emerged on an open walkway. The central atrium was not as large as that of the *tanyen* hotel, and was a tube rather than a cone, with alternating layers of walkways and private terraces. It contained a gently rotating light sculpture, but, Bez was glad to note, no bugs. Vines laden with creamy, bell-shaped flowers had been trained up the walls between apartments.

Her glasses directed her to the correct door, which opened at her approach. The Graceni's apparently trusting nature might stem from their high moral standards, but, according to the guidebooks, it was backed up by draconian punishments for lawbreakers, whether local or offworld. Bez reminded herself that what she was doing was not actually illegal, and went inside. The apartment was empty of both people and furniture. Bez let the door shut then called up an interface with the local systems direct from her headware. There was only minimal security, which she defeated easily; once inside, she found the overlay data sparse and the set-up basic.

She stayed in the apartment for as long as someone looking to rent might do, using the time to fully explore the limits of the local infoscape. When she left she called the elevator, getting off on the next floor up. She strode around the walkway with a confidence she didn't feel, heading for Cusa Foelin's front door. Even before she came to a halt, she had blinked herself into the house system using her comshades, which gave a more comprehensible interface than her hub-orientated headware.

The set-up was essentially the same as the empty apartment, and it did not take long to fool the lock. However, unlike the apartment, this door did not open immediately. If local systems were going to react to hacking with delays, she needed to make allowances. As the lock finally clicked, Bez pushed the door.

It swung open to semi-darkness. The apartment she had just visited had lit automatically; perhaps some residents modified this default to save power. Bez had not seen anything in the house systems to indicate this; maybe there was a manual control somewhere near the door. She dialled up her visual acuity—

And froze as she made out the figure standing in the unlit corridor, no more than three metres away. The figure had something in its hand that looked an awful lot like a weapon.

RISK FACTORS

As far as I know, the Sidhe don't have anyone in the Commission. This appears to be related to an aversion to hubs. The only explanation I can think of is that, while the hub-points are the heart of human commerce, the Sidhe's interests lie elsewhere. But it's still odd, given that although the Commission's hand is light, the Treaties they enforce are ubiquitous throughout human-space.

<file under: Unqualified Data>

'Do not move.'

Bez squeaked, 'M— my mistake. Wrong door.'

The woman shook her head. 'Liar,' she said. She sounded as scared as Bez felt.

'Is that a gun?' Bez asked the question to buy herself time. What for, she had yet to work out. She had briefly considered trying to get hold of a weapon herself before coming to Gracen, but had discarded the idea, both because of the impracticality and because if it came down to pointing guns, she had already lost. She regretted her decision now.

'Aye, 'tis a gun.'

'Are you going to shoot me?' Another dumb question, but looking down a gun barrel did nothing for her ability to reason her way out of situations.

'No,' said the woman. 'But thou will come inside, moving slowly.'

'So you can kill me without witnesses?' Bizarrely, the longer the insane conversation went on, the less actual fear she felt. Probably her body over-compensating.

'So I can speak with thee.'

'I much prefer talking to shooting,' said Bez, earnestly.

'Then enter!'

She could still try to escape, and hope the woman's nerves threw her aim. Some hope. She stepped into the hallway. The door closed behind her and the lights came up.

The woman standing before her had ash-blonde hair and skin so pale it was almost translucent; behind her comshades she wore a resolute expression. She held the compact weapon in both hands, grasping it like a talisman. It looked like a dartgun, probably firing tranq, but that didn't make it any less dangerous.

'See thou this?'

Bez realised the woman meant the gun. 'Oh, yes.'

'Thou would be shocked to know how I gained possession of it.'

Bez had no idea how to respond to that.

'We shall talk through here.' The woman nodded towards a half-open door. 'Thou first.'

Seeing no alternative, Bez pushed the door open and walked in. She found herself in a comfortable, lived-in lounge complete with soft furnishings and knick-knacks. Being in such a personal space added an extra level of unease to the already grim situation.

From behind her the woman said, 'I know thee.'

Bez paused. And she had thought this couldn't get any worse.

'Or rather,' she continued, 'I know *what* thou art, what thy plans entail. Or what thou claimed to Khea, anyway.'

'So you're Cusa.' Though it was the logical conclusion, Bez had not wanted to make assumptions.

'Of course!'

Bez's gaze fell on a holo on the shelf in front of her. This woman and another, somewhere dark with strings of gaily coloured lights in the background; they were laughing, happy and at ease. Cusa and Khea, together. And Khea's name was still on their voicemail. Bez said, 'Where's Khea?'

Cusa said, 'Turn around.'

Bez obeyed, careful to keep her hands in sight.

'Now sit thee down.'

Bez lowered herself onto the saggy couch, perching on the edge of a buttock-shaped indentation.

Cusa remained standing and said, 'Thy expectation was that I would be at my work-place.'

'Yes.'

'What didst thou plan to do here?'

'I wasn't sure. I'm trying to find out what happened to your wife.' There was no point dissembling.

'Thou travelled all the way from the hubs in search of Khea.'

Bez wasn't sure if this was a trick question – or even a question at all. She decided to stick with honesty. 'I came here because she had uncovered something important.'

'Important to the fight.'

Bez decided to interpret that as a question. 'Yes,' she said, 'something that could help our cause.'

'Khea said thou nurtures deep hatred for them.'

Bez relaxed a fraction; as she had hoped, Cusa shared her wife's worldview. Of course, *them* in Cusa's mind was not the Enemy themselves, but the Ascensionists who worshipped them; and the hatred was not between races but between religions. The net result was close enough for Bez to say in all honesty, 'I'd give my life to bring them down.'

Cusa inclined her head in what might have been a nod of approval. 'I have heard it said that there are worlds that actually permit Ascensionist Chantries.'

'Yes, though not many.'

'The Sidhe worshippers have embraced evil. Each and every one will burn in hell.'

Bez was stunned by the woman's quiet, matter-of-fact fanaticism. Destroying the Enemy was one thing; presuming to know what happened to them after they died was another. It was ironic that one of the reasons Ascensionism was almost universally reviled was due to its 'ridiculous' insistence that the Sidhe were not, in fact, dead.

'And what of the hub-points?'

'What do you mean?' asked Bez in return.

'Do those who rule the hubs tolerate Ascensionists?'

'No. Absolutely not.'

'Yet thou hailst from the hubs.' Cusa frowned.

'I do. And it's because of people like me that the hubs remain free of Ascensionists.' Bez hoped Cusa was as willing to swallow that explanation as Khea had been.

The other woman pursed her lips; the tip of the gun sagged slightly. Then Cusa asked, 'What use have Ascensionist heretics for false identities?'

Apparently, Khea had confided extensively in her wife. 'Like I told Khea, they insinuate themselves into positions of influence.'

'Aye, but 'tis a considerable effort. Surely one skilled in data manipulation could achieve the same without recourse to such complex deception. Thou art the possessor of such skills thyself.'

Bez did not like where this line of enquiry was going. 'I am, yes. And that means I know the limitations of hacked IDs. They're fine if you move around a lot. If you want to stay in one place, maintaining a consistent identity while you amass power and influence, you need something solid, something that will stand up to detailed background checks. An arrangement like the one here, where someone is re-activating the identities of children who died young, provides that.'

'But would those perpetrating the deception not require bio-metric information for the individual they are creating the identity for?'

Khea had been more fiery in her fanaticism, and less rigorous in her logic, than her wife. Cusa appeared to be the brains behind the outfit. 'You're right. It does require a lot of organisation. What I believe happens is that the g— young person who will be assuming the new ID travels to this system but doesn't make planetfall. The necessary samples are smuggled down, then shortly afterwards the new ID is smuggled offworld and the person it refers to is listed as having emigrated.'

'So our records would show these individuals as godless children who opted out of their crèche to request fostering with offworld heathens?'

'Yes.' That was one way of putting it.

'Such an arrangement requires the collusion of corrupt officials.' Cusa did not sound surprised at the possibility.

'I imagine so.'

'It would also require access to considerable resources, that these children may enter and leave our space undetected.'

'Yes, it would.' Of course, it helped if your resources included freetraders who could bypass normal transit-paths.

Cusa shook her head in dismay. 'Would Khea had never encountered thee, and been dragged into this.' She looked straight at Bez, eyes narrow and glistening. 'Do ye have mourning leave in the hubs?'

Bez had no idea what she was talking about. 'No, we don't.'

'No, ye would not. Here, when someone close to us goes to the Lord of All, we are given time to adjust. During that period we are under no obligation to work, nor to receive visitors. We pray and grieve in our own way.'

'She is dead, then?' asked Bez quietly.

Cusa's tears spilled over, and her face twisted. 'I wish I knew,' she whispered.

'Oh.' This was getting more complicated by the moment. 'Listen, maybe I can find out. If you tell me everything you know, I can try to track down the truth – and finish what Khea started.'

As Cusa opened her mouth to reply, a weird sound filled the room. Bez looked around in panic: the pained, high-pitched squeal was coming from nearby. Cusa jumped, but there was something about her expression, not afraid, but concerned—

Bez realised what the noise was. 'Limitless void, you've got a child!'

'That is my son,' said Cusa, her voice barely audible over the breathless infant screams. She started to turn towards the door then appeared to remember herself. 'Thou must leave us now.'

'Cusa, I can help you, help you find out what Khea—'

'Go!'

Bez saw her last chance slipping away, and against all her instincts, said, 'I'll give you my ID, in case you want to get in touch.'

'I have thy details. The house system harvested them when thou tried to hack my lock. Thou art not alone in having some skill with data, Medame Shiqua – or whatever thy true name may be.'

'Oh.'

'Go. I must tend my child.' She pointed the gun at the door.

Bez took a deep breath and went out. The front door opened automatically, and closed behind her.

Back in the building's lobby, Bez tried to make sense of the encounter. It alarmed her that Cusa had subverted her hack so easily. How competent a databreaker was she? Not an expert, presumably, or Khea would have utilised her skills. Unless she didn't want to endanger her spouse. Then again, maybe Bez's failure with the house system was merely due to lack of experience with the unfamiliar infoscape.

Perhaps a more important question was: how much did Cusa know? More than she was telling, obviously. And she had apparently gone to extreme lengths to get hold of a weapon. Who, or what, was she so frightened of? Presumably the traitor that Khea had found ... and who had found, and possibly killed, her. But who was that? What resources did he or she have?

When her taxi picked her up, Bez considered hacking it to delete any record of the trip, but her experience with Cusa warned her off, at least until she was more at home in Gracen's infoscape. She did take a physical precaution, ordering the cab to drop her at a women's gym she had looked up earlier. The lobby was light and airy and smelled faintly of labouring bodies. Bez expected the building's reliquary to be a holy drop of sweat or a running shoe, but it was another bone, albeit from a saint's foot.

A woman came in just after Bez, heading for the lifts; she gave Bez a curious glance in passing but didn't say anything. Once she was gone, Bez took the building's secondary exit, which led to a different road, where she picked up a new taxi. She had no idea if such a move was adequate, or even necessary, but it helped reassert her sense of control over the situation.

By the time she got back to her hotel, it was dark; the heat of the day had disappeared with the light, and Bez shivered as she walked up the path. Once inside, she called the starport. There was still space on tomorrow morning's starliner. She thought long and hard, but in the end held off booking a place. There were not enough risk factors to force her to abort just when she was finally getting somewhere.

She ate with the other women then returned to her room. It took her a while to get to sleep, though when she did her rest was mercifully undisturbed by dreams.

The next thing she knew something was buzzing insistently. Not her com, although she had set an alarm to wake her so she didn't miss breakfast again; this was an unfamiliar external sound. She opened her eyes. A light was flashing, next to the recessed handset. Bez stumbled out of bed and snatched up the device. 'Yes?'

'There is a message for thee,' said Dena, over the crackly line.

Bez was instantly alert, her mind flooded with unpleasant possibilities: Cusa had shopped her; the authorities were on to her; the Enemy had finally tracked her down. She made herself reply, 'Who is the message from?'

''Tis from thy husband.'

TAGS TO USE

Although the attached files contain the unpalatable truth about transit-kernels, you won't find much on beacons. That's because there isn't much: I don't know what beacons really are; I wish I did. One thing I do know: the Sidhe don't need them to shift, so Sidhe ships can do things human ships can't, and that's a worrying thought.

<file under: Unqualified Data>

Bez shook her head, as though that would make the impossible news go away. 'My *husband*?'

'Aye. Thou never mentioned being in wedlock.'

Bez's mind worked furiously. 'Are you sure this man's got the right person?'

'He called from the starport and asked for thee by name.'

Or rather by the name she was currently using. Surely this was a case of mistaken identity? That was the only plausible explanation. 'Right. And what is the message?'

'He has taken a room in the Hotel Fiviel and wishes thee to go there in order to meet him.'

'Right. Er. Sorry, I've only just woken up. I need to …' *Run! Escape!* '… get washed and dressed.'

'Thy bill will await thee when thy ablutions are complete.'

'I wasn't planning to leave—'

'This is a *tanyen* hotel, a place for unmarried women.' Her host's sniff was audible over the primitive com. 'Had I been aware of thy status, I would never have opened my house to thee.' She cut the call.

Bez showered, her mind racing. Best-case scenario, this was a mistake. Worst-case, it was a trap. She slung her bag over her shoulder and walked into the central atrium. Her com pinged immediately, with her bill. Ignoring it for now she called the starport. As she feared and expected, this morning's liner was already boarding and she was too late to get a ticket. She booked herself onto the next flight out. She could try moving to another hotel, but he had found her here, so he could find her there. Whoever he was. She ran through the men she knew, male agents she had long-standing relationships with. None of them had either reason or means to follow her here.

She considered leaving the city, picking a place and heading out, returning just in time to catch her flight. But the guidebooks had stressed the inadvisability of travelling too far from the starport. Meneske itself, for all its foibles and potential problems for the unwary traveller, was at least used to dealing with outsiders. Besides, without a local persona in place, the only way to disappear effectively would be to get offplanet without going through the starport, and that was not an option now she no longer had access to a freetrader who owed her favours.

She looked up the Hotel Fiviel, a name she remembered from her initial research; it was one of the more upmarket tourist hotels. She accessed their public records. The hotel didn't reveal who had which room, but it did list everyone currently staying there. Bez scanned the names; most of them meant nothing to her, but then why should they? Names were tags to use. Then she saw it: *Imbarin Tierce*. Any remaining hope that this was an unfortunate coincidence vanished.

Her only choice, insane as it seemed, was to go and meet him. After all, the first time they had met he had been friendly enough; possibly too friendly. She could always run afterwards, once she had some idea what he was up to.

She commed his hotel and asked them to pass on a message, hastily declining the offer to be put through to Sirrah Tierce. Instead, she asked the receptionist to tell him to meet her in one of the hotel bars in two hours' time.

She checked out of her current hotel then called a taxi. She changed taxis once, via the lobby of the local equivalent of a shopping mall, one of the few secular mixed-sex spaces in the city. All the time she kept expecting a call from Tierce. The uncertainty gnawed at her and she found herself unable to come up with a coherent plan.

She arrived at the Fiviel early. This hotel was as gaudy as the *tanyen* hotel was restrained. The lobby had the mandatory reliquary (the thumb of Saint Parsevus, famous for starving himself to death in order to achieve holy visions), but the item was tucked into a hidden niche, and Bez only spotted it because she knew to look.

Reception was at the bottom of an atrium several times bigger than her last hotel's. The various in-house entertainments – bars, restaurants, casino – gave off the atrium, and in the case of some structures, intruded into it via walkways or balconies. The cantilevered clear-sided swimming pool on the upper levels was particularly impressive; from ground level, the naked swimmers showed merely as brownish blobs in the green-lit water. Although about half the tourists, and all the staff, were wearing standard robes, a number of visitors had dressed to show off their physical attributes. She had the unpleasant impression that she was in a minority by not expecting to have sex in the near future.

She went to the quietest bar and took a table near the door. She was trying to decide whether to order a drink when Tierce walked in, five minutes early. She was relieved to see he was fully dressed, in a robe whose semiotics, if Bez read them correctly, said he was mainly heterosexual but open to suggestions. He waved and came straight over.

She had rehearsed possible ways of greeting him, but in the end her apprehension snapped into sudden and unexpected fury. 'What in the void's name are you doing here?' she hissed.

'And it's lovely to see you again too.' He made to sit down next to her.

'Over there, please.' She nodded at the seat opposite.

'Would you prefer to talk somewhere quieter?'

'If you think I'm going to your room—'

'Our room.'

'*Your* room. Just answer my question: what are you doing here?'

'For a start, I'd like to buy you that drink.' He sat, and tapped the table to bring up the menu. 'Caf? Or something stronger?'

Apparently, they did have caf here, presumably for the tourists. 'How did you find me?' she asked. Her nervous anger was burning off in the face of his insouciance.

'With great difficulty.'

'Right.' It would be too much to hope that he would just tell her. 'And you followed me halfway across the sector to buy me a *drink*?'

'For starters, yes. We can talk over a caf; what could be more civilised?'

'Talk about what? I don't even know who you are.'

'Really? You're normally so assiduous in your research, Orzabet.'

'*What did you just call me?*'

He leaned forward, and Bez flinched back, concerned he might try to touch her. 'Much as I like games, denying what we both know qualifies as fucking about, and that I *don't* tolerate.'

Bez caught her breath. 'All right, let's assume for the moment I am who you say I am. And who precisely are *you*, Sirrah Imbarin Tierce?'

He beamed. 'How long did it take you to find out *my* name? Not long, I'd guess, given you're the greatest databreaker in human-space!'

She ignored that. 'So far, all I know for sure is that you work for Tarset station. Aren't you a bit out of your jurisdiction?'

'Interesting point. Yes, and no. But to get back to your original question, I'm here to help.'

'To help? In what way is turning up out of the blue and claiming to be my husband helpful?'

'Pretending you were my wife seemed like the obvious solution to the sexual segregation problem. The local customs are a bit quaint.'

'You got me thrown out of my hotel.'

'My point exactly.'

'Well, I'm not married to you. I don't even know you.'

'I realise that. But I'm here if you need me.'

'To do what?' She paused then decided she had nothing to lose by asking, 'Why do you think *I'm* here, Sirrah Tierce?'

He didn't hesitate. 'You've had a tip-off important enough to your fight against the Sidhe that you're following it up in person.'

Bez struggled not to let her shock know. Finally, she managed, 'The Sidhe are dead.'

Tierce dropped his voice. 'Remember what I said about not fucking about? We both know those bitches are still around. Don't pretend otherwise.'

'Even if you believe th— they aren't all dead, what's *your* interest?'

'I'm fighting the Sidhe, just like you.'

'How? You're some sort of enforcer on a hub station.'

'I'm also part of a larger organisation devoted to opposing the Sidhe.'

'An organisation I've never heard of? Impossible.'

'We're very careful.'

'And you know about me?'

'Indeed we do. We have been following your activities with interest for some time.'

Their drinks arrived, brought by a robed waiter. They both shut up. Bez tried to use the pause to think, but it was too much to take in. She sipped her caf, and for a moment lost herself in that simple pleasure. Unfortunately, when she looked over the rim of her mug, Imbarin Tierce was still sitting opposite her.

'Has anyone ever told you you're beautiful?'

'*What?* Of course not!' She had paid well to have her face re-sculpted, leaving it carefully average, as forgettable as possible. 'I would appreciate it if you refrained from these ridiculous court-ship games, Sirrah Tierce.'

'I was just expressing an opinion.'

'You were about to tell me whom you work for,' she prompted.

'We don't have a name as such. We like to stay in the back-ground.'

'So how many of you are there in this nameless organisation?

How long have you been fighting the Sidhe? And why haven't I come across you before?' She tried to load as much scepticism as possible into the questions but deep down she was panicking. If Tierce was telling the truth, it could change everything.

'To answer your first question: I can't give you an exact number, because we're ... let's call it a cell structure.'

'You can at least give me some idea.'

'Dozens ... no, more like hundreds. Yes, let's say a few hundred.'

Was he making this up? He appeared pretty casual and ill-informed. 'Less than the number of Sidhe in human-space?'

'Probably, yes.'

'"Probably"? "A few hundred"? You can't really expect me to believe you when you give such vague answers.'

'Like I say, I know what is going on locally, but not elsewhere.'

She had to concede this made sense: any hypothetical human-space-wide resistance would have to operate as autonomous cells, given the Sidhe's ability to prise information from unwilling minds. 'And how long have you – your cell, anyway – been around?'

'We've been around for a long time, but until recently our activities have been very low-key. Monitoring Sidhe influence, rather than confronting it.'

'What changed?'

'They made hostile moves against us.'

'They know about you, then?'

'Oh, yes. For much of recent history, a balance has existed. They have upset that balance, and we are responding.'

Which might be why he was making contact now. His explanations were beginning to look unpleasantly plausible. 'What prompted them to move against you?'

'A good question.'

But not one he was going to answer, apparently. 'So the reason I haven't come across you before is because you haven't been actively pursuing the fight?'

'That's right.'

'But now you are?'

'Right again.'

'Are you trying to *recruit* me, Sirrah Tierce?'

'Not at all. We are merely offering assistance. After all, we are fighting the same war: you in your way, we in ours.'

Bez received an interrupt from her comshades. When she checked the tag she saw that the call came from her previous hotel. She looked through the display at Tierce. 'I need to take this.'

He shrugged and sat back.

It was Dena. 'A visitor arrived for thee.'

'Who?' Bez sub-vocced back.

'She refused to leave a name. She had a babe with her.'

Cusa. 'Where is she now?'

'I told her of thy new hotel.'

Damn. 'When did—?' But Dena had already hung up.

'I have to go,' said Bez out loud.

'Must you? I thought we were getting on pretty well.'

'Thanks for the caf.'

As she hurried away he called after her, 'You'll find me a very useful ally.'

She commed reception to check if anyone had been asking after her. No one had. Tierce's bombshell had shaken her, and it took a few moments to decide on her next move; she kept walking anyway, just to get away. Then she instructed reception to tell her if any visitors arrived for her and took a lift further up the atrium, going into a space her overlays labelled as a 'women's bar'.

She realised her mistake at once. She was the only person wearing robes, or in fact much at all; this was a bar for tourist women to meet each other. But at least Tierce couldn't follow her here. She found a quiet table, facing the door.

She kept replaying the conversation with Imbarin Tierce. All these years she had been sure she was passing undetected through human-space, and now she found she was being watched, monitored. It was unthinkable. Assuming he was telling the truth. But he had found her here. And why would he lie? What else could his agenda be? Not to stop her: he could have done that already.

She felt as though she had stepped out onto a tightrope; she was too terrified to turn back, and had no choice other than to keep going.

She did a comprehensive search for traces of Imbarin Tierce in the local infoscape, but found only what she expected: someone of that name had disembarked from this morning's starliner and checked into the Hotel Fiviel. If there was further data on him, she couldn't access it.

'This seat taken?'

She started, expecting to see Cusa, but it was a slender woman whose cut-out bodysuit showed off some surprising piercings.

'I'm, uh, waiting for someone.'

'Suit yourself.' The woman wandered off.

Her com made her jump, but it was only reception, informing her she had a visitor who would not give a name but had a child with her. Bez told the receptionist to send her up.

ESTRIS
(The Ice Coast, Tetrial Beta, Tetrial System)

Everyone has secrets.

It doesn't matter whether you want them; they just arrive in your life, and mess it up.

Estris had been in Astren's house for three weeks now, and she had developed a routine of sorts: a bracing run along the beach first thing, then a day divided between light reading, watching holodramas and browsing for jobs until the time when most folk finished work, at which point she spent a while chatting on the comnet to those of her friends who still wanted to talk to her; in the evening, there was the family dinner.

The fateful conversation happened over lunch; even with the children away at school and her husband working in his study, Astren insisted on a formal sit-down meal at midday. Estris, used to eating at her desk or on the streetcar, found this adjustment one of the hardest to deal with.

Astren was serving the samphire salad while Estris aired her grievances: how unfair the agreement was, how it made her feel so worthless, so frustrated, almost like a prisoner despite the nominal freedom afforded her by the accompanying pay-off. Astren put down the spoon and said, 'So try beevee.'

Estris stared at her sister, confused. 'What do you mean?'

'Well, your non-disclosure agreement has plenty to say about not passing information on to, um, "any individual or organisation", or discussing the matter on – what was it they said, exactly?'

'"On any network, chatgroup or other means of disseminating defamatory accusations through the infoscape,"' finished Estris, reciting the infuriating terms a little impatiently.

'What I'm saying is, while Dynosys have covered themselves thoroughly here on Tetrial, from what you said, there's not one mention of other systems in the document you signed.'

'I …' Trust Astren to think of that. 'I'd have to check.' Before her sister could object, Estris got up and strode down the corridor to her room. Hail rattled against the window as she dug her slate out from under a pile of discarded clothes on the floor.

Returning to the table, she found Astren pointedly waiting to start eating. 'You're right,' said Estris, smiling to emphasise the point and offset her rudeness, 'there's nothing specific about not using beevee. Just the local comnet.'

She sat down before murmuring a blessing over the meal. As she ate she thought through the implications of Astren's offhand comment. She made herself wait until her sister offered seconds, which she accepted – Astren's love of health foods meant Estris was perpetually hungry, even if her figure was benefiting from the regime – then said, 'Were you offering to let me use your uplink?'

'Of course.'

'I'd pay for my time on it.'

Astren shrugged. 'If you wanted to make a small contribution towards the bill, that would be appreciated.'

'Are you sure, though? I mean, I could take the sled into Hunterport.'

'A public uplink would cost you ten times as much. Don't waste your money.'

'I don't want to be any trouble.'

Astren gave her *that* smile, the one that said, *You're always trouble, little sister, but I love you anyway.* 'This thing is eating you up, Est; you need to let it out.'

'Yes, but … over *your* uplink? What if my messages are traced?'

'I'm not sure that's even possible. Anyway, aren't you being a bit paranoid? No, a lot paranoid.'

'You've read the agreement! If I mention anything about … what I found, Dynosys will take back my severance payment and sue me!'

'They don't want anything that can come directly back at them over the nets. I doubt they'll even *know* if you talk to people out-of-system. Unless you found evidence of Dynosys being part of some deep interstellar conspiracy when you came across the suppression notices?'

'I ... didn't.'

'Well, then, if you really need to speak out, do it where Dynosys won't be listening. Although' – Astren raised a cynical eyebrow – 'I should warn you that the less tightly regulated beevee boards attract a certain type of person with too much time and money on their hands.'

'Rich kooks like you, you mean?' Estris grinned to show she meant it as a joke.

Astren mimed taking offence, frowning hard. 'Those rich kooks help pay for all this, you know!' She swept a fork around to indicate the glass-walled dining area, the low sofas and the glowing firewall.

'So you research your books from the beevee boards, do you?' Estris played along, happy to see her too-serious older sister lightening up.

Astren leaned forward and whispered, 'Yes. Just don't tell my editor.'

'Don't want her complaining the next time you ask for a deadline extension, do we?'

Astren grunted. 'As if I ever did.'

'You could, though, if you had to.' Estris was considering taking up writing; it was a career her sister thrived on. She had the money to support herself while she retrained, and Astren had the contacts to sell whatever she came up with. 'I mean, pan-human histories are selling like spiced cake right now.'

'Yes, well, when a nation's licking its wounds it likes to hear about mistakes and failures in faraway cultures.'

The sisters lapsed into bitter silence, remembering their nation's recent defeat. Not that anyone close to them had been killed in the war; it had just knocked them back as a people. Estris finally blurted out, 'That's what really irks me. We could have won, with that sort of technology.'

'The power source, you mean?' Astren spoke cautiously; she was the only person Estris had trusted with the truths she was now legally bound not to reveal.

'Unlimited free power would have given us a massive advantage! And it wasn't just that. The files I saw ... all those projects, vetoed. And I think I only found out part of it. What if there were weapons that could have beaten the Inensians swiftly and decisively, except their development was stifled?'

Astren grimaced: unlike her sister, she had moved on from the recent defeat and embraced the ensuing peace. 'Those vetoes were on religious grounds, you said. Which is fair enough.'

'That technology wasn't blasphemous! All right, perhaps the new energy source, if you've got a very limited idea of how much of creation the Almighty is happy to let us access. Maybe even the improved neural interfacing, although if you grant that such things are allowed at all then why can't people have a faster and more invasive version? It's their choice. And that alternative comp paradigm? What's wrong with that? As for a brainwave reader that detects a particular class of abnormal mental signature: in what way is *that* offensive to God? No, Astren, it looks to me like whenever Dynosys's R&D came near certain breakthroughs, someone jumped on the project. As for who, how and why, I have no idea.' Estris realised she was ranting. She took a deep breath.

'I wish I could help you,' her sister said. 'Honest to God, I do. But I don't have any more idea of what was going on at Dynosys than you do.'

'You're sure it wasn't Inensia, though?' Apparently an Inensian had taken over Estris's old job. Everyone was meant to be friends now, in this new era of peace.

'If they had that sort of clout inside a company owned by their enemies, do you think the war would have dragged on for as long as it did?'

'I guess not.'

Estris was wary at first, choosing an obscure pseudonym and carefully tailoring what she gave away about her background.

When there was no word from her ex-employers after a month of sporadic contact with the rest of human-space, she started visiting some of the more fringe sites. It was something to do while she tried to find a new job. Her experience was too broad, too vague: yes, she was an excellent administrator and researcher, but those were hardly vital skills for a nation rebuilding itself after a war. She found herself looking forward to her daily beevee download of distant news, after the constant disappointment nearer home.

Astren was right about one thing: there were some odd people out there, airing some wacky views. At first Estris found the level of belief comforting: if she posted a comment about a conspiracy to suppress energy generation via multidimensional sources, then a dozen others would agree that, yes, such hidden manipulation was widespread. But she soon came to realise that most of these responses sprung from uncritical credulity; she could have claimed invisible aliens were tampering with the water supply on all the hubs, and someone would say they had seen evidence of that too.

Yes: a lot of kooks.

She also browsed the more respectable boards, the sorts of places her sister used to research her books, but they tended to go the other way, favouring conservative views of history and culture, expressed in technical terms and obscure references.

Her frustration grew. She had wanted to vent her fury with the company that had shafted her; to share her secret with people who would listen, not pander to idiots who would either believe everything she said, or conservatives who would believe nothing.

Then she found someone who, for all their interest in off-the-wall subjects, didn't appear to believe wholesale in whatever anyone else dreamed up. Whoever 'Orzabet' was, he or she was no credulous kook. And they were genuinely interested in what Estris had to say.

Estris was intrigued. Dynosys hadn't spotted what she was doing: or if they had, they didn't care. She decided, after some thought, that she would share what she knew about her ex-employers with her new out-of-system contact.

THE DARKNESS BENEATH

Designation: Target399
Human alias: Nema Lastre
Position: Chief Research Officer of Dynosys
Technologies
Location: Tetrial
Vulnerabilities: Target399 is likely to have been involved in
the suppression of technology within Dynosys, a corporation
based on Tetrial who sell patents to out-of-system third
parties. No concrete proof of her actions is available at this
time.

<file under: Target List>

Cusa looked distinctly out of place in the bar. She wore her hood up and carried her child in a sling across her chest.

When she paused at the end of the table, Bez gestured and said, 'Have a seat. Did you want, er, anything? To drink or eat.'

'This is a fast day for me.'

'Right.' Bez stared at the top of the baby's head and wondered, irrelevantly, if it was a fast day for the baby too. Presumably not. The other woman sat down opposite then reached past the baby into her robes. Bez tensed, remembering the gun, but Cusa merely brought out a pack of *cigrenes*, offering one to Bez first. Bez took it, mindful of social convention, and allowed Cusa to light the stick. Cusa took one too: presumably today's abstinence did not extend to smoking.

After both of them had inhaled and exhaled a couple of times, Bez said, 'So, do you want to carry on our conversation now?'

'Thou art not a great one for pleasantries,' observed Cusa.

'Not when something's important, no.'

The baby squirmed, possibly disturbed by the smoke. It opened its mouth in an unfeasibly wide yawn and punched blindly at the air with a tiny fist. Bez stared in fascination: she had minimal experience with children, but was suddenly struck by how odd it was that this defenceless, barely sentient creature would one day become an adult human being.

'He is named Gion,' said Cusa.

'Hello, Gion,' said Bez. It was a pointless greeting, given the baby's level of cognitive development, but it appeared to please Cusa.

'I carried him,' said Cusa, her free hand resting lightly on the infant's head. Gion had thrust his fist into his mouth and gone back to sleep. 'But Khea was the primary. There were complications, and he was born a month early, only two days after we moved apartments.' She took a long draw on her *cigrene*. 'Three weeks later, Khea was gone.'

Bez said carefully, 'Gone, as in ...?'

Cusa narrowed her eyes and started to speak in a low, even voice. 'One day she did not return from work. Her com was offline. The next morning I called her office, as at times she would work late, though never without calling me first. Her colleagues said she had left at her usual time the previous evening.'

Through the smoke, Cusa's expression became more distant. The *cigrene* smouldered over the table, unregarded. Bez was about to prompt her to continue when she said, 'I tried to report her disappearance to the monitors. They directed my call to a family liaison officer. She expressed concern for my loss, and asked if I wished for counselling. I was confused. This made no sense. Eventually, the officer forwarded me Khea's death certificate. I did not believe it.' She flattened her lips in a grim smile. 'I shouted at her. My call was cut. But I still had the certificate. And when I checked the infoscape, Khea had no presence there. It was as though she had been erased.'

'Couldn't you challenge this? Go to the authorities? You have an elected government, don't you?' The Graceni were a religious democracy, not a full theocracy.

Cusa glanced down at her son then drew on her *cigrene*. 'I tried. I called the monitors and contacted our local deacon; I even spoke to a presbyter. Each and every one referred me to the death certificate, which stated that Khea had gone to the All-Father due to natural causes on the night she went missing.' She gave a bitter laugh. 'I imagine they thought me unhinged by grief.'

'How about using your skills to uncover the truth? Hospital records and such.'

'My skills?'

'With data.' Bez put her *cigrene* in the tray, deciding Cusa was unlikely to notice.

'No. I feared that, whatever fate had overtaken my wife, I could be next. Because we are a spiritual, moral people who live easy and comfortable lives, we believe all is well with our world. Provided we behave according to the Lord's tenets and the laws of the land, our system will treat us fairly. Or so I thought. Now I know different. I have seen the darkness beneath.'

Bez thought of the first time they met, and what Cusa had said about the gun: *Thou would be shocked to know how I gained possession of it.* 'Even if you don't know what happened to Khea surely you must have ... suspicions.'

'Aye, sister. I do.'

Bez forced herself to wait for Cusa to tell her in her own time. The other woman shifted in her seat, taking a last draw on her *cigrene* before stubbing it out. 'The ministry where Khea worked is a large and complex place. In its higher offices there are perhaps a dozen people who exercise enough authority, if they are careful, to insert a death certificate and remove other records. Of those, only one is also in a position to re-activate inactive personnel records: a man called Tren Valdt.'

'So he's the one who's creating the false IDs?' Part of Bez wanted to know why Cusa couldn't have just told her this straight off, but it was a part she found herself obscurely ashamed of. She resisted the urge to immediately search on the name.

'So Khea believed. I warned her against acting on her suspicions, but she was holding to a promise – one made to thee – and she meant to keep her word.'

Cusa might blame her for Khea's death. And she still had that gun. But the other woman appeared composed, almost resigned. 'Was Khea investigating this Tren Valdt when she disappeared?'

Cusa gave a weary smile. 'I do not know: although we had no secrets, she spared me some details. Those we love we shelter from the world.' Cusa reached inside her robe again, her hand brushing her baby lightly as she did so. This time she withdrew a dataspike, which she pushed across the table. 'All that she had gleaned on Administrator Valdt is here. Not much, but I give it freely, to use as thou may desire.'

Bez took the 'spike, glancing around even though no one was paying them any attention. 'Thank you. Will you …' She tried again, not sure how to put it. 'Is this Administrator Valdt the reason you got the gun?'

'I acquired it for the sake of my child. Thou art not a mother.'

Bez realised it was a question. 'No, I'm not.'

Cusa said, 'My mourning leave ends this week. Then I must return to work – in the same building as *that man*. I need a job to fund my son's future in a crèche.'

'That's normal here, isn't it? Being brought up in a crèche, I mean.' Bez was uncomfortable with the thought that the small being that seemed almost part of this woman would soon be taken from her.

'Aye, once a child reaches the age of eight. But it is different if there are not two parents to share the care. I have applied for visiting rights to Gion's crèche, but whether I get them …' She shivered. 'If Administrator Valdt seeks to punish me further by blocking my application, then the weapon I whored myself for is likely to see some use.'

Bez was suffering the weirdest feeling, something she could not immediately identify. 'I hope it doesn't come to that,' she said.

''Tis in the All-Father's hands. I will leave thee now, sister.' She got up, careful not to disturb the sleeping infant. 'I doubt we shall meet again.'

'Thank you,' said Bez, 'and good luck.'

It was only after Cusa had gone that Bez put a name to the unusual emotion: empathy.

She sat perfectly still, letting unaccustomed feelings wash through her. Then she stood up and walked out of the bar. She commed reception and asked to book a room. They were understandably confused, given there was already a suite reserved in her husband's name, but she insisted. She took the cheapest option, initially just for one night.

Once in her room, she rummaged in her bag for the slate she had purchased on the starliner, and slotted the 'spike.

Cusa was right: the info was sparse. She had the man's home address and basic personal details, plus a lot of supposition; enough to make him worth following up. Her best bet would be to check out his home. This time she would be more careful. She would make sure her target really was at work, and not assume that, just because the locals didn't maintain a virtuality, their systems were primitive.

A com call interrupted her. She was dismayed, if unsurprised, when she saw who it was. 'Yes?' she snapped.

'I just wanted to check everything is all right.' Sirrah Tierce sounded genuinely concerned.

'Everything's fine.' *Like it's any of your business.*

'Could we maybe continue our discussion now?'

Bez wanted to say there was nothing to discuss, but patently he was not going to leave her alone. 'All right.'

'I'm still in the bar, if you—'

'Com's fine.' She had had too many face-to-face conversations recently.

'Fair enough. With video, perhaps?'

She patched the call through to her slate; she didn't want him in her visual cortex.

'That's better,' he said, then frowned. 'Hey, that looks like a hotel room—'

'It is. So, what did you want to say?'

'Firstly, I wanted to apologise.'

'Apologise?'

'Yes. I've obviously discomforted you by turning up like this. That was not my intention.'

'And what was your intention? Because you have, by your own admission, gone to a lot of trouble to find me.'

'I want to let you know that I'm – we're – here for you. To help.'

'I don't need your help.'

'I beg to differ. You do. You just don't know it.'

'Oh, really?'

'Yes. There's no easy way to say this but ... we already *are* helping you, whether you like it or not.'

'In what way?'

'Covering up your mistakes, for a start.'

'I don't make mistakes.'

'You're arrogant, which I can understand, but perhaps you should ask yourself whether it is *truly* feasible in the interconnected universe we live in for one person to constantly get away with the sort of heists you keep pulling?'

'Heists?'

'Thefts. Of data. Credit. Identities. That sort of thing.'

'I have no idea what you're talking about.'

'Please don't fuck about. It wastes both our time.' He looked pained. 'All right: an example. You and I might not be having this conversation now were it not for a perfectly timed com call to First Detective Hylam on Tarset station a few weeks back.'

Bez actually felt her jaw drop. She snapped it shut. She had thought the distraction that had let her walk free on Tarset was convenient. It had not occurred to her it could have been contrived. 'Wait, you ... how in the void's name could you be responsible for that?'

'How is not relevant. The result is. We're looking out for you.'

This was not something she could run from. This was something that had been shadowing her, unseen but constant, possibly for years.

Tierce appeared to take her silence as acquiescence. He said,

'So, given we're on the same side, do you have any leads?'

'Leads?'

'Yes, that urgent com call you took; was it relevant to your investigations here?'

'My ... investigations? Y— No. I mean. I need to think about this, Sirrah Tierce. About what you've said.'

'You've got my number. Just call.'

After he hung up, Bez did some calming calculations. Then she tried to grasp the enormity of what her alleged ally had said. The worst of it was, his claims made sense. There had been occasions in the past when events had appeared to conspire in her favour, or useful data had become available at just the right time. She had dismissed them as happenstance but Imbarin Tierce might be exactly what he said: the representative of an organisation whose aims paralleled hers. Even if he was, that didn't mean she should automatically trust him.

While her unconscious tried to assimilate this shift to her worldview, she went back to the task in hand.

Her research into the apartment where Administrator Valdt lived soon revealed a problem: Valdt was an unmarried man, living in a building of unmarried men. The physical set-up of the block was similar to Cusa and Khea's place, with a semi-public atrium. If she could get through the main entrance, she could hack the lock to Valdt's place. Perhaps she could fool the building sec from the surface door, or maybe hack her comshades temporarily to ID her as male. But that was risky, and she might still need to provide the system with a reason for visiting. There were no apartments for rent in this block. How about deliveries? Graceni ordered most of their supplies via the comnet, so provisions companies brought food and suchlike all the time.

There was something about deliveries, something she had seen in Valdt's file ... She checked again. One of his hobbies was sand-yacht racing, and he sometimes had components sent to his home; there was a standing order in place allowing certain companies to leave deliveries in the lobby of his apartment. She could use that. She looked up the companies referred to. She would like to get hold of one of their courier uniforms, though as with everything else here, it came down to the symbols and insignia on your robes, which should make it relatively easy to fake.

That just left fooling the lock with her gender. Tricky, for even if she spoofed her shades, she could not be sure what trackbacks were in place: a female tourist visiting women's accommodation was unlikely to get flagged up; a tourist whose gender had apparently changed probably was.

She needed a man's comshades. Or a man.

Bez briefly entertained the paranoid possibility that Imbarin Tierce had somehow known she would need his help and turned up at the right moment.

Tierce obviously had considerable resources. Even if his aims only temporarily coincided with hers, she could use him to get what she wanted, then disappear – or try to. The thought that there was an organisation out there that knew what she was up to left a cold hollow in the pit of her stomach. But she was not going to let that knowledge derail her plans.

She commed him. 'Before we go any further,' she said as soon as he picked up, 'I need you to answer a question for me.'

'Ask away.'

'Let's assume for the sake of argument that I believe you. Let's say your people have been present in the background all the time, even though I've never come across any sign of them. Furthermore, let's say they've been helping me out behind the scenes.'

'It's the truth.'

'If that's the case, then you – your organisation – has a void-eating amount of power. Why in the name of deep entropy do you need me?'

'Two reasons. Firstly, we value your talents, your *considerable* talents, which lie in subtly different areas from ours. Secondly, our power is localised and quite specific. Limited, even. You, however, see the bigger picture. You treat all of human-space as your domain. You go wherever you need to, and do whatever you have to, all in the cause of destroying the evil that is perverting human destiny. You're our greatest asset.'

'Let's just get one thing straight here,' she said slowly. 'I am not your, or anyone's, *asset*. I'm a free agent, and if that means we're on the same side for the moment, then so be it.'

'So you're willing to let me help you?'

She paused, then said, 'For now, yes.'

TROPHY PIECE

Some things we believe about the Sidhe do appear to be true. For example, I've found no evidence of any of the old, powerful Sidhe males anywhere in human-space. It's logical to conclude that the received wisdom may be correct in this case: the true male Sidhe are all long dead.

<file under: Unqualified Data>

As Bez followed Tierce up the path, she wondered when she had started taking such risks. With every step closer to Valdt's apartment complex, her breathing got shallower and faster. Such drastic action, taken so impulsively. Not her style at all.

Tierce had initially suggested she need not accompany him to Administrator Valdt's home, but Bez insisted she would. This was her mission, and he was only involved because she had decided to let him assist her.

Getting hold of male robes had been straightforward: the hotel had its own laundry, and entrances to the service areas were protected by nothing more than warning signs. Tierce had sneaked in and brought back a selection of disguises. She chose clothing that marked her – or rather him – as a male of low rank. In the privacy of her room, she lightened her skin and hair until it was close to local norms, and scraped her hair back so that, with her hood up, she could pass at a glance for a boy.

If Tierce had been surprised at her radical change of appearance when she turned up at his suite, he didn't say anything.

She had no idea how Tierce got hold of a set of comshades that were – so he claimed – the property of a reputable courier company. He had simply used the word 'borrowed', smiling as he said it.

They approached the door to the complex's lobby with Bez a pace behind Tierce, jointly carrying a package fabricated from the central spine of the clothes stand from his bedroom, dismantled and rewrapped in plasticised sheeting. It was long and bulky, but if they were posing as a pair of couriers, they needed to be carrying something that required two people. Getting the package out of the hotel had involved going through the service areas, an experience that put her on edge even before they left the building. She had relaxed slightly when Tierce paid for the cab: if he was willing to take risks on her behalf, far be it for her to argue, although such behaviour was at odds with his assertion that his people were as careful as she was. Perhaps he had backup, maybe even a data-breaker running interference in the infoscape.

They stopped outside the door and Tierce used the courier's comshades to request entry. After what felt like several seconds, a synthesised male voice asked politely, 'Kindly state thy reasons for visiting this address.'

Bez had dealt with a similar security interface when she visited Cusa. 'A delivery for Sirrah Tren Valdt,' said Tierce, sounding bored.

'Sirrah Valdt has not given notice of any deliveries today.'

Tierce, apparently unconcerned, said, ''Tis from Sand Aero. The mast-strut he had on back-order; he did not expect it yet.' He pointed with his free hand to the end of the package under his arm, for the benefit of whatever surveillance might be trained on them.

Building security systems varied massively both in their paranoia and intellectual capacity. A similar set-up on a hub might well ask for the second person's ID at this point, in which case they would have to abort. The voice said, 'Sirrah Valdt has previously notified this system of deliveries from that company. Ye may enter, as per his standing instructions.' The door opened.

Bez smiled in gratitude at the trusting nature of God-fearing societies.

Inside, the building was marked as male territory by the prevalence of straight lines over curves, and the colour scheme, which was russet highlighted in dark brown and black.

Getting the package into the elevator proved mildly challenging. En route to Valdt's floor, the lift stopped. The elderly man who got in looked askance at Bez, who had kept her hood up even though they were indoors. Then his gaze fell on the wrapped package propped up across the back of the elevator. 'What is that, brother?' he asked.

''Tis a weigh bar for, ah ...' – Tierce made a show of blinking into his comshades – 'Sirrah Sriden.' Despite herself, Bez was impressed at Tierce's ability to mimic local speech patterns and effortlessly deploy disinformation.

'Hah,' said the older man. 'Why will the man not use the house gymnasium like the rest of those body-sculpt boys!' Then he looked at Tierce more closely. 'Art thou unwell, brother? Thy skin is dark as a hellbound sinner's.'

'I have been ill,' said Tierce, his tone full of embarrassment.

'Huh,' said the man, apparently satisfied, or possibly repelled.

The man got off at the next floor. She and Tierce carried on to the bottom level, where the most expensive apartments were. The square atrium featured a small park and the gymnasium the man in the lift had referred to. Bez was relieved to see only one person working out, too distant and too stoked on endorphins to pay them any attention.

The outer door to Valdt's apartment had no lock: in a luxury block like this, apartments needed lobbies to facilitate the many collections and deliveries that kept the residents' lives effortlessly opulent. Valdt's lobby contained a bag of dirty washing and several items that probably really were destined for his sand-yacht. Bez and Tierce propped their package up against one wall and went over to the door to the apartment proper.

'Did you want to do the honours?' he asked.

By way of an answer, Bez blinked her headware fully online. Her intrusion suite was set to go, and the lock looked as simple as the last one she had cracked, but given she had failed to spot Cusa's ID-harvesting retrohack, she took the job slowly.

Finally the door gave a barely audible *click*.

'I'm assuming you would have told me if there was any additional security.'

Tierce's voice, right by her ear, made Bez jump.

'Of course!' she retorted in a harsh whisper. 'But feel free to go in first anyway.'

He did. She followed. From the look of the wide hallway, Administrator Valdt was a collector of large-canvas 2-D artworks, mainly of the erotic variety. He was also untidy, as might be expected from a busy man who lived alone.

She followed Tierce as he made an initial recon of the apartment. They found the rooms to be large, well appointed and, with the exception of the main lounge, unoccupied. This room housed, along with hardcopy books, expensive furniture and a comprehensive ents unit, a half-metre-long, lizard-like creature, which dozed under a sunlamp in the terrarium along one wall.

Tierce said, 'How about I do a full physical search while you see what you can find data-wise?'

Bez found his tendency to give her first refusal on everything simultaneously reassuring and irritating. 'Agreed.'

On the few previous occasions Bez had searched people's accommodation, she had known what she was looking for – usually dataspikes – but this was a trickier proposition. And although she had commed Cusa to confirm that Valdt was still at work before they had set out, he could have arranged for the building system to alert him if anyone turned up unexpectedly. Even now, he might be rushing home to find out what that anomalous delivery was ... Bez applied the best-case principle and halted further unhelpful speculation.

She moved around the different rooms, accessing the house system direct from her headware. She was increasingly at home in Gracen's infoscape, and confident her personal tech would leave no trace. There was no internal security, and she found only the expected environmental controls and monitoring systems linked to supply/re-order routines. Scanning recent purchases, Bez was mildly disconcerted to find that Valdt's pet preferred live food; young avian-analogues by the look of it. She also discovered a booking for an additional pickup of recyclables outside the building's scheduled collections.

'Found this.' Bez, standing in Valdt's gleaming if over-full kitchen, looked up at Tierce's voice. He held out a slate. 'It was in a desk drawer,' he added.

Bez put the slate down on one of the clear surfaces, leaving Tierce to continue searching the apartment. She interfaced with the slate by degrees, wary of security. A lot of what she found was office work, the kind of complex mundane trivia she would expect on the personal comp of a high-ranking bureaucrat. But she also got his diary, which included a couple of interesting entries.

As Tierce was still busy, she dug deeper into the personal files on the slate and found various image stashes. Some were family/social snapshots, but others, protected by Valdt's amateurish attempts at encryption, were porn of the hardest variety. Between the apartment artwork and what she had found on the slate, Bez had already worked out that Valdt preferred women to men and liked his sex somewhat rough, but some of the hidden files turned her stomach. When she came across high-definition footage of a young girl being beaten and kicked by a pair of obviously aroused men carrying short batons and wearing nothing but masks, she blinked herself back into the real and went to find Tierce.

He was standing in the living room, hand on chin, looking pensive. The room was somewhat untidier than it had been. 'Did you find anything?' she asked.

'Possibly. Here.' He held out a narrow strip of highly patterned fabric. 'You've been here a while: what does that look like to you?'

'Robe decoration,' said Bez, examining the fabric without touching it. 'From a woman's robe – see the colours and the way the patterns flow into each other? Is that all there is? I can't tell much from such a small sample.'

'This is all I found. It was in his bedroom cabinet. It doesn't smell too good.'

Bez was glad she hadn't touched the cloth, even though she wore gloves. But what Tierce said chimed with her earlier findings. 'I think I know where there might be more of this.' She turned, not waiting to see if he followed her.

When she reached the apartment's lobby she stopped. The prophylactic gloves were sufficient to stop them leaving DNA traces, but they were also gossamer thin, so as not to cause loss of sensation when put to their more usual uses. Bez had no intention of thrusting her almost-bare hands into a pervert's filthy clothes.

When Tierce came up to stand beside her she pointed at the bag she had originally taken to be dirty washing. 'In there,' she said.

'What makes you think that?'

'Valdt's getting this lot picked up for recycling tomorrow. An additional collection.'

'Disposing of the evidence, you reckon?' Tierce sounded almost gleeful.

'Possibly, although it's been several weeks since my agent disappeared.'

'But you reckon it's worth a look.'

'Yes.'

'And you're expecting me to do the actual looking.'

'Yes.'

Tierce affected a sigh and crouched down next to the bag. Bez stood back and checked the time. This was taking too long; they needed to think about leaving soon, whether or not they had anything conclusive.

Tierce straightened. 'How about this?' he said. It was a larger strip of fabric, perhaps the bottom third of a robe. Bez spotted a familiar motif. She moved up to get a closer look. 'I know this pattern,' she said. 'Cusa wore a variation on it. I think this is Khea's robe.'

'So, it looks like he might have killed her,' said Tierce thoughtfully. Bez had had no choice other than to give him the gist of her findings on Alpha83. 'Have there been any other collections for cloth recycling recently, scheduled or otherwise? I'm thinking he's been getting rid of the incriminating evidence in several, non-suspicious bits. Other than his trophy piece.'

'This sort of recyclable is collected every two weeks.'

'Perhaps he sent off the first piece then got cold feet.'

'Perhaps. I found some other unusual activity in his diary.'

'Such as?'

'He's taken a lot of leave from his job recently, some of it on short notice.'

'Interesting, but not conclusive.'

'Also, he's been trying to set up a visit to SA-19.'

'The archive facility?'

'That's the one.' Good: so he had read Cusa's file thoroughly.

'What was your agent after anyway? I'm guessing it's to do with IDs.'

Bez hesitated. So far she had given Tierce only intel pertinent to this part of the mission. Now, briefly and uneasily, she told him what she had recruited Alpha83 for. He caught on at once, finishing the explanation for her:

'... and SA-19 is the only offline storage facility that keeps ID data – the *original* ID data for everyone ever processed by Valdt's office – in perpetuity.'

'Indeed it is.' Bez felt oddly warm all of a sudden.

'Hmm. Then I'd say Valdt's our man.'

The warmth might be a physical response to having given so much away to her new ally ... No, she was experiencing a blast of heated air from somewhere. Was her robe malfunctioning?

'Bez? What is it?'

'The heat.'

'What about the heat? Oh yes, it is getting warmer, isn't it?'

'Valdt leaves his apartment at ambient when he's at work. But he's got a link to his desk at the ministry; when he signs off for the day, it signals the building's maintenance system. The heating just came on. That means he's on his way home.'

'Oh dear.' Tierce didn't sound overly concerned.

She needed to remove the slate from the kitchen, and Tierce would have to put that vile scrap of fabric back. Not to mention getting rid of the package they had come here with; they hadn't even discussed what to do with that. This was what came of acting without proper preparation! Then Bez remembered the state of the living room. 'What did you do to the lounge?' she asked.

'I searched it.'

'And you made a mess, didn't you? More of a mess.'

'I thought the idea was to search quickly but thoroughly. You never mentioned anything about *tidily*.'

'We have to clear up! He'll know someone's been here!'

'I imagine he will,' said Tierce.

'But that wasn't the plan!'

'I don't remember us discussing what would happen if we didn't find any incriminating evidence.'

He was right, damn it. She knew what she would do, but it was different once you started working with someone. You had to *explain* everything. 'We'd leave, making sure he had no way of knowing we'd been here! What other logical course of action is there?'

'Ah. You can go if you want. I thought I might try … other avenues.' He reached into his robes.

'You're not thinking of staying? This man is almost certainly a murderer!'

'In that case,' he said, producing a small but deadly-looking gun, 'it's a good job I brought this, isn't it?'

TOO MANY GUNS

Designation: Target416
Human alias: Utenia Mandrew
Position: Vice President, Currency and Investment, First
   Allied Bank
Location: Luftain
Vulnerabilities: Accused of fraud (two counts) and
manslaughter (one count) but never brought to justice.
She has already been the subject of investigations on her
homeworld; the authorities there may be amenable to
accepting any evidence presented to facilitate her arrest.

<file under: Target List>

'You've got to be joking!'

Given Gracen was meant to be a peaceable and spiritually inclined world, Bez was seeing far too many guns here.

'No. Although I enjoy humour on occasion, this is not one of
those moments.'

Bez remind herself of his role on Tarset station: security without
portfolio. Naturally he would have a gun. She wondered whether
his secret society had helped him smuggle the weapon down
to Gracen. It looked like a needle-pistol, a nasty little weapon
favoured by more dubious spacers because it was easily concealed
and fired flechettes instead of slugs.

'What are you going to do?' she asked as evenly as she could.

'Get some answers.'

'Right.' The situation was becoming more insane by the
moment.

'You can go if you want to, although I could use a hand.'

'A hand? Doing what?'

'We'll need to restrain Valdt. That's quite tricky when you're training a gun on someone.'

'So you want me to tie him up?'

'Not *tie*, as such. He's got some … specialist equipment.'

'I'll bet he has,' she said grimly.

'So, are you staying?'

Although her instinct was to leave, that would not stop Tierce doing whatever he was going to do. And it might be too late to get away anyway; Valdt's office was close enough to his home that she risked passing him on her way out. How would she react if she saw him, knowing what she now knew? 'Yes,' she said. 'I'll stay. But only to help you restrain him.'

'That's all I'm asking.'

They moved the package into the spare bedroom, so Valdt wouldn't suspect anything when he came in, then Tierce went to fetch the restraints. When he handed her the cunning contraption of chains and bars, she had to force herself to take it. He also had to show her how it worked. She decided not to consider how he knew. 'Why don't you wait in the lounge until I call you?' he suggested.

Bez nodded, happy to stay out of the way until Tierce needed her. She threw the bondage set onto a chair and stood in the centre of the room, taking deep, careful breaths. Whenever dread threatened to get a hold on her, she made herself think of Cusa looking down at her sleeping baby. This was not the way she worked, but perhaps this time, in these circumstances, it was the right way.

She heard a faint click from the hall.

A man said, 'What in the name of the All-Father—?'

'Don't move.' Tierce issued the command casually, almost like a suggestion.

But it was a suggestion backed up with a gun, and Valdt's voice showed fear as well as bravado when he said, 'Thou must know I am not a man to be toyed with.'

'Me neither. Hands on your head, please.' Tierce sounded like he was enjoying himself.

A pause, presumably while Valdt obeyed. Then Tierce said,

'And if you'll just make your way into the dining room, we'll be joined there by my lovely assistant.'

Bez picked up the restraints. When Tierce called back cheerily, 'Sirrah Valdt is ready for you now!' she took a deep breath and left the room.

Tierce had positioned his captive at the head of the impractically large dining table, with his back to the door. Bez was glad of the arrangement as she clicked and ratcheted him into his chair. If she had had to look at the man's face she might have lost her nerve. Her nostrils were full of the rank stench of his fear, and his voice was low and harsh, alternating between cajoling and threats. 'I see thou art an offworlder, sirrah, so I would surmise someone has hired thee, possibly on false pretences. Let me go and I shall double whatever fee they offered.' Then, when Tierce didn't respond, 'Thou shalt live to regret this outrage! I hold great power here!'

Despite her eagerness to get away, Bez double-checked the bindings before she straightened.

Tierce, speaking for the first time since she had come in, called past the bound man to her, 'See you back at base, then.'

To her own amazement, she shook her head. 'No,' she whispered, 'I'll stay, in case ...' In case what? 'I'll wait,' she concluded. If she left now, whatever Tierce found out would belong to him.

Tierce smiled, although it was not a pleasant expression. 'In that case,' he said, 'why don't you turn on the ents unit? Cover up any sounds from in here, if you see what I mean.'

Unfortunately, she did.

When she returned to the living room, the lizard was awake. Its triangular head swung round towards her as she came in. Bez was irrationally convinced it knew what was happening to its master next door. She looked away, and located the controls for the holoset.

The choice of shows was limited. Bez settled on a gaudy biopic exploring the life of one of Gracen's most famous saints. She kept glancing over at Valdt's pet until it finally lowered its head and closed its eyes.

She tried to give her attention to the improbable life story of an unknown stranger. If nothing else there was an engaging absurdity in the way the biopic tried to combine sentiment, melodrama and outbreaks of gore and nudity – not to mention more of that overtonal singing – with piety.

After one particularly bizarre sequence in which the subject of the biopic rejected both her lovers in order to grow closer to 'Universal Love', the action was replaced by a panning long shot of her walking barefoot into the desert. As she receded, so did the soundtrack, becoming no more than a faint thrum.

Someone screamed, close by. A man, quickly cut off.

Bez swallowed bile.

Another sound: sobbing.

She changed the channel on the holoset, settling on a game show, which had the advantage of providing constant noise. She sprang to her feet and began to pace, careful not to touch anything. After a surreptitious glance at the sleeping lizard to gauge its dimensions, she set about calculating its approximate internal volume: a pleasingly complex problem. The holoset's drawl receded to white noise.

It took her a moment to register when the door opened. Tierce came in and strode straight over to the terrarium. He opened the lid with one hand, reaching in with the other.

The lizard went from apparent somnolence to vicious motion in a heartbeat. Tierce whipped his arm out and slammed the lid down as snapping jaws closed on the empty air where his hand had been a fraction of a second before.

He muttered something under this breath that sounded like, 'Thought so,' then drew his needle-pistol. He raised the lid high enough to point the tip of the gun inside, and pulled the trigger. Purple-red blood spattered the inside of the terrarium.

Bez turned the holoset off. In the deep silence that followed, Tierce finally acknowledged her presence with a nod. Then he turned his attention back to the mess in the terrarium. He rolled up his sleeve and reached in, feeling around the floor of the gore-spattered enclosure. Bez cringed; even with gloves he was going to end up covered in reptile remains.

Tierce said conversationally, 'Sirrah Valdt claimed this critter was harmless, but he struck me as the sort of man who would keep something nasty then train it to go for strangers.'

'Actually,' said Bez, calming down in the wake of Tierce's sudden violence, 'its bite is poisonous. Was poisonous.'

'Really?' Tierce reached in further.

'I can't imagine any other reason for keeping a supply of anti-venom in one's cooler.'

'Right.' Tierce frowned, then said, 'Got it.' When he withdrew his arm, his unpleasantly stained hand held a small case that Bez recognised as a protective carrier for dataspikes.

Suddenly nothing else mattered. 'Is that it?' she whispered. 'Is that the ID data?'

'It's part of what we came for. As for the rest ... I'll explain en route.'

'En route where?' Just when she thought she had a moment to come to terms with events, they moved on.

'Initially back to the hotel. As soon as we're in the atrium, I'll call us a taxi.'

'We can't go straight back! Not after ... what's happened here. At the very least we need to change taxis.'

'I guess that might be wise.'

Bez was stunned at his recklessness. 'And you need to get cleaned up,' she added.

'Good point. I'll use the guest bathroom.'

'Um, make sure you wipe your cheek.'

'My cheek?'

'There's a smudge on it. I think it's blood.' Red blood, not the purplish stuff from the lizard.

'Thanks. Won't be long.'

The lizard carcass was beginning to smell, but Bez was loath to leave the room for fear of finding worse outside. She clenched her fists, calculated a few cube roots from her chrono, and concentrated on not being sick. By the time Tierce stuck his head round the door, she had her physical responses under control. 'Let's go,' he said.

157

The hall was empty. Seeing her gaze slide towards the closed door to the dining room, Tierce said, 'Administrator Valdt has left a message at his office saying he's been taken ill. However, when he was, ah, speaking to me a little later, he claimed to have an important meeting tomorrow as a result of which someone is bound to com him in the afternoon.'

'Was he telling the truth?'

'Mainly he was trying to save his skin, but I think what he said about the meeting was true. By that point he was pretty much beyond lies.'

Bez suppressed a shudder. 'So we need to be on the next flight out.'

'Yes, we do. But first we have to get what you came for.'

They said nothing as they exited the building. Bez kept expecting some alarm to sound or the local law to turn up, but all was quiet. In the upper lobby they encountered a couple of residents; Bez kept her head bowed and hurried past.

Outside, night had fallen. The world's single large moon had risen and painted the barren landscape in silver. For the first time, Bez looked up; the starry night sky was a lot less intimidating than the burning daytime one, even if the horizon was too far away and the stars twinkled disconcertingly.

As they walked through the silent garden to the taxi she felt compelled to ask, 'Is he dead?'

'Oh, yes.'

'And Khea? Did he kill her?'

'Eventually.'

Bez tried not to think about the footage in Valdt's personal files. 'And is the dataspike he hid in the terrarium a list of all the fake IDs he fabricated?'

'Indeed it is. One hundred and eighty-two of them, covering nearly forty years.'

'So he planned to visit SA-19 to purge the original records?'

'That was his intention. Up until recently, he wasn't unduly worried about the archived data. No one had any reason to access it, so no one would ever know it had been tampered with. Once he interrogated your agent and discovered what she was after, he changed his mind. He requested a visit to the archive facility, but he wasn't in a hurry because he didn't want to arouse any suspicions. That's how I knew he was telling the truth about the meeting tomorrow, by the way. He told me all about his current project, how he was going to wait until that was out of the way, then arrange for a little bit of data destruction.'

They reached the gate, which opened automatically. The cab arrived a few moments later. As with the journey here, Tierce paid. She was happy to have his ID be the one linked to the scene of the crime. Once they had pulled away Tierce said, 'Do you reckon you could hack a set of comshades?'

Bez looked at him sharply. 'I'm not sure we should be—' She gestured to take in the taxi.

'Don't worry, no one's monitoring us.'

'I'd still rather not talk in here.'

'As you wish.'

Rather than returning directly to the hotel, they visited a mixed-sex tourist bar. Bez positioned herself carefully so as to have as good a view as possible of the main entrance and as bad a view as possible of the show being staged in the centre of the room. This was not sacred ground, so at least they wouldn't be expected to participate. 'In answer to your earlier question,' she said, speaking just loud enough to be heard over a soundtrack of chanting and primal sleaze, 'I'm sure I can hack a pair of shades. Presumably we just need to fake an ID?'

'That's right.'

'So you, uh, persuaded Valdt to arrange his visit to the archive facility for tomorrow.'

'Indeed I did.'

'What if someone cross-references his request for sick leave with the visit?'

'Not a problem: he's not going. He'll be sending a minion.'

That made sense; after all, Valdt's face might be known. 'So you'll be posing as someone from his office?'

'Not me,' said Tierce. 'You.'

Bez stared at him. 'No,' she said.

Tierce reached forward. 'Leaving aside the fact that you're eminently equipped to deal with any data issues, there's two reasons why you're the right choice. Firstly, gender – these are women's records – and secondly, colour.' He pointed at his hand. 'Tourist,' he said. Then, briefly touching her paler one, 'Local.'

Bez pulled back, saying nothing. He was right, damn him to the void.

UNRELIABLE SENSES

I realise there is a possibility that, should we succeed, the surviving Sidhe might mount a raid into human-space. That would be bad news for whichever system they picked on, but it would be a desperate strategy.

   People would certainly mobilise against them if they turned up in force, and even if the Sidhe numbered several million they'd be facing trillions of humans united by a hatred of their old oppressors.

<file under: Unqualified Data>

Back at the hotel, she turned down Tierce's suggestion that she come back to his suite, and renewed the reservation on her room. She went to work on the set of comshades they had used to get into Valdt's apartment. Tierce had persuaded Valdt to make an appointment for a Gena Markin, a statistician from his department, to visit SA-19 as his deputy. Bez's job was to make sure that the woman who turned up at the archive facility in the morning would be ID'd as Markin.

   Comshades were relatively primitive, little more than ports into Gracen's comnet, with the additional ability to transmit an ID and tap into the owner's verified funds. Given Bez only needed to make the shades ping-back a false ID, not actually access Markin's personal data, the job did not take long. She commed Tierce to tell him she had succeeded.

   'Great,' he said. 'You can come and have dinner with me.'

   'I don't think so.'

   'Why not? It would reinforce our cover. We are meant to be married.'

   'Don't you think that's a bit pointless, given I've taken a separate room? And why do you think it's so important to maintain the charade anyway? Is there something you're not telling me?'

'Not at all. I just thought you might like to go out for a meal.'

'We've got an early start tomorrow. I'd rather get an early night.'

'As you wish.'

The call did remind her that she needed to eat. She commed room service. Her meal arrived with a human waiter rather than on a bot trolley, and Bez realised afterwards she should probably have given the girl a tip. This business with Tierce was damaging her ability to present a non-memorable front. But whether she liked it or not, they were now linked by their complicity. This thought was not unbearable, provided she didn't dwell on what he had done to Administrator Valdt. Allying herself with Tierce was achieving her aims, however dubious his methods. She wondered if her uncharacteristic lack of caution was due to one uncertainty too many recently. Was she losing her objectivity? Perhaps, but she was also getting results.

Valdt had not only confessed to Khea Foelin's murder, he had told Tierce where to find the body: he had buried her out in the desert, near the remote racing station where he kept his yacht.

Bez's half-remembered dreams that night were filled with moonlit chases ending at a shallow grave.

She awoke to the sound of her alarm, and met Tierce in the atrium at the prearranged time.

Their taxi initially took them to the only cultural attraction open this early – a museum which the guidebooks suggested as a side trip for any tourists interested in the elements of Graceni society not devoted to sex or religion. The establishment still displayed an assortment of Aesir reliquaries and a collection of shrines to the various incarnations of the Manifest Son.

They spent a few minutes wandering round in uneasy silence. Bez had not wanted Tierce to come along, but he insisted on accompanying her and paying for the cab, just as he had yesterday. Although this was a weight off Bez's mind, she wondered at his motivation: it was almost as if he didn't care if he left traces.

Unless he was trying to *protect* her? But even if his peculiar attempts to initiate intimacy were genuine, such ridiculous selflessness belonged in romance holodramas. For now, she would take advantage of his foolish generosity, however distasteful she found the implicit debt.

Having established basic cover, they ordered another cab to take them out of town. The change from urban to rural was gradual, with wider spaces between surface structures, less cultivated areas and, finally, an end to the fences that kept the food-stock animals off the roads. As the already minimal data in her overlays dwindled further, Bez grew increasingly nervous.

The terrain changed, undulating with gentle hills. In the distance she saw tracts of yellow grassland with brown and black dots on them – presumably more farmed animals. On the flatter sections they passed fields of monocultures: long lines of bushes with silver-green leaves shading bright clusters of red berries, gnarled trees whose entangled branches formed a canopy hung with pendulous fruits, and tall strands of green-and-russet grasses with hand-sized golden seed heads arranged in spirals round their stems. They encountered occasional ground vehicles, some quite large; one slow-moving truck was pulling a trailer containing about a dozen long-necked ungulates with patchwork hides; the animals swayed in time and looked around curiously. Overhead, the turquoise sky remained bright and empty.

With the exception of brief identifiers when she focused on passing vehicles, Bez's overlays were entirely empty now. She reminded herself that this was how humankind had lived for most of history, but not having any input beyond her unreliable senses made her feel untethered and unreal. Rather than stare at an unaugmented world, she reviewed her research data. Tierce made no attempt at conversation, for which she was grateful.

After three hours, the cab began to slow down. Its synthesised voice stated that authorisation was required to complete the journey. Hired transport would either take passengers to a named location or to a grid reference; Tierce had used the latter request when he ordered the cab, but the machine's primitive brain must have finally registered where they were heading and was querying the request.

Bez donned the hacked comshades then used the Markin ID to instruct the cab to continue its journey. Although she was confident she had managed to spoof the shades, this was the first test. She was relieved when the cab acknowledged her authority and began to accelerate.

The archive facility itself was a typical Graceni building, complete with perimeter fence. Bez's comshades listed it as a 'government storage facility'.

As the cab slowed outside the gate, Tierce hunkered down. There was no obvious surveillance but it was a wise precaution. 'You're not going to stay like that the whole time, are you?' asked Bez out of the corner of her mouth.

'Only until you get out. Then the cab will go wait in the vehicle depot round the back of the complex.'

Bez should have known that; she had read up on this place too. She cursed her slip, born of nerves.

The gate opened when she transmitted 'her' ID. She tried to stride confidently up the path, but she was sweating hard enough to test the cooling abilities of her robes.

The building had two doors, one for each gender. The women's entrance brought her into a small lobby. The guard sitting at the desk had her hood down, and smiled when she saw Bez. Bez located and kissed the reliquary, after which the guard said, 'Greetings, sister.'

Bez replied, 'And to thee.' At least she would not be expected to kiss the guard.

'Thou art early.'

'Is that a problem?' Bez winced inside, unsure of her intonation.

'No,' said the guard slowly, 'it is not.'

'If thou would be kind enough to show me to the correct vault.' Bez had practised that sentence, along with others she expected to use.

'As thou wishest.'

When the guard got up she noticed a miniaturised holoset at

her station, its volume muted, showing a cheesy-looking drama. Spending your days in a place like this on the offchance some bureaucrat wanted to access offline storage had to be a pretty boring job. And thanks to their stupid gender laws, there would be an equally bored male guard on the far side of that wall. What a way to run a world.

The elevator arrived. Bez followed the guard inside.

'I have a cousin in Administrator Valdt's office,' said the guard conversationally.

Bez stared at the guard, dumbstruck, then made herself say, 'Really?'

'Aye. Her name is Mila. She is a researcher. As art thou, I believe.'

'I am newly come to my position.' Tierce had made sure she would be impersonating a recent employee, but even though that was a sentence she had practised, Bez was sure the guard suspected something.

'I ask because she is a statistician by training, which I thought thou might be also. I know 'tis often said that numbers are man's work. So I just thought thou and she might have met—'

'No. Sorry.'

A nasty silence fell. Bez, expecting the guard to draw her weapon at any moment, made herself ask, 'Did thou see that holo on Saint Leta last night?'

'Sorry?'

''Twas on Prime. Quite early.'

'I was on lates. It was good?'

'Aye,' said Bez as decisively as she could. ''Twas excellent.'

'Ah,' said the guard.

The elevator stopped. The guard did not draw a weapon or say anything. Bez exhaled quietly as she was led out of the lift. She stayed a step behind the guard as was proper, and memorised their route through the near featureless corridors. The guard stopped at a door labelled:

CRÈCHE MORTALITY (FEMALE, PRE-PUBESCENT) c.880–c.950

As the door opened the guard said, 'I shall leave thee to thy work.' Then she turned and walked off.

Inside the room were racks of storage devices: not dataspikes but cubes, an older, less efficient technology that was nevertheless highly resilient. Information could be stored on a cube for a thousand years with little risk of degeneration; add the protection of several hundred metres of rock and a controlled environment, and the info in here might still be accessible when Gracen's sun finally swelled to make this dustball entirely uninhabitable.

The racks had hardcopy labels, faded strings of letters and numbers. There was a small, primitive comp on a spindly table at the end of one rack. Bez tried to interface with it using her shades before realising it actually had an ON switch. The screen sprang to life, displaying a simple search menu: touch the criterion required (*date, region, crèche, cause of death* or *other*) and speak the parameter. Bez investigated the *other* option and confirmed that it was possible to name the person in question. Good: searching through every dead child in the period covered by the false IDs was impractical.

Even so, the work was slow: the comp gave her a cube reference for a name on Valdt's dataspike; she then had to find the cube, mount it in the comp's reader and scroll through to find the info she wanted. Fortunately, the set-up assumed users would want to take a copy, so that required just a single voice command.

Valdt would have been trying to actually delete this info in order to stop anyone doing what Bez was doing now. Unsurprisingly, there was no *delete* option, which was probably another reason the late Administrator had not managed to destroy the evidence yet. Perhaps he had been trying to hire a female databreaker who could delete the data for him. It was even possible that, had events gone differently, he might have ended up paying Bez herself to do it.

She reined in that disturbing thought and got back to the job in hand, applying the best-case principle to any stray flashes of paranoia: Tierce had abandoned her; the guard had checked with Valdt's office and discovered the deception; the info she was accessing wasn't really offline and was triggering an alarm.

She and Tierce had nominally agreed a base time of four hours. It took three hours to get the first hundred names. But she persevered: every name represented one of the Enemy who could potentially be removed from human-space. And, by the same token, every name she *didn't* match was a Sidhe who would probably escape justice. She carried on.

She got back to the elevator five hours and thirty-four minutes after first arriving. As soon as the elevator neared the surface, her headware pinged. It was Tierce; she acknowledged the contact.

The security guard raised her eyebrows when Bez emerged, then asked distantly if she had got everything she wanted. 'Aye, I did,' said Bez, heading for the door. *Any moment now she's going to tell me to stop and turn around—*

But she didn't. Bez walked out into the sunlight, its spectrum reddened with the advancing day.

The taxi was waiting for her at the gate. She glimpsed the top of Tierce's head as she approached.

As the cab pulled away she said, 'You see, you didn't need to come after all.'

'I was beginning to worry,' he said, getting back up on to the seat.

'I wanted to be thorough.'

'I've noticed that about you.'

His comment made her face feel hot.

Her thoroughness made them late. Their luggage had been safely despatched to the starport, and they commed to pay their hotel bills as the cab carried them through what passed for rush hour in Meneske's evening streets. Bez found herself looking over her shoulder every time they turned a corner.

They reached the starport to find the reception area empty. The tail end of the queue on the far side of the barriers disappeared as they entered. By mutual consent they ran, side-by-side.

The ship was still loading, and the starport staff hurried them through. Bez took one last glance back before turning the corner, but no one was coming after them.

As she set foot on the starliner she smiled to herself. She – *they* – had done it.

JIO
(Port Viridian, Tethisyn Alpha, Tethisyn System)

Everyone has secrets.

Jio Maht devoted his life to helping other people, *especially* those with secrets. He had a face and manner that inspired trust; he was one of nature's born confidants, and helping people gave him considerable satisfaction. Any large corporation needed counsellors like Jio, positioned far enough outside the system to be perceived as neutral and safe. He had an enjoyable career that provided a decent living.

If only they knew.

It had begun twenty-eight years ago, when he was first starting out as a vocational stress consultant. Clients sometimes fixated on people in his profession. More rarely, the converse occurred. A good counsellor has the insight to see into a person's heart and the empathy to not be repelled by what they find there. But there is a risk, however unprofessional it might be, of falling for someone you are trying to save.

Not that what he had with Merice was exactly *love*. From the start, it was a very physical relationship. She had been in a junior position back then, but he had recognised her obsessive need to succeed. He remembered being surprised and impressed that someone with such drive also possessed the humility and self-knowledge to seek a counsellor of her own volition. When she had told him about her strange, loveless childhood on a distant anarchic world, he had felt deep and genuine sympathy.

He had also, from the instant he saw her, wanted to go to bed with her.

They had moved on to discussing boyfriends, of which she had

had many. She freely admitted to valuing her career over interpersonal relationships. What she really wanted was a man who would get close when the time was right, but otherwise keep his distance. Jio tried hard not to start thinking of himself as that man. She was his client, and to take advantage of the trust she put in him was an abuse of power. He saw too many victims of abused power in his work: ThreeCs was like a parent in both good and bad ways.

After three months of weekly sessions, he started to believe she felt something for him too. Part of him desperately hoped she did, because he was beginning to obsess about her. Part of him hoped he was wrong, because he needed to disentangle himself before something irrevocable happened.

When something irrevocable did happen, she initiated it. All these years later, the details were both clear as crystal and hazy with nostalgia.

He had become concerned she was holding something back; when he'd finally coaxed out her secret, she had confessed to falling in love with him. At least, that was how he remembered it. The cause mattered less than the effect: amazing sex, in his consulting room. Such a cliché. Such a transgression.

Naturally he insisted they could not go on as client and counsellor. She said – and this he did remember perfectly – that she saw no reason why not, given she had no intention of ever sleeping with him outside his office.

He had been incredulous and appalled. She had been adamant: if he wanted her, those were the terms of the relationship. From the way she had said *if*, she made it clear from the outset that any other possibility was unthinkable.

Not that they just had sex. Sometimes Merice wanted to talk. That was difficult. Sometimes she wanted to talk about her other lovers: that was almost impossible. He challenged her on this once, confessing how hard he found it to provide objective advice when jealousy impinged. She had pointed to the door and said, 'Beyond that, you are not mine and I am not yours. Those are the rules.' Then she had leaned close, and he'd had no choice other than to agree.

Merice had been coming to him for about a year when she got her first big promotion. Her workload forced her to reduce her counselling sessions to once every two weeks, then to once a month. Jio did as she said, and lived his life fully; he had various girlfriends, and plenty of friends. His obsession with Merice became firmly compartmentalised, a process he observed with professional interest.

He had just moved to a larger office when he met Rhenery. Initially he had no idea she was the woman he would marry; it took three years, and some agonising, before he decided that his future was with her. He never seriously considered telling her about his occasional lover.

By the time they married and moved to the large apartment in the heart of Port Viridian that came with his promotion, he only saw Merice every couple of months. Sometimes she cancelled at short notice. He tried to use these disappointments to harden his heart, to purge himself of her. Instead the sessions she missed only made the next meeting more piquant.

He had been sleeping with Merice for eighteen years when he decided to re-evaluate his life and relationships. Rhenery was having problems, largely as a result of their daughter's growing pains but also due to the inevitable reassessments that come with middle age. Jio knew that if he told his wife about his long-term infidelity, their marriage would be over. He thought long and hard whether he wanted a clean break with Rhenery, or whether his love for her was still strong enough to fight for.

He decided it was. From this conclusion it followed that he had to get Merice out of his life. The thought of doing so terrified him; he would be bereft, incomplete, without her. Merice was a constant, and she had wormed her way into his soul. He had come to embrace, almost to cherish, the ongoing weakness she represented. But he saw his lover only once every few months. Rhenery was his wife.

It was one of the most difficult things he had ever done. He remembered the sweating palms, the racing heart. When Merice came in, he launched straight into the speech he had considered, revised and rehearsed more times than he could remember. He had uttered about a dozen words when she held up a hand.

He stopped talking. There was no volition in it, he just shut up. It was as though he had forgotten how human speech worked.

Merice began to laugh, a low, sexy rumble. The most intense flash of lust Jio had ever experienced ignited him. She sashayed across the room. And that was that.

Afterwards, she raised herself up on one elbow then traced a finger along his collarbone and said, 'You're mine. Don't ever think otherwise.'

She rarely used endearments, even such disempowering ones, and before he could help himself he said, stupidly, 'I love you.'

Merice sighed, the exhalation chill on his cooling flesh. 'Yes, but that's not the point.'

Her refusal to acknowledge his feelings made him angry. From the start she had never used the word 'love', and he had tried not to either, because those were the rules. Now he had, and she had dismissed it! Even as his professional mind analysed the games she was playing, the pain made him snap, 'Then what's the point? Because I meant what I s— what I *tried* to say earlier. We can't go on.'

She rolled over, away from him. 'Of course we can,' she said laconically. 'You can't reject me. I won't allow it.'

A new chill settled over him; Merice was rising fast through ThreeCs' political hierarchy. On a world effectively run by a single company, people like her held considerable power, the power to make or break careers, even lives. 'Are you talking about blackmail?' he said, fighting to stop his voice falling to an appalled whisper.

She laughed. 'No. Not that.' She was playing with him, speaking as though he was a child. He refused to rise to it.

Then he had the weirdest thought: the way she had shut him up, her arrogant manner, even the phenomenal sex: it was almost as though, impossible as it seemed, his mistress was – and he had an urge to smile at the crazy idea – a Sidhe.

'Yes.'

He looked over to find she had turned to face him again. She lowered her chin onto his shoulder, at the same time reaching down to cup his balls.

Trying hard to ignore what she was doing he said, '"Yes" what?'

'What you were thinking,' she said conversationally, 'about me.'

'And what was I thinking about you?' Other than that if she kept doing that he'd lose the ability to speak again.

'You were thinking that, impossible as it seems, I am not human, but am one of the semi-mythical race humanity is so very proud of apparently wiping out.'

'Why—' He swallowed, managed to get some spit into his mouth, and continued, 'Why would I be thinking something like that?'

'Because it's true.'

'You're not serious?' Although Merice kept parts of herself – too much of herself – locked away, he thought he knew her well enough to have spotted the sort of near-psychotic delusion that led someone to claim they were an alien.

'Totally.'

Both instinct and training instructed him to humour her, all the while looking for a way back to rationality. But this wasn't just a client; Merice was—

He went blind. Blind and dumb. He was in utter darkness. His existence was instantly reduced to primal, animal fear.

He had no idea how much time passed before sensation and rational thought returned. One moment he was in an endless terrifying nightmare, the next he was back in his office, lying on the rug with his lover. His heart was still thudding madly, but other than the aftermath of the fear response, he was unharmed in body or mind.

Merice whispered, 'Most, though not all, of the legends are true. Including the one about us being able to kill with a thought.'

Her words didn't scare him as much as they should, even though he knew she was speaking the truth. Ridiculous though it was, there was no other explanation. He tried to think through the implications, to work out what would happen now the world had changed for ever. Obviously he could never tell anyone. And he could hardly break things off with her. Beyond that—

'It'll take a bit of getting used to,' she said, almost as though he had spoken out loud. Which, he supposed, he might as well have. She laid a hand on his chest. 'But I wouldn't have started fucking you if I didn't think you were strong enough.'

He felt a ridiculous warmth at that, an almost childish joy at having pleased her.

Merice continued, 'Actually, when it comes to sex, I've been holding back until now. If you'd like to cancel your next appointment I'll show you a few more' – She gave a throaty, ironic giggle – '*legendary* tricks.'

She was being absurdly coy, but all he could think of was that she was giving him a real choice. She would still do that, and he could still refuse.

As if he would. He made a brief com call, pleading a booking error. In return, Merice was as good as her word. After that, he could never give her up.

Ten years on, his feelings hadn't changed. He and Rhenery were still married; he still loved his wife, and they still had sex occasionally. They had a granddaughter now, and she was a joy.

But in this office, once every few months, he was Merice's, utterly and without reservation. She was a genuine, impossible fantasy. She had all the power, and knew all his secrets. Which, though they never discussed it, may well include other people's. He was under no illusion about how useful he was to her: he was one of the top counsellors in Port Viridian, perhaps in the whole of the Tethisyn system. All sorts of people confided in him.

He also knew she could break him – his career, his life, his mind – but that was a spice missing from the lives of most people in his situation, safe and comfortable in a corporate enclave. A surprisingly high number of his clients had problems that came down to just such a lack of danger; in response he sometimes advised taking up deep-dive hunting, jet-skimming or freefall splashdown (with the usual caveats about personal safety). Without Merice, he might have resorted to such extreme hobbies himself.

This next session was before lunch, to allow them maximum time, and give them the opportunity to get showered and respectable again afterwards. The client before cancelled; he'd considered calling Merice to ask if she wanted to bring her visit forward, but there was no point. He didn't get to set the schedule.

Between sessions with Merice he barely thought about her, yet the knowledge of what they did together had come to define him. Today, waiting for her, he'd had too much time to think. He had been her lover for half his life, and though his appetite for her remained undiminished, even with modern medicine there would come a time when he might not be able to satisfy her. Unless the Sidhe had a solution for that too.

Then again, over the last few years they had spent as much time talking as screwing. He would like to think this change reflected a deepening in their relationship, especially as she had finally begun to share some of her problems with him – almost as though he really was her counsellor. But he suspected her change of attitude reflected something larger, something that reached beyond ThreeCs. She had intimated as much, even mentioned specific concerns, going so far as to name a few names. She couldn't be the only member of her race in human-space, and he had no doubt they held power elsewhere too. It was not a thought he liked to dwell on.

The door chimed. The familiar warm rush lit him up from groin to back-brain. He smiled, and let her in.

SAFER NOT KNOWING

Designation: TargetZero
Human alias: Merice Markeck
Position: Director of Corporate Strategy, ThreeCs
Location: Tethisyn
Vulnerabilities: None
Note: Unlike many Sidhe in human-space,
TargetZero has not made any effort to tone down her striking
appearance.

<file under: Target Listing>

The elation was disconcerting. Bez felt childishly, uncomplicatedly joyful. Rather than hiding in her cabin, she stayed with Tierce in the starliner's day lounge. Tierce, eager to celebrate their success, ordered and paid for a stupidly expensive bottle of double-fermented Eiswein. Bez allowed him to pour her a glass, but when the first few sips increased her light-headedness, she put the drink to one side.

Although they were using one of the lounge's privacy booths, they initially kept their conversation vague and innocuous. Then, with Gracen reduced to a brown smudge in the observation window behind him, Tierce asked Bez for a copy of the data from the archive. Her instinct was to refuse, but he had after all helped her secure the info. She asked what he intended to do with it.

'Initially, nothing,' he said, refilling his glass. 'As far as I'm concerned, the next move is yours, Orzabet.'

Bez looked around nervously at the use of that name. Without thinking, she whispered, 'If you aren't going to stick to the cover ID, then you'd better call me Bez.'

'Bez it is.' He smiled broadly at her, and took a swig of his drink.

She felt her face reddening. Why in the name of the screaming void had she told him her real name? That drink must have gone to her head after all. But she could hardly take her words back. Tierce lowered his glass. 'And you should call me Imbarin.'

'Why?' asked Bez defensively. This conversation was unpleasantly close to one she had had over a year ago with Captain Reen.

Tierce raised an eyebrow, miming offence, though his voice was light when he said, 'Because it's my name.'

'Really?'

'Amazing though it might seem to you, some of us get by on a single identity.'

'Despite being part of a secret organisation apparently working towards the same aims as me?'

'We employ a different modus operandi.'

'So you keep saying. How does this nameless secret society work, exactly? If we're to be allies, I need to know more about you – and your group.'

'Much as I'd like to tell you, believe me when I say you're safer not knowing.'

Annoyingly, Bez could see his logic: what she didn't know couldn't hurt her – or, rather, couldn't hurt his people if she fell into Enemy hands. And any additional info Tierce provided would further entangle her with him. Their goals coincided and they had worked well together, but that was as far as it went. 'All right,' she said.

'Is that "All right" as in, you'll let me have a copy of the data?'

In itself, the existence of more than one copy of the original ID records posed no threat. 'Yes.' She considered sending the info direct to his headware then changed her mind; she had managed to avoid such close contact with him so far, and wanted to keep it that way. 'I'll write a dataspike.'

'Whatever works for you.'

'And I think I'll get some rest before the transit,' she said.

'So I'll have to finish this wine all by myself, then?'

She stood up. 'I'm sure you'll manage.'

*

Bez was too hyped to sleep. Instead she lay in her cabin considering what possession of the Sidhe ID data would do for her mission. She was no longer accumulating intel: she was planning how to use it. R-Day had gone from an aspiration to an event in the foreseeable future.

She needed to work out the most efficient way of disseminating this new intel to the right people at the right time. Some previously important avenues of investigation could be dropped, while hitherto minor contacts would need to be developed. Delta contacts would become Betas or Alphas; a number of Alphas would no longer have such a vital role. The changes would mean reconfiguration across her entire hyperweb.

When the announcement came for passengers to proceed to the stasis room, Bez recorded a com message. She had thought long and hard about this, as it gained her nothing and in the long run would irrevocably fry her current ID.

The message was for Cusa Foelin, despatched with a delay of two days – long enough for Administrator Valdt's body to be discovered and for Bez to be far beyond Graceni jurisdiction. It was one line of text – *You were right: he killed her. Look in this location* – followed by the coordinates of Khea Foelin's grave. As far as Bez was concerned, once you were gone you were gone, but the Graceni believed that the soul only ascended to 'heaven' if the body went through the correct ritual processes. Giving Cusa the chance to indulge her beliefs felt somehow … appropriate.

She ran into Tierce in the stasis room. He appeared nervous, far more so than during their operations on Gracen. When she looked askance at him he gave a thin smile and said, 'I hate stasis.'

She nodded as though she understood, though such a phobia was at odds with everything else she knew about him. His aversion to travel did support her assumption that his movement operated locally, one cell per hub, with little or no overlap. As she lay in her comabox, the numbing chill of stasis creeping over her, she wondered if the existence of such an organisation explained the lack of Sidhe influence on the hubs. If so, the implication was that while she knew nothing of Tierce's people, the Enemy did. And they apparently steered clear of them.

She worried at that thought again in the fuggy aftermath of stasis, before deciding to put the possible connection – or disconnection – to one side for the moment. The mutual exclusivity of the hub rebels (as she had come to think of them) and the Sidhe was significant, but she lacked the intel necessary to work through the full implications.

A transit away from Gracen, the elation from her success should have passed, but she still felt a residual warmth, as though some dark, hard place deep inside had lightened and softened a little. She resolved not to let this unexpected emotional weakness affect her judgement. While she had to acknowledge Tierce's usefulness, she did not share his assumption that they were automatically allies. She was also starting to find his physical presence disconcerting. She refused an invitation to eat with him, and took the post-transit meal in her cabin.

The starliner made a stopover after the first transit. The system was not a hub-point but it had good shiftspace connections and natural features of interest to tourists. She took the chance to despatch a few messages, preparing the way for the deployment of the Sidhe ID data. She needed to secure more funds soon but that was best done in the busy heartland of the hubs, where the subtle skims she used to siphon off credit could pass undetected amid the welter of legitimate transactions.

She was mildly surprised to find a message in her permanent datadrop. She anticipated it might be from Captain Reen, still trying to convince her that he was on her side, but it was from a storage company on Xantier hub. The decrypted text was succinct: *An unsuccessful attempt was made to access your package: we have responded as per your standing orders.*

The package in question was the original memory-core of the *Setting Sun*, as – apparently – liberated by Captain Reen. Bez had spent several intense days decrypting the core, which was designed to only be accessed by the *Setting Sun*'s own comp. When she finally cracked the memory-core, she had copied everything she could get off it. Retaining the original device had been a failsafe; while she thought she had all the data, the necessity of bypassing normal access methods had resulted in a chaotic download of unsorted files. There was a risk she might need to return to the source later.

And now, apparently, someone had attempted to get their hands on the memory-core. But who? Who even knew it was on Xantier? The answer to that was simple: Jarek Reen. She had originally suggested he keep the core on his ship, but he had refused. One logical reason for him coming after it now would be that, having subsequently fallen under the sway of the Enemy, he was having second thoughts. But she had given him a full copy of everything she had extracted. Unless she *had* missed something vital and he had recently discovered this and was after the core itself, either to stop her getting it or because it contained info he now needed.

She spent a while considering alternative scenarios, but no other explanation fitted the facts.

Reen hadn't succeeded in accessing the core: the storage company she chose was Hawk Consignia, who prided themselves on discretion and security. Hawk had been instructed not to release her sealed package to anyone unless that person arrived with a recorded voice authorisation from her, speaking a prearranged code phrase. Failure to follow this protocol resulted in the message she had just received, and in increased security on the package. As a result, Hawk Consignia would only release it to her in person now. If she wanted the memory-core back, she had to fetch it herself.

The timestamp on the message was four days ago, which meant there was a risk Captain Reen was still at Xantier, but her success on Gracen had banished some of what she now thought of as her excessive timidity. She would be using a persona he had no knowledge of, and she would plan carefully before making her move.

If she was going to Xantier she needed to switch ships here, rather than head back towards Tarset. She checked some local message boards and found a freetrader going the right way; the trader's scheduled run would take her within two transits of

Xantier, so Bez should only have to change ships once. Even so, the journey would take several days and eat up the last of this persona's credit. That was acceptable: Xantier's infoscape was well suited for credit skimming and redistribution.

She made the initial reservation, and had just started packing when she remembered Tierce. She commed him; he answered quickly.

'Hi, Bez, changed your mind about letting me show you the sights? We've still got a few hours here.'

'No, I've changed my mind about going back to Tarset.'

'What?'

'Something's come up.'

'What sort of something?'

She tried not to sound smug when she said, 'You'll be safer not knowing.'

'Touché. Can you at least tell me where you're going?'

'Xantier.' She trusted him enough to tell him that.

'Xantier? I'm not sure that's a good idea.' He sounded alarmed.

'Why not? What's the problem with Xantier?'

'Nothing, probably.'

'Tierce – Imbarin – if there was something you thought I needed to know, I hope you'd tell me.'

A pause. 'Perhaps if you explained why you need to go to Xantier ...'

'It isn't anything to do with you.'

'But if it's something we can do from Tarset, then I've got access to considerable resources there, so maybe—'

'There is no "we".'

'All right, I'm being a bit forward. But even so, Tarset's safe ground, the nearest you have to a home. I like to think it's some-where you feel comfortable.'

'I thought that once. Then someone set me up.'

'What do you mean?'

'Oh come on! The first time we met? When you conveniently happened to stop hub-law from arresting me for databreaking?' She hadn't intended to mention it, because dwelling on those events undermined her decision to trust him, but she was riled now.

His image smiled unconvincingly. 'Yes, that was lucky, wasn't it?'

'Luck had nothing to do with it! If you've got the means to get a priority call placed to a First Detective at exactly the moment I'm walking past her in disguise, then you've got the means to shop me to the law while I'm virtual. Not to mention organising a real break-in at the Alliance offices to distract them from following up on me.'

'All right, I admit it. I arranged a few things that evening. But I went to all that trouble because I wanted to meet you. You are so elusive, Bez! And leaving aside my personal feelings, you have to believe that everything I've done is—'

She cut the call.

He gave up trying to com back after the fifth attempt. She got a steward to give him the dataspike; however uncomfortable he made her feel, he had played fair by her, and she would do the same by him.

When she left the liner, Tierce was waiting for her in the departure lounge. She tried to get by with a farewell nod, but he spread his hands. 'I'm really sorry about what happened on Tarset. Will you forgive me?'

'One day, perhaps. But right now I'm going to Xantier.'

'Is there any anything I can say to persuade you to change your mind?'

'No.'

'Right.' She saw, for the first time, a twist of anger on his face. 'You know, for someone so obsessed with the truth, you're far too comfortable with lies.'

'What do you mean?'

'Your every persona is a lie. Do you even know who you are any more?'

This was not a discussion to be having in a public place. 'I am an instrument of vengeance,' she hissed, wincing internally at how pretentious that sounded.

Quietly, he asked, 'And when your vengeance is done?'

She had no answer for that, so instead she looked him firmly in the chin and said, 'Thank you for your help. I'll be going now.' Then she walked out.

ROUNDING ERRORS

Perhaps you've wondered about the odd requests I've
made, when I've asked you to dig into an individual's past or
gather information on an apparently innocuous company or
organisation. Now you know why: it's because I suspected
that person or group was involved with the Sidhe, perhaps
a knowing part of their unseen web of influence, perhaps an
ignorant tool. They were part of the problem: you've already
been part of the solution. That's why I need you to carry on my
work now I'm gone.

<file under: Conclusion>

The staff at Hawk Consignia's Xantier office were embarrassingly
helpful. Bez expected nothing less: she paid well for the company's
premium service. In fact she paid them several times over, via various personae, in order to maintain accounts with the company on
a number of different hubs. She was probably their best customer,
had they but known it.

The final section of the journey had been with a freetrader
outfit that provided cut-price passenger transport as a sideline. In
order to keep costs down, their refitted tradebird had dormitories
not individual cabins. Rather than sleep in a room full of strangers,
she had paid extra, signed the relevant waivers and spent most of
the trip in stasis.

While the tradebird cruised in from the beacon, she had checked
the public listings of ships currently docked. No sign of the *Heart
of Glass*. Immediately after arriving and before switching identities to her preferred local persona, she did a little light hacking in
the port authority system to find out if Captain Reen had visited
Xantier in the last few weeks; this also drew a blank. He could

have hired an agent to do his dirty work, although she wasn't sure he had the resources for that.

Regardless of who was behind the attempt on the memory-core, she needed to move it to a new hub. Once relocated, she could examine the core at her leisure and work out what she had missed.

'Did you keep any record of the voiceprint?' she asked the Hawk Consignia clerk. She had already reviewed Hawk's surveillance footage; it showed a man she had never seen before asking for the memory-core, apparently on Bez's behalf. His ID claimed he was a local citizen who worked in the hub admin offices. That might even be true.

'Unfortunately not, medame. However, although the voice authorisation was rejected automatically, the clerk on duty did make a note on your file saying he suspected the voiceprint was a composite.'

'Composite as in someone had recordings of my voice from which they snipped out the relevant words?'

'Precisely, medame.' The woman leaned forward slightly. 'Sadly, this does happen. It's usually someone known to our client.'

Bez had spent several days on Reen's ship; long enough for him to record her speech. At the time, excited by the prospect of getting her hands on the *Setting Sun* data and believing he was on her side, such duplicity had not occurred to her. But, if Captain Reen had recorded her voice while she was on his ship, that implied he had already been turned when they first met; and that threw the *Setting Sun* data into doubt again. But why record her on the offchance? He didn't strike her as someone who planned far ahead. Unless that was merely an impression he gave.

Still too many unknowns. Until and unless the *Setting Sun* data was proved unreliable – and it had been solid so far – she had to assume it still had value. The fact that someone was after the original core supported this supposition.

She had a choice when it came to relocating the memory-core: deception or force. She could either have the package loaded onto an outgoing ship quietly and discreetly, or she could take advantage of Hawk's 'escorted delivery' service to ensure it left obviously but securely. Generally she preferred deception over force, and that was also the cheapest option. However, if Reen's agent was local and was still keeping watch, an attempt to spirit away the memory-core might come to his attention. He would definitely see it go if she chose the less subtle approach, but unless he wanted to pick a fight with armed security, he wouldn't be able to do anything about it.

Hawk Consignia were happy to oblige. From the moment it left their offices at Xantier until it reached the Hawk storage facility on the next hub, the item would be watched over by a pair of guards licensed to use lethal force. Bez herself would travel independently and pick up the package at Catherli, the adjacent hub she judged safest as a repository for the core.

After making the booking she found a cheap hotel in the vertigo district, where prices were low. Xantier was a hollow earth, though cylindrical rather than spherical. Most visitors preferred the 'floor' of the massive cylinder because although the habitat's real estate wrapped itself around you wherever you were, at the bottom your view was across other buildings, with a 'sky' above you. The further upslope you went, the more disconcerting the outlook, until the periphery of the habitable zone provided a choice of looking 'down' over the sprawling sweep of buildings or 'up' across a thin band of crops and parkland into the artificial sky. Bez, having spent her late teens in a hollow earth, was not overly concerned about this.

She had three days until the memory-core was due to be despatched. She began honing her plans, mentally assigning each compromised Sidhe ID to a trusted agent. She also geared up for some serious financial hacking; remembering Imbarin Tierce's reaction when she said she was coming to Xantier, she made all her enquiries virtually, and stuck to her secondary persona for any transactions aside from those with Hawk Consignia.

While she would have preferred to see the memory-core safely despatched before doing any databreaking, she needed credit in order to book her onward passage. Once she had the core she could work her way back towards Tarset. Despite his excessive influence on the station, there was some truth in Imbarin Tierce's assertion that Tarset was somewhere she thought of as a safe haven.

She decided to address the problem of her credit balance the evening before the core was due to ship out, taking advantage of the nightly data propagation routines.

Although she had no specific virtuality ingress points on Xantier, she knew what she was looking for: somewhere quiet, anonymous and private near the physical and virtual heart of the station. The obvious choice, and one she had used before, was an elsewhere suite in the downtown district.

She booked a premier booth at the Vision Tree franchise on the edge of Xantier's congested downtown. Unlike a lot of elsewhere suite operators, Vision Tree catered for customers seeking full-immersion virtuality for reasons other than the obvious. They also had a rep for respecting customers' privacy; even so, when she had been passing earlier, Bez had taken the chance to look them over virtually from the café across the way, double-checking that none of the booths had any monitoring equipment beyond the legally required health feeds.

She paid for three hours. Although she should automatically be alerted if anyone opened the booth door, she set up spotcams to watch over her. Then she sat on the couch, using a careful finger to push the various attachments out of the way. Another thing she liked about Vision Tree was that they cleaned their booths properly. The place smelled faintly floral, without a whiff of bodily fluids.

Going into a veebooth and not actually running anything would look suspicious, so she picked a near-orbit freefall over a world with, so the hype claimed, spectacular scenery. Her body would be subject to odd gravitational and temperature effects as the booth added subtle physical enhancements to the program, but she would be tuned into the local virtuality by then, free of fleshly distractions. The program was just over an hour long; the sort of databreaking she was about to engage in was time-consuming, and there was a risk she would still be deep in the virtuality when the program finished. She hesitated then selected a second option, labelled 'Demon Lover'. After all, that was what most people used these booths for. Perhaps, if she finished in time, she might enjoy the program herself, by way of a small celebration. She eyed up the relevant apparatus, wondering how many other women had used it. Perhaps not.

She sat back, forcing herself not to tense as the couch reclined. She ran through her current headware set-up, performing a last systems check on the hacking suite. Then she pulled the booth's headset down onto the cushion beside her head, started the program timer, and went virtual independently.

Xantier's virtuality did not employ the standard architecture but mapped closely onto the real. There were differences – the streets and buildings were brighter and more stylised, and the icons representing people floated above the streets rather than walking along them – but the structure was the same: a huge, hollow cylinder.

Bez ramped up the anonymity setting on her icon; the infoscape wasn't crowded but anyone who happened to look her way would see an already unexceptional icon become pale and translucent. Her real weaponry was hidden too well for anyone to spot. She drifted for a while, running subtle sweeps to pick up any interest. All was quiet.

Time to change the game. So far she had been skating on the surface. When she saw the brightening in the 'sky' that indicated the arrival of the nightly updates, she sank towards and then through the 'ground', venturing into territory most virtual denizens had neither the skill nor inclination to enter.

As the illusion of Xantier city dissolved, so did the comforting biofeedback from the surface virtuality: the crackle of data, the sharp scents indicating different flavours and strengths of system security. She felt as though she were falling, the wind in her face – an illusion possibly backed up by her body's current experiences in the veebooth.

Finally she was deep in the rarely visited base level of the infoscape, experiencing raw and unfiltered data ebb and flow around – and through – her. But though the sensation recalled her data nexus dream, this was no physical titillation, no bodily arousal; it was perfect synthesis. When she'd accessed the freetraders' stream during the quarterly update on Tarset, she had experienced the dataflow peripherally. Now she was inside it. She knew how seductive this nowhere/everywhere place was, how easily she could lose herself in it. But she had work to do.

Hubs received three types of beevee transmission: messages, secure data and streamed pay-per-view entertainments. Unknown to most people, the latter high-volume channel contained additional verification keys for the two more secure lines, with partial decryption/re-encryption applied down here at the base level before the datastreams split off again, heading for local planetary systems or adjacent hubs. The filtering, splitting, decoding, re-encoding and packaging occurred at consolidation nodes, structures only accessible from within the inchoate data sea of base virtuality. The minuscule delays at these consolidation nodes as the data were processed formed the spacetime where she did her deepest magic.

She drifted over to a node she knew was particularity productive, hosting as it did transactions for several of the major pan-human banks.

The operation of interstellar finance relied on encryption that, while fiendishly complex, was in theory breakable. The combination of a deep understanding of the principles behind it and possession of a number of highly illegal encryption algorithms gave Bez an unfair advantage, as did the computational power she carried in her head. As the node advanced to fill her consciousness, she sensed her awareness drift through its firewall, the code in her head engaging with and defeating the node's countermeasures.

Inside, the flow was tornado strong, thousands of transactions combining and splitting. Although any discernible analogue to reality was lost in the maelstrom — her normal senses had been banished to save them being overloaded — Bez weathered the storm instinctively.

She began with some simple shunts: one advantage of hacking at Xantier was that accounts in several of her still-sound IDs were easily accessible from here. She instituted basic commands that would take a while to propagate, but would eventually result in safely laundered funds from a number of her hidden stashes becoming available to key personae she expected to use over the next few months. Small amounts only: although she possessed large financial reserves, moving them would attract attention. More importantly, that credit was earmarked to pay the agents in her network who would enact her will. She would work double shifts cleaning toilets while living in the ducts before she drew on funds required for the mission.

The easy part completed, she moved on to more challenging work, insinuating herself deep into her chosen node and deploying the relevant virtual tools. Such direct hacking took advantage of every aspect of financial transactions, from minute variations in exchange rates to fraudulent fee requests. Many of her routines hinged on the rounding errors which had been exploited ever since humans first started to record their finances. Bez was patient, and never greedy, taking fractions of credits from the millions of transactions opened up by the nightly update, gathering in a slow and steady harvest, never taking too much too quickly.

With her routines initiated and the credit beginning to trickle into a spread of holding accounts, she began to relax, to settle into this unthinkably strange, pure existence.

EVERYTHING—

No warning: unreality dispelled. Disorientation, blind attempts to reconnect, to sense, to feel—

—IS—

Ripping through defences, through thought. Down deep, below consciousness, where the wondrous world of data is—

—GONE—

PART TWO

REMILLA
(New Salem, Quondat, Quondat System)

It wasn't an auspicious location for an epiphany. Crates and storage drums lined the walls of the back-street warehouse, and the dust kicked up from clearing the space in the centre still hung in the air, lit in slices by dilute sunlight slanting in from the high windows. Remilla wrinkled her nose rather than give in to the urge to sneeze. The reek of biofuel and damp stone was seeping into her already unsettled stomach. But she understood why the miracle must occur in such a place: the true path is only vouchsafed to the persecuted few. She put aside the physical discomfort of cloying air, gnawing hunger and aching knees, and tried instead to do as Frej had instructed: *Review your life, ready to bring the best of yourself to the fore when the time comes.*

She'd find it easier to stay focused if she hadn't recognised one of the other supplicants. He hadn't given any sign of knowing her when the five of them had been led in by their sponsors. Mind you, the last time they'd met he'd been too busy ramming his prick into her arse to pay much attention to her face.

Since meeting Frej two years ago, life as a whore had become both harder and easier. Harder because she was trying to wean herself off the drugs; easier because now she had something else, even if it wasn't always enough. Knowing she had someone to share her spiritual life with had awoken Remilla's soul. True, Frej's faith would have got her hung and burned by the Community. But when Frej started to discuss her creed – in a straightforward, no-nonsense way – it made more sense to Remilla than anything she had heard when she was growing up. 'We all got a bit of the Divine in us,' claimed Frej, 'and we all got the potential to become more than we are. We gotta remember that spark, that responsibility, and choose the right path. Course it ain't easy, but it's never too late to put things right.'

Never too late to put things right. Just hearing that made Remilla's heart leap. Frej had taken a few weeks to introduce the wildest concepts: that you could be saved without submitting your will to the Manifest Son; that the concept of a single God was wrong; and that you needed to live more than one life in order to achieve salvation. Finally Remilla dared ask the question that had been nagging at her from the start: 'What do you call your religion? It's not like any sect I've ever heard of.'

'That's cos it ain't any breed of Salvationism, sis. It's Ascensionism.'

Remilla hadn't heard the term before. 'And it's called that because … because you evolve through your many incarnations, and eventually ascend to become reunited with the Divine?'

Frej smiled broadly. 'Praise the Devas, she sees the light!'

Remilla smiled back, raising her face to the yellow-grey sky; they were in one of their favourite haunts, a dead-end alley with sealed dumpsters that made passable seats away from the rats and skitterbugs. For once, it wasn't raining. She looked back to her teacher and friend. 'The Devas? You've mentioned them before.'

'Sure have. The next step, remember?'

'Yes, I remember. You said, um, that it's possible to eventually get re-incarnated as a Deva if you remain true and prove yourself willing to sacrifice all for the Divine.'

'Right again! Want to know a secret?' Frej leaned close, and Remilla was reminded of the way Armina used to share confidences. Remilla nodded eagerly. She was sure her sister would have liked Frej.

'One day, if you keep on the path, you might meet one.'

'Meet a Deva? How?'

'They travel around, inspiring the faithful.'

'But you said they're full of Divinity, and are as gods themselves—'

'Goddesses, yeah. But they're still part of the universe. They

194

know that when they die they'll ascend fully, so they make it their mission to help others take the next step.' Frej turned and looked at her intently. 'Y'know, you're very lucky.'

'I am?'

'Yeah. Most people get fed a load of shite about the Devas. You're coming to this fresh, without prejudice. That makes you special.'

Remilla smiled. No one had ever told her she was special.

A year later, she took an oath to follow the Ascensionist faith. And now, a year after that, her time had come. She had made it to her twentieth birthday. Whether she would make it beyond that was about to be decided.

The pain in her knees was moving from distraction towards agony, and someone's stomach had started to rumble. Keeping her head lowered, she glanced over at the man she recognised. Though she was used to seeing him in a suit – or rather, out of it – like all the supplicants he wore a plain white robe.

She realised the rumbling wasn't the john's empty belly: it was a low drum-beat. The sound grew, setting off odd grumbles in Remilla's own guts and making her feel light-headed. It hadn't been hard to fast for two days: hunger had always been part of her life. And she saw the need to cleanse her body, to make it as pure as soiled flesh could be. She had expected the mamas to be unhappy at her going so long without any trade, but Frej said she'd fixed that. Not having a breath of Fume for so long had been harder, but if she was going to be saved, she needed to get clean.

The music became louder with a faint fluting overlaying the hypnotic beat. Remilla smelled something new: incense? The scent was heavy and sensuous. The drum gave three firm beats then fell silent. She did as Frej had told her: bowed her head lower, raised herself to kneel up, and readied her mind.

She sensed the change and, despite herself, looked up.

Before her stood a Goddess.

Remilla had expected an offworlder, and she knew how tall they were. But the Deva's presence filled the room; all light focused on her, as though she were its very source. Her perfect beauty made Remilla want to cry.

The Deva didn't speak. There was no need.

She strode up to the first supplicant, a well-turned-out woman who had given Remilla a sour look when they first came in. The woman bent her head back as the Deva lowered a hand to gently touch her cheek. What seemed like scant moments later, the Deva stepped away again. The woman sat back on her heels, eyes closed and a dreamy smile on her face.

Next was a man, the only other male chosen beside the john. Remilla, mindful of Frej's instructions, tried not to watch this time, and instead concentrated on preparing herself.

She looked up at a *thump*, the sound painfully loud in the otherwise silent room. The man lay face down on the ground, unmoving. Remilla knew he was dead. The Deva stepped around the body. Beside Remilla, the john drew a panicky breath.

Remilla wasn't panicking. She was calm. She would accept her fate, even if that fate were death.

Another woman next. Remilla didn't intend to look, but again she was distracted by the noise: not a thump this time but a sob. The woman collapsed and began crying wildly. She sounded like someone who'd lost everything.

For the first time, Remilla doubted. Death she would willingly accept, but more pain, more despair … there had been so much of that already. *Please,* she prayed to the Divine spirit that had replaced the Salvatine God in her heart, *no more suffering. Oblivion, yes, but not pain.*

The john looked terrified as the Deva reached for him. His epiphany took mere moments, and at the end of it he too collapsed, though not in pain. His eyes rolled upwards and he made a noise Remilla had heard him make before, hands clutching at his groin.

Then it was her turn, the youngest and least worthy. She should have ignored the others, should have concentrated instead on her own ordeal!

The Deva's long, cool fingers brushed her face.

Images, sensations, memories, whirled through her head, too fast to catch and then—

Settled on the tearing emptiness inside when she mourned her dead sister, and knew the only person she loved and trusted was gone for ever—

Settled on the indignant bruising pain when Pol beat her, resenting the obligation to do so even as he raised the rod—

Settled on the obscene suffering inflicted by three strangers in an alleyway, who saw her as no more than warm flesh that would be dead and cold at the end of a long, terrible night. She remembered all the details, every last thing they did to her, with her—

Except, it no longer hurt. The pain was gone. All of it: mind and body. She knew, as surely as she had sensed the Goddess enter the room, that she need never experience such pain again. Her past was absolved. She had been washed clean. Reborn.

<Are you ours, child?>

It took a moment for Remilla to grasp this last miracle, though Frej had told her that the Devas sometimes spoke directly to a person's soul. She composed herself as best she could then projected unconditional and wholehearted acceptance.

<Good. Such commitment pleases us. Your life serves a higher purpose now, Remilla.>

Remilla was held in a state of grace such as she had never dreamed possible. The Deva's words had become the only meaning in the universe.

<We shall send you to a place with no sky, from where you will further our cause.>

<And I will go!> thought Remilla ecstatically in return. *<I will go!>*

CURRENTLY INACCESSIBLE

Falling.

FallingFallingFalling.

Shivering and falling and ...

... not falling.

There was something beneath her. She twitched. Bounced. Fell again, more slowly.

And settled.

Her body was stretched out; confined, feather-light, nauseous and chilled to the core. Everything was dark. No, not everything: numbers flashed at the edge of vision, counting, regular. She took comfort in them.

Aside from the numbers ... sensations and images skittered beyond consciousness. Something bad had happened, something unexpected and very bad, and now she was strung up in a cold place where she weighed too little. It was like that story, the bad child in the spider's larder. She needed to escape, before the spider got her. If only she could move ...

Wait: being restrained didn't matter because there was something else, a remembered impulse. Yes, she knew what she needed, what she did, what she *was*! She exhaled and tuned out of the nightmare and into the comfort of the virtual world.

An unseen force drove a spike into the base of her neck. She shrieked.

Someone said, 'Easy, girlie!'

The pain in her head eased and suddenly she was fully awake and in the moment. She opened her eyes wide. It didn't help: she could see nothing. She could smell, though, despite the freezing air. This place stank.

'Heh, heh, girlie.'

Light flared, cold and white. Next to the light was an impossible figure, long thin limbs bundled in rags and topped by a crazy halo of tangled hair. The figure was pulling itself free of some sort of cocoon, its shadow dancing across the curved walls. *The spider, come to suck out her innards!*

She tried to cry out, but the noise caught in her throat. Helplessly she watched as the apparition unfolded itself and punted off the floor towards her, coming closer, closer ... Animal terror overwhelmed her. Warm dampness spread out from her groin.

'Easy, aye, see what old Kety's got fer you.'

The figure bent over her, blotting out the light. This was no monster; it was a person, albeit an appallingly tall and thin one. The vile stink increased, masking the other smell: in her stupid, unthinking weakness, she had wet herself like a frightened child.

A tube was thrust into her mouth; she tried to turn away, but only managed to bruise her lips.

'Drink, girlie, drink. Kety has fresh water, clean and pure!'

Despite herself she sucked at the tube, her body knowing what she needed even if her mind didn't. She kept drinking until the tube was snatched away.

'Little by little. Don't wanna hafta scrape yer puke off the wall, do we?'

Whoever this person was, she – and it was a *she*, at least if the voice was anything to go by – didn't appear to mean her any harm. She let the woman remove the tube, swallowed carefully, then tried speaking again. 'Wh— where?'

'Aha. Better? Better. Heh, heh.'

'Where ... is this?'

'Safe. Safe in the tunnels.'

'The tunnels?' Should she know what that meant? She was lying in her own urine, imprisoned in a strange place by a crazy scarecrow. Nothing made sense. But if she let go now, she might never regain control.

'Tunnels, aye.' The woman smiled, revealing a vague assortment of discoloured teeth. 'With Kety, eh?'

She latched onto the name. 'Kety?'

'Aye, girlie.'

'You're … Kety?'

The scrawny woman moved back, pointed to her chest and nodded vigorously.

'And I'm …' Did Kety know? 'Who am *I*, Kety?'

Kety shook her head.

'Please, I can't remember! You have to tell me!'

Kety patted her arm. 'Sleep again now,' she said gently, 'sleep and dream.' She turned in a swirl of rags and loped away, then reached for the light.

'Please, leave it on!'

Kety looked over her shoulder, and chided, 'No fuel for night-time.' The light went out.

She fought the urge to scream as the darkness returned.

She sniffed, then sobbed, before focusing on the numerical display in her vision. As she watched the digits click over she felt herself becoming lighter, as though she could float away from the horror of her situation, up into the darkness.

When she awoke the light was turned up fully and the woman who called herself Kety was fussing around the small space the two of them shared.

She wriggled, testing her bindings. She was tied into some sort of hammock, suspended a few centimetres above a hard, curved floor; the bindings were uneven, with one leg held slightly crooked, and her arms tied across her chest. Like the spider's cocoon … She watched the numbers until that thought went away.

If she bent her body, she could touch the floor with her head and feet, but she had no way of getting any purchase. The movement reminded her of what had happened earlier; her groin was cold and sticky, the smell appalling. She began to gag. Kety's head shot up, and she came over. The way the thin woman moved …

the gravity was wrong, far too low! Swallowing vomit, she clung to that observation, desperate to build on it.

Kety arrived in a gaggle of limbs. 'Awake again now, eh, girlie?' she asked.

'Uh.'

Kety wrinkled her nose. 'Oooh. Best get you cleaned up.' The woman reached into the cocoon, zeroing in on her charge's lower body, loosening ropes and pushing down leggings to expose what felt like some sort of nappy. She fled back to the numbers. They made more sense now: a count, measuring out time. Measuring out time because ... because ... there was something important she had to do. If only she could remember what.

She only realised she was whimpering when Kety made shushing noises, sending gusts of warm, reeking breath across her face.

She looked beyond Kety, though her vision was jumping due to the chattering of her teeth, which in turn was due to the touch of freezing air on bare, damp flesh. She was stretched across a tunnel, smooth-walled and about twice as wide as she was long. From the look of the other, empty, cocoon-like hammock and the bags and nets of random junk tacked around the walls, this was Kety's home.

She turned her head the other way. On her right the tunnel was blocked by hard-set yellowish foam. She suspected she had once known the name of that substance. She suspected she had known a lot of things, once. That reminded her of the alternative to this reality and, desperate to escape, she tried again to tune in to the virtual.

The pain was instant, sharp enough to make her buck and squeal.

Kety grabbed her then made soothing noises and stroked her forehead before going back to the nappy. By the time Kety finished dealing with her bodily functions, she had calmed down enough to speak.

'Kety,' she said as evenly as she could.

'Aye, girlie.'

'You're my friend, aren't you?'

Kety smiled. 'Aye, girlie. I'll keep you safe.'

'So ... will you untie me? Please. I won't go anywhere. I just can't bear this ... Please, I won't run, I swear.'

The woman looked down at her, and shook her head slowly.

'Please! I'm begging you, just—'

Kety raised a hand, palm chopping upwards, 'Hush! No shouting now. Quiet, quiet, girlie.'

'Why be quiet? Why?' Her voice ran away with her, control slipping. Kety was kind but she was also her jailer! 'Why be quiet when I'm trussed up and you won't tell me why or where or even who I am!'

'Nameless!'

'What?'

'You're nameless. Nameless but safe. But *only* safe if you stay quiet and still. Understand?'

'No.'

Kety mimed preparing to deliver a slap.

She took a breath. 'Yes. Yes, Kety.'

'Good. Enough questions.'

She shut up, and watched the numbers.

Kety refused to speak to her for the rest of the 'day' – the period the light was on. Her host – or jailer – spent her time working through piles of junk, fiddling with this, trying to fix that, humming tunelessly as she tinkered. She broke off long enough to give her charge more water and spoon tasteless goo into her mouth.

She spent the time thinking, but her memory had stalled. All she knew for sure was that for whatever reason, the unreal world, her other – true? – home was currently inaccessible. She was a prisoner in her body, and her body was a prisoner in this cocoon.

Yet she had an odd intuition that, grim though her situation was, this was not the worst thing that could have happened, not the eventuality she feared the most. She had no idea what was.

Although virtual space was forbidden to her, she still had the display that counted time. Those numbers led to others that existed purely in her head. She recited comforting sequences, performed arithmetic operations, counted and calculated.

That night she dreamed she was walking in a garden (normal grav, noted the detached self, observing the dreamer); she was with a boy and they were happy. The sky in the dream curved up and over them. Was that somewhere near here? She woke up, infuriated by her inability to make sense of anything, only to slip back into sleep.

Kety fed and cleaned her again the next day. Her jailer refused to answer direct questions, though her mutterings included a reference to an 'open above'. Was that where the boy from the dream lived?

Eventually Kety went out, having first explained how important it was for her guest to stay 'quiet and still'. She took the light with her, briefly revealing the fact that this tunnel curved away sharply beyond their living space.

She had already examined her cocoon as closely as she could from within it while Kety's back was turned. It was based on a loose mesh hammock bound into a tube by additional scraps of rope, string and rags. The tube tapered off to a single, thicker rope at the foot – and presumably the head – which was looped round a hook driven into the tunnel wall. She hung slackly and was permitted some movement in the cocoon, but not so much that she could dislodge the looped rope from its hook.

Kety – or whoever had put her here – had lashed her limbs to the cocoon, but her legs weren't bound tightly and she reckoned she could kick and contort her lower body free, given time. But first she needed to untie her hands.

There were tight loops around the wrists; a separate thicker rope coiled around her upper body, binding her crossed arms over her chest. The wrists were the weak point: if she pulled one she felt a faint tug on the other, which meant they were held by a single rope threaded behind her back. Free one hand, and she could free the other. But to do this, she needed to get her wrist to her mouth.

She eased her right hand up her chest. When the rope was at full stretch, she raised her head, which wasn't tied, towards the hand. She was asking a lot from unused muscles, and in normal gravity she doubted she could hold this position for more than a few seconds, but, after some flexing and straining, she managed to butt the back of her hand with her chin. The cord on the back of her wrist was easiest to reach but if, as she suspected, it would take more than one session to get through it, Kety would spot what she was up to. She turned her wrist as far as it would go; the cord bit painfully into her flesh. She felt the warmth of her breath on her wrist, but it took more effort, neck muscles spasming, before her lips brushed the cord.

She paused then opened her mouth, catching the cord in her teeth. Ignoring the repellent taste, she bit down. The cord caught, then slid away. She tried again but only succeeded in grazing the inside of her wrist.

The cord *would* break, because it had to. She just needed to adapt the plan. The problem was the angle: the binding was vertical, running across her mouth. So, rather than catching and biting, she needed to cut across it.

She opened her mouth wider, pressed her lower jaw to the cord, and moved her head fractionally from side to side, sawing at the cord with her lower teeth. After several minutes, during which her neck muscles burned and twitched, she felt part of the cord break. She wanted to rest, but she made herself probe her handiwork with her tongue. From the feel of it there were three strands making up this binding, and she had severed one. Forcing herself to ignore her aching neck, the revolting taste in her mouth and the slippery coating of saliva, she began worrying at the next strand. When her neck muscles cramped, making her bite her own wrist, she gave up. What mattered was that escape was possible.

Kety came back soon after. By then she had turned her wrist over to hide her handiwork; Kety frowned at the drying drool on her prisoner's chin, but made no comment.

CHANDIN
(Cyalt Hub)

Chandin stared at the envelope. Actual paper, with his first name written on it in a spidery, unsteady hand. It was lying innocuously in his desk drawer. Someone had got into his office, and left a handwritten note for him.

He should call security ... but he recognised that handwriting. He reached into the drawer, picked up the envelope, and ripped it open. As a result of his lack of experience with the medium, he managed to tear the rough sheet of paper inside, though he could still read the message, which was also handwritten. It said simply: *I got news. Meet me at 20h at the Razzle Do – your da.*

When Chandin was growing up, the Razzle Do had been a Floorville bar frequented by the semi-reputable poor, drowning their sorrows after a long shift scraping pipes or grading resyk. If his father was still drinking there, that was probably still true.

But why, after nearly two decades without any contact, did 'Da' want to talk to him? What news was so important? Going on past performance, it probably involved credit, and Chandin's access to it. His initial instinct was to ignore the note. But perhaps the time had come to reconnect with the family he had left behind; it felt apt, now the family he had chosen was entering a new phase.

He tried to concentrate on the day's work, but with the handover to Tanlia finally complete, and his new subordinates carrying some of the weight while he settled in, he was not overly busy, for once. He distracted himself from his father's note by browsing old records, under the guise of getting familiar with some of the more obscure historical precedents in Treaty history. He had come across some odd references he wanted to follow up.

Meanwhile, his subconscious was working out how he might – if he chose – keep tonight's appointment. Chandin could request an armed escort if he felt he was in personal danger – which he could be down in Floorville – but such a request would be logged, and though he had no immediate superior to question his actions, the Commission prided itself on its oversight apparatus. Someone, at some point, would ask why he had visited such a dubious part of the station. So, no guard. And if he went dressed like this, he was asking to get mugged.

Perhaps he should destroy the note and leave the past safely locked away.

But then there was the *other* recent message, received less than a week ago by means as hi-tech as this morning's letter was lo-tech. He had no idea if the two were connected, but given the inscrutability of the former message perhaps he should pursue the latter.

If he did go, he should go armed, although getting his hands on a gun would be complicated. Not impossible, though. He checked the station directory. This just took a bit of thought.

His subconscious appeared to have made the decision for him.

The Razzle Do hadn't changed. The same worn-out furniture, the same worn-out staff, the same dim-enough-not-to-show-the-wear lighting. There was even the inevitable terceball holofeed in the corner, turned up just loud enough to disturb a quiet drink.

Chandin sipped his watery beer and watched the door. So far, so good. His plan had started with a trip partway down the wall, to a mid-level exchange boutique where he had pawned his expensive suit for a shabbier one and some scrip; this had, in many ways, been the riskiest transaction, because there was a chance, however slight, that the pawnbroker might recognise the new Prime Commissioner Legal by sight. If the slovenly woman behind the glass did know who he was, she didn't respond and, now suitably attired, Chandin used the public chainway to make his way further down the crater wall, his gaze carefully fixed on the carriage's grubby floor. He stopped off to visit a second, less salubrious establishment, whose listing in the station directory omitted certain details that Chandin was relieved to find still held true. Here he used some of the scrip to buy an antique-looking dartgun; the shopkeeper admitted that the design was so old he would have trouble getting reloads, but Chandin was only carrying it for peace of mind, and planned to ditch the weapon at the end of the evening.

Now he had reached his goal, he was wondering if all that effort was in vain, because the time was coming up to twenty-thirty and there was no sign of his father. So far the only person to pay him any attention was a woman with too much makeup and a weary smile, presumably a prostitute.

He decided to finish his drink then go. He had a third of a glass left. He was debating whether or not to leave a sealed note behind the bar when his father walked in.

Chandin was shocked. If the sagging belly and jowls were anything to go by, twenty years was a lot longer down here than up on the rim. Then again, money kept the signs of age at bay. But it was still dismaying to see the changes to the familiar face.

His father came straight over and sat down opposite him. While Chandin was going through the conversational openings he had mentally rehearsed, his father said, 'You're looking well!'

'Thanks.' He couldn't bring himself to lie in return.

'So, a drink?'

Chandin remembered that tone. Rather than give in to his irritation – because *obviously* the drinks would be on him – he made himself smile and said, 'Of course: beer?' When his father nodded eagerly, he tapped the table and ordered two more.

'You got my note, then?' said his father, pointlessly.

'Yes. I did wonder how you got that to me.'

'Oh, I knows a man, who knows a woman who's got a TopTier cleanin' contract.'

'Right.' It was odd to hear his home district referred to as TopTier. Then again, those who inhabited the bottom of the crater rarely used the term Floorville. 'So what's this news, then?' he prompted.

His father had been looking longingly at Chandin's glass, but now his expression fell. 'Your mother ...' he began.

That was what Chandin had suspected. 'She's dead, isn't she?'

His father stared at the table. 'Yeah,' he said slowly, 'she is.'

'Was it the Mathors?'

'Yeah. Got 'er in the end.'

Mathors Syndrome wasn't curable but it was treatable. In the circles Chandin now moved in, sufferers could live a long and relatively pain-free life. But those treatments were not cheap. He refused to feel guilty. Thanks to his father's actions – and his own, long ago – he had had no way of helping his mother. 'She fought it for a long time,' he said. He would have liked to have said goodbye to her properly, but that was the other thing about the cheaper treatments: one day they stopped being effective, and that was that, sometimes in a matter of hours. He had come to terms with never seeing his mother again some time ago.

'Yeah ...' His father was still looking at the table, and an unpleasant suspicion began to dawn on Chandin. At that moment the barman brought their drinks. From the look he gave the older man, the barkeep knew him well, and had his suspicions about who Chandin was. Chandin wished his father had chosen a more discreet place to meet.

When the barman was safely out of earshot, Chandin leaned forward and said, 'When did she die?'

His father was busy with his drink. When he put his glass down he mumbled, 'Oh, comen up fer six years gone now.'

'Six years!' Chandin refused to lose his temper: he should have known. 'So why are you only telling me now?'

'Well ... I was waitin' fer the right time.'

'And why is this the right time?' Six years: a long time, but also a significant one.

'She missed you, y'know, right up till the end.'

'Why did you ask me to meet you here today?'

'S'bout Maira.'

'My sister.' An alien word implying kinship, familiarity. He had seen Maira three times in his life, and not at all for the last nineteen years. 'What about her?' Then, despite himself, he said, 'Is she all right?' His most recent memory of his only sibling was of a round-eyed child barely old enough to know who he was.

'She's fine. Grand and sweet.'

'Good. I'm glad.' Right now he missed the sister he barely knew more keenly than he felt the estrangement from his father or the death of his mother. He wanted to ask about Maira's life, but that would make her more of a stranger, not less.

'Thing is, she's—'

'Is it Mathors?' The condition wasn't usually hereditary but it was all Chandin could think of.

'No. Not that. She's finally got 'erself sorted, see. And she wants another child.'

So much left unsaid! Chandin forced himself to ask evenly, '*Another* child?'

'Yeah, see, after her little girl, what she 'ad when she were dancin'—'

'Dancing where?' Not in the aeroballet, that was for sure.

His father flicked a hand. 'Clubs. You know.'

Chandin didn't know, but he could guess. He reminded himself that when he was growing up, jobs like servicing ducts, tending bars or being the sort of entertainer his sister had apparently become were nothing to be ashamed of. He had no right to judge her life choices. 'Is she still ... dancing?'

His father shook his head. 'No, she's outa the clubs now, works in a dockside beauty parlour, doing touro ladies' nails an' stuff. Married a shift supervisor on the facilities maintenance crew; they got themselves a top-floor apartment. It's real nice.'

Chandin remembered that tone; the pride in his father's voice. Sweet void, that's how he'd sounded when he had talked about Chandin thirty years ago. *My son's trainin' fer the Commission, he is.* And his mother had wept with joy. This despite the pitifully low pay for the first few years. He put those feelings aside. 'But you say she already has a daughter.' My *niece*, he thought with a jolt.

'Yeah, but she lives wi' her da, see. And now Maira and Jold want their own litlun. So I was wonderin' if you—'

'No.' Last time he had said yes. Not again. Never again.

'You ain't even 'eard me out.'

'I don't need to. I'm not repeating that mistake.' Twenty-five years ago he had been a junior administrator sending a percentage of his pittance wages back to his family. But he had known – and they had known – that he could get his hands on more credit. Corruption was rife in the lower ranks of the Commission, but rather than fight a losing battle against it, those above used the endemic culture of bribes and kickbacks as a self-selection process: a low-paid employee who got caught taking advantage would have a note put on his or her file and never attain high office. Chandin had been determined not to fall into that trap. But then he found out about his mother's illness; add that knowledge to his residual shame at his humble origins, and he had weakened when his father had begged. It had just been a single lump sum, taken from a contractor bidding for courier franchise rights. The whole amount had gone direct to his family. No one had known. But that had only been part of The Mistake.

'It ain't about credit, son!'

He wished he wouldn't call him 'son', for all sorts of reasons. 'It wasn't about credit last time, was it?' Chandin failed to keep the bitterness out of his voice. Some of the black-market credit *had* gone on treating his mother. The rest … His father had friends in low places, some of whom had interesting talents. One of them had managed to hack the station's ID database and reset the family's status to 'childless'. With her son gone on to higher things and her own mortality brutally brought home to her, his mother had been desperate for another child. He had tried not to be hurt at being edited out of his family; after all, the further he moved up in the world, the more their initial pride soured to resentment. He was happy in his new life; happy, if he was honest, to be free of them.

'No, you see, it's about the lottery.'

'The lottery?' Chandin refocused; his father must mean the licence lottery, run to redistribute unallocated child licences. 'What about it?'

'Well, what with you bein' up with the authorities these days, I wondered if you had any influence—'

'Of course I don't!' But he did have a spare child licence. No, that was stupid: to donate it to a random low-life would raise questions; thanks to the databreaker his father had hired, station records contained no link between himself and this man. If he donated his licence to his father, he may as well just turn himself over to IDOB and confess to The Mistake straight up. *Yes, I took a bribe, and yes, I am aware that a major ID infringement was paid for using the credit I appropriated. Just escort me back down to Floorville right now.*

'Oh. Right.'

Presumably the databreaker who had hacked the family's records last time was no longer around. Or perhaps his father thought manipulating the lottery was an easier option. Did he really believe his son could pull those sorts of strings? Quite possibly: Da had never been one for holding realistic expectations. 'Even if I could, I wouldn't. You know that.'

His father's face took on a cunning cast, and Chandin felt the chill of uncertainty. Was there any connection to the other, virtual communication, the one simply signed 'Orb'? It had been a short and simple message: *The time is coming. Our deal still holds. Save this key.* When those words had popped up unexpectedly on his screen last week, it had taken Chandin a few moments to recall his only other contact with 'Orb'. That had been six years ago. Now he knew about his mother's death, he suspected the timing was related: the truth about Chandin's past might have been briefly exposed when his late mother's records were updated, and whoever 'Orb' was, he or she could have spotted the anomaly then.

His father said, 'It'd be a shame if anyone ever found out about what happened, y'know.'

'Yes,' said Chandin tightly. 'And how were you thinking that might happen?'

'Well, I dunno. Anonymous tip-offs? You say yer Commission is hot on those oversee— oversights. Course, a little credit would, er, distract me from that, like.'

Chandin fought the urge to smile. That his father was an idiot was nothing to be happy about. 'Have you any idea how many libellous, accusatory or simply unhinged messages the Pan-Human Treaty Commission receives *every day*?'

His father looked hurt, and in that moment Chandin had the odd impression that, regardless of biological age, he was now the older one. He also knew that, despite his fears, there was no link between this pathetic, foolish man and the mysterious 'Orb'. His father's expression underwent another open transformation, becoming the very essence of the put-upon elder. 'I'm sorry,' he wheedled, 'I shouldn'ta said that. But you know, you could just remember your ol—'

Chandin held up a hand, forestalling him. 'I'm glad Maira's doing well, I really am. I hope her number comes up in the lottery. But this has *nothing* to do with me.' He stood up. 'And neither, I'm afraid, do you. Not any more.'

His father watched him walk away, for once lost for words.

TRYING TO SURFACE

The following night, she bit through the second cord.

Now it was just a matter of waiting, using the numbers to keep herself sane.

Kety went out late the next day. Even before the light had fully disappeared, her wrist was in her mouth. She gnawed at the last cord with frantic speed. Finally it gave.

She let her head fall back with a sigh. But there was no time to rest. She pulled her left wrist, wincing as the binding stung raw skin. She freed both wrists and wiggled her fingers, ignoring the painful pins and needles. Then she used her numb hands to ease the thicker but looser bindings around her chest down her body.

At the same time, she kicked her legs, twisting to pull them free. One heel hit the ground with jarring and unexpected force, and she gave an involuntarily grunt of pain.

She eased the bindings down over her stomach. From here it was relatively easy to disentangle herself from the cocoon, pushing rope down and away, and finally flopping out from the filthy, torn netting like a beached fish. She eased her left leg free from the final loop of rope, waited a moment to catch her breath, then used the hammock to pull herself upright.

It was only when she stood up that she realised her head was still constricted. She reached up and felt her skull. Some sort of tight-fitting cap covered her from her forehead to the nape of her neck, secured under her chin. She could ease a finger under the strange headgear, but found no way of getting it off. She decided that removing this last, non-restrictive binding was less important than getting out of here. Kety could come back at any moment.

She eased one foot forward, then the next one, letting go of the cocoon. She had estimated the distance to Kety's cocoon in the light, and – foolishly – assumed she would be walking, not shuffling. She kept expecting to come across it, and when she finally did, she inevitably tripped over the damn thing.

The fall wasn't hard, but it still shocked her. She lay where she was for a moment, heart thudding, working out what to do next. Given the sloping floor, utter darkness and weird gravity, crawling made more sense than walking. She raised herself onto all fours and began to crawl, taking it slowly because if she did encounter anything now, she would be meeting it head first.

When she put her hand down on something sharp she recoiled, then paused, arm upraised. She lowered her hand gently and tapped at the sharp object with a fingertip. It was some sort of ceramic knife, serrated along one side. The other edge felt blunt, and the knife had a plasticised handle. Moving carefully, she felt all around the knife, then picked it up. She had no idea whether she could use a weapon but she liked the idea of having one. Sitting back on her haunches, she tucked the knife into the waistband of her leggings. When she bent forward again, it fell out. She pushed it deeper, working it down between her clothes and her bulky underwear. This time it stayed put.

She set off again, crawling along the bottom of the tunnel. The path curved, as she expected. When she came to an odd bit of floor, she paused, visualising the set-up; Kety's tunnel must have met another intersecting one. She took the left-hand path. All was silent, still and dark, and she began to get up a bit more speed. When she reached another intersection, she went left again: she had a vague notion that always turning left worked in these situations, and even if it didn't she was out of other plans. Kety's lair only had one exit, so at least she wouldn't end up back where she started.

The next left came up quickly. She took it. It curved to the right, which she decided was a good thing.

She was getting tired, and the knife had worked itself round to scrape the delicate skin at the top of her groin. She sat down and adjusted her clothing. As she did so she remembered the strange headgear. There was something about that, a lost memory trying to surface … She felt her head again. The cap was a skin-tight lattice made of thin strips of cold, rubbery material.

Feeling along the chinstrap, she failed to find a catch or buckle; but although the strap was too tight to work up over her chin, it was just loose enough to get a finger underneath. She reached carefully into her clothes and withdrew the knife; then, before she could think better of it, she tipped her head back. Holding the strap away from her neck with a crooked finger, she worked the tip of the knife under it, careful to keep the serrated edge pointed outwards. The dark worked in her favour: if she had actually seen the knife she had just put to her own throat, common sense might have got the better of her.

She began to saw at the strap, using tiny, measured strokes.

It was tough going. By the time she was halfway through, her sweaty hands were making the job dangerous, so she paused, knife still stuck absurdly and dangerously into the chinstrap, and wiped her hands on her clothes. Then she carried on.

The strap finally gave. She put the knife down then pulled the cap off.

It was as though a veil had lifted. Memory and ability flooded back. She knew who she was, and where: this was Xantier. She must be in the hab-rat tunnels, which burrowed through the natural rock of the hollowed-out, elongated planetoid that formed Xantier station; hence the low grav and stinking air. With that knowledge came fear, and a myriad of other questions.

First things first: she blinked up the function that intensified her night vision. It worked, but the act hurt her head. A residual effect of the inhibitor cap, perhaps? She wasn't sure. She felt muzzy, slow. Drugged.

Bez's final memories before waking up in the tunnels began to trickle back. Something had attacked her in Xantier's infoscape; whatever it was had been powerful, unlike anything she had encountered before. It had ripped through her defences effortlessly.

She was shivering: she caught herself, clenching her teeth

against cold and fear. Her first priority was to get out of the tunnels. Once back in the station proper, she could work out how to get off Xantier safely, ideally to Catherli. She blinked her chrono out of its default setting of hours, minutes and seconds to show the full date. Four days had passed since the virtual attack, so the memory-core *should* be safely away.

She could risk walking, now she could see. Her instinct was to access a map, but it was unlikely anyone had uploaded schematics of this place; besides, she was right on the edge of Xantier's virtuality, and if whoever put her here was still watching the infoscape, such activity might alert them.

She picked up the knife and stood slowly.

She had only taken a couple of steps when she froze. A flicker of light was coming from a side tunnel up ahead. She began to turn, ready to run, but missed her footing. She slipped on the smooth, curved tunnel floor, falling onto all fours. The knife went flying. Even as she scrabbled to get up she heard muffled voices.

'Like rats, heh?'

'Nah, rats taste good.'

Laughter, suddenly cut off.

Then, clearly, 'What the shit-eatin' fuck?'

She turned towards the voices, sitting upright in the centre of the tunnel. She found herself facing four boys, filthy and leggy, bundled in rags. One of them held a lamp like Kety's. Another danced past his companions to come right up to her and crowed, ''S a touro medame! She seriously lost!'

She leaned back, away from his stink, trying not to panic. Where was the knife?

The boys seemed more curious than hostile. One of the others said, 'Not touro all ragged like that. Street-above.'

'Not gonna be missed, then,' said the nearest one, and reached for her. She brought her right arm round, trying to fend him off, but only succeeded in falling backwards. Now she was lying down, sprawled and defenceless.

'Heh, *yeah*!' The boy loomed over her.

She should say something, do something, but this was too far outside her experience. She had no idea how to react.

A brief call and the others were there too. Someone grabbed her breast; someone else began fumbling with her clothes lower down. She squeezed her eyes shut.

'Ah!' Rancid smell of old urine. 'Fuckin' too-grim.'

'Just pull it off! Still warm crack underneath, ain't it?'

Deep inside she was appalled and disbelieving, but action, even speech, was beyond her.

Another boy said, 'Ah, wait. This the one, y'know. Kety's?'

'What?'

'Like jujuman said? Keep her alive?'

'Ain't gonna *kill* her, yer doik!' A weight pressed down on her belly.

'Yeah, but Kety ...'

'Kety what?'

Her heart jumped at the familiar voice.

The pressure eased. One of the boys said, 'Heh, heh, bag-hag!'

'You leave her now. She's mine. Gonna save her.'

'Like you saved yer little girl, heh?'

Kety said, 'That's past. She's my girl now. Jujuman says so.'

She should try to get free, use the diversion and *run*. But she could barely breathe.

'Not gonna kill this one. Just play.'

Kety's tone was firm. 'You tell that to the jujuman.'

'She's right,' said one of the boys. 'She's blessed by him now, y'know. Food, water, everything, all fer free.'

Kety said, 'Right, Kety's his special friend. You cross Kety, you cross him.'

A pause, then the vile touches withdrew. The nearest boy said, 'You keep her close, then, hag. Keep her close or we'll cut her, jus' like we did yer girl.'

Bez waited until the boys had moved off before opening her eyes. Kety was crouched next to her. The other woman's long face had a look that might have been sympathetic before the shadows got to it. The loose net of the inhibitor cap dangled from her hand.

'All safe now,' she said. 'But poor nameless needs her crown. Needs her crown to be happy.'

'No.' She must not let Kety put the cap back on. She had to get out of here. She got as far as raising herself onto one elbow. Kety reached forward with the crown, lamp held high in her other hand.

Bez lashed out, fooled by the low gravity into thinking she could overpower her more delicate opponent. But the blow was badly judged, and Kety batted her hand away; on her home territory she had all the strength she needed. Her expression hardened. 'Bad nameless!' she hissed, bringing the lamp round in a wide arc to connect with Bez's head.

Bright light was followed by utter darkness.

She had an idea she knew this place, knew the scarecrow woman who fussed over her. The woman said she was called Kety. Perhaps she was. Apparently she herself had no name. Kety said she didn't need one, and given Kety looked after her, she had no reason to doubt this.

Whenever she felt afraid, she deflected the dread with the numbers in her eyes, and the numbers in her head. The numbers were always there for her, reliable and constant.

Sometimes as she slept, her mind dredged up fragments and images: a luxurious room of bright furnishings; long square corridors; a man sitting opposite her, talking earnestly; crowds surging while she watched from above; a bright, infinite sky of burning turquoise; floating over rooftops, full of secret potential; the feel of the boy's hand in hers as they meander through the park, at peace with the world and each other; a glass tank spattered with purple blood.

While she experienced them, the dreams were vivid and vital; when she awoke, sense fled and she felt bereft, then confused and angry. In rare moments of lucidity she wondered if the nightly images had their roots in real memories and were part of the puzzle of her past. More likely they were mere illusions of an uncontrolled mind. Perhaps, if she embraced the numbers fully, the dreams would eventually stop haunting her.

One day when she opened her eyes the light was wrong and came from beyond Kety's cocoon. She blinked uncertainly.

Someone cried out. Kety's hammock jerked, and was still.

There were people here. Two of them, pushing past the limp form in Kety's cocoon, filling the room. They were bundled in fabric and had lights on their shoulders. They shuffled along the floor like they were stuck to it.

One of them said, 'Holy Christos, what a fucking mess!'

They were both men. She had an idea that men had tried to hurt her once. And they'd already hurt her friend. 'Kety!' she called out.

'Who the fuck's Kety?' said the first man.

The second one replied, 'No idea,' then looked directly at her and drew a stubby knife.

She shrieked. It was too late to stay safe and quiet.

The first man reached forward and clamped a hand over her mouth.

She bit him, as hard as she could.

He sprang back with an oath, shaking his hand. He came for her again, fast but careful. He turned her head to one side. She tried to resist but something cold touched her neck, and then there was nothing.

<file under: Temp>

We met at a party.

I only went to shut Chellis up. She was my facilitator – that's what ThreeCs called the handlers who managed mavericks like me. She said I should get out more. So I got out. The party was to celebrate someone's promotion or suchlike.

The first thing Tand said was, 'Are you the numbers girl?'

I remember thinking, *Oh, give me a break*.

But he looked as uncomfortable as I felt. And when we got talking it turned out he actually knew what a beevee cryptographer was. He was probably the only person at that party who did. He was a freelance researcher. 'I study the patterns of history,' he said, then pulled a face and added, 'Yeah I know that sounds pretentious. Actually most of the time I freelance for the Holo-Ents division; hardly intellectually challenging but it pays the rent.'

We spent the rest of the evening sitting in a corner and talking, ignoring everyone else.

Three days later, on our first proper date, I drank too much and did my party trick, testing an ancient conjecture said to have first been postulated on Old Earth: I got Tand to give me a high-value even integer, then told him which two primes it was the sum of. Most people get bored after a couple of numbers. He gave me seventeen, and only stopped because the waiter came to ask if we wanted dessert.

I went back to his apartment that night.

The next morning we walked in the park. Because Tethisyn-Delta's a hollow earth, the park runs round the top edge of the inhabited district. I used to hang out there because I liked the illusion of solitude. I'd also walked there with my previous boy-friends. All three of them. That morning, with Tand, it was like the whole place had been newly created for us. We watched the mist over the ponds, kicked up leaves under trees, and looked for flowers in the long grass. Then he took me to one of the bridges, a steep, elegant curve of red metalwork. 'Watch this,' he said, and ran up and on to the bridge. At the top of the curve, he jumped—

—and didn't come down. Or, rather, he came down slowly, gracefully, tracing a parabolic trajectory to land ten metres along the path. There was a dodgy grav-plate, he said; the utilities board hadn't got round to fixing it yet, and because the bridge let you start your jump a few metres above ground level, you didn't come down at once. I had a go. It was exactly the kind of craziness that'd been missing from my life.

For the next three weeks, Tand and I spent all our free time together. When Chellis noticed me making mistakes at work, she was annoyed. Then I admitted I had a boyfriend and she was delighted. Suddenly I was normal, rather than the difficult girl-genius who didn't make small talk or go to parties.

By then I was closer to Tand than I'd ever been to anyone. I began to suspect there was something he wasn't telling me.

It came out after we had our first row. We argued about money. Being a freelancer, Tand couldn't afford the time he was spend-ing with me. I offered to help. He refused, saying he didn't need charity. The row went on, backwards and forwards, not getting out of hand but not resolving either. I guess people in long-term relationships learn how to argue, but we had no clue.

Eventually I accused him of hiding something. Idiot that I am, I even said, 'If you love me, you'll tell me what the problem is.'

He said it wasn't relevant to our relationship. That just made me more determined to find out.

He said I'd think he was crazy. I said I'd never think that.

So he explained. It was about the patterns in history he'd talked about when we first met. Someone was messing with them at a level so deep, so universal, that no one suspected. He used the beevee network as an example, claiming that using its capacity as the basis for a universal currency shouldn't work. A construct like that was too unstable, too vulnerable to greed and short-sightedness; he said he'd found several examples where unexpected corporate altruism appeared to have averted a human-space-wide financial crisis. Someone was saving us from ourselves, just like the Sidhe had always claimed they were. When he mentioned the Sidhe I flinched, because that *did* sound crazy.

I said something about the inherent illogicality of human systems. I may even have called him paranoid. I didn't tell him that I already had my own doubts.

But he wouldn't let it go. He gave other examples, such as the scarcity of shiftships, and humanity's failure to rediscover lost technologies like zero-exchange power generation: he said that *someone* was controlling the supply of ships, and stifling research that got too technologically advanced.

Even though I didn't think it could be the Sidhe, I admitted my own doubts then, because this was Tand, the love of my life. My problem was with beevee. I knew about the different channels and the prioritising systems, but my area was encryption: attention to detail, not the big picture. Even so, I'd spotted some anomalies: encoded priority messages that made no sense even when deciphered, odd redundancies, apparent repetitions. Nothing to compromise the data I was paid to protect, and up until then I'd believed some sort of concerted beevee conspiracy to be as unlikely as someone manipulating human history.

Unless someone was using beevee as a means of bypassing normal communication channels *in order to* manipulate human history.

Put together his supposition and mine, and suddenly they both got more plausible. But that didn't mean this potential conspiracy was down to the Sidhe. They were all dead, I told him. He said he hoped I was right, but he couldn't see who else it could be. He'd looked into the historical sources in depth and found missing data and anomalous accounts relating to their apparent extinction. It was possible, he said, that not all Sidhe had been killed when the Protectorate fell.

I didn't mean to tell Chellis. It just came out. She asked how things were with me and Tand. I said we'd rowed, she came across all sympathetic, and I fell for it. I guess I needed someone to talk to. Not my mother, obviously, and I didn't have friends as such.

Looking back, I see that I was incredibly naive. But I got on all right with her, and she showed an interest. Besides, I wanted to know what other people thought about Tand's theory, the sort of people who watched lifestyle holos and socialised with their colleagues and knew what to say to strangers.

I didn't mention my doubts about beevee. I wasn't that stupid. I just said my boyfriend had this really wild theory about the Sidhe still being around. Chellis raised an eyebrow and said I should check his apartment for medication next time I stayed over. I didn't mention it again.

When I told Tand I'd spoken to Chellis, he was furious. We argued again. Then we made up. Then he got me to apply cutting-edge encryption to his research files, and sent a remote copy off to a secure storage service.

Things cooled off a bit between us. I'd damaged our relationship, and it was going to take a while to mend.

Two weeks later I received a meeting request from a Holo-Ents exec called Merice Markeck. I began to understand Tand's paranoia. But to refuse the meeting might arouse suspicions.

I checked her out: she was young and ambitious and she was visiting Delta from Port Viridian for various face-to-face meetings with people way above my level. When I met her we chatted about my old home city. I remember thinking how nice she was, how open and friendly. I liked her. Trusted her.

She'd heard that I knew someone who'd unearthed a really interesting, potentially important story. I said I had, and told her about Tand's findings. She listened, nodding, then said this was something humanity needed to know about. Those were her exact words: *something humanity needed to know about.* At least, that's what I remember her saying.

We talked some more: trivial, easy stuff. Then she offered to fund a docudrama. I said I'd put it to Tand.

He was sceptical. But the money was good, the piece was going out in prime-time and he'd have full artistic freedom. Besides, thanks to my loose tongue, his secret was already out.

I persuaded him that this wasn't a disaster but was actually the break he'd been waiting for.

The programme aired a couple of months later. We were at my place, because I'd got a better ents system, though soon it would be *our* place: he was moving in at the end of the week.

The feature was called *The Hidden Empire*. It started with an attention-grabbing reconstruction of Protectorate days: humans as willing slaves of the Sidhe, building a shiftship. It employed rather more melodrama than I'd expected, and the Sidhe wore rather less clothing than I'd expected, but as Medame Markeck had apparently said during production, 'First, you have to grab your audience.'

Then, apparently, you have to reassure them. Reassure them that while there are some crackpots out there who think the Sidhe aren't dead, these people are lone cranks. Such people should not be believed.

Everything Tand said had been carefully edited to make him look like a fringe loony. Talking-head academics vaguely but vitriolically deconstructed his evidence.

I believe the technical term is 'hatchet job'.

Tand watched in silence. After a while, tears started running down his cheeks. When it was over, I tried to comfort him, but he shrugged me off. He said he needed to be alone. I let him go.

After an hour, I commed to see if he was all right. I got no reply. I gave up after the seventh attempt.

I didn't sleep much that night. The next morning he commed and we talked; he said he didn't blame me, but he needed more time alone, to think.

A day passed. Two. I'd pretty much given up on sleep and food. I went to work, but got almost nothing done. I had a new co-worker, whom I ignored. (Chellis had suddenly and mysteriously transferred to another department, which was probably for the best, as otherwise I might've tied her to a chair with elastic bands then used my hard-copy cutter to slowly skin her alive.) I considered resigning, but though my work wasn't the most important thing in my life any more, it still mattered to me, and ThreeCs was the only place I could do it.

Four days after the broadcast, I had the news on in the background while I cooked a meal I had no appetite for. I stopped, knife in hand, as Tand's picture appeared on the holo. I dropped the knife and shouted the volume up.

'Witnesses say they saw the young man in the park early this morning, though no one was nearby at the time of the incident. After the utilities board traced the cause of the anomaly, the local surveillance footage was reviewed. This is what they found.' Cut to a silent recording of Tand, walking through the park, head down, coming into shot from one side. He speeds up. He's running now, along the path to our bridge. When he reaches it, he pelts up the smooth curve, arms pumping. At the highest point, he jumps.

This time, he doesn't come down. He just floats up slowly, until he's out of shot.

Someone chimed my door. It was the police.

They'd sent a man and a woman, not in uniform, looking glum and formal. When I let them in the woman spotted the newscast and said, 'I'm so sorry: the media got hold of it at the same time we did.'

I was confused, so she explained, gently, how my boyfriend had used a faulty grav-plate to jump high enough to escape the field generated by the habitat floor, then carried on upwards until he eventually fell into the nearest source of gravity.

Suddenly I knew what the news report had meant by 'the cause of the anomaly'. One of my random acts of teenage rebellion had been to throw a ball that had once been a favourite toy straight up as hard as I could, to see whether it would come down. It didn't. Mother told me sternly that it had fallen up into the sun. We hadn't got into trouble because the ball wasn't big enough to register on the utilities board's read-outs when it hit the fusion sphere at the heart of our hab. Apparently a human body was.

I didn't take it well. The police were very understanding, and did their best to comfort me. But when I'd calmed down they insisted I go and stay with my mother. They probably didn't want two suicides in one week.

Mother was as sympathetic as she ever got, which wasn't very. A couple of days later, she told me ThreeCs had got hold of Tand's suicide note. The authorities had originally found the recording when they went to his apartment, and they had asked if I wanted to hear it then. I'd said no. It would be too painful. Now everyone except me would be hearing it, courtesy of my employers.

Make that ex-employers.

I sent ThreeCs my resignation, waiving my severance payment.

Later that day I had another visitor, a lawyer. I hadn't realised Tand had made a will, but he had, just before the damned-to-hell programme had gone out. My lover had left me everything. The will also specified that his possessions be left exactly as they were when he died. Apparently the hab authorities had honoured his wish. After all, there was no criminal investigation as a result of his death.

It was still two more days before I could bear to visit his apartment. If I'd had a friend, I'd have asked them to come with me.

The place looked just like I remembered it. I spent a while wandering round, picking stuff up, smelling his clothes, sitting on the bed.

Finally I turned my attention to his comp. Ignoring the flashing message icon, I checked the secure files.

All gone. Deleted.

Were the law in on it? Or was it ThreeCs themselves?

I commed the data storage firm he'd left the back-ups with. They told me the back-ups had been deleted.

Who by? I asked.

By the account holder, they said.

I checked the log on Tand's comp. It was encrypted, but I'd written the encryption, so that wasn't a problem. The files had been deleted one hour and seventeen minutes before Tand's leap off the bridge. As far as I could tell, they'd been deleted by him.

This made no sense.

I acknowledged the message icon, because I'd run out of other places to look.

Tand stared out of the screen at me. He looked calm and sad, like a man who has reluctantly reached the only logical conclusion.

'Bez, I'm so sorry. I've been such an idiot. I've wasted my life on this crazy obsession. I've finally seen it for the paranoid lie it is, but it's too late. You ... you were almost enough to make me want to carry on. But then, someone like me, I'd be no good for you, not in the end.'

Tand's gaze sharpened. He was looking straight at me now.

'I love you, and I hate how it will hurt you, but I *have to* do this.'

The recording ended.

The image of his face blurred as my tears started. It was a while before I could see or think clearly again. When I did, I thought of his expression: so intense, like he was trying to tell me something he couldn't voice.

I have to *do this*.

I went back into the base directory and accessed the suicide note from there. As I expected, the file was too big. About five times too big.

It wasn't hard to find the embedded file. It was another vid-and-audio, far longer than the original note.

It started similarly, with Tand sat at his desk, but the perspective was different. This recording came from the spotcam hidden inside the frame of one of the poster prints on his wall. The recording showed him stopping work, and looking up. The audio was faint, but I thought I heard him say my name.

He got up and walked towards the door.

The camera didn't cover the door. Audio caught his voice, *Who are—?*

A pause. No audio, nothing in shot.

Then Tand backed into sight. He was moving oddly: not like a man who was facing a threat; more like he was dazed. The figure that shadowed him wore a dark, hooded tunic, but from the way she moved I knew it was a woman. Tand stopped in the centre of the room. So did the woman, standing toe-to-toe with him. Neither of them spoke.

She reached out a hand to his cheek, like a mother caressing a child who's fractious or upset.

For a minute and a half the two of them stood there, not moving, not speaking.

Then the woman turned on her heel and left.

The screen went blank.

I checked the timestamp. Exactly two hours before he jumped.

I'd been sustaining myself on hatred for ThreeCs, but my emotions were misplaced. ThreeCs were amoral and venal but they weren't the ones calling the shots. They were just like any other big organisation: they did whatever it took to survive.

It occurred to me later that maybe Tand didn't hide that surveillance file after all; maybe I was just meant to think he did. Maybe the bitch who killed my lover let him leave that clue. Maybe she even *made* him do it. Perhaps my untimely death would have been one odd event too many — better just to warn me off.

If that's what the Sidhe intended, then their plan seriously backfired, didn't it?

FULL CIRCLE

Bez hesitated, then played back the recording. The sound of her unguarded words made her cringe. But it proved the diary still worked.

Up until a few hours ago she had been sleeping, dreaming constantly. Eventually, the dreams had begun to make sense.

When she had finally regained consciousness, she was lying somewhere comfortable, in normal gravity. She had examined that thought, *normal gravity*, and processed the idea further to disentangle the weight of dreams from her last dose of – highly unpleasant – reality. She had taken a moment to remember the strange woman who had looked after her; Kety was almost certainly dead. Then she had checked her chrono. She had been out of circulation for twenty-seven days.

That in itself was cause for panic. Then there was the memory-core. And she wasn't even sure where she was. She had been kidnapped by men who, initially, she had feared would attack her. It was possible those men were working for the Enemy. That would be the worst thing that could have happened. The question was, had it?

She had risked opening her eyes to slits and seen the sort of recovery room – soft and floral – that expensive medical insurance paid for. Not that such physical luxury meant anything. She closed her eyes again.

She wanted to go virtual. Having regained her memory and sense of self, the lack of access to the world of data nagged like a missing tooth. As far as she could tell, she was not wearing an inhibitor cap, but there was more than one method to block abilities like hers once someone recognised them.

She had decided to take things slowly. She considered calling up some of her stored data but suspected the violation that had occurred on Xantier had been aimed at the information in her head. She wasn't ready to risk accessing it yet.

The diary, however, was another matter. She could test that relatively easily and safely, without tuning in; all she had to do was make an entry and play it back. She knew at once what she would record: the events that had set her life on its current course.

Now, listening to her whispered recollections, she thought how she had come full circle: her crusade against the Sidhe had started in one hollow earth, and whatever had brought her to this pass had occurred in another one. She rarely considered her part in the plan she lived to carry out – she was no more than a means to an end – but recent events had begun to change her perspective. Everything was becoming more personal.

By the time the recording ended, she was blinking back foolish tears. A few moments later the door opened. She opened her eyes, ready to face her fate.

'Tierce?' she said, amazed.

He smiled warmly at her. 'The very same! And she still won't call me Imbarin ...' He was carrying a bunch of flowers, which he thrust forward. Then he frowned. 'Are you all right? You look like you're c—'

'I'm fine,' she said quickly.

'Right. I brought you these. I believe it's traditional in many cultures.' He waved the flowers vaguely.

'Er, thanks,' she said. 'I'm not sure what you expect me to do with them.'

'I'll put them here.' He placed the flowers on the bedside table, then perched on the end of her bed.

She eased herself up onto her pillows. She felt all right, just a little weak. 'Am I on Tarset?'

'You are!'

She relaxed a little. 'And how did I get here?'

He steepled his fingers and looked grave. 'With considerable difficulty.'

'It was your doing?'

'I organised your extraction, yes. There were numerous complications I won't bore you with, save to say that while you were safely unconscious, there were a few exciting moments for the pair I hired, including, they tell me, a fire-fight on Xantier's docks. Mind you, bounty hunters are prone to exaggeration.'

'You hired *bounty hunters* to get me out?'

'Yep.'

'Why?'

'Because I wanted to save you. Feel free to thank me.'

'I'm grateful, of course I am. I'm just surprised you went to that much trouble.' Especially given they hadn't parted on the best of terms. Not that she intended to mention that.

He leaned forward. 'I should have stopped you going to Xantier. I bear some responsibility for what happened to you there. Naturally I was going to do my best to get you out safely.'

She was not sure his logic was sound, but she was hardly going to argue, given the result. 'What exactly *did* happen to me on Xantier?' She had an idea, but she wanted independent confirmation.

'You were hacked. Your headware's deep storage was compromised; there was also some coincidental damage to your organic memory, possibly due to drugs, although that's on the mend now.'

She strove to keep her voice even as she asked, 'The data in my deep storage, was it taken?'

'We can't be sure what was actually stolen; as well as the most efficient mass storage I've ever seen, and all sorts of dubious data-breaking tech, you've got some impressive scramblers installed in that pretty li'l head of yours. But a large volume of the data you were using in your fight appears to have been lost or corrupted.'

She refused to give in to despair at having her fears confirmed. Instead she asked, 'Do you know who hacked me?' Not Jarek Reen: he didn't even have an implanted com. It could have been someone he hired, assuming he knew anyone that good at databreaking. His pilot? No, the boy was just a kid. The more she thought about it, the less likely his crew's involvement was.

Tierce pulled a face. 'I think it may have been my counterpart on Xantier station.'

'*What?*'

'When I said we don't always work well together, I wasn't kidding.'

'But your organisation is meant to be fighting the Sidhe! Why in the void's name would one of you hack *me*?'

'I'm not sure. But things have changed recently.'

'What things? Changed how?'

'For a start, our conflict against the Sidhe is hotting up.'

'So you said, back on Gracen. What exactly has happened to make your people stop watching and start acting?'

'A good question.'

'But not one you're going to answer.'

'No,' he said, 'I can't.'

'Can't or won't?'

'I can't.'

Bez wished she were better at spotting lies. 'Was there something else?' she asked.

'Hmm?'

'You said "For a start" when you talked about reasons I might have been hacked. Was there something else?'

'Possibly. Arguably I shouldn't have taken you into my confidence the way I did.'

'By telling me about your group in the first place, you mean?'

'That's right.'

'But if each cell operates independently, how did the Xantier cell even find out you'd spoken to me?'

'Good question. Spies, perhaps.'

'You *spy* on each other?'

'Sometimes.'

'Void's sakes, no wonder you need me to fight the damn Sidhe for you!'

He looked embarrassed. 'Your point is valid. Given what

happened, would you be willing to tell me why you went to Xantier? Was it something relevant to the fight?'

'Yes.'

'Anything I can help with?'

She thought for a moment. 'Possibly,' she said.

'Well, let me know. Which reminds me: I have something you may need. Now, where did I put it?' He patted his suit. 'Ah, here.' He extracted a dataspike from an inner pocket.

'What is this?'

'Don't you recognise it? You gave it to me.'

'Oh. The Sidhe ID data.'

'Precisely. Just in case your copy was corrupted.'

'Right.' She thought for a moment, then added, 'Thank you.' She would have asked him for a copy if necessary, but she appreciated him offering the 'spike straight off. 'Presumably, while I was unconscious, tests and such were run on me?' She tried not to shudder at the thought.

'You were examined and, as far as you could be, healed. Or perhaps "fixed" might be a more accurate term.'

'Am I safe to go virtual?' She had so much catching up to do, so many agents needing instruction, so many lines of enquiry requiring follow-ups.

'You are, though I'd appreciate it if you avoided doing anything too, ahem, naughty while you're on my station.'

'I just want to reconnect with my network.'

'Yes, I imagine you do. Those bounty hunters I hired tell me you had an inhibitor cap on when they found you. Whoever hacked you wasn't taking any chances; they wanted you stuck in your own head. Which kind of begs the question why they didn't simply kill you.'

Bez had an idea why: Kety's 'jujuman' had taken pains to keep her breathing because he must have believed, correctly, that her headware incorporated a dead-man's switch. If all brain activity ceased, a databurst would go out, propagating rapidly throughout her network. Her diary plus a zipped subset of supporting intel would be transmitted, multi-encrypted and auto-spoofed, to her most trusted agents.

'Bez?'

'Yes?'

'I just wondered if you had any theories as to why you're still alive.'

She smiled tightly. 'Some,' she said.

'I suppose it was too much to hope you would tell me. Well, for the record, I'm glad you are.'

'Thanks. I need to rest now.'

Imbarin Tierce's smile told her he knew what she really wanted to do, but he left her alone anyway.

She tensed as she tuned out of the real, but the transition was painless. She eased herself into Tarset's infoscape slowly, then, when she was sure all was well, interrogated her permanent datadrop, which was as full as she had ever seen it. As she suspected, her recent absence had caused some confusion.

While she read through her messages, a meal was provided and a female medic fussed over her.

Alone again, she performed a full diagnostic on her internal memory.

She concluded that the damage was severe but selective. The data she had laid down herself had fared best: her diary was intact, as was most of her 'everyday' data, such as contact details and protocols for her agents, and her dossiers on Enemy targets. She had lost the decryption algorithms she had used on the *Setting Sun*'s memory-core, which meant that even when she got the core back, it would take time to reconstruct the data from it. And she *would* have to reconstruct it: over ninety-three per cent of her imported-and-zipped info, including the compressed download of the Sidhe memory-core, was gone. To have so much of her precious, hard-won intel torn from her head was a violation of a magnitude she found hard to contemplate. Instead she decided to be grateful for what had survived, and focus on the future.

She answered the most urgent queries then initiated rerouting protocols from nearby transient drops. Physical pick-ups of data-spikes would have to wait; she had more than enough to deal with already.

By now she was ready to rest, but first she commed Imbarin Tierce. Some time in the darkness of the last few weeks her sub-conscious had come to accept him as a possible ally – a conclusion borne out by her subsequent rescue.

'Do you have contacts on Catherli?' she asked when he answered.

'Depends what you mean by contacts,' he said. She got the impression she might have woken him up. A glance at her chrono confirmed that this was likely.

'Would you be able to find out if a certain shipment sent with a secure courier had arrived there?' The person that Hawk Consignia expected to collect the parcel had never reached Catherli. However, if Imbarin Tierce's influence was typical of that wielded by his organisation, and he had allies on that hub, perhaps he could find out for her.

He looked pensive. 'I reckon I could. Might take a few days.'

'Then I'd like you to do that for me. If you don't mind.'

'Sure. Did you want anything done about this shipment? That could be more complicated.'

'I … no. I just need to know it's safe.'

'Send me details and I'll see what I can do.'

In the event, it only took two days. Hawk Consignia had received a package conforming to the memory-core's specification. It was in their secure storage facility on Catherli.

By then she had been discharged from Tarset's medical facility; the doctors and technicians assured her there was no lasting dam-age. Her usual procedure when she expected to be in one place for a while was to arrange untraceable accommodation – hacking the security on a unit awaiting renovation was a trick she had used before here – but mindful of Imbarin Tierce's request that she stay within the law, she once again took up the inconspicuous but clean Kenid Sari persona then booked herself into a cube hostel. At least this identity now had some funds available, courtesy of the transfers Bez had initiated before she was hacked in Xantier's infoscape.

When Imbarin Tierce commed her with the news about the memory-core, he asked if she'd changed her mind about getting her 'mysterious package' back.

'No,' she said. The core mattered less than the Sidhe ID data now. There was also the residual taint from the *Setting Sun*'s association with Captain Reen, although she had been following up on his recent movements and nothing she had found gave cause for further suspicion. If Captain Reen *was* working for the Enemy, he was playing a very deep game.

'That's a relief,' responded Imbarin Tierce. 'I've rather used up my favours in that neck of the woods.'

'At least you had some to use on Catherli,' she said. 'Unlike Xantier.'

'Quite,' he said slowly.

'I have a theory about Xantier.' She had thought long and hard about whether to share her thoughts, but decided his reaction could tell her a lot.

'You do?' His image in her visual cortex took on an expression of interest.

'Yes. I think I was set up. I think your counterparts gave me a reason to go there in order to hack my internal storage.' It was the most logical explanation: even if the hub rebels on Xantier wanted the intel on the memory-core, why go to the effort of stealing and then decrypting the base files (assuming they even could) when they could just read the decoded data direct from her head? Making a failed attempt to steal the core had brought her running so they could do just that. Not that they had succeeded; at least a third of the info had auto-erased before it could be read. She was strung out between smugness at having cheated the thieves and sorrow for the data now lost for ever.

'I think you might be right,' said Imbarin Tierce. 'Not everyone holds you in the same high regard I do.'

Bez snorted. 'That's one way of putting it.'

'I wouldn't take it personally. We've always tolerated you,

because we're all on the same side. But it appears certain of my people have decided you're a bit of a loose cannon, and they could make better use of your findings than you're likely to.'

Bez tried not to let that comment chill her. It was bad enough not knowing how comprehensive the hub rebels' knowledge of her was – pretty far-reaching, on the evidence so far – but the realisation that some of them still believed she couldn't bring down the Sidhe was deeply disheartening. 'But you don't feel that way.'

'No. Most of us don't.'

'And when it comes to it, would the others in your organisation try to stop me?'

'Depends on your definition of "it" ... but, generally, no. Xantier's the exception, not the rule.'

'Good,' she said and signed off.

Her life's work was a complex, living hyperweb of many intersecting networks of human contacts, flowing data, transferable funds and carefully constructed personae. With the acquisition of the *Setting Sun*'s memory-core, this hyperweb had become more focused and better informed. Getting the Sidhe ID file had honed her plans, moving her closer still to her goal.

Yet thanks to a minor miscalculation, one piece of missing intel, she had come close to losing everything.

She could not afford another mistake like that.

R-Day was going to be coordinated from Tarset, with Imbarin Tierce's help. And it was going to happen soon.

DERN
(Olympus Orbital, Ylonis System)

'Why the sudden interest?'

Dern looked across the table at his mother. 'I was just curious.'

She snorted. 'Don't tell me you're still trying to impress those out-of-system kooks with your knowledge of Starscape?' She said the name of her almost-ex-employers with a mixture of venom and wistfulness.

Dern shrugged. 'Not so much these days, no. But someone told me Fera Yasmie isn't from Ylonis, which I thought was a bit odd given her position in the company. Hence asking.'

'I see. To be honest, I'm not sure.' His mother was humouring him, but he expected nothing less. They still observed the ritual of eating dinner together and talking about their day while they did so, even if the dining area was rather less grand than he was used to; the family had been in their new apartment for a week now, and Ma still seethed at the imposition, although she acknowledged its necessity. She had even sold some of her precious vases.

'You've never met Medame Yasmie, then?' He tried to keep his voice neutral.

'I have, as it happens.'

That wasn't good news. 'Oh. Often?'

'No, but we're both – we *were* both – in the same division.'

'Is Medame Yasmie …' He struggled for a way to put it that wouldn't set her off. 'Does she still work full-time?'

'I believe so.' His mother frowned, remembering. 'And you can tell your conspiracy-freak friends that she probably *isn't* local. She's very pale-skinned.'

'How did you get on with her?'

238

'What do you mean, "get on with her"?' Ma was on her third glass of wine, and her patience was fraying.

'What did you think of her, when you met?'

'Well, it was only a handful of times, at corporate functions. She struck me as eminently competent. The fact she still has a job, with her area of responsibility, supports that.'

Given the slurred bitterness in his mother's voice, Dern decided to drop the subject. He had the answer he needed.

His father, who had been concentrating on his food, looked across the table and said, 'I've noticed you don't spend so much time chatting to your out-of-system friends these days.' His tone made it obvious how pleased he was with this development.

'He can't afford to,' said his mother tightly.

'That's true,' acknowledged Dern. His job as a junior utilities technician paid enough to contribute to the household budget, but left him little spare credit. The days when his hobbies and interests were automatically funded by his parents were gone for ever.

'Actually,' said his father, 'I was referring to Jerine. I think she's good for you, Dern.'

Dern smiled. 'So do I.' Whatever he thought about his menial job, he couldn't bring himself to regret it, not when it'd led to meeting Jerine. He was trying to be mature and careful about their burgeoning relationship. He'd had plenty of sexual experience, including the sort most young men dream about. Back in his terce-ball days he'd had his pick of fan girls (and boys – he'd tried all the options before deciding he preferred the opposite sex), but that had just been fun, easy and meaningless. Jerine wasn't a terceball fan, and they had been going out for several weeks before they'd gone to bed together. She also viewed work for the hab's utilities office as a step up, not down; her family had never had anyone in Starscape. She wasn't even good-looking compared to a lot of the girls he'd been with. But he loved her. That was new, and just as amazing as those stupid songs claimed.

'You're certainly spending a lot of time with her,' said his father.

Dern's smile became wry. This was the closest his parents had come to explicitly mentioning how few nights he'd slept in his own bed over the last month. The only reason he had come home today was because he and Jerine were on different shifts this week, and he needed some actual sleep. Good job he'd returned when he had, given the package that had been waiting for him in his room.

'She seems quite nice,' added his mother. Dern heard the unspoken coda: *for someone from that background*.

'She is.' Life was so much simpler if he just agreed with everything his parents said.

No one felt compelled to carry on talking, and the meal trailed off into silence.

Back in his room, he wove a path through the boxes to his desk. Several of those boxes contained his animatronics collection, which this new, smaller room had no place for. And neither did he, really; not anymore. Mother had started selling her vases; he should sell some of his models. He needed to adjust to their new lifestyle. That was something else he'd learned from Jerine: how it was possible to still enjoy life without those activities and luxuries you couldn't afford. They had a place to live and enough to eat. The other stuff was pleasant but ultimately optional. As long as he had Jerine, the lack of credit or fame, even the shitty job – none of that really mattered.

But there was one thing that did matter, something that went beyond his personal happiness.

He picked up the dataspike and slotted it into his slate. Weeks without any contact from Orzabet, and now this. Time was, he'd have welcomed such personal attention from his mysterious co-conspirator. Well, not exactly welcomed, given the contents of the 'spike, but it would have energised him into action. He saw now that his interest in possible conspiracies stemmed in part from a desire to recover the excitement of his failed sporting career. But that was before Jerine. She complicated his decision immensely, because life wasn't just about him anymore, it was about the two of them.

Although he had been through everything on the 'spike twice since he first opened the package this morning, part of him still wished he could dismiss the contents, put them down as a hoax or mistake. But all Orzabet's protocols were in place. He played the audio file yet again. The more he listened to her intensely spoken words (Orzabet was female: that had been a surprise), the more real and inescapable their sense became ...

'I'm going to tell you the truth about transit-kernels. In return, you're going to help me expose a lie that's gone unchallenged for a thousand years.

'You take an interest in such things, so you know the accepted story: how transit-kernels were developed by the Sidhe, and how the technology was stolen millennia later by the rebels who overthrew the Protectorate. Well, it wasn't quite like that. Yes, transit-kernels are Sidhe tech, but they can only be made by Sidhe. That's as true now as it was during the Protectorate.

'The Sidhe are alive, Dern. Not many of them, but enough to impact on the future course of human history. One of the ways they shape and manipulate us is by controlling interstellar travel. And they do that by controlling the supply of transit-kernels.

'Every one of those black boxes was once a living being; each transit-kernel contains the central nervous system of a Sidhe. That's right: the Sidhe put their own people into transit-kernels. Or, rather, they put the few surviving male Sidhe into them. Young boys, mentally limited ones at that. This all happens some-where far from your home system; I've included further info on this dataspike.

'I've also provided the shipping schedules that brought some of the recent deliveries to Ylonis, along with the results of my in-vestigations into the companies who create and distribute transit-kernels. It's a twisted path; as you'll see when you check the data, the real origins are well hidden.

'You're at the sharp end, Dern. What you see is the final result: technology capable of propelling a ship through shiftspace. I'm sure most people at Starscape never consider the source of the ker-nels. But there are individuals in that company who are in on the secret. More importantly, you have a Sidhe agent in your midst:

she's aware of the full truth and determined to keep it hidden. Her name is Fera Yasmie. I've given you everything I have on her.

'*As a result of events elsewhere, I can confirm that the supply of transit-kernels has dried up for the foreseeable future, possibly for ever. I'm sure you're smart enough to work out that this has serious implications for human-space, but you have to remember that the way things are now is a lie, a sham. We aren't free of the Sidhe: they're still here, hiding in the shadows.*

'*Fera Yasmie is a blight, a cancer in the heart of Starscape. She has to be removed.*

'*I'm not asking you to do anything illegal or dangerous. The info I've provided is enough to incriminate her. When you go through it you'll see that her actual crime, the law she has broken, is use of a false ID. That alone is enough to have her up before the Commission. And once someone like her comes under close scrutiny, it'll all fall apart. The Sidhe only maintain their hold while they remain out of sight.*

'*Some of the enclosed data will go to others in positions of power in your system, but that's not enough. I need you to bring Yasmie to the attention of the authorities at Ylonis at the same time as other action is taken. Do it anonymously if you must, but there has to be corroboration, more than one voice calling for action. I need you to make the actual request to apprehend this Sidhe menace. You are a vital part of my plan, Dern Morvil. I implore you to do what you know to be right.*'

Even before he had invested himself in a worldview and subculture where people entertained unlikely possibilities, Dern had had an interest in such things. Given the evidence – which Orzabet had provided – he was ready to believe. But was he ready to act?

ESTRIS
(The Ice Coast, Tetrial Beta, Tetrial System)

Estris never told her sister about Orzabet. However, she continued to use the beevee connection even after it stopped being a tool to relieve her anger, even when her job-hunting began to pay off and the first interviews came in. She stayed in touch with Orzabet because this was one thing in her life her older sister had no part of.

Then the package arrived. It came in the same week as her trial period with her new employers. The job paid less than her old one and it was only in Hunterport, so she was unlikely to be moving back to the capital anytime soon. On the other hand, she could commute from Astren's place until she found her feet and sorted accommodation nearer the office.

The package had customs stickers, which confused her: who, for Mithras' sakes, would go to the expense of sending her a *physical object* from another star-system? It wasn't until she opened it and found the dataspike that she linked the delivery to the cryptic transmission she had received from her out-of-system contact a couple of months back. Alone in her room at the beach house, she applied Orzabet's codekey to the 'spike. Snow flurries hurled themselves against the window as she listened to the female voice explaining intently how there was indeed a conspiracy to suppress certain technologies, and how this conspiracy was ancient and widespread. Dynosys were involved in something huge, just as Astren had jokingly suggested. And now Estris had a chance to act against her ex-employers; more than that, she could be part of a fightback taking place across human-space.

Suddenly light-headed, Estris paused the recording. Perhaps this was what she had seen in Orzabet, what had made her stand out from the delusional idiots who posted their crazy theories without any corroboration or logic. Orzabet was onto something big. She smiled to herself: Astren might write about history, but Estris was being given the chance to participate in it – if she dared. She took a few calming breaths and restarted the recording.

Orzabet wished her to forward certain information about a particular individual in Dynosys to the branch of the policiat that dealt with extra-territorial crimes. Orzabet said she could give the tip-off anonymously – Estris's smile turned grim at that comment – but she had to make her report at a specified time. Estris recognised the name of the individual in question: she was the head of Dynosys's R&D division, one of the most powerful people in the company. Estris had never met Nema Lastre, but it was reasonable to assume she was ultimately behind the suppression of the tech breakthroughs, and hence responsible for Estris's own woes. Odd that it was just one person; much as Estris liked the idea of there being a single focus for her anger, she had expected the problem to be more widespread.

As though anticipating the question, Orzabet's recording went on to explain who – or rather what – Nema Lastre was.

When the recording finished, Estris stared at her slate. Then she replayed the last segment. *The Sidhe?* For Mithras' sakes!

But Orzabet was perfectly serious. Her delivery didn't falter. She really believed that this otherwise plausible-sounding conspiracy originated with long-dead aliens.

Apparently one of those aliens had indirectly shafted Estris. And now she was being asked to return the favour. Not anonymously, though. Orzabet obviously didn't realise how the policiat worked. Estris's name would be associated with whatever action was taken, possibly openly via the news media. That definitely broke the terms of her non-disclosure agreement. Was it a price worth paying to get revenge?

And then there was Astren. Estris could picture her sister's face when she found out that Dynosys's actions allegedly originated with a *Sidhe*. Astren had a distinctive laugh, a sort of dismissive snort, which she used whenever she came across people who expressed half-baked knowledge of the subject she had studied in depth. Estris could hear her now; Astren would say something like, *Don't confuse fairy tales with facts, little sister.* And she was right: when it came to history, Astren knew what she was talking about.

Estris sighed, and ejected the dataspike.

CHANDIN
(Cyalt Hub)

This message from 'Orb' was far longer than anything Chandin's mysterious contact had sent him previously. Or, rather, it came with a significant volume of associated data. It also arrived via an unexpected route.

Although the Commission had access to priority beevee channels, its officers avoided squandering the taxes they took from every inhabitant of human-space, even if those taxes amounted to little more than the price of a round of drinks in a given individual's lifetime. Therefore high-volume, non-urgent data was transported on dataspikes. This particular dataspike contained scans of some of the oldest Treaty records, the ones recorded on actual paper and kept in temperature-controlled vaults on hubs with the facilities to store such delicate material. The bulk of the documents had been requested by one of his top company-law specialists, who was seeking a ruling on a particularly obscure dispute within a trans-system corporation. However, Chandin had appended a 'would be nice' request, asking for records related to the Sidhe's demise, a cleansing whose efficiency and brutality would be horrific had it had not come at the end of millennia of tyranny.

Finding a second dataspike in the package was a shock. After having applied the best data-cleansing routines he possessed to the mysterious 'spike, he checked its contents and found hundreds of individual datafiles, and one audiofile, all of them encrypted. He concluded that this dataspike might well originate with his mysterious blackmailer. His father could learn a thing or two from Orb, he thought wryly. (As he had expected, there had been no further developments since their last, uncomfortable encounter. He doubted he would hear from the man again.)

Chandin was no expert at databreaking, but it was logical to assume that all the files had been encrypted in the same way. Sure enough, when he applied the key Orb had transmitted previously, it unscrambled a file he picked at random from the dataspike.

He decoded the audio header file. It was a recording of a woman, speaking low and earnestly.

'Use these files to help humanity. That's what the Commission is for, and that's what I need you to do.

'Assuming you do as I ask, you have my word that all records of your indiscretion will be wiped. No one will ever know what happened twenty-five years ago.

'If you choose not to act, then I have nothing to lose by making certain of your colleagues in the Commission aware of—'

He paused the recording. He could visualise Tanlia's face when she heard the news. Part of her would be genuinely apologetic as she took away everything he had worked for. But part of her would be triumphant. And Gerys: how would she react? Would their marriage survive if his wife discovered he had hidden something so important from her for all these years?

He could lose everything. But he doubted Orb would have gone to this much trouble unless she was about to request something major. And if he complied, doing her bidding might destroy his career just as effectively.

He restarted the recording.

'—your mistake. More importantly, if you don't do this, you are a traitor to our race.'

'Orb' obviously believed what she was saying but that last comment smacked of mental instability. He tuned back in to the recording.

'This dataspike contains intel on over five hundred individuals. Wherever possible, these individuals must be apprehended and detained. The information I have provided is enough to build cases against nearly half of them. As for the rest … I'm under no illusions: we can't get them all. But we have to try.'

As Chandin wondered how she expected him to go about this near-impossible task, the recording continued:

'I realise the Commission has no jurisdiction over individual systems. However, the strongest cases are against those who have perpetrated inter-system ID-fraud, and that is your responsibility. You can request investigations into at least one hundred and eighty-two people on those grounds.

'I know how these things work: you put in a request, acting on information the Commission has uncovered, and your liaisons in local law decide the best way to implement it. Sometimes they'll stall, because they have more pressing business, or because of local politics you're unaware of. Other times, they jump. This will only work if they jump. In most of the systems in my files, your official request won't be the only one they receive. Local agents in possession of the same data will be reporting to the authorities in their home systems.

'As I'm sure you appreciate, timing is key. Your messages need to arrive in coordination with those from my agents. The data must *be transmitted, and the requests made, on the date I specify.'*

Shocked and disturbed as he was, Chandin couldn't help but admire Orb's ambition. She wasn't messing around.

'I would prefer to use dataspikes, but that isn't practical. Therefore you will need to employ the Commission's own resources, utilising priority beevee services with maximum encryption.'

Sweet void, she wasn't asking much, was she?

'There's one more thing, and I wasn't sure whether to tell you this, but it's only fair that I do.'

For the first time Orb's voice showed uncertainty.

'When you check the files you'll notice all the targets are female. There's a reason for that, and it's one you may find hard to credit …'

Chandin listened to the remainder of the recording in horrified fascination.

When it finished, he walked over to the window. Evening was falling and the roofshine had deepened from azure to bronze, painting the hab's terraces in a warm golden glow. This was real: Cyalt station, the Commission offices, the people he cared about.

Not some crazy conspiracy in which the Sidhe – the Sidhe! – were alive and well and still secretly in control. Orb had been painfully sincere as she matter-of-factly explained how the culture Chandin had sworn to protect was not what he thought it was. That didn't mean she was right. He would be as crazy as her if he abused Commission resources, not to mention impugning the Commission's integrity on the word of a single lunatic, no matter how fervent and apparently well informed she was.

But if he didn't, then she would destroy him.

He returned to his desk and unmounted Orb's dataspike then slotted in the other, expected, one. He needed to ground himself.

The files he had requested for his colleague were all in order so he sent them straight over. On a whim, he opened the archive scans he had asked for under his own auspices.

As darkness fell outside, he lost himself in momentous decisions he hadn't had to make. Some of the choices taken during the formative years of the Treaty Commission had been perceptive and wise, the wisdom of lone voices that saw the way forward despite opposition. Other choices had, in hindsight, been nearly disastrous. A lot of the latter were made by people who had underestimated their enemies.

The female Sidhe had always been a minority, ruling largely through fear and ignorance. The males had probably been even less numerous, and had already disappeared from history by the time the Treaties were drawn up. (Or possibly been written out: Chandin had found some interesting if obscure references to the old machine-melded males and their antipathy towards the other half of their race. He hoped to find time to follow up on this some day.)

Once humanity had finally woken up and turned against the female Sidhe, their extinction had been swift. But had it been complete? Millions of Sidhe had been killed in coordinated action; those who escaped had been ruthlessly hunted down. Just as the male Sidhe's final fate never made it into the surviving accounts, the human records of the fall of the Protectorate focused on humanity's victories, and glossed over the failures. From what he had read, in these files and others, it was possible that a few Sidhe had got away.

What if Orb wasn't crazy after all? What if she was the lone voice of reason, however unlikely that initially appeared?

He was an agent of the organisation set up to restore humanity after the dark days of the Sidhe Protectorate. If Orb was telling the truth, he could not afford to ignore what she had sent him.

NEWSHOUND

The two months leading up to R-Day were the busiest of Bez's life.

She could never have brought everything together so quickly while living her usual peripatetic lifestyle. As it was, the task of priming her agents and securely distributing the intel they would need kept her busy twenty-plus hours a day. She paused only grudgingly, when physical distractions like hunger or exhaustion began to affect her judgement and performance.

Imbarin left her alone unless she asked for his assistance. However, he had, without her asking, provided a secure apartment and unlimited beevee access. Both were essential if she were to implement her plan in her chosen timescale, so whenever the thought of being in his debt worried her, she turned that concern into an urge to work faster and better, the sooner to be free of the need for another's generosity.

As she worked, she visualised the transformation she was preparing to trigger throughout her network. For nearly two decades she had built up the web that allowed her to work towards her goal, using it to collect and collate intel. Now the flow of data was about to be reversed.

Overnight, her hyperweb would go from intel-gathering tool to trap.

R-Day itself was an anti-climax. She spent the preceding day setting up the last of her newsfeeds. At the moment her chrono indicated the start of another arbitrary unit of beacon-maintained time, she paused to watch the count: 24:59:59 to 00:00:00 ...

Nothing changed, of course, save the knowledge in her heart that the next twenty-five hours would bring the culmination of her life's work.

When twenty minutes passed without news or incoming contact – not that she had expected any yet – she decided to get some rest, although she had to resort to a sedative to overcome her nervous anticipation.

When her alarm woke her six hours later, the first report was just in. It came from Ylonis, one of the two systems that produced shiftships. The other shiftship construction company was under the control of an untouchable Sidhe agent with a solid ID. But the Sidhe on Ylonis, Target93, had just been arrested pending an investigation into corporate malpractice and identity fraud. Bez smiled for what felt like the first time in weeks.

The shift from instigator to observer turned her into a newshound, obsessively reviewing events from systems where her agents had been charged with carrying out her will.

By the time a week had passed, the initial surge of arrests was tailing off. After two weeks she had to acknowledge that in some systems, such as on the chilly and factional world of Tetrial Beta, her agent had failed to act. And there was one Sidhe in particular that she waited in vain to hear about.

Too many of the Enemy remained free. She hadn't won yet. Despite all the effort she had put in, there was no guarantee she would.

Even so, she began to think about the future. There was still work to do, follow-up intel to distribute, further investigations to lend her aid to, but the time would come when, whether or not she succeeded in breaking the Enemy's hold over humanity, she would have done all she could. When that happened, would she really be able to settle down in one place, living out her life as one person? Or would she continue to travel, and databreak, because that was all she knew?

A lot of her time was spent on analysing events in systems where the Sidhe had escaped initial attempts to apprehend them.

She needed to turn more near misses into ultimate successes. Earlier today she had received a full newscast from Bryntarin, a one-world system two transits from Tarset. When Imbarin Tierce commed her, she was watching it for the fifth time.

The footage showed the launch of a ship, one of the superliners that circumnavigated Bryntarin's equatorial ocean. The world was a capital-based democracy, ultimately run by corporations. The Sidhe there, Target258, was the head of a major company and a member of the ruling elite. Her company had built the superliner, and now she was launching it.

The hovercam recording showed a crowd of the great and the good, filling the parade deck of the ship. The Sidhe was standing on a low dais against flower-covered railings, making a speech that Bez had sat through the first time but now muted. Three minutes and twenty seconds into the speech, Target258 made an extravagant gesture, then dropped. When Bez had watched this section with the sound up, enduring the Enemy's glib words, she had clearly heard the *whistle-crack* of the projectile shot at this point. The Sidhe ducked at exactly the moment the assassin took his shot. All around, heads were turning. The viewpoint wobbled as the cam's controller tried to work out what was happening.

By the time the cam stabilised, chaos had broken out. The assassin was now shooting into the crowd. Even without the soundtrack of screams, it made grim viewing: an elderly man was spun around by a shot, his female companion falling when he did, clutching at him open-mouthed; a child was kicked to the floor and trampled; a young, pretty woman stood still, too shocked to move, until another shot punched her to the deck in a spray of red.

This time though, Bez wasn't looking at the mayhem in the foreground. She was focused on the figure of Target258, standing aloof behind the crush of desperate humanity. The Sidhe hadn't run or taken cover. Instead she had climbed up on to the railing among the flowers, making herself an obvious target. She was staring across the cam's field of view over the heads of the panicking crowd. Even after four viewings Bez couldn't be certain, but the sims she had run strongly indicated that the Enemy was looking directly at the assassin, who according to later reports was stationed in one of the dockside towers.

When she got an incoming com call, Bez froze the image. She knew how the rest of the newscast played out: there was another thirty seconds of death and mayhem before the security forces managed to locate and take out the assassin, then started dealing with the casualties.

The call was from Imbarin Tierce; she cut across his greeting. 'Have you seen the news from Bryntarin?'

'I'd heard about it, yes. Not seen, though. You requested a full cast?'

'I needed to see for myself. I hope that's all right.' She cursed her timidity; he had given her the beevee account, it was up to her how she used it.

'I guess so, if you felt it necessary to actually *watch* what went wrong ...' She was getting better at reading his moods, and even with no visuals she could tell he wasn't convinced.

'I did,' she said firmly. 'Seventeen dead, Imbarin. Seventeen innocent people whose deaths that bitch was responsible for. Eighteen if you count the assassin; he'd have escaped if she hadn't forced him to shoot into the crowd. And she got away without a scratch.' More than that: to Bez's deep disgust, the report from Bryntarin said Target258 had been awarded a medal for her courage during a 'devastating and unprovoked terrorist attack'. She was likely to remain at large: if they had had enough intel to take her out legally, then Imbarin wouldn't have had to resort to hiring a local assassin in the first place. Another favour he had done for her, albeit one that had gone horribly wrong.

'We knew they wouldn't go quietly,' said Imbarin.

'Next you're going to tell me it's a small price to pay.'

'It is. You know it is, rationally. You're just letting your emotions get the better of you.'

Not something she remembered anyone accusing her of before. 'Those emotions are what make me human.'

'So they are. Anyway, I actually called to ask you out to dinner.'

'Dinner?' Her overlays were full of people running, panicking, dying. 'I'm busy.'

'Busy punishing yourself over things you can't change?'

'I have to know which fail-points can be salvaged.' But he had a point: Bryntarin's Sidhe wasn't going down.

'Yes you do. But you also need to eat. I've managed to get a reservation at Cherry. It's the best restaurant on Tarset.'

'That's not saying much.'

'I'm hurt, Bez. Really, I am. You can be very rude sometimes, you know.'

'I thought that was what you liked about me.' Odd how easily they fell into this casual, friendly banter. 'And if I don't like the place, you'll be paying for me to be rude in public,' she added. She was trying to rationalise Imbarin's continuing outlay on her behalf as only fair given that she was refraining from databreaking at his request, but she wanted to remind him she wasn't comfortable being beholden to anyone.

'I'm willing to risk your sarcasm. The reservation's at twenty hundred.'

'I'll see you there.'

EVOLVING WILDNESS

The restaurant was in a respectable lower block in the quietest part of the dockside mall. When she arrived, a uniformed server tried to intercept her, but she spotted Imbarin sitting at the back, dodged the waiter, and went straight over. Her heart did a stupid little double-trip when Imbarin caught her eye. She fought the urge to sigh at herself. That kind of crap had been happening all too often recently. She appeared to be developing feelings for the man.

He was wearing the style of dinner suit tourists favoured for formal meals on starliners, and Bez felt suddenly self-conscious, even as he said mildly, 'You'll set a trend.'

She was so used to considering clothes as costume that it hadn't occurred to her that, when not actively impersonating someone, she might wear something other than a plain coverall. People were looking at her. Heat rose in her cheeks and she sat down abruptly.

A server slid a hardcopy menu into her hand. Addressing Imbarin, he said, 'Your drinks will be along shortly, sirrah.'

Imbarin nodded an acknowledgement and said to Bez, 'I took the liberty of ordering wine.'

'Thanks.' She glanced at the menu, which was printed on embossed card. Phrases like 'truffle soufflé' and 'tenderloin cutlet' leapt out. Also, logically enough, a lot of dishes involving cherries. There was a note at the bottom of the page stating that all the fruit used was imported from farms on Alixer; having to actually ship the main ingredient in from a nearby planetary system might explain the exorbitant prices. Good job she wasn't paying. She had planned to suggest Imbarin order for her, but now she changed her mind and read the whole menu.

The wine arrived and was served, after which the waiter took their orders, claiming insincerely that every choice they made was 'Excellent'.

When they were alone again, Imbarin raised his glass in a toast. 'To victory.'

She tasted the wine; it was, as she was sure the waiter would say, excellent. She took a second sip and put down her glass. 'Let's not be premature.'

Imbarin's sparkling smile dimmed fractionally. 'Fair point.'

'Take Bryntarin,' she said, fighting the distracting rush of alcohol from tongue to blood to brain. 'I didn't watch that news-cast just to satisfy my curiosity.'

'I thought you already extrapolated what must have happened: the target spotted the assassin and took control of him. That is what you found, isn't it?'

'It is,' said Bez slowly. 'But I wanted to know if she knew some-one was there. She responded very quickly.'

'She could have sensed the assassin, if she was paranoid enough to be scanning for threats. It's equally possible she was lucky, or the assassin was shoddy. I told you when I hired him that all I could get was a local contractor. Let this one go, Bez. Bryntarin isn't a key system.'

He was right, damn him. She should focus on what was import-ant, and could be influenced. 'I found something interesting on one of the alternative channels out of Mercanth.' Imbarin grunted encouragingly, so she continued, 'They've made the connection with, well, not the Sidhe per se, but the pundits there are talking about disconcerting echoes of Protectorate times.' Bez realised she had just unhesitatingly named her enemies in public.

'Well, if the trusted and well-trained men and women you send after your suspects keep going mad or suffering brain haemorrhages, then something odd has to be going on, doesn't it? That's good news: we need to win the public over if we're going to catch the ones who've got away so far.'

The idea that the Sidhe's continued existence might one day be accepted as fact had been one of Bez's great hopes, yet now the possibility was being acknowledged it made her oddly nervous.

Imbarin was saying, 'What is the current score, anyway?'

'It can only be an estimate.' Commercial newsfeeds were hardly a reliable way to gather statistics. 'We have fifty-six probable kills and another eighty-one detentions. In addition, there're at least seventy systems where warrants have been issued.'

'So that's just over a third actually exposed.'

'So far, yes.' Not as many as she had hoped. 'Do you really think the others will run?'

'When they realise there's no chance of regaining control, yes. The point at which those targets we haven't yet touched start to disappear is the point at which we know we've won.'

'I'll drink to that,' she said, and did.

The waiter approached with their starters. Bez had ordered roasted sour cherries with curd cheese. The dish looked like a work of art. It tasted good, though: tart yet creamy. She allowed herself to enjoy the sensual pleasures of food and wine for a while, although she ended up leaving some of the extraneous leafage.

She had just put down her fork and taken another sip from her newly refilled glass when Imbarin said, 'I have an apology for you.'

'An apology? Why, what have you done?' Just when she thought he was trustworthy ...

'It's not from me. It's from Xantier.'

'I'm sorry?' The unaccustomed alcohol must be going to her head.

'Well, when I say Xantier ... my counterpart there. The one who abducted you. In the light of recent developments, he regrets his earlier actions.'

'You mean ...' Bez was caught between incredulity and fury. Fury won. 'You mean he's sorry he *nearly killed me then left me to rot in the hab-rat tunnels?*' she whispered.

Imbarin grimaced. 'Yes. That. He'd temporarily lost sight of who the real enemy was, the idiot.'

She sat back and crossed her arms. 'Well, that's all right, then.'

Another visit from the waiter, this time to remove their plates, shut her up. By the time they were alone again, her anger had subsided. Perhaps it was the soft glow of food and drink, or perhaps it was Imbarin himself, who looked genuinely, almost comically, pained.

She leaned forward again. 'You know, if everyone in your organisation had just cooperated with each other – and me – from the start, we might have eradicated the Sidhe completely by now.'

'I'm not disagreeing with you there.'

The next course arrived: seared pork fillets on stir-fried something-she-had-forgotten. But her appetite was not up to the cuisine. Pushing food around her plate she said, 'Take beevee.'

'What about beevee?'

'Do you monitor it?'

'That would be illegal.'

Bez laughed. 'Yes, and neither of us would *ever* do anything illegal. But if your group did somehow get access to a suspicious beevee transmission, possibly from our adversaries, would you have passed it on to another cell?'

'Probably not,' he admitted, 'though now, with success in our sights, it's more likely. But that assumes we could spot the suspicious transmission, then break the encryption on it, and *then* decode any meanings hidden in the plaintext. Something like a stock investment report might contain a brief but vital message only comprehensible to someone aware of the encoding regimes in place.'

She smiled and said, 'Oh, don't I know it.'

'So to answer your question: no, we haven't done that well at spotting and intercepting the Sidhe's use of beevee.'

'You know what the problem is, don't you?'

'At a guess: ThreeCs.'

'We need to take out the head Sidhe there, Imbarin.'

'I agree. And knowing you as well as I hope I do, I can't believe you don't have a back-up plan in place to do just that.'

'I did.' The wine was making her careless. She knew what he would ask next.

'But not anymore? What went wrong?'

She could have claimed the intel she had needed was among the stored data she had lost, but she disliked lying to him. Instead she said, 'I made an error of judgement.'

'Ah. Is the situation salvageable?'

'Possibly.' In theory she – or he – could engage a professional assassin to travel to Tethisyn and take out TargetZero. But as events on Bryntarin showed, that was a risky proposition. A criminal gun-for-hire would never be as effective as an Angel.

'Just let me know if I can help.'

She wondered if Imbarin himself had the skills she needed. He had certainly surprised her so far. But she did not like the idea of him putting himself into direct danger.

The waiter took their plates. Silence fell while they waited for dessert. Every time she met up with Imbarin, she gave away more of herself – yet she didn't mind. *Should she?* She still knew so little about her new ally, for all she wanted to trust him. More than trust him, if she was honest.

The next course arrived: cherry mousse. It was so light it evaporated off her tongue, leaving tingling fruitiness in its wake. Somewhere along the way they had acquired another bottle of wine.

'Can I ask you something?' said Imbarin as she sat back after finishing her dessert.

'Yes,' she said warily.

'Why do you hate the Sidhe so much?'

'It's personal.'

'I see.' She hoped he wouldn't pursue the matter and wondered what she would tell him if he did. Then he added, 'Is that all?'

'What do you mean, "all"? Trust me: it's enough.'

'I understand: that's a very … human … reason. But is there something more? Something ideological, perhaps.'

Despite the wine, she saw what he was getting at. 'Depends what you mean by ideological. I truly believe that humanity – possibly the universe itself – would be better off without them. They're an aberration. A force for chaos.'

Imbarin smiled broadly. 'That's my girl.'

Bez was still deciding whether to be patronised or amused by his comment when Imbarin's eyes glazed over. When he focused on her again, she asked, 'What is it?' She liked to think he would only be accepting urgent calls right now.

'Good news. Events are moving ahead of schedule.'

'What events?'

'I've got a surprise for you, Bez.'

'I don't like surprises.'

'It's true that you might not like this one, at least not initially.'

'That's not what you're meant to say. Now I'm definitely worried.'

'You might not *want* this, but you *need* it. Trust me.'

'Void's sakes, Imbarin, just tell me what you're on about!' The frivolous verbal jousting was fun, but he was beginning to worry her.

'Finish your wine, then we'll go see.'

'Go see what?'

'Finish your wine.' She complied; it fitted in with the evolving wildness of the evening.

When she lowered her glass Imbarin's expression was just regaining focus, presumably after paying the bill. 'Right,' he said, standing up, 'let's go.'

'Go where?'

'To experience the fruits of victory for ourselves!' He took her hand and pulled her to her feet, then swept her out of the restaurant.

She couldn't remember the last time anyone had touched her like that. She grasped his hand hard in return. Should she interweave her fingers in his?

She told herself to get a grip, and not on his hand. 'Where are we going? I need you to tell me.'

'We're going to meet a Sidhe.'

THE ECSTASY OF OBEDIENCE

Bez stopped dead, pulling her hand free. 'No! Absolutely not. Never. Are you *insane*?'

'They've been haunting you for too long. You've just admitted that something unpleasant happened to make you what you are. Now you're finally winning it's time to face your fear.'

That last comment reminded her of her old shrink, back in her youth when ThreeCs were intent on keeping her stable enough to be of use to them. 'There's a reason I'm scared of them, Imbarin. Those stories about how Sidhe can twist your mind, make you kill, or die? They're not just stories you know.'

'I know. Believe me, I know. But this one's no threat. She's been sedated ever since she was captured, not to mention being restrained and kept under guard. I've waited for this moment for a very long time. I'd like you to share it with me.'

When Bez still didn't move, he turned to face her, taking both her hands in his. 'Please,' he said.

How could being touched be so damn distracting? She had a stupid urge to lean in towards him. Two nights back, she'd had the data nexus dream, and the face that had triggered her orgasm was not Tand's, but Imbarin's. Looking back on her recent actions, she saw her foolish desire to go to Xantier unprepared as an unconscious attempt to escape his orbit. And since she had resigned herself to staying here on Tarset with him, she had felt an enervation beyond that resulting from the culmination of her mission. If her body had its way, she might end up having sex with Imbarin Tierce. 'I'm not comfortable with this,' she said, aware of the layers in that statement.

'I know. But you'll be safe. I promise.'

'Let me think about it.' The shock had gone some way to sobering her up, but she knew her judgement was still impaired.

'I understand your reaction, but she won't be here long. The prisoner is passing through en route to a Commission hearing.'

'I had no idea they'd started!'

'Hers is the first.'

Despite herself, Bez was intrigued. 'Really? Who is it?'

'Utenia Mandrew.'

'Target416.' That made sense: Target416 was local, and had a long charge sheet. 'That's great.' She looked it him hard. 'And why in the void's name didn't you tell me about this earlier?'

'I only just got confirmation myself. Listen, Bez, she's only on Tarset for a few hours while she changes ships—'

'I still don't see why we have to see her at all.' Just knowing she was on the same station as one of the Enemy made Bez's skin crawl.

'Because you need this. I need this. And I'm going to eyeball the bitch whether you're there or not. But if you do bug out now, I think you'll regret it.' He leaned closer. 'Come with me, Bez. View your vanquished enemy from a safe distance, and know that you – that we – are going to win.'

'I ... all right. If you insist.'

'I do.' He leaned forward and planted a quick, confident kiss on her cheek. 'You won't regret it.'

The Sidhe was in a custody suite on the docks. There was a reassuring level of security in place although Imbarin's ID opened every door, and he got Bez through those checks her current persona might fail. She even endured a body-scan, although Imbarin had a brief word with the officer wielding the scanner, and he stopped at neck level.

Finally they were shown into a small, bare room with a one-way glass panel in the wall. On the far side of the glass was another room containing a medical gurney with a figure strapped to it. A stocky-looking figure in uniform stood off to one side. Bez, unwilling to look directly at the Enemy, focused instead on the guard. She was young, her uniform ill-fitting and her unruly red hair crammed under her cap, but she wore a hard, determined expression.

As Imbarin strode up to the panel, the officer who had accompanied them said, 'Wait! That guard!'

Imbarin turned to her. 'What about her?'

'The Commission sent a Levy-trained guard with a high mental resilience. It was a man, an older man.'

Bez, still looking into the other room, saw the young guard raise her gun. She tensed, thinking she was going to shoot out the glass, but then the tip of the gun jerked upwards. There was a flash, and the lights in the other room went out.

'Fuck!' Imbarin sprang back from the window.

'Sirrah,' cried their guard. 'Stay here, please. Everything's under control.'

Imbarin was already pushing past Bez.

The guard said, 'You can't go in there!'

'I can,' said Imbarin. Even as she turned to follow, Bez wondered at the slight emphasis on the 'I'. Bez and the guard followed him at a cautious distance. Imbarin pointed at the door to the holding cell. 'Open this, please.'

'Sirrah, wait! Reinforcements are on their way.'

'This door is kept locked, yes?'

'Yes. As soon as the pair arrived, we locked them in as per the Commission's orders.'

'Then either your older Levy-man has magically turned into the young woman who just shot out the lights, or *this cell is not secure*. Now open the damned door!'

The guard still hesitated.

'The longer we stand here, the longer that Sidhe agent in there has to help her mistress get free. Open the door and give me your weapon.'

'Yes, sirrah.' The guard stepped past them, thumbed the door control and looked into the scanner.

As the door slid open Imbarin turned to Bez, saying emphatically,

'You should run now.' Then he took the guard's proffered gun and rushed into the room.

The traitorous guard stood by the gurney, but she was already turning as Imbarin entered, her own gun raised. Imbarin moved fast and low; the shot zipped past him – and past Bez. Even as fear froze her, she heard their own guard curse.

Imbarin squeezed off a casual shot at the Sidhe's guard without slowing down. The diminutive woman ducked and ran straight for him, head-butting him in the gut. Something small went flying.

Bez stood transfixed by the unfolding scene. Imbarin moved with the confidence of someone used to combat, but the woman fought with mad passion, and she was strong and fast. The pair rained blows on each other, neither giving ground.

It would be a good idea to pick up the gun.

What gun? thought Bez, even as her eye fell on the object near the head of the gurney. *Ah yes, that gun.*

She was two steps into the room before her conscious mind put in an interrupt. This wasn't right. She looked around, confused. Then she did something she regretted for the rest of her life: she looked directly at the figure on the gurney. The Sidhe was a dark shape in the half-light, but her eyes glittered. No, they *shone*, bright as any suns.

Everything fell into place.

Bez experienced an enormous rush of wellbeing. Her life would make sense, and be complete! All she had to do was just—

<Pick up the gun.>

As she bent down the contact faltered and somewhere in another dimension the real Bez started screaming. Then she was standing up, gun in hand, mesmerised by the twin suns of the Sidhe's eyes.

<Wait for my command.>

She raised the weapon slowly, simultaneously entranced and repulsed at the inevitability of her actions.

<Now.>

She had practised using a gun, learning the basics in case she ever needed them. She had never shot a living being before.

There ... A *hiss-pop*, and the taller of the two shadowy figures fell to the ground.

Deep inside a voice called out, *Imbarin!* But the cry was drowned by the ecstasy of obedience. She had done what was asked of her and all was well.

The shorter figure disentangled itself and hurried to attend to the Sidhe. Bez also went over, delighted to be allowed closer. The Sidhe reached out and grasped her hand. A sensual warmth flowed from the contact. Bez exhaled dizzily. She turned, because that was what her mistress wanted, and pointed the gun at the open doorway, ready to shoot anyone who dared show themselves.

The inner voice still howled. She ignored it, because now the Sidhe was stroking the inside of her wrist, and the arousal was moving up into her hind-brain and down into her groin. She had never felt anything so wonderful.

No one came through the door, though she could hear sounds outside; distant shouts, and the whine of an alarm.

After a short while the Sidhe moved. Bez stepped to one side, feeling the loss when her hand was released, eager to lend whatever assistance she could. The Sidhe sat up, shaking the last of the broken restraints away. She turned to look over her shoulder at the other servant; for a moment the horror was back and Bez was free to think: *The worst possible thing has happened, is happening!*

The short woman ducked down out of sight, and the Sidhe's full attention returned to Bez. All her doubts were blown away. She felt a brief stab of jealousy, knowing her mistress favoured the other above her, but perhaps now they were alone she could prove her worth. She offered the gun to the Sidhe but the mistress shook her head; she already had a weapon, presumably from the other servant.

The Sidhe came to stand in front of her and reached back to take Bez's free hand. Bez smiled to herself.

They walked out of the room together, Bez in front, the Sidhe holding her hand loosely.

A uniformed woman sat on the floor outside, legs outstretched. She had a hand pressed to her shoulder. Even as she struggled to stand, Bez felt part of her mistress's attention switch to the guard, who twitched, then crumpled over herself.

They paused before the next corner, and the Sidhe projected a wordless image of the situation up ahead: three people, waiting in ambush. She and her mistress ran around the corner, firing wildly. Two figures went down. Something stung Bez's arm. A fraction of a second later, the other figure fell.

They ran on past, now side-by-side. The Sidhe caught her hand again. The pain in her arm disappeared. For a brief moment a stray thought intruded – *I held Imbarin's hand like this!* – but it was quickly replaced by elation: *I'm with Her now; the two of us against the world!*

If only she weren't so damn tired all of a sudden. She faltered, feet dragging. The Sidhe slowed, then cursed – the first sound she had made – and let go of Bez's hand. Bez whispered urgently, 'Don't leave me!'

She sensed the Sidhe evaluating the situation, and willed her mistress not to discard her so easily. Sounds of pursuit closing in came from nearby. The Sidhe snatched the spare gun from Bez's hand and turned, not giving her a second glance.

Bez's legs buckled. She slid down the wall, forlorn tears spilling over her cheeks. To touch such majesty then lose it ... The Sidhe was most of the way along the corridor now. Bez glanced down at herself, cradling her rapidly numbing arm. The wound was small: presumably some sort of drugged dart.

Deep inside, the voice of reason was crying for attention, but she wasn't listening.

She looked up at running feet. A man, not in uniform, was moving speedily up the corridor. He had a vicious-looking gun in his hand.

The mistress hesitated at the end of the corridor; she had her back to the approaching man. Bez realised she could still be of use, and cried out. The Sidhe turned, and Bez felt a flash of triumph. She waited for the man to fall over, or turn his gun on himself. He didn't. The Sidhe threw herself to the floor as he paused to raise his weapon.

The man lowered his gun and ran past Bez. The Sidhe scrabbled up into a crouch and disappeared round the corner.

The memory of a man falling in a darkened room pressed in on Bez's clouded mind.

The stranger put on a burst of speed and hurtled round the corner after the Sidhe.

Bez blinked, strung out in a limbo between two selves: the Bez who had been – controlled, stitched up tight, always alone; and the Bez who now was – who acquiesced, who relaxed into pleasure and service and—

BLAM!

Was that a shot or an explosion? Even as Bez wondered, the Sidhe glamour evaporated. Reality slammed back into true focus.

She screamed.

She kept on screaming, as though that would expel the poison. As though she could undo the violation she had permitted – not merely permitted but *welcomed*.

It was a mercy when one of the guards ran up and shot her.

DERN
(Olympus Orbital, Ylonis system)

It was fortunate Dern knew the route from Jerine's place to his parents' apartment by heart, because today he was paying very little attention to his surroundings. Before he left this morning, Jerine had suggested he move in with her, and he had accepted. It would mean big changes in his life, and he had no idea how his parents – especially Mother – would react.

Then there was the news, also this morning, that Fera Yasmie had been apprehended trying to board a starliner. She had escaped custody three days ago, then subsequently been tracked down to the commercial docks. She had been seriously wounded during her recapture and was in a critical condition. Dern hoped she wouldn't pull through. Although the law were true to their word and hadn't released the source of the original tip-off, he'd still had to complete formal documents in relation to her initial arrest. Complete anonymity had proved impractical. For the last three days, he'd lived with the nightmare that the renegade Sidhe might turn up on his, or worse, Jerine's doorstep.

Part of him wanted to tell Jerine about his role in recent events; another part warned against it, because although he was proud of his actions, they belonged to his old life. His future was with Jerine.

If his parents saw a link between his odd question a few weeks back and current events in Ylonis and beyond, they made no comment.

Opening the door of the apartment he heard voices. He assumed Mother was accompanying her afternoon's drinking with a holo-drama until he heard her distinctive laugh. She never laughed at the holo. Surely his father wasn't home yet? Not that she laughed much with Da these days either.

Dern walked cautiously up the short corridor to the living room.

A man sat in the chair Da normally used, glass in hand, looking comfortably at home. As Dern came in, his mother gestured to the visitor, 'Ah Dern, this is Anand. He works at Starscape.'

Dern stared at the visitor, hoping he was wrong. The visitor stared back.

His mother wittered on, 'Anand and I only know each other vaguely, but he was passing so he dropped by to tell me how things are—'

Anand moved first, hurling his glass away and reaching into his jacket. Dern, used to sizing up opponents – albeit in a different arena – wasn't taken entirely by surprise.

As his mother's voice trailed off, Dern assessed what he had to hand. Anand had already drawn his weapon – a knife, not a gun, thank Adonis – but unexpectedly, he didn't go for Dern. Instead he stepped sideways, towards Ma. He reached her before Dern could react. Dern's mother shrieked and flailed. Her drunken panic gave Anand momentary pause. She fell, smashing the fragile table next to her seat.

Anand stood over her and addressed Dern. 'Now I'm going to take away what *you* love. Then I'll kill you.'

As Anand bent towards Ma, Dern grabbed the vase from the table beside the door, and hurled it. The vase wasn't as aerodynamic as a ball, and Anand was partially in cover, but his opponent wasn't moving and the gravity was constant, which were two advantages over the terceball court. The vase hit the chair his mother had been occupying moments before, and smashed. Fragments of glass flew up. Anand staggered back, slapping a hand to his face.

Mother began to crawl off, barking out small noises of panic.

Anand looked at her, then wiped blood from his cheek and rushed at Dern.

There were no other vases within reach, nothing else to use as a weapon. Dern, his mother's cries in his ears, ran forward. After

270

all, he thought absurdly, a good team member can block as well as throw.

When their bodies impacted, both men paused for a fraction of a second, winded. For the first time Dern felt fear; the man's actions, his eyes, his whole being, had an air of repressed insanity. As Dern tried for some sort of hold on his opponent, he wondered if every Sidhe thrall went this crazy when they lost their mistress.

Something pricked his leg, but he ignored the pain and, getting a hand free, landed an inept punch on Anand's neck. Anand grunted but didn't let go. Instead he hugged tighter. Hot breath and warm spittle hit Dern's cheek and his ears were filled with his opponent's laboured breathing. At least Anand had dropped the knife. Without it, they were evenly matched.

Dern glimpsed movement behind his opponent. A fraction of a second later there was a nasty thud. Anand tensed, then slumped. Dern pulled back as the other man slid to the ground.

His mother was holding up that awful metallic statuette of Dern as a young boy that she kept in the niche behind her chair. She looked down at Anand, who wasn't moving, then gave a short, hysterical laugh, dropping the statuette. Dern heard it hit the carpet.

The sight of blood on Ma's face turned Dern's stomach. 'Are you all right?' he asked.

'Me?' His mother frowned as if the question were unexpected, then touched her face. 'Oh, that's nothing. You ...'

Dern followed his mother's gaze. Anand's knife stuck out of his thigh. Tiny rhythmic pulses of blood forced their way past the buried hilt. 'Oh shit,' he said stupidly.

His mother caught him as he fell.

He felt her hand press against his leg, even as his old coach's words rang in his ears: *The worst injuries are the ones you don't feel at the time, son.*

'I'm calling for help, Dern. You just hang on, you'll be fine.'

His mother's eyes glazed over. Now he knew it was there, the wound's pulsing filled his entire being. Despite the pressure of his mother's hand, he could feel his blood, his life, oozing away.

'Dern! Open your eyes, Dern!'

He hadn't realised his eyes were closed, but he opened them anyway. Mother's face swam above him. 'They'll be here as soon as they can. Just stay awake. You have to stay awake, Dern. Who *was* that? Tell me!'

Talking was a lot of effort, but Ma was as insistent as ever. 'Worked for ...' Oh yes, that whole mess. No way did he have the energy to explain right now. He was beginning to feel cold; not an unpleasant sensation, but disconcerting.

'For Starscape, yes. But he knew you. Why did he attack you?'

She deserved to know. 'Check my slate. Password's *Jerine4ever* – that's ... the number four.' He experienced a brief flush of embarrassment at his sentimentality, but he wasn't going to think about Jerine now, because that would hurt too much.

'You can tell me yourself, Dern! You just have to hold on.' Then, so quietly he barely heard, she added, 'Damned low-budget medical cover! Where are they?'

'Look after Da,' he managed, though he was down to whispering now, and he wasn't sure she heard him.

His mother leaned closer. Something wet – tears? Blood? – dripped on to his face. 'You saved me, Dern. I'm so proud of you.'

Actually, he wanted to say, *I saved all of us*. But speaking was too much effort. He closed his eyes. No amount of shouting from his mother was going to make him open them again.

THE BEST WEAPON

She must remain unconscious. Awake, it would all come back and that *must not* be allowed to happen.

But unwanted images and feelings intruded:

—Imbarin, falling—

—Shooting wildly, people screaming—

—Running through dark corridors—

—Warm and mindless obedience, the deepest and most glorious violation—

That did it.

Bez opened her eyes and lunged for the side of the bed. Her stomach was empty, so she only coughed up bile. Afterwards she lay sprawled face down over the covers. There was no point moving.

Someone came in. She let them lift her and clean her. She was awake now, awake enough to check her chrono: it was three days since—

—Imbarin, falling—

She grabbed the woman who was wiping her down and rasped, 'Is he dead?'

The woman flinched, pulling away. 'I'll get someone,' she said, and hurried off.

Bez waited, trying to suppress the images playing out in her head. But oblivion wasn't going to come just because she wanted it.

Finally a man she vaguely recognised came in. 'Imbarin?' she said, her voice weak and small. Then with a start, she realised her mistake. 'Is ... what happened to Imbarin Tierce?'

'I'm sorry,' said the man.

Some part of her had been holding onto the hope that, because she was a bad shot, because she hadn't been able to see very well, that whatever else had happened, Imbarin had survived. That she hadn't murdered him.

She couldn't breathe. Then suddenly she could, but only by drawing deep aching breaths that came out as huge, bone-wrenching sobs, violent enough to tear her apart.

Hands tried to hold her down. She fought them. She lost, and got the oblivion she was desperate for.

Periods of half-wakefulness.

More stupid tears. A lifetime of suppressed emotion leaking out.

Waking began to outweigh sleeping, but that was all right. Everything had become soft and distant. Bearable. The memories were there, but somehow dimmer and less excruciating.

She registered where she was. She wondered if this was the same room in the same medical facility. Not that it mattered. Nothing mattered.

People came and went, tending her body. She let them.

Time passed. She let it.

One day, as she was about to sink back into the soft chemical embrace after a period of semi-wakefulness, she noticed someone different in the room. A man, standing at the foot of the bed. She blinked. He didn't go away.

She opened her eyes fully and said flatly, 'I killed him.'

The man answered at once. 'No, you didn't. The Sidhe killed him.'

Using me as a weapon. 'Is she dead?' He didn't look like a hallucination, but Bez was in no state to judge.

'Oh, yes.'

She had an idea where she had first seen this person. 'You killed her.'

'Yes.'

There was such finality, such satisfaction, in that tone that Bez whispered, 'Good,' and closed her eyes.

When she opened them again a few seconds (Minutes? Hours?) later, the man was still there. Feeling marginally less bemused, she thought to ask, 'Who are you?'

'I'm a close associate of Imbarin Tierce.'

Another of the local rebels. But not the one she had become attached to. Not the one she had shot. She made herself focus on her visitor. 'What's your name?'

'You can call me Arnatt.'

'He never mentioned you. At least, I don't remember him mentioning you.' She should probably be concerned at talking to a stranger like this, but, between the trauma and the drugs, she appeared to have mislaid her paranoia. Ah yes, the drugs. 'Just what have you people given me anyway? I can't feel, not properly.'

'I think the term is "a chemical cocktail".'

She snorted. He even spoke like Imbarin.

'We can reduce the dose, if you like.'

'I do *not* like.'

'That's understandable.'

'So, while what you tell me can't hurt, why don't you explain how the— the prisoner got free?' Details still nagged, puzzles needed solving. Other details, those that challenged her sanity (*You let the Enemy dominate you!*) and tore her heart out (*You killed the only person you've cared about since Tand!*), she was not going anywhere near.

'In addition to the agents we know about, the Sidhe sometimes use sleepers,' began Arnatt.

'Wait. What d'you mean, agents "we" know about? You …' Some vestige of habitual caution surfaced. 'I don't know you.'

'I realise that,' he said gently. 'But Imbarin and I shared everything. You can assume I know anything he knew.'

Bez wasn't sure how she felt about that. Then again, she wasn't sure how she felt about anything right now. 'All right. Carry on.'

'The Sidhe sometimes put individuals attuned to contact with them in failsafe positions on hubs. Most of these sleepers never get the call. This one did. Because she was attuned, the Sidhe managed to make contact with her while semi-conscious. We believe the sleeper was living as a hab-rat. She got into the custody suite via tunnels too narrow for a normal human. She's small, presumably because she originally came from a hi-gee world.

'She entered the cell through a wall panel out of sight of the guard. She tranqed him then dragged him into the ducts, where she slit his throat. We found his body crammed into a crawlspace. She gave the Sidhe a patch of strong stim, which had just started to take effect when you and Imbarin arrived. When the Sidhe sensed you, she acted.'

Bez skipped past the unbearable part. 'What happened to the Sidhe when you caught her?'

'I shot her with a monofil gun.'

'And the hab-rat?'

'We'll find her.'

Bez wanted someone to pay, wanted to see justice done. 'She deserves to die.' Bez was shocked at this new emotion, this hot desire for vengeance; such strong feelings chipped away at the careful chemical calm. 'I want to sleep again now,' she said.

'Of course.'

The next time she awoke, some of the fuzziness was gone. For the first time she considered her physical state. She was unharmed, so presumably she had only been shot with tranq. Then again – she checked her chrono – eight days had passed since the Incident. She tuned out and took a shallow dip into the local infoscape. Everything appeared to work, although the drugs dulled her mental reactions.

When a medic next came in with food Bez asked why they had reduced her dosage of sedatives.

'Because we're in the business of healing people, not letting them wallow in their pain,' she said primly.

'What if I *want* to wallow?' she asked.

More gently, the medic said, 'See how you go, all right?'

She ate the meal, insisting on feeding herself. Then she blinked herself virtual and accessed her datadrops. She was curious how the quiet revolution she had initiated was progressing without her.

Arnatt arrived while she was checking her messages. She banished her overlays and said, 'Have you caught the hab-rat?'

'Not yet, no. She's not a priority.'

'What is?'

'Finishing what you started.'

'And how is that going?'

'Not as well as it could be, frankly. We need you back, Bez.'

'Don't call me that. You're not Imbarin.' Damn: saying his name actually made her throat close.

'No, I'm not. But I share his vision. Your vision.'

'I've done my part. It's happening. Happened, possibly.' She had earned a few months of medically supervised drug abuse. *And maybe, one day, I'll manage to forget what She made me do.*

'It *hasn't* happened. We haven't won. And I'm not sure we will. Not unless we can take down ThreeCs.'

'Target Zero,' she breathed to herself bitterly.

'You called her that because you suspected she's the most important single Sidhe in human-space. You're right. We've removed about a third of them; a few dozen others have fled. But most of the Sidhe infiltrators remain untouched. They haven't given up. And they won't, not while they have someone in an unassailable position of power who can facilitate secret communications. If we're to stop them regrouping, we have to take out Merice Markeck.'

'Don't you think that if I had anything on her I'd have used it by now?'

'I'm not talking about having her arrested.'

'Oh.' In her current state it took Bez a moment to catch his meaning. Then she said, 'I'm not an assassin. If you know someone who can kill her, why don't you just send them in?'

'Because it's not just about killing her. If, as we believe, she is coordinating the Sidhe fightback, she's going to be in possession of vital data: codekeys, details of Sidhe agents, beevee logs. We've taken this as far as we can with the intel we have. If we can get hold of that additional data, we can follow up on those Sidhe who have escaped so far.'

This enticing possibility had occurred to Bez, but she had discarded it as impractical. 'She's not going to store such sensitive data anywhere easily accessible.'

'True, though it won't be in her head, so we can get to it.'

'They don't use neural implants, do they?' Bez had surmised as much; presumably headware interfered with Sidhe abilities.

'No, they don't. There's another reason we need that info: as well as making sure the remaining Sidhe stay united, she can use her position in ThreeCs to gather intel on *us*. Specifically on our agents, and actions.'

'I'm careful with my messages, Arnatt.' But he had a point. If you had full access to all the corroborating data, any message could eventually be traced back to its source.

'I know, and it'll take her a while, but the time will come when she can turn the tables on us. Given the choice between waiting for the Sidhe to take out your agents, and getting the data you need to neutralise more of theirs, which would you choose?'

'You know the answer to that. But it isn't that simple. That woman is one of the most important corporate executives in human-space. We can't touch her, and we have no means of accessing any data she chooses to keep offline.'

'It's not like you to give up.'

'How dare you!' Fury at the man's presumption cut through the chemical haze. 'I don't even know you. Don't assume you know me.'

'Sorry. You're right. But just think about it. Please.'

'All right. Now kindly go away.'

She did think about it. If nothing else, Arnatt's proposition distracted her from the constant replays of Imbarin's death.

He commed the next morning, initially making polite enquiries about her health. She ignored them. 'All right, what's your plan?'

'My plan?'

'I assume you have one. One that includes me.'

'It does. In short, we would make a physical penetration of ThreeCs HQ, with a view to killing TargetZero and getting hold of her secure data.'

He made it sound so simple. 'When you say "we", who exactly do you mean? Are you intending to come along?'

'I wouldn't be the best choice. But there are people ideally equipped to deal with the physical aspects of the mission.'

'Bounty hunters, you mean?' Presumably if Imbarin had had access to such types, Arnatt did too.

'Actually, I was thinking of Jarek Reen and his crew.'

'What?'

'Well, you've met them. Him, at least.'

'How do … what makes you think that?'

'You had a meeting with him here, on Tarset, about a year and a quarter ago.'

A meeting she had gone to considerable efforts to keep secret. 'And if I did?'

'You both came out of it alive, which implies you trust each other. We also believe you've been in contact since. To be honest, we'd assumed he was part of your plan, even if he didn't make the news.'

'He was, originally.' The comment slipped out before she could stop it.

'And?' prompted Arnatt. 'What happened?'

'I didn't like the company he was keeping.'

'You mean Nual?'

'You *know* about her?'

'Oh yes. We know about her.'

'So why are you even *suggesting* I have anything to do with Captain Reen?'

'Nual's a rebel, Bez. In some ways she – and her companions – are the best weapon we've got against the Sidhe.'

Bez said nothing. When Captain Reen had tried to convince her that the Sidhe he travelled with was a friend, he could have been under Nual's direct influence. But there was no way Arnatt could be. His organisation knew of the alleged Sidhe renegade and apparently agreed about her status. And nothing Bez herself had found out actually pointed to Captain Reen being an agent of the Enemy. She had to acknowledge she might have been wrong.

'Bez?'

'I told you not to call me that.'

'Sorry. Will you at least talk to him?'

'We didn't part on the best of terms.'

'He strikes me as a pretty forgiving type.'

She nearly said, *But I'm not*, then caught herself. This wasn't about her. She could not let a previous mistake jeopardise future success. 'I ... maybe. If you think his people are the best choice for this.'

'They're the only choice.'

Bez thought for a moment, then said, 'All right.'

PREDICTABLE GRACE

It took Captain Reen a week to arrive, after she had summoned him using protocols she had never thought to use again. While she waited, she started weaning herself off the sedatives and mood-lifters. Not entirely, though: after a lifetime avoiding mind-altering substances, she allowed herself some leeway, especially given the alternative. She had no desire to experience fits of listless crying or to see Imbarin die whenever she closed her eyes. Given the choice between breaking and cheating, she chose to cheat for now.

She moved back to the apartment Imbarin had secured for her. She continued to monitor the progress of her plan, tweaking where she could, feeding through additional intel to those agents who were continuing the fight. Although belief in the Sidhe was gaining momentum, the Enemy themselves were proving elusive. Arnatt was right: the final outcome was balanced on a knife-edge.

When the *Heart of Glass* arrived in-system, Arnatt organised a privileged link into traffic control. She waited until Captain Reen was forty minutes out from Tarset station: close enough to avoid signal-lag but far out enough that if the conversation went badly, his permission to dock could legitimately be revoked.

Against her instincts, she made the call with full holo engaged. Usually she avoided such overt contact, but she wanted to see his face.

He took a while to accept the call and when he did his expression was one of bemused surprise. 'Bez? I assumed you'd want to meet in person with the usual, uh, precautions.'

She said quickly, 'I owe you an apology.'

'An apology? You mean for running off like that on Eklir?'

'Yes.'

He shrugged. 'Well, yeah. Apology accepted. You've realised I'm not your enemy after all, then?'

She nodded tersely. 'Yes. I was wrong.'

'Would you like to tell me what changed your mind?'

Bez thought for a moment. 'No,' she said. Then added, 'Not yet, anyway.'

'Fair enough.' He smiled his irritatingly engaging smile. 'Listen, I – we – wanted you to know how impressed we are. No, impressed isn't the right word. Amazed.'

'Amazed? By what?'

'Bez, all we've ever managed to do is trash a couple of Sidhe ships, and that was essentially self-defence. You took out their entire fucking network! Most of it, anyway.'

Bez felt the unaccustomed pull of a smile on her face. 'That was always the intention.'

'Yeah, well, I'd drink to that if I had anything appropriate to hand.' He made a show of looking around, then focused on her again. 'But the job isn't entirely finished, is it? Unless you only summoned us here to apologise.'

'Correct again. But first … first I need to speak to Nual.'

He looked taken aback. 'Uh, sure. If you like. I'll call her up.'

'Wait – I want you to stay as well. While we talk.'

'Whatever you say.'

He turned and shouted over his shoulder. Bez reminded herself that the *Heart of Glass* wasn't a very big ship.

While he waited for his crewmate, Captain Reen said, 'Anyway, it's good to see you again.'

She nodded, then remembered to say, 'And you.'

He stood up and his place was taken by the beautiful creature Bez had last seen asleep in Captain Reen's comabox. He stood behind her, fuzzily in shot.

'Hello, Bez,' said the Sidhe.

Bez stared at the projected figure's chin and forced herself to respond normally. 'Hello.'

'What can I do for you?'

'I wanted the first time I talk to you to be ... like this.'

Nual gave a faint smile. 'Because my powers won't work over a com, you mean.'

'Yes.'

'A reasonable precaution.'

Bez was also made vulnerable by their chosen method of communication. The Sidhe might have been robbed of her ability to persuade and influence, but Bez was showing herself on an open coms channel, rather than hacking or employing some other deception. The parallel stung.

Nual said, 'Did you want to ask me something?'

Bez had had plenty of time to consider all the questions she might ask this alien, but now only one mattered. 'Why you?'

'You mean, why did I rebel?' For a moment Bez wondered if the Sidhe *was* reading her, despite the distance, before deciding that, no, she was just perceptive, able to guess people's motivations in a way some ordinary humans were.

'Yes. You're ... different, aren't you? From the other Sidhe, I mean.'

'I am. As for exactly how and why, I'm not sure myself. All I know is that as I grew up I grew apart from my sisters, until one day they excluded me. They would have been wiser to kill me, but before they could I made contact with Jarek. He helped me escape.' Her smile became bitter. 'I've been doing my best to wreak havoc on the rest of my race ever since, although you've achieved more than I ever could.'

'That was a compliment,' said Bez warily. She let her glance dart up to meet Nual's eyes. They were as mesmeric as she had feared.

'It was a statement of fact.'

Bez looked away. She had proved she could deal with this atypical Sidhe. That was enough for now. 'I'd like to speak to Captain Reen again.'

'Of course.' Nual stood with predictable grace.

As Captain Reen sat down Bez said, 'I need to see you in person.'

'Just me?'

'No. All of you.'

Arnatt arranged for a hardcopy message to be handed to Captain Reen by a customs official, telling him when and where to meet her. He also arranged for the location Bez chose – a public one, in contrast to her previous meetings with the freetrader – to be under surveillance by trusted, armed guards. 'If the Sidhe tries anything, they'll shoot her,' he said succinctly.

Assuming they got the chance, Bez thought but didn't say. Instead she asked, 'Will you be around?' Her feelings for Arnatt were nothing like those she had developed for Imbarin, but she trusted him to support her mission.

'I'm afraid I have business elsewhere. But I'll keep an open com, and my men won't let anything untoward happen. Not that I think it will. Reen's as fanatical about the Sidhe as you, in his own idiosyncratic way.'

The bar she chose was relatively respectable with a rep for good live music. There was no band tonight but it was pretty full of people getting food or meeting friends for a drink. She arrived early and waited. Captain Reen turned up on time, his two companions walking a few paces behind him. He wore drab spacer's coveralls, but the other two dressed with more style; in the boy's case, conspicuously so, though given his height he was never going to be inconspicuous. The Sidhe wore dark glasses, hiding those dangerous eyes.

Reen paused, waiting for Bez to invite him to sit. After she'd done so, he squeezed in next to her. The other two slid across to the far side, Nual sitting as distant from Bez as possible.

'Order what you like,' said Bez, who had a beer in front of her. They selected from the table menu, Taro taking twice as long as the others. Bez tried not to stare at the Sidhe and to get a grip on the mixed emotions her presence was triggering.

Once the orders had been placed, Bez engaged the table's privacy screen. She had chosen this bar because its private booths employed a good range of countermeasures.

'So,' said Captain Reen, rubbing his hands together distractedly.

'Let's wait for the drinks.'

'All right.'

The drinks arrived swiftly so the awkward silence did not last too long. When the server had departed – having brought beer for everyone except the boy Taro, who had ordered some sort of ridiculous cocktail – Bez said, 'We need to finish the job.'

'Agreed,' said Captain Reen. The others nodded. 'How can we help?'

'We have to hit ThreeCs.'

'The media corp? They've taken a pretty big hit already, haven't they? They had a lot of Sidhe working for them.'

'I'm not talking about their regional offices. We need to go to Tethisyn, their home system.'

'Wasn't the Sidhe at the corp HQ arrested?' He looked over at Taro, who blinked carefully. Bez resisted the urge to smile: the boy was still getting used to his headware.

'Er, yeah,' Taro said after a moment. 'Woman called Lana Crais. She's currently awaiting trial on a shitload of offences, including ID fraud, wrongful imprisonment and attempted murder.'

'Crais was one of *two* Sidhe agents at ThreeCs' head office,' said Bez. 'The corp is sufficiently important to them that at any one time they have someone at the top, with another infiltrator being groomed to take over when she retires. It was all in the *Setting Sun* data, Captain Reen.'

'That's Jarek to you, Bez. And I'm afraid we aren't as familiar with the intel from the *Setting Sun* as you are.'

'No, I suppose not.' She had another thought. 'You didn't try to get hold of the ship's original memory-core, did you?'

'No,' he said, looking confused. 'Why would I want to do that?'

'No reason. It's not important anymore.' He did have a copy of the data, though; she could ask about that later, and restore what the Xantier rebels had taken from her. 'We need to concentrate on ThreeCs.'

'Wait,' said Taro, 'when you was on about me taking someone out last time we met, was that this other Sidhe in ThreeCs?'

'Yes. The head Sidhe at ThreeCs is probably the most firmly

entrenched and powerful representative of her race in human-space.'

'And you want us to kill her?' Taro sounded eager enough.

'Yes.'

'If she's so powerful, ain't that gonna be tricky?'

'Possibly. I have a few ideas and some inside knowledge. But I'll need you to get me there. And there's something else we have to do on Tethysin. Something I have to do, rather.'

'Which is?' prompted Captain Reen – Jarek.

'Get hold of the data we need in order to finish the Sidhe for ever.'

'You'd be the woman for that job,' said Jarek. 'So, what you need from us is help getting in, support once you're inside and for one of us to kill the Sidhe in charge?'

'Precisely. Obviously your previous debts to me would all be discharged with this mission.'

Jarek made a dismissive gesture. 'It's not about money or favours, Bez. It's ... Do you mind if I discuss this with my crew in private?'

'I guess not.' Such were the perils of working with others. 'Did you want to stay here?' She didn't like the idea of them going back to their ship and running away now they realised what she intended to do.

Taro chipped in, saying, 'I like making decisions where there's a bar within easy reach.' Jarek nodded. Nual inclined her head.

'I'll leave you to it, then,' said Bez, and got up.

She half expected Arnatt to be waiting for her outside, but he wasn't. She wandered Tarset's familiar byways, lost in thought. Although Jarek owed her, it was not a debt she could force, and the decision had to be one his companions agreed with. They were an odd trio: the trader, the boy-assassin and the renegade Sidhe. She wondered if Nual's opinion carried equal weight in their little band. Probably. However mismatched, they appeared to function as a team.

Staring unseeing into the window of a workwear emporium, she asked herself whether, if they did refuse to help, she would try to take on ThreeCs herself. The data made it worthwhile, even if she had no chance of killing Markeck. So yes, she would. Somehow.

The incoming com call was Jarek. All he said was, 'We're in.'

REMILLA
(Tarset hub)

The moment she felt the Deva die was the worst moment of Remilla's life.

After months hiding out in this alien, godless place, the call had finally come. She had gathered the materials she needed, gone into the ducts, and done the Deva's bidding.

The guard had had to die: he opposed Divine Will. She also understood why the Deva had chosen another to accompany her out of her captivity. The unwilling thrall the Deva recruited in the holding cell was unworthy, but she was also expendable. Remilla was more valuable than that.

She had revelled in the Divine connection the Deva had awoken in her, and in the glorious knowledge that she was rescuing a goddess from the infidels. Everything before – her repressive childhood in the Community and the sordid years in New Salem – had led up to this.

Then, suddenly, the Deva was gone.

At the moment it happened, Remilla was paralleling the Deva's course as best she could, scrambling through the hidden spaces behind walls and above ceilings. She was not in a position to see anything, but she had heard the fateful shot and felt the sacred connection die.

If the murdering heathens had found her then, she would have fought back with all her might in the hope they would kill her. She had wanted only to die for the Divine and follow the Deva beyond death.

But no one had known she was there: why would they, when she was in a place too small for these oversized hub-dwellers to reach? After a while, jammed in the corner of a duct, Remilla had come to her senses and fled back to her echoey lair.

None of those among whom she made her home knew she had been involved in the events on Tarset's dockside. Not that she lived closely with the other inhabitants of this dark and derelict corner of the station. Most of the time her neighbours ignored her; and the empty, crud-encrusted tank where she slept was accessed only by a pipe, which was a squeeze even for her. When she first started living among Tarset's hab-rats, the combination of her 'home defence' knowledge from the Community and her relative strength in the lower gravity had allowed her to defend herself. But she had soon realised there was a better way. She made herself of interest to the most powerful gang leader, initially just for her body – which he took more as a dare than because he wanted her, so she got a beating too – and then for her ability to go places others couldn't in order to spy on the gang's rivals and pilfer supplies from 'citizen country'. The gang viewed her as something between an indulged pet, an occasional runner and a whore of last resort, but that didn't matter. She obliged them: in return they made sure she was left in peace.

She followed up on the incident at the docks as best she could, eavesdropping on locations where such matters were discussed, peering out from her hidden perches to view public newscasts, and listening to local hab-rat gossip. In the latter case she was careful not to reveal her interest: showing you cared about something was a weakness that could be used against you. She discovered, to her fury, that the thrall recruited by the Deva had survived the incident. Worse than that, the woman was said to be in cahoots with station security. Remilla became certain that this wretched individual had directly contributed to the Deva's death. She was still perplexed as to why, when the woman and her male companion had first entered the Deva's cell, the Deva had insisted Remilla attack the man, given he had been the greater threat and therefore the more useful person to enthral. No matter: he had died. But the woman – apparently her name was Kenid Sari – had not.

Remilla also discovered that she herself was wanted as a result of the incident; they broadcast her ID, which she hadn't used for months. However, they also put out a description, which was more of a problem given her distinctive appearance. So far, no one had said anything – hab-rats generally enjoyed seeing citizens inconvenienced – but now there was talk of a reward. To be turned in by fickle allies was not the ending she had in mind.

The news from further afield was bad too. From what she had managed to glean, action was being taken against the Devas – the Sidhe, as unbelievers called them – all across human-space. The Divine spark was being extinguished, a thought which made her want to weep.

These days, Remilla spent all her free time praying. To come so close to saving a Deva, and then to be betrayed! The resulting desolation was almost enough to sap her will. Almost.

ILLOGICAL CONVICTION

'You need to see this.'

Bez blinked away her overlays. At least Captain Reen had commed her rather than just yelling down from the bridge. The curtained walls of her makeshift 'cabin' replaced the tiled newscasts – three text, one talking-head – she had been reviewing. She tried to keep the irritation out of her voice when she responded, 'What is it?'

'It's easier if I show you.'

'All right.'

She had noticed a change in the media reports over the eight-day journey to Tethisyn. The possibility that there had been a scattering of Sidhe living among humanity for centuries was now being openly discussed. A few – non-ThreeCs-owned – channels were even calling for a 'Revelation Purge'. But too many of the Enemy remained safely ensconced in their positions.

Bez pulled back the curtain to see Taro loping across the rec-room towards the galley. He gave Bez a cheery wave, then called over, 'Wanna caf?'

'In a minute,' she called back. Then added, 'Thanks.'

Taro and Nual had been polite if distant during the trip here. Nual in particular was careful not to crowd her or initiate conversation. The two Angels had spent most of the journey in their cabin. Bez avoided thinking about what went on in there. Those lurid legends of Sidhe sexual appetites were surely exaggerated. Then again, Nual could just be sleeping off the back-to-back transits.

She had a clear path across the rec-room, which made a change. She knew the crew were trying to curb the chaos that pervaded their ship, but Jarek had the ability to make a space untidy simply by walking into it.

Up on the bridge, Jarek was hunched over a flatscreen display. He straightened as Bez approached. 'Recognise that?' he said, pointing to a line of highlighted text.

'Yes,' said Bez grimly. 'I do. Are these the ships currently in-system?' She was used to seeing this sort of data in raw, not-entirely-legal form rather than laid out prettily for people – like freetrader captains – who could legitimately access port records.

'Yep.'

Bez blinked to bring up details on the ship he had indicated from her internal storage. The *Lambent Spire* was a medium-sized tradebird currently hauling an assortment of luxury goods bound for ThreeCs' top execs but it was captained by a Sidhe. 'And this is their arrival timestamp?' she asked, pointing to a set of digits.

Jarek nodded.

The ship had been in-system for two days. Looking at the location code, she realised it was on Tethisyn-Alpha right now. She swallowed and said, 'They're berthed at Port Viridian.'

'Indeed they are. Do you want to carry on?'

She stared at Jarek. 'We can't abort.' Then she added, with more confidence than she felt, 'Viridian's a big place. It's not as though they know your ship ID.'

'No, but they know me.'

'You were thinking of staying with the ship anyway, weren't you?'

'Yes. Now I definitely will. And I won't be trying to trade.' The *Heart of Glass*'s hold was half full of refined metallic components, chilled natural-reared meats and a few cases of fine wines; an odd combination, but the best cargo Jarek had been able to rustle up to provide cover for coming to ThreeCs' home system.

'Prime,' said a voice behind them. Bez turned to see Taro hovering – literally – in the hatchway up from the rec-room. 'Means I finally get a go at yer actual freetrading, don't it? After all,' he added, raising the bulbs of caf he held in either hand, 'reckon I've paid me dues as driver and bevie-boy.'

Jarek chuckled but Bez couldn't help thinking about the young man's original, darker vocation.

She didn't watch the final approach to Port Viridian.

Taro would have patched the bridge visuals through to her overlays if she'd asked, and she had been tempted. Not for nostalgia's sake: quite the opposite, she wanted to get any emotional responses to her childhood home out of the way before they could impede the mission. If that meant watching the city of crystal towers gain definition across the calm orange ocean, she would have done so, and worked through any feelings the view stirred in her. But she had something more important to watch: trash. Now they were in range of Tethisyn-Alpha's comnet, she was sorting through the thousands of channels looking for the sort of lifestyle shows her mother had so adored; vapid programming that devoured and regurgitated titbits of the lives of the rich and famous. And, sometimes, the rich and secretive. She had data-agents trawling the morass of trivia for keywords such as the relevant name and job title. Unfortunately, her own intellect was the final arbiter, so she had to watch a certain amount of dross in order to extract the few relevant facts.

Jarek was sharing the burden of viewing the mind-numbing 'entertainment', possibly to stop himself worrying about his junior partner, who was currently speaking to local officials. He had assured her, with a somewhat unconvincing grin, that Taro was quite capable of acting like a grown-up when he put his mind to it.

When Taro called Jarek up to the bridge, Bez paused the playback. Had the authorities identified the *Heart of Glass*? She was sure the ruse she had used to rename his ship had worked, but that had been over a year ago and he could have been careless since then, and revealed himself ...

Jarek came back down a few minutes later and she asked him if there was a problem.

'Nothing a bit more freetrading experience won't teach the boy,' he said wryly. 'We've put out preliminary feelers to sell the cargo – anything else would be suspicious – but Taro learned his bargaining skills in a rather different environment. He needed a bit of guidance.'

'How about the authorities? Any trouble?'

'Christos, no. We've already landed, in fact.'

As though on cue, one of the two cabin doors opened and Nual came out. Taking a moment to consider it, Bez realised it probably *was* on cue.

A few seconds later Taro floated down from the bridge. The boy used his flight implants casually; she doubted he even knew how they worked. Then again, neither did she.

'So,' said Jarek, 'everyone set?'

'I'll get my bag.' Bez fished out an inconspicuous carryall from her curtained-off space. Unlike the Angels' luggage, hers was exactly what it appeared: clothes and personal effects, suitable for the paying passenger she was impersonating.

They had already agreed she would disembark first, so she headed for the airlock. Jarek called out, 'Good luck,' and she raised a hand in acknowledgement.

Immigration took their time with her. She had been concerned they might. Port Viridian floated on a fertile, weed-locked ocean, and parts of the outer perimeter were indeed oceanic ports, but even in this busy planetary system, interstellar traffic amounted to no more than a dozen ships a week. Port Viridian might have only needed a single starport if not for the complicated logistics of disseminating different cargoes throughout the massive complex of floating hexagonal tiles. The *Heart of Glass*, with its mixed load, could have made planetfall at any of the city's three starport tiles. Jarek had wisely chosen one of the two not being used by the *Lambent Spire* – or by anyone else. As a result, the bored staff gave Bez their full attention. She was glad she had allowed herself a dose of medication before disembarking; the artificial calm helped her keep her cool.

The salty, algal tang of 'the riches of the sea', so familiar from her childhood, hit her as soon as she emerged on to the open concourse. The rapid development of the Tethisyn system in the post-Protectorate era had been largely down to its main habitable planet being one big, wet repository of aquatic protein. The world's two permanent settlements were located in stretches of becalmed deep water on opposite hemispheres, where the orange tangle of brineweed extended from horizon to horizon, further dampening the ocean swell and providing a basic foodstuff, supplemented by the myriad of animal life in the planetary ocean. The weed-and-seafood diet was one of the many things Bez did not miss about Port Viridian. Although she had expected the smell, it still set off the ghost of memory. At least the reek no longer held associations of 'home' in the way it had whenever she'd returned to Alpha during the first few years after moving out to the Tethisyn-Delta hab.

Here on the edge of the city, decadent architecture and conspicuous decoration took second place to the utilitarian functions of the twin ports, stellar and oceanic. She looked up past offices and warehouses to the clouded lavender-grey sky, pleased that she had managed to quash any uncalled-for bouts of nostalgia.

In a public convenience she changed her colouring and clothes to match the local norm. She would have liked to change to a new persona too, but this was not an option. She wondered in passing if her original, legal identity was still on record. It might be, given she had simply disappeared twenty years ago, but trying to find out would be foolish in the extreme.

She dumped her bag in a charity bin then consulted the local comnet to find the nearest tubeway station. The entrance had the archway she remembered so well, twinned green fronds coming together to form the double-T logo of Tethisyn Transport, one of a handful of nominally independent companies ThreeCs suffered to exist in their system. She selected the day-pass option and boarded the train, then settled back in her seat to tune into the local infoscape. As her consciousness rose through the glamorous virtual representation of the city's bright towers and glowing walkways, she felt a twinge of foreboding, an illogical conviction that she should never have returned.

Non-confidential schematics of the central tiles of Port Viridian were freely available; however the lack of detail and the large swathes of the map marked 'private' made this intel insufficient for their purposes. But it was a start, and the alternative, to hack directly into more sensitive datastores, was too risky at this point.

A pop-up in her overlays informed her that the train was approaching its first interchange. By now the two Angels should have disembarked from the *Heart of Glass* and be making their way to the rendezvous point. Assuming all had gone to plan with customs. She had a sudden thought, something she didn't remember anyone discussing. Too late now. Unless she wanted to break com silence she had to assume the others had thought their plan through fully. After all, despite the impression the pair gave, they were professional assassins.

She changed trains at the next interchange, blinking her overlays transparent as she crossed the central hall. The holo-ads were as intense as she remembered: husky voices whispered enticingly in her ears and the hall's six exits were all but hidden amid the welter of imagery, much of it from the latest beevee soaps or blockbuster holodramas out of Seaview City. (That name had always irritated her: of course you could see the sea from Port Viridian's sister city: it was *floating on it*!)

Jarek had timed their arrival for early evening, and the hall was crowded with workers travelling back to their homes from the port and light industry tiles at the city's edge. Bez followed the discreet arrow in the corner of her visual cortex to the correct exit and waited for the next train. She recognised one of the ads playing over the tunnel wall: the Aqua Zoo had been her favourite tile as a child; she had forever been bothering her mother to take her there, to let her swim through the enclosures containing some of Tethisyn's more manageable sealife. She had missed the Zoo desperately when they moved out-system, missed the comfort of being among incurious beings who accepted her, yet demanded nothing of her—

She jumped as the ad was eclipsed by the smooth arrival of a train. Stepping aboard, she told herself to stop dwelling on the past.

No need to change for the next three tiles, so she could start amalgamating the city plans she had downloaded with the data she and Jarek had extrapolated from the ents feeds during the flight in.

'Bezea?'

Bez's attention snapped back to the real. As she stared at the man standing in front of her, everything stopped: she was fifteen again, screwed up, hormonal and confused. 'Doctor Maht?'

'It *is* you! I wasn't sure; you've certainly changed, though your eyes are still the same, if you don't mind my saying so.'

Once, such a comment would have sustained her for a week. At the time her mother had first sent her to see Doctor Maht, to deal with her 'behavioural issues', Bez had been disdainful and angry, obstreperous as only a lonely genius teenager could be. But he had listened to her, and he was kind and good-looking. Naturally, she had developed an infatuation for him. For the first few months after she moved away, she had pined pathetically for her ex-shrink.

Right now he was the last person she wanted to see.

She swallowed and said tightly, 'You've mistaken me for someone else.'

'Uh, no, I don't think so.' He was smiling that smile, that trustworthy, I'm-on-your-side smile, and looking straight into her eyes. 'I never forget a client.'

Bez turned her head, looking for escape. She shouldered her way past the woman standing next to her, earning a sharp look.

'Bezea? Come back. I'd love to catch up ...'

She carried on, pushing through the complaining commuters, her heart tripping. When she reached the end of the carriage she paused, expecting him to come after her, but he was hidden in the crowd. The next time the train stopped, she hurried off.

She had an irrational desire to run. Instead she paused and glanced over her shoulder. Doctor Maht was still on the train, looking out through the crowd at her, his expression perplexed. She turned away, taking the stairs up to the central hall two at a time.

At the top she paused, pressing herself into a corner out of the main flow, and called up her overlays. What was the man's first name? Jio, that was it. Jio Maht was a relatively common Tethisyn name, and it took a few moments to locate the right directory entry. He was still working as a mental health professional; his office and residential address were listed, both of them on respectable inner tiles. According to his profile, he spent a couple of days a week helping out at less well-funded health centres on poorer tiles on the edge of the city. One of the clinics was nearby. So, he had been travelling home after a bit of charity work and she just happened to be on the same train. Given she used to live here, there was always a small risk of meeting someone who recognised her despite her changed appearance. It should not be an issue, unless he mentioned their meeting to someone. But then, why would he?

She decided, on balance, that this disturbing coincidence did not warrant calling off the mission. If the chance encounter hadn't been with someone she had such an awkward history with, she wouldn't have let it disturb her so.

The train with Doctor Maht on would be long gone now. She turned around and returned to the platform she had come up from.

She called up the data she needed, but kept her overlays shallow. When she made her next change she paid careful attention to the people around her. No one gave her a second glance.

The intel she was preparing still required work but her encounter with Doctor Maht had left her running late, so she banished her overlays as she came out of the tubeway station at her destination.

This tile was one of the central cluster of seven at the heart of Port Viridian, a fairy-tale world of high, bright towers linked by delicate-looking bridges; more commercial than the heart of Seaview City, but still a place where dreams were peddled: dreams, and power. The people were perfectly groomed, the streets wide and airy and paved with possibilities; even the ads were subtle enough to be more decoration than exhortation. Bez had dressed appropriately in a low-level exec's smart day suit, albeit not in the latest fashion.

She slotted herself into the polite crush of foot traffic, taking the opportunity to work on her data when she found herself on a moving walkway.

She peeled off at the appropriate side street, walking past bars providing early evening relaxation and appropriate settings for casual business deals. Between two of these establishments she paused for a momentary look around, and then, when she was sure no one was watching, she slipped down a narrow alleyway.

She came to an intersection: to the left was the back entrance of a bar where her mother, in one of her rare periods of gainful employment, had waited tables. She turned right. Twilight was falling and she jumped when she saw two figures at the far end of the alley, silhouetted against the glow of the central tile beyond. She caught herself even as the taller one of the pair straightened and said, 'We were beginning to worry.'

'I'm sorry, I got, uh, distracted.'

'Distracted?' This was from Nual, who had paused in the act of swinging a slender black case off her shoulder. 'By what, if you don't mind my asking?'

Bez did, but she knew better than to dissemble. 'Someone recognised me. Someone from my past.'

'That gonna be a problem?' asked Taro.

'I don't believe so.'

'Good,' said Nual. Someone else might have asked if Bez was sure.

'You didn't have any trouble with customs, then?' Bez addressed the question to the air between the two assassins.

'Nope,' said Taro laconically. 'The cove operating the scanner got a bit freaked at his readouts, but then Nual had a quiet word with him 'n' he calmed down real quick.'

'Won't there be a record? In the scanner, I mean.' That was what had been worrying her earlier: the Sidhe's powers of persuasion might influence a human official to forget the Angels' implants and the contents of Nual's case, but the incriminating scans were still in the system.

Nual had crouched down with the case on the ground in front of her. She looked up and said, 'He decided to delete the records then forget he had done so. There might be a problem at the next audit but we will be long gone before then.'

Bez had to admit that having a Sidhe on your side had its advantages.

Nual continued, 'I'll need a couple of minutes to assemble the gun.'

'That's fine,' said Bez, not looking at the case. 'I'm still collating my data.'

'Right,' said Taro, 'I'll keep watch.' He strode past Bez and up to the corner.

Bez retreated into her head. By the time she returned to the real, Nual was standing up again. The slender, black long-arm slung across her back looked too delicate to cause the kind of damage x-lasers were reputed to be capable of.

Taro padded back; he moved pretty quietly for someone of his stature. 'You got some plans for me, then?' he said.

'I have, but bear in mind that I've had to employ a degree of extrapolation.'

'Did you want more time?' asked Nual. 'We can wait.'

Bez wished Nual wasn't being so considerate. It was disconcerting. She debated taking a last look through the ad hoc database she had constructed from the lifestyle programmes combined with the legitimately downloaded city plans, but she was confident she had got all she could. 'No, I'm ready.'

'Is it like you remember?'

She looked up at Taro's question. 'Port Viridian, you mean?'

'Yeah. Yer home city.'

'Yes. It is.'

'Ain't it odd to be back? I mean, you moved away when you were, what, fifteen?'

'Fifteen, yes.' Despite some emotional issues, that had been a good year, the year she became the youngest person ever to gain a place on ThreeCs' prestigious 'R&D FastTrack' programme. The necessary move to Tethisyn-Delta – or 'Cryptoball', as some of her peers disparagingly referred to the home of ThreeCs' Secure Communications Division – had not been one her mother had welcomed, though she had been happy enough to live off her daughter's generous grant. Was her mother still on Delta? Was she even still alive? Bez decided, on balance, that she didn't want to know.

'Bez?' She focused on Taro again. He gave an awkward smile. 'Lost in the past, eh?'

Bez cleared her throat. 'I'm ready.'

'Let's do it.' He came to stand in front of her. Bez had to crane her neck up to meet his eyes. It had been years since she had prac-tised such open datasharing, and it made her feel exposed. Taro's inexperience – it took four attempts to blink their overlays into sync – didn't help. Finally she managed to transfer the annotated plans of the city's central tile to the boy's headware.

Looking over at Nual she was momentarily confounded to find that the Sidhe had partly disappeared. Then she registered what she was seeing: Nual had donned her mimetic cloak, another item in the Angels' arsenal. Taro began shaking out his own cloak.

'There's no air traffic out there right now,' said Nual. 'Shall we go?'

Bez looked across the water at the jewelled wonderland of Port Viridian's central tile, known simply as Central by the city's inhabitants, most of whom would never set foot on it. She walked up to stand next to Nual, and said again, 'I'm ready.'

She flinched at Nual's touch but didn't pull away. A moment later, Taro took her other arm. She hugged herself to give the pair a stable hold, trying not to think about the close contact and whom it was with. Had there been any other way, she would have taken it, but the tubeways and airbuses into ThreeCs' corporate heart employed stringent ID and weapons checks, and the few private aircars in the city were strictly for the elite. At least no one was going to expect them to arrive this way.

'Here we go,' murmured Nual.

The Angels lifted off slowly, taking Bez with them. They had already practised carrying her in a short flight around the *Heart of Glass*'s rec room but she still froze, animal terror getting the better of her as they rose the three metres over the plexiglass wall edging the tile. The drop down to the shadowed water on the far side was higher because the tiles rose proud of the sea by a dozen metres. The dark line of a tubeway floated half out of the weedy surface; in the fading light, the caging that kept the tube from getting tangled in the brineweed was invisible.

The Angels accelerated hard. In the relatively clear water beside the tubeway, Bez glimpsed a turn and flash of scarlet-and-gold, like a living string of lights, there then gone. A glowstinger, probably. She tried not to think of the infinite sky above and the deep ocean below. At least the repulsion fields on the undersides of the tiles and tubeways deterred the larger and more vicious sealife.

Halfway across, the Angels jinked to the left, making a subtle but firm course change. Given neither had spoken, Bez drew the obvious, unpleasant conclusion as to how they coordinated their actions. She squeezed her eyes shut, willing the flight to be over. A few moments later she opened them again; they were descending, coming down to land in the mouth of an alleyway just inside Central's outer wall. Bez exhaled as her feet touched the ground.

The Angels stepped back to let her stand. Her legs hardly shook at all. The alley walls were stacked with shadowy shapes: bins, trolleys and other maintenance equipment.

Taro said, 'Can you do the hack from here?'

'It's as good a place as any, provided no one disturbs us.'

Nual said, 'No one will.'

Bez decided not to consider the implications of that assertion. Instead she tuned out of the real.

Most hubs sexed up their virtualities, adding colour and flash both to help in navigation and to further glamorise the alternate reality. In the heart of Port Viridian, the glamour was already there, notwithstanding their immediate surroundings. The crystal towers were somewhat brighter and more translucent, but other than that the change was seamless. Her experience of going virtual in Port Viridian was limited: she had still been too young for full implants when she left, and her youthful exploration of the info-scape had been on outer tiles.

Now, with two decades of databreaking experience, Bez knew the right path almost instinctively. She took her awareness down, as she had on Xantier. This time she was not looking for secure transactions but basic ones, the unseen parallels to the grubby alley where she was physically located. A brief memory intruded: aged fourteen, she had considered the very hack she was about to perform; then it had been an act of rebellion, a daydream of vengeance against the uncaring world. Not something she would ever have dared actually to *do*. Whereas now it was a prelude to far more drastic action.

The system was simple enough; there was protection, but nothing compared to the sort she habitually defeated on financial systems in the hubs. She bypassed the security, found the correct virtual switch, and flicked it.

Blinking herself back into the real, she heard a faint rising tone singing through the air.

'I'm hopin' you did that,' said Taro.

'I did.'

'And they'll definitely believe it's the real deal?' Taro's face was indistinct in the twilight but he sounded young and uncertain.

She resisted the temptation to snap back that she would never have suggested this plan otherwise, and instead said, 'If a pod of megafins did get through the under-shields then chewed their way up through the weed and decided to have a go at your tile, you'd want to be in the core shelter.' A wildlife invasion was only one possible emergency, but faking a storm – the most common cause of an alert – was not feasible. There were also other reasons for alerts that rarely made the news: civil unrest, lone loonies and violent protests. And right now there were a lot of paranoid people in ThreeCs. 'No one takes chances with a shelter warning,' she concluded.

Taro took her arm and Nual came round to her other side. As they got into position Bez asked the boy, 'You're clear on where we need to go?'

'Got it netted,' he said. 'Here, mind if I tuck this in? Help keep us out of sight.' He pulled the edge of his cloak round, stuffing it down between her arms and her chest. Bez endured the intimacy, reminding herself that it was a necessary precaution.

They took to the air.

FAR FROM DEFENCELESS

They rose up the outside of the nearest tower. Although shelter warnings were rare, the possibility of such excitement in this superficially tame and boring environment had perversely delighted Bez when she was a child. Whenever her tile held its annual shelter drill, she had experienced a secret thrill at this tiny bit of – ultimately safe – uncertainty and adventure.

They needed to get further in, which involved flying directly past the homes and offices of some of the most powerful people in ThreeCs. She reminded herself that it was dark, that they were camouflaged with stealth technology and that, with an alert in progress, no one should be looking out of windows anyway. She saw signs of movement – figures inside apartments, lights going off – but no sign of panic. People might assume it was a drill but they would still head for the core, or face a fine from the city authorities.

Despite his assurances that he knew where he was going, Bez was following Taro's chosen course on her headware. At one point he took what she thought of as a wrong turn. She bit back a comment; a few seconds later he corrected their course. Bez concentrated on staying silent and not looking down. The Tethisyn indulged the human foible of equating height with power, and some of the structures on Central reached up for over half a klick.

They were coming up on TargetZero's apartment. There were lights on but the shades were drawn. Every window was closed, as were the sliding doors leading on to the balcony.

In Bez's ear, Taro muttered, 'All locked up. Bollocks.'

'It was always a risk,' whispered Nual, presumably for her

benefit. 'Bez, we're going to put you down on that balcony to your left while we break in.'

Bez blinked for data on the apartment the Sidhe had indicated, but her information was too sketchy. 'Wait—'

'It will only be for a few seconds. I can't use the gun while I am holding on to you.'

Bez swallowed. 'All right.'

The balcony Nual had chosen was dark, the door open a crack. Bez was so busy trying to work out if anyone was inside that she failed to see the plant stand in the corner. She ran into it as she stumbled out of the Angels' grasp; the pot of foliage rocked then fell with a crash.

'Shit!' muttered Taro. Nual had already flown off.

Taro put himself between Bez and the door, facing the apartment: covering her. Despite expecting the light to come on and someone to rush out at any moment, Bez's gaze was drawn to where Nual must be. The Angel showed as a patch of uncertain shadow in the night, hovering outside TargetZero's balcony. A thin rod emerged from the shadowy form. Bez thought she heard a faint sound over her racing heart, something between a sizzle and a hiss. There was nothing to see: the gun fired coherent light beyond the visible spectrum. Then the gun-barrel disappeared again, and the shadow rippled, coming towards her.

The apartment behind remained dark. This time when the Angels gathered her up Bez all but threw herself into their grasp.

They ferried her across to TargetZero's balcony. As they landed Bez was careful to watch where she put her feet.

Nual's gun had cut an inverted U-shape into the glass of the balcony door. The cut itself was barely visible but it was picked out by damage to the hanging blinds behind, which had a neat arch cut out of them.

Taro stepped up to push the glass in, just as Nual hissed, 'Wait!'

They paused. Nual frowned and muttered, 'There are two people in there.'

Taro turned to her and whispered, 'People as in …?'

'Just humans.'

'Can you show me where?'

Nual nodded. Taro put out a hand, which she caught in hers. Both Angels went silent and still.

Bez had almost got used to working with the Sidhe, but the easy intimacy she showed with Taro turned her stomach.

A moment later Nual let go of Taro's hand. 'They're in the office,' he whispered.

'Can you tell what they're up to?' Bez asked, doing her best to remain calm.

'Not from here,' said Nual. 'If I had to guess I would say our target has her suspicions about this alarm and has left a couple of expendable staff behind just in case.'

Bez had to accede to Nual's knowledge of Sidhe psychology. 'You said they were in the office. Given she doesn't have any head-ware, might they be copying or even deleting incriminating data from her deskcomp?'

'That is a possibility.' She turned to Taro. 'Can you deal with the opposition so Bez can get to the data?'

'Sure,' said Taro laconically.

Bez could see Nual's logic: if Bez had to choose one of the assassins to stay with her, it wouldn't be the Sidhe.

'Then I'll hit Markeck alone.'

'How you gonna find her? I got the plans.' Taro tapped his head.

'Show me what I need to know.' Nual stepped close again, this time taking both his hands. Bez counted ten frantic heartbeats before the Sidhe stepped back. They paused for a moment more, hands still clasped. Then Nual turned and leaped into the night.

Taro grinned at Bez. 'Knew I shoulda borrowed Jarek's needle-pistol.'

'You haven't got a gun?'

''Fraid not. The more shit we tried to smuggle in, the harder it'd've been for Nual to make sure no one rumbled us. Don't worry: I'll improvise.'

Bez reminded herself that, even without visible weaponry, Angels were far from defenceless.

'Ready?' said Taro. When Bez nodded he pushed gently at the cut section of glass. It fell neatly onto the carpet on the far side. Taro went first, cloak pulled tight, stepping to the side as he entered.

'All clear.' Bez jumped at his voice in her head, then reminded herself that, along with the map, she'd given him her preferred com channel.

'Coming,' she sub-vocced, and followed him in. She noted in passing how thick the glass was: only the best and most secure for those living at this elevation.

'Stay behind me,' murmured Taro, unnecessarily. This room was the lounge; as Bez expected, Taro moved through the open arch into the dining room. Then, assuming her plans were correct, there was a short corridor leading to the apartment's on-site office. She tensed as Taro opened the door, but the space beyond was empty. He stopped just inside the corridor, and pointed to a spiral shell on a stand; soft light emanated from the shell's pink mouth. 'That ain't gonna bite me, is it?'

'Er, no,' said Bez, bemused. Her mind was trying, irrelevantly, to identify the species of sea creature that had been so tastefully converted to a lamp.

'Good.' Taro picked up the shell, hefting it to judge its weight. He paused outside the office door. Then, in one movement, he opened the door and bowled the shell in, low and fast. Thanks to his cloak, all Bez saw were his feet and the shell appearing from nowhere.

Then even the feet disappeared as he drew them up and took flight. He pushed the door wide and flew in, no more than a faint disturbance in the air.

There was a *swish-thwack* sound. A woman shrieked, the sound cut off with awful suddenness.

A thud, then a grunt. Was that Taro? What if he needed her help? Bez looked around frantically, as though lethal and easy-to-use weaponry might suddenly materialise next to her.

Someone laughed – that *was* Taro – and she heard another swish. Something fell heavily. There was a burbling squeal.

'All clear,' came over the com. Taro sounded surprisingly calm.

Although Bez expected the aftermath of violence, the scene in the office still shocked her. Taro was leaning over a figure lying face down beside the desk in a pool of blood. He was wiping his blade on the figure's back. A man sat up against the wall, hands pressed to the gaping hole in his neck. His eyes were open and his legs were twitching. Blood welled out from between his fingers; from the look of the impressive spray across the pale carpet, he wouldn't be alive for much longer.

Taro looked up, silver blade snicking back into his forearm. 'Sorry 'bout the mess.'

'I just need ... to get to the desk.' Being so close to violent death was making her guts heave.

'Sure, I'll er ...' He looked at the body at his feet, his expression mirroring some of Bez's disgust, then bent down and pushed it out of the way. It was a woman, and like the man she wore a dark uniform, somewhere between that of guard and servant. Bez was glad of the colour; it didn't show the blood. When Taro rolled the body over, the mixed stench of urine, faeces and warm blood grew stronger. Death really did have a smell all of its own. Bez pressed her hand over her mouth.

The desk had all the functionality any top exec would require, but as Bez had expected, the indentation for TargetZero's personal slate was empty. She would have that with her.

'Least we got a gun now.' Bez looked over at Taro, who had picked up a small pistol, presumably from the hand of the other guard who had, mercifully, stopped kicking and gurgling.

She lowered her hand. 'You take it. I ...' She gestured at the desk.

'Yeah. Sorry.'

She wondered if the guards had had the opportunity to raise the alarm. It was unlikely. Even if they had, Markeck would be most of the way to the shelter by now. She blinked up an overlay image from the spotcam Nual wore on her collar. Bez hadn't explained why she wanted to witness TargetZero meet her doom. Perhaps Nual had, through some combination of intuition and unholy talent, worked out that this was a matter of personal vengeance, but Bez no longer cared. She just needed to see Merice Markeck die.

Nual was still flying through the residential district. Bez minimised the overlay.

Rather than dive straight into the personal system of her ultimate Enemy, Bez did a visual check of what she had before her. The deskcomp appeared to be on standby, at least as far as an unenhanced observer was concerned. Presumably the dead servant had been interfacing directly via headware. In theory, given Taro had surprised her, the system should still be wide open.

Her minimised view of Nual's progress showed a brightly lit, clear-walled passageway far below. Bez maxed the image. Every tile had evacuation channels like this one, sloping gently downwards from multiple levels to allow residents to reach the shelter at the heart of the tile as quickly as possible. In Bez's old home they had been crowded during drills, but on Central, with a permanent population of fewer than two thousand, the emergency passages were almost empty – this one entirely so. Nual turned, simultaneously losing height, checking back along the passage. There were figures there, and for a moment Bez's heart leapt. But Nual was presumably able to see – or otherwise sense – that this was not her target, for she turned and flew further in, her course paralleling the passage.

Bez attempted a low-level interface with the deskcomp. Her progress was blocked with the red *access denied* icon every databreaker knew all too well. Damn. TargetZero's servant must have had time to lock the system. She would have to hack it.

As she activated her full databreaking suite Bez kept half an eye on the feed from the spotcam. There was another group of figures in the tunnel ahead. A long way ahead: Nual needed to hurry. As though sensing Bez's urgency (which, Bez decided firmly, she couldn't), the viewpoint sped up.

Bez's virtual sortie failed. More than that, the icon remained constant in her vision. That was odd: she had the best tools available and even if they weren't up to penetrating the system security, she expected enough feedback on the fail-points to allow her to hone her attack. Then again, the information on this system could bring down worlds. Naturally Markeck would have applied the best possible encryption.

Bez devoted a few seconds to calling up some of her more militant virtual weaponry, routines that mimicked truly destructive and virulent attacks. Once she unleashed them, she would need to watch carefully or she could end up trashing the very info she was trying to retrieve.

She paused and changed focus: Nual was closing in on the fleeing party, who had slowed to deal with the shallow steps at the passageway's steepest point. There were half a dozen uniformed figures clustered around a smartly dressed woman. From behind, her dark curls bobbed as she descended the stairway.

To Bez's frustration, Nual paused. Then a slender black barrel swung into sight, held loosely in front of the assassin. Nual carried on, hurrying to overtake the group below. Bez would have been happy for her to take the shot then and there, but she acknowledged that they had to be sure. Nual and Taro had both studied publicity shots of Merice Markeck, though Bez liked to think ThreeCs' Director of Corporate Strategy would not be looking quite so suave now.

Nual passed the group, getting a little ahead before she turned. Bez saw TargetZero's face, distant but familiar.

The viewpoint halted, the gun sweeping up into Nual's eyeline in one smooth motion. Bez clenched her fists, waiting for the perfect, awful moment.

Nual failed to take the shot.

'Kill her! Kill her now!' Bez was vaguely aware of speaking out loud.

Nual lowered the gun.

Bez howled. Nual hadn't been able to do it, hadn't been able to shoot one of her own! *Damn her to the void, the Sidhe had betrayed them after all!*

'It's not her!'

Bez looked round wildly at Taro's shout. 'What?'

'Nual says ...' He blinked hard, his expression simultaneously vacant and intense. 'She reckons that's some sort of double; she looks like Markeck, but she's an ordinary human.'

'But – where's the real TargetZero?'

'Nual thinks she's still—'

The door burst open.

'—*here!*'

THAT SPACE IN MY HEAD

Jarek was pondering the relationship between friendship and respect.

He had immense respect for Bez. She was a genius, and had devoted her life to the cause they shared. But she was not someone he considered a friend. She was too distant, too asocial. In some ways she reminded him of the Consorts. She had the same other-worldly outlook, the same obsessive interest in matters normal mortals failed to see the significance of. He didn't dislike her. He just didn't want to be trapped in a confined space with her for any longer than necessary.

Having said that, she'd changed since the last time they met. There was a fragility, a humanity about her that hadn't been there before. As a result, the journey to Tethisyn had been less stressful than expected.

He wondered if the mellowing of her character was related to the allies she had mentioned. She had let slip that she had a contact on Tarset who was helping her. Apparently he had provided a haven she considered safe – no mean feat – and had even taken part in ongoing operations against the Sidhe. Exactly what part, she refused to say. But Jarek had his suspicions about Bez's new-found friend. A powerful man who knew all about the Sidhe: that sounded awfully familiar. Not that he'd say anything to her until and unless he had enough information to be sure—

His com chimed. The caller was listed as a Frex Drelle, company name Bluewater Imports.

Jarek was torn: he was meant to be lying low, but he had already revealed that the *Heart of Glass* had someone on board besides its nominal owner when he'd corrected Taro's attempts to list their cargo as open commodities – not something you did on a corporate world unless you wanted to be ripped off. And the quicker they sold their trade goods, the sooner they could make a speedy and inconspicuous exit.

Jarek answered. 'Can I help you?'

'Good evening. Who am I speaking to, please?'

'Amad Kelsor.' That was the name of a fictitious business partner briefly associated with the *Heart of Glass*; he doubted this trader would have the inclination or means to check his story.

'Well, Sirrah Kelsor, I'm interested in some of your cargo, specifically the meat and wine.'

'Both rare items here, I understand,' said Jarek, falling back into freetrader banter.

'There's always a market for such goods, yes.'

'Given you've gone to the effort of contacting me outside normal office hours, I'd say quite a lively market.' Jarek had already done a quick survey, and he'd been pleasantly surprised by the kind of prices being quoted for the 'luxury' part of his cargo.

'I prefer to discuss specifics in person. Could we maybe meet up for an informal chat?'

That wasn't an unusual request; such business was often conducted face-to-face, where the parties involved could assess each other as they bargained. 'Normally I'd agree but I'm not currently in a position to leave the ship.'

'Is there another member of your outfit there, someone else who could meet me?'

'Unfortunately, that's not convenient just now. Perhaps if you come back first thing in the morning?'

'I'll be frank, Sirrah Kelsor: there is a lot of interest in your cargo, especially the meat. It's been a while since anyone brought in any plains-reared fleshstock.'

'Which is why I decided to ship some.'

'And given you don't have much to sell, no doubt you will be holding out for the best deal. That's why I wanted to make contact with you promptly. I would be happy to buy you dinner while we discuss what I can offer you.'

'Thank you, but as I say, I need to stay here.'

'Then perhaps I might visit you on your ship. I could bring some bluefin sashimi and weedwine: not as rich as the fare we would be bargaining for, but a token of Tethisyn hospitality.'

The man was certainly persistent. To refuse would be suspicious, and Jarek's experience and instinct said this was a genuine offer. 'All right. Just give me a while to get a few things sorted here.'

'Would an hour be enough?'

'That'll be fine.' An hour would be long enough to take precautions – hopefully unnecessary ones.

Even as the word left Taro's lips, Bez was already diving from her chair. A shot zinged overhead.

She landed behind the desk. With something solid between her and the Sidhe, she risked a glance to the side. There it was: the door to the executive gym suite that lifestyle holo had mentioned. And it was ajar. She smiled.

The smile died when she saw what Taro was doing. He stood, swaying on his feet, staring out into the room with a glazed expression. As Bez watched he turned – awkwardly, slowly, inevitably – towards her hiding place.

TargetZero was going to use the Angel to kill her. She had to get to that door. But everything was moving too slowly, her body lagging behind her will.

Taro lurched towards her in a jittery shuffle, jerking his gun up as he moved. He was blinking rapidly, his face shiny with sweat.

She was going to die like Imbarin had, only knowing what had happened. In some ways that was worse.

Her world narrowed to the barrel of the weapon pointing at her. Behind it, barely in focus, Taro was trying to speak, his mouth working in comical exaggeration. Finally, he rasped out one word:

'Run!'

Then, like a spring released, he pivoted round to fire at Markeck.

Bez didn't wait to see if he hit her. She bolted through the door.

The room beyond was unlit and filled with odd shapes, presumably gym equipment. She avoided the large treadmill but failed to see a loop on the floor, which caught her foot and almost tripped her. While she was still trying to get control of her adrenalin-wobbly legs, someone grabbed her arm and a familiar voice said, a little breathlessly, 'Wanna try that "Run" thing again?'

She nodded and let Taro half drag, half guide her through the room of shadowy obstacles. She dialled up her visual acuity; the confidence with which Taro was moving implied he could already see in the dark.

The darkness suddenly diminished; someone had opened the door to the office. Bez tensed, ready to sprint for it, but Taro hissed, 'Here!' and pulled her down behind a rowing machine. She wanted to obey his first suggestion, and keep running.

'There's three of them, but I reckon I got one,' he whispered. 'I think Markeck's sent in the other guard an' gone round to flank us.'

Bez called up the apartment layout. The boy was right: if the Sidhe went back out into the corridor and along towards the kitchen, she could get between them and the front door. 'So what now?'

'I sneak back towards the guard. You stay here, then when I com you, run across an' hide behind that thing with the pedals. Make as much noise as you want.'

'You want me to be your *decoy*?'

'Got a better idea?'

She didn't. 'All right.'

He slid away, melting silently into the gloom. She concentrated on trying to breathe as quietly as she could.

'Now.'

At Taro's relayed whisper Bez forced her rubbery legs to move, stumbling across to the piece of gym equipment he'd indicated. She tried to shout but only managed a sort of strangled squeak.

The hiss of a silenced shot came from across the room. Then Taro's murmur in her ear: 'Got the fucker.'

The lights came on.

Bez ran back towards the office. Somewhere in the back of her mind was the thought that although Markeck might believe she was cutting them off by getting between them and the apartment door, she wasn't, because they hadn't come in that way.

Taro was crouched over a body sprawled in the doorway. There was no blood.

He handed her a small, compact gun, then pulled his cloak back round himself and stood up. 'Let's go,' he said.

Bez took the weapon. It was a dartgun, probably only firing tranq: easier to procure than lethal weaponry, and ideal if you wanted to capture someone alive and question them.

The office was empty, save for Taro's two original victims. 'Shit,' breathed the Angel, 'must've missed that first bastard.'

So: one guard and one Sidhe to go. 'What's your plan?' hissed Bez as they ran out into the corridor.

'Stay out of Markeck's way until reinforcements arrive,' Taro said grimly.

'But you resisted her!' Now she considered Taro's actions, Bez was amazed: she would never forget how utterly the Sidhe on Tarset had subjugated her.

'Yeah, well, that space in my head's already taken, ain't it?'

Bez supposed it was.

Taro continued, 'What d'you reckon: bedroom or through the diner?'

'Back the way we came.' Not that she could escape that way: it had taken two Angels to fly her here. But it beat running towards the Sidhe.

They ran through the dining room and into the lounge. Taro hesitated, looking towards the door to the kitchen; Bez carried on, towards the balcony. 'Bez, wait! You know I can't carry you!'

Her options had narrowed: die, or kill. Try to kill, anyway. No choice, really, not with TargetZero. 'We can set an ambush on the balcony. She'll know we're here, but the blinds'll hide us visually so she'll have to come out to get us.'

Taro thought for a moment then said, 'Right you are.'

317

Bez stepped over the glass; Taro followed close behind. Once out on the balcony she broke left; he went to the right.

'You stay there, close up against the window,' said Taro, moving towards the balcony rail.

'Wait—' He was going to fly off. Not that she blamed him.

'I ain't leaving.' He gave a low chuckle. 'Jarek'll have my balls if I come back without you. Nah, we just need to set up a crossfire: you're on the inside, I'm on the outside.'

'Of course. Sorry.'

Bez raised her weapon. She was shaking so much that, small though the gun was, she had to use both hands to steady it.

A figure burst through the door. Bez fired, pressing the trigger convulsively, once, twice, three times. She had no idea if she hit anything. The figure faltered, slammed into the balcony rail, then bounced off, falling towards the hazy space where Bez had last seen Taro. She heard a soft impact, saw vague movement.

Someone else came through, moving with far more control. Bez knew who it was even before Markeck turned and focused on her. Bez squeezed the trigger but her aim was wild and the shot went wide. Then the Sidhe's will reached out to her: Bez reacted to the instant compulsion to drop her gun but the connection was fleeting. She backed away, looking around frantically at everything except her Nemesis.

On the far side of Markeck she glimpsed a pair of indistinct figures struggling on the floor. Bez was sure the Angel could beat Markeck's guard, but by then it would be too late. It would only take a moment for the Enemy to ensnare her.

Now her choices had changed: be dominated, or flee. No choice, really, even though there was only one place left to run.

The balcony's railings were ornamental as well as functional, constructed of the organic curlicues Bez always associated with Tethisyn-Alpha architecture. Markeck reached for her, but she was already leaping for the railing, propelled by a fear greater than that of death. Her left foot lodged in an ersatz metal frond halfway up the barrier. She grabbed the top of the railings with her left hand, right arm flailing.

The Sidhe advanced. Her face, mercifully, was in shadow. In a voice of silk and honey she said, 'We can discuss this rationally, you know.'

For a fraction of an instant Bez almost acknowledged the sense of the Sidhe's words. Then in her mind's eye she saw Imbarin, falling.

She threw herself off the balcony.

Her left foot caught, and she pivoted as she fell. Something in her leg went *crack*, even as that same leg was brushed by a fleeting, glorious touch. Not enough to hold her. Not enough to stop her.

I'll die free.

The thought had barely begun to form before someone grabbed her. *Markeck!* She tried to fight her off, then realised she was mistaken and relaxed. She was still falling, albeit more slowly. More slowly because …

Everything jumped into perspective.

It was Taro. He was trying to save her, the foolish boy!

In his efforts to slow their descent, he had got underneath her. She found herself facing upwards, looking at the distant figure leaning over the balcony. Abruptly Markeck's head disappeared. A moment later something warm and wet spattered Bez's face.

She was too busy being terrified to work out what had just happened. They were still falling, faster all the time. She wondered vaguely how fast: perhaps she could calculate the impact speed before they hit? No, she knew the approximate height and local gravity, but not the extent to which Taro had slowed her fall. Not enough, if the way the walls were rushing past was anything to go by. Would the boy let go in time to save himself?

His grasp tightened. Apparently not.

But that wasn't Taro. She felt the other presence, another body supporting her, wrapping itself – herself – around her. The rush of scenery began to slow.

The screaming wind abated as they decelerated. She could hear the Angels' harsh breaths in her ears.

Individual features sprang into focus: signs, windows, external lights. They were almost at street level. She closed her eyes.

The landing sent spikes of agony through her leg. She tottered and fell backwards. She gasped, winded, then opened her eyes wide to the vision of shining crystal towers stretching up into a purple-black sky.

IMPRESSIVE CARNAGE

Bez decided to stay where she was for now. When Taro bent over and asked if she was all right, she waved him away.

Nual came into view, crouching down beside her. 'We need to go back for the data.'

Ah yes, the data. 'But the Sidhe—'

'She's dead.'

Bez remembered the soft, warm rain. She sat up abruptly and began scrubbing at her face.

Nual continued, 'Can you stand? Your knee—'

'My knee?' She lowered her hands then made the mistake of looking down. 'Oh.'

'You're in shock, so you aren't feeling it yet. We don't have a med-kit and although I could solve the problem myself' – Her gaze flicked to Taro – 'that is not an ideal solution.'

Bez raised her gaze and wiped her hands firmly down her flanks. 'There'll be medicines in the apartment,' she said.

'Good idea. Here, let us help you.'

Bez didn't object. They had to complete the mission. She did ask, as Nual and Taro were getting into position ready to carry her, how come Nual had failed to spot Markeck was still in the apartment.

'She hid her presence, and that of her close bodyguards,' said Nual. Then she smiled nastily, 'I did the same, just before I killed her.'

'So she suspected a trap and set her own?'

'Precisely. It appears we underestimated her paranoia.'

By the time the Angels had flown back up to the apartment,

Bez's knee had started to send out tendrils of pain. They landed carefully. There was no avoiding Nual's handiwork. Markeck's body lay sprawled across the balcony. Her head was missing. Blood, tissue and bone fragments were spattered in a wide radius around where it had once been, including up the walls and across the glass door. Apparently the x-laser's reputation for being able to literally blow a person's head off was no exaggeration.

Bez could put off her physical reaction no longer. Taro held onto her while she threw up. If he objected to getting vomit on his boots he didn't say. After all, they both had worse on them already.

Once she had retched herself dry, the Angels picked her up and flew her over the impressive carnage on the balcony, then through the apartment to the office. When they reached it, the scene inside looked almost tame in comparison.

'I'll go and find something for your leg,' said Nual after they had lowered her into the office chair. Taro stayed; he didn't need to, and Bez had work to do, but she found herself unexpectedly glad of the company. Before she turned her attention back to Markeck's deskcomp she asked, 'Out on the balcony, after I jumped: why didn't you just go for TargetZero? She couldn't control you, and you had the weaponry to take her out.'

'Because then you'd have fallen and died,' he said.

Bez nodded, as though it really were that simple, and turned back to Markeck's comp. When her more measured attempts still weren't getting anywhere, she wondered about the Sidhe's slate. She probably still had it with her, and it might have less security on it. She was about to ask Taro if he minded searching Markeck's body when Nual returned with a small box. 'It's an all-purpose trauma splint,' she explained.

'With painkillers?' Bone-scraping agony was a distraction she couldn't afford.

'Yes.' Nual crouched down beside her. Bez winced as the Angel pulled away the shreds of torn fabric from her knee. The act of easing the flaccid split kit around her leg set off whole new cascades of pain. 'Sorry,' said Nual, 'I need to position this correctly.'

'Just ... hurry up, please.'

'Right, I'm done. Are you ready for me to pull the tab?'

'Oh yes.'

For a moment the agony spiked, as the splint inflated and pressed on her shattered kneecap. Then her whole leg went cold and wonderfully numb.

'Are you getting anywhere with the comp?'

Bez focused on Nual. 'Actually, no.'

'Ah.'

'What do you mean, "Ah"?'

'I know this is usually your area, but do you mind if I have a look?'

'If you like.' Bez eased her chair back, careful of her splinted leg.

Nual leaned over and tapped a couple of keys. A menu screen came up.

'What did you do?' she asked.

'Touched it. I've seen this before: some Sidhe genelock their tech.'

'Genelock?' Bez had heard of such measures, but genelocking was tricky, expensive and, in many systems, illegal. Also, it tended to be for a given individual. 'How come you can access it?'

'It's specific to Sidhe gene-markers, not to a specific individual. In theory, any Sidhe has access to any other Sidhe's knowledge – and thoughts. We're big on unity.' Nual's voice was heavy with sarcasm. 'You should be able to get around the system now; once they've unlocked their tech, they tend to let their minions do the actual work.'

As Nual moved back, Bez asked a question that had been bothering her for a while, but which she hadn't felt comfortable voicing before now. 'What are the Sidhe? Your biometrics – the ones Jarek gave me to get your false ID – they're human, right down to the signature sequence.'

Nual shot her a wry sideways smile. 'It's a good job the Salvatines got their own way. If it was acceptable to hold complete genetic profiles for everyone, I'd never pass for human.'

'So Sidhe are mutated humans?'

'Yes. They diverged from humanity several millennia back.'

Bez digested this. She couldn't decide whether being not-truly-alien made the Sidhe better or worse. 'Is that why they didn't just leave us alone after the Protectorate fell? Did they feel ... some sort of kinship?'

Nual laughed, an unexpectedly light and carefree sound. 'Not exactly. The Protectorate was accurately named: the Sidhe genuinely believed – and still believe – that their destiny is to shepherd the poor, unfortunate lesser race.'

'I never thought about it like that.'

More quietly, Nual said, 'When humanity turned on them, it made the Sidhe reconsider. But they stuck to their principles. Even after the combination of monomaniac vision and limited resources led to stagnation, my people kept the faith.'

'Yet you rebelled.'

'Yes,' said Nual. 'I did.' She straightened. 'I'll leave you with Taro now. I need to sort out some loose ends.' By which she presumably meant those of Markeck's servants who had only been tranqed, not killed outright.

After she left, Bez said to Taro. 'And you, uh, love her?'

'More than life itself.'

Bez turned back to the deskcomp. That, at least, made sense.

Now she had access, Markeck's system was easy to crack. And there was so much here.

She only spotted the com call because it was in the 'recent activity' file, and she was curious about TargetZero's final actions. She scanned the file while downloading a listing of Enemy agents in this sector. The message was voice only, and if she hadn't spoken to him recently she would never have recognised the caller as Doctor Maht: *Merice, this is probably nothing, but you remember that hacker girl from a couple of decades back that you said might not be dead after all? Well, she isn't: I just saw her on the tubeway; I think I spooked her. I thought you should know.'*

That explained their reception. She considered keeping quiet about her findings, then decided not. She'd tell her allies later. Right now, she had a rich seam of compromising information to mine.

'Er, Bez.'

She glanced up. Taro stood next to her, looking vaguely apologetic. 'Yes?'

'Don't wanna disturb you but Nual needs to know how much longer you're gonna be.'

Bez checked her chrono: she had been in Markeck's system for eighteen minutes. 'Is there a problem?' Given that none of the night's mayhem had taken place anywhere public, and the original alert was over, she had not seen any reason to hurry.

'No problem,' said Taro, 'Nual just wants to know whether she needs to keep the servants under for longer.'

'Wasn't she just going to ... finish them off?'

'Nah, far better to plant a few false memories then let 'em loose. That way, the authorities'll be looking for a gang of local coves.' Taro raised his gaze, as though conjuring facts from the air. 'They were dressed as ThreeCs security but probably weren't, and they surprised Markeck on her doorstep, made her go back in, trashed the place a bit and knocked out her guards; they must've killed her with some sort of explosive round to the head.' He looked down at Bez. 'Somethin' like that.'

Bez could see the logic of this. 'If I can have another fifteen minutes, I'll have cleared the system out.'

'No worries.'

Bez wasn't sorry to have two fewer lives on her hands.

The *Heart of Glass*'s external cameras showed a man matching the publicly available holos of Frex Drelle. He was approaching the ship's airlock carrying some sort of covered tray. He appeared to be alone.

Taro had just commed to say they were about to leave the target's apartment. Jarek considered stalling his visitor, but to turn him away now would sour any possible deal.

Jarek threw himself out of his chair and hurried down the ladder. His com went; Sirrah Drelle was formally requesting permission to board. He ignored it for a moment while he double-checked the set-up in the rec-room. Then he went to stand at the end of the corridor to the airlock; the only other door off that corridor led to the ship's cargo bay, and that was locked. A glance at the cam feed on his com showed movement outside the airlock, but the angle of the camera and the tiny screen didn't give him much to go on. It could just be his expected visitor. Jarek ordered the corridor lights up full, then answered the call. 'Come on in, Sirrah Drelle.'

The airlock didn't need to cycle so it opened immediately. Jarek thought he caught a glimpse of something or someone behind the man standing there. He tensed.

Drelle smiled broadly and advanced into the corridor brandishing his tray. 'As promised, some light refreshment.'

And there she was, flitting out of the open 'lock like a shadow, still partly hidden behind the grinning merchant. *I fucking knew it!*

Jarek turned on the spot. He'd paced this out, calculating his moves exactly. The first part of his plan, to run, required no effort. Sidhe generally had that effect on him.

One step. Two.

He heard a noise of masculine surprise: the kind of sound a man might make if his host suddenly turned his back on him ... or if someone unexpectedly barged past.

Three, four steps.

A crash, as of a tray falling to the floor. Everything was simultaneously too fast and too slow.

Five, six.

And now the tricky bit. There was plenty of debris on the rec-room floor to choose from, but he'd selected something soft when he walked this through; a black, narrow-brimmed hat that Taro thought, incorrectly, looked pretty stylish. All his pursuer would see was a small dark obstacle which—

—he tripped on.

He didn't fall flat: that would be suicide. He ducked and rolled, just like he'd practised. The impact still winded him. No time for that, keep it fast and smooth; either panic or hesitation would be fatal.

He rolled to the side, half sitting up as he did so, risking a glance back in passing.

The Sidhe had reached the corridor, no doubt eager to get control of the situation – of him – before he fled into cover.

One of the trickiest elements of the plan had been deciding where to put the gun. He'd tried wearing it on his hip, but there was a risk of losing it when he fell, and not being able to draw it quickly enough after he landed. Instead he'd left it on the floor, among the other mess, exactly where he expected to fall. And had fallen. His hand closed on the butt of his pistol.

If the Sidhe had a gun too, he was screwed. But why risk smuggling weapons through customs when you can disable or even kill with your mind?

He looked at her.

That act took considerable willpower, overriding instinct and bitter experience, but when he saw the Sidhe's face he knew at once that his plan had worked.

She was confused. And unarmed. Her fiery gaze had absolutely no effect on him.

Jarek shot her.

A needle-pistol was a less extreme weapon than the Angels' laser, but at close range it still made a nasty mess. The shot caught the side of her face, slicing off skin and flesh in a rain of accelerated micro-projectiles. The Sidhe shrieked and threw her hands up. Jarek fired again, because when it came to the Sidhe, you didn't take chances. The second shot turned her chest to bloody pulp. She span and fell.

Jarek began to laugh, not caring what his other visitor thought.

Bez had had enough of blood for one day; perhaps for one lifetime. Jarek had cleaned the worst off the rec-room floor by the time she and the Angels got back to the ship, but she still got a whiff of that too-familiar smell, the same for Sidhe as for true humans.

She looked over at the stranger sitting at the galley table. He shot back a look of naked curiosity. Jarek had said it was all right for them to come aboard, so she wasn't going to let the presence of a bemused local merchant get between her and the medbay. Jarek was probably assuming that if the man gave them any trouble,

Nual would simply edit his memories. Bez no longer found that idea as appalling as she once had.

'I want to see the body,' she muttered to Taro, who was currently acting as her crutch.

'Don't you wanna get that leg seen to?'

'Yes. But I have to do this first.'

Taro helped her to the hold, where Jarek had bagged up the body of the Sidhe. Bez knew who it was and, though she had wanted to see the evidence, she had no intention of actually opening the bag. Target204, solo freetrader, thirty-four years old ... She called up the full file, which confirmed that this wasn't someone she would otherwise have got. Jarek had been rash to take on one of the Enemy alone – even with his secret weapon – but after her experience on Tarset station, Bez understood his reasons. He too knew what it was to be enthralled by a Sidhe. And with the Sidhe in human-space about to go on the run, taking out their freetraders was a priority.

Bez looked over at the comabox with the Consort in. It was still in the corner of the hold nearest the rec-room. According to Nual, the three of them had carried out extensive research to determine the exact range at which a Consort could nullify a Sidhe's power. Jarek had had to partially wake the boy to utilise his abilities, but he was safely back in stasis now.

'I'm done here,' she said to Taro. He supported her while she made her way out of the hold.

Back in the rec-room the merchant was discussing the current market in fresh foods with Jarek. Apparently he might buy their cargo. Bez glanced at Nual, busy deploying the medbay's foldaway bed on the far side of the room. Apparently he might even do so of his own volition.

As Bez let the Angels ease her onto the bed, the hapless trader was saying, 'I'd heard a bit about recent events elsewhere – not officially, you understand, ThreeCs haven't been reporting it, for some reason – but it never occurred to me that I'd actually meet a Sidhe! I mean, it's unbelievable.'

'And she convinced you to come here without you realising you were being compelled to?'

'Exactly! That's the worst part: I really thought it was just a good idea to trade with you; I had no conscious thought about the involvement of ... that person.'

'And do you still think it's a good idea to trade with me?'

'Well ...' The man sounded embarrassed.

'I'd be willing to give you a very favourable price.'

'Thank you. It's just ... all this ...'

'Yes, most irregular. Presumably you were logged coming through customs, so if anything odd *were* to be reported ...' Bez got the impression Jarek was enjoying himself.

'I've certainly no desire to involve the authorities. In fact, I was wondering about the, the body—'

'This is a water planet with, I believe, quite a lot of carnivorous wildlife.'

'Ah. Yes.'

'So, then, shall we open negotiations?'

'I can certainly discuss the purchase of a percentage of your cargo.'

'Excellent. If you're over the worst of the shock then perhaps you'd like to open that bottle you brought.'

'Excellent: you're not limping.'

'I'm fine. The knee's almost healed.'

Arnatt still insisted on moving the seat back for her. Bez wanted to be annoyed, especially given this was just a dockside bistro and not some smart restaurant, but instead she found herself amused. The more she got to know Arnatt, the more he reminded her of Imbarin, with his wilfully eccentric mannerisms and sardonic view of life. When she'd pressed him, he had admitted they were distantly related.

'Sorry I haven't had time to meet you in person for a few days,' he said. 'Been busy.' Arnatt was on Tarset's Board of Directors, and hence more actively involved in running the station than Imbarin had been.

'That's fine, you don't have to buy me dinner now.' He had also been busy when Jarek and his crew had dropped her back at Tarset last week. Given he considered Jarek such a useful ally, Bez found Arnatt's tendency to avoid him rather odd. Or perhaps it wasn't Jarek Reen but one of his companions that was the problem. That he avoided Nual implied Arnatt had something to hide, but Bez was satisfied that on the important matter of the Sidhe he could be trusted.

'It's no trouble.'

She and Arnatt chatted as they ate, going over recent developments in the ongoing fight.

Markeck's files had provided a whole new network of Enemy agents whose names Bez was in the process of disseminating to the relevant parties, supplemented by the recovered *Setting Sun* data.

Meanwhile, more Sidhe were going to ground, disappearing before human vengeance caught up with them. Some would escape via the surviving Enemy freetraders, but at least they would be out of human-space. Bez found herself wondering at the symbiotic relationship between human and Sidhe. Nual had said the Sidhe were trying to save humanity from themselves, and it was true that some of what they did – such as the creation of transit-kernels – was in humanity's interest. Bez had broken that symbiosis and her actions would condemn the remaining Sidhe to a slow and lingering decline. She was not as pleased with that outcome as she expected to be.

Today's big news was the Commission's announcement that they intended to investigate ThreeCs. Bez could see the battle between the two great powers running and running, but she didn't greatly care; without any direct Sidhe influence, ThreeCs was no longer a threat. The events she had initiated had already moved beyond her control.

Bez only realised as she finished her spiced rice that they hadn't engaged the table's privacy screen, a lapse that would have been unthinkable a few months, even weeks, ago. Then again, if the other patrons worked out what they were talking about, then rather than considering them insane as might have been the case until recently, they would probably congratulate the two of them for their pivotal role in uncovering Sidhe influence.

Arnatt ordered a dessert; Bez didn't, and as he ate she said, 'I'm thinking of leaving Tarset.'

Arnatt swallowed, and raised his eyebrows. 'Is it something I've said?'

'Of course not. I'm just not used to staying in one place for this long.'

'I realise that. But you have everything you need here.'

'Yes, I know and—'

'Is this about credit?'

'Frankly, yes. I'm grateful to you for honouring Imbarin's wishes and continuing to provide an apartment and beevee access, but my personal funds are about to run out.' She had decided to keep her promise to Imbarin and not do any financial hacking while on Tarset. But she had no intention of living off charity either.

'But you would come back here?'

'I ... well, yes, obviously I'd come back here some time.'

'I meant to stay.'

'Stay?' She looked at him hard.

'I was thinking of offering you a job.'

'A job?'

'I know you can live off your wits, but I'm guessing that you've been justifying your career as a data thief as a means to an end. And one day, in the foreseeable future, that end will, um, end.'

Bez glanced around at his tactless comment, but no one was paying attention. 'Your point is valid,' she conceded softly. There was also the matter of the other hub rebels. They had turned a blind eye to her more dubious activities when they served the same cause, but might not be so forgiving now.

'In that case, I might be able to put a word in. Correct me if I'm wrong, but your background is in cryptology, isn't it?'

'Yes.'

'Obfuscating or illuminating?'

'What? Cryptography originally.'

'Excellent. I think that when you're ready, a post can be found.' He went back to his meal.

'Thank you,' she said, somewhat to her own surprise.

'Not a problem,' he said, through a mouthful of compote. 'I like having you around.'

By the time they left the bistro, Bez was giving his offer serious consideration. Back before she gained possession of the *Setting Sun* data, she had never considered what her future might hold after her mission was complete. Looking back she now saw that she had perhaps expected to die trying to bring the Sidhe down. When the memory-core had fallen into her hands, she had acknowledged the possibility that she might not only win, but survive; that there was an *after*. Getting the Sidhe ID data had confirmed that possibility. And now it had come true.

Up until now, she had assumed that once she had done all she could, she had two choices: to settle down and retire using her remaining funds, or to carry on databreaking and travelling. The former would require picking the right persona – the Estrante ID would have been a good one – and might involve the kind of luxury she found annoying. Certainly there would be a risk of boredom. The latter was neither morally defensible nor, given the power of the hub rebels, advisable.

But she had worked as a cryptographer once, and enjoyed it. Perhaps she could take the job Arnatt was offering on her terms, with scheduled time off to visit other hubs and planetary systems of interest. Travel wasn't a habit she wanted to break. But she had already begun to think of Tarset as home. She felt comfortable here.

Not that Tarset was everybody's idea of a pleasant place to live, as was proved when they reached the main concourse and saw that one of the elevators was out of order, yet again.

Arnatt mimed an exasperated sigh and rolled his eyes theatrically as they stood in the grumbling crowd. Bez remembered waiting at this very spot, all those months ago, with hub-law. So much had changed. By the time the car finally arrived, Bez was smiling to herself.

No lovers this time, but the car was crowded. Bez tolerated the press of humanity with equanimity.

More passengers got on at the upper concourse, but as the car rose through the station it began to empty. One of those who got on after her was a stockily built child, travelling alone. Bez was uncertain of its sex as it wore a heavy coat and hat. Presumably some parent had told their offspring to wrap up when travelling through the hub; though if they cared that much, why weren't they with it? Bez suddenly found herself considering children as something other than small and unpredictable humans. As something, perhaps, she could let into her life. That was a shocking idea: shocking, but not entirely unthinkable. She already had one legacy, unseen and abstract. How would it be to have living descendents? How would it be to give love to someone who gave unquestioning love in return? Perhaps she should start with a pet—

Something smashed, a dissonant, unexpected *ksshckt*.

Even as she jumped, yellow vapour billowed up from the floor. On the far side of the car she saw that the child had lost her hat. Except, this was no child. Bez recognised the face, the unruly red hair. The Sidhe sleeper agent. Even as the shock hit, the girl's face creased in pain and Bez's throat began to burn.

The lift stopped. Bez waited for the doors to open, poised to make a run for it.

The doors remained shut. Her eyes were smarting now, but through the tears she saw the Sidhe traitor watching her even as she coughed and retched.

Every breath was agony. She made herself stop breathing, but she could still feel the corrosion burning into her lungs.

She closed her eyes, not giving up, but changing focus. Tuning out and going virtual.

The panicking passengers faded and the walls became translucent. Beyond them, the representation of the car's braking mechanism glowed red: some sort of emergency override? She was aware of another presence – Arnatt. She tried to sub-vocalise, to ask if he knew how to disengage the lock and open the doors, but even that small physical movement made her damaged throat convulse, almost dumping her from the virtuality.

It occurred to her, in a distant way, that she should be frightened. But the only emotion she felt was a deep disappointment at having been caught out so easily.

She looked further afield, searching for some virtual tool she could use, some way to escape the trap she had stupidly fallen into. Arnatt hovered beside her, his silver icon reaching out to pull data from the air, sorting and discarding.

Suddenly he stopped and turned to her. He was close now, as close as it was possible to get to anyone in the infoscape; their unseen processes meshed, disrupting each other in subtle ways. She resisted, because this was a distraction, and if they were to stand any chance of surviving the situation in the real, they needed to keep focused in the virtual, and look for a way out.

She shifted her perception, keying into the lift's surveillance. It was futile and only made the inevitable more painful, but she had to know. The feed was vid only: she could still hear the screams and cries for help through her physical hearing, but they were distant, almost irrelevant.

Her body had fallen to the floor, along with the assassin and almost everyone else in the lift. Arnatt was still half sitting up, and his eyes were open if streaming. A heavily built man was trying to force the doors. Then he too fell to his knees.

Through the yellow air, Bez saw her body twitch: despite her will, a last, desperate breath had been taken. She was vaguely aware that, somewhere deep inside, soft tissue was being burned out, irrevocable destruction being visited on flesh that no longer had a strong connection to her.

Even as she watched the life seep from her body, she clung to Arnatt's virtual presence, striving for that last shot at existence, determined to somehow persist beyond bodily annihilation, if ...

only ...

for ...

... a moment.

CHANDIN
(Cyalt Station)

This is becoming a habit, thought Chandin, staring at the box on his desk. He'd got his security people to take all the usual precautions, scanning the package for explosives, drugs, nanites, the works. He had also tried, without much expectation of success, to track down the source of this apparently anonymous delivery. Somewhat to his surprise, the item had come through a partially traceable channel, via the courier company Hawk Consignia. Unfortunately, when he queried them they said that the account that had sent the package had since been closed.

He had a good idea who it came from. Not that he had expected any further contact, given the transmission he had received six weeks ago. Then again, that had been via beevee. A physical delivery would take far longer to reach him. He was ashamed to recall his guilty relief on finding that Orb – or Orzabet or whatever her real name had been – was no longer in a position to release the incriminating material she had held on him.

When he first took the actions Orzabet had blackmailed him into, he had received considerable attention from his peers. There had been talk of a possible Oversight Committee. But the Treaty Commission was nothing if not pragmatic, and when his actions had started getting dramatic results the investigation requests had been dropped. After the ThreeCs story broke, he was given the resources to set up a dedicated subdivision.

Tanlia had been key in getting the newly formed – and, Chandin thought, rather dramatically named – Revelations Bureau off the ground. In his darker moments he almost expected to see Tanlia herself exposed as a Sidhe agent, but unless Orzabet had missed something vital, there *were* no Sidhe in the Commission, nor in any positions of power in the hubs. He would have loved to know why that was, but with Orzabet dead, he doubted he would ever find out.

The Revelations Bureau certainly had their work cut out. For every Sidhe in human-space there must be dozens of knowing collaborators and hundreds of unknowing agents. Orzabet's data – the original dataspike, the subsequent transmissions and her final, posthumous databurst – had given the organisation enough to get started, but there must be more.

Chandin would go down in history as the man who had exposed what the media had dubbed the Hidden Empire – even if most of the credit wasn't his – and he intended to finish the job. He had lived his life assuming humanity was free of Sidhe influence; he wanted to die knowing it really was. That was why, after much discussion with Gerys, they had decided to donate their second child licence to the lottery. His work was his legacy.

He opened the box. As he hoped, it contained dataspikes. Seven of them in a holder, each with a printed label: *General/Govt. 1, 2* and *3*; *Corp 1* and *2*; *Misc, inc. Freetraders*; and *ThreeCs.*

Chandin had a ridiculous desire to punch the air. Instead he lifted the first *General/Govt.* 'spike out, eager to see what he had. Given how much data a single 'spike could hold, he was going to need more resources.

Underneath the 'spike was a piece of hardcopy paper with some writing on it. He lifted out the holder to reveal a high quality printout of just three words: *Use them well.*

Chandin had every intention of carrying out Orzabet's last wish.

SO HE DOES

The reproduction is perfect, down to the sycophantic waiters and the residual sweet/sour/smooth tang of roast cherry and curd cheese on a tongue she no longer possesses.

The only anomalous detail is her dining companion. The man who sits across the table looks like Imbarin Tierce ... until he doesn't. As she watches, his face changes again, to become that of Arnatt. Before (*There was a 'before'?*) he was a stranger, though one she felt she should know. The constant metamorphosis is one clue that none of this is real. Another is her last clear memory before this current period of awareness, which is of watching herself die.

Thoughts trickle through her mind, many of them related to how come she still has a mind for thoughts to trickle through. Her ability to reason is coalescing, returning after an unspecified absence.

Imbarin/Arnatt watches her silently, fork poised above his plate.

There is only one logical conclusion. 'I've been uploaded,' she says out loud. The act of speaking feels as real as the ambience of the restaurant and the flavour of the food.

Her companion's face settles back into Imbarin's features. He smiles and says, 'Correct!' He sounds pleased, and exactly like Imbarin.

'That's not possible,' she states flatly, despite the evidence to the contrary. 'I'm experiencing continuity of consciousness.' Holodrama makers' flights of fancy and databreaker legend notwithstanding, it was impossible to upload a human consciousness into a virtuality. Memories could be stored and incorporated into limited intelligences, but the personality would be disrupted for ever. The

Salvatines were fond of citing this as evidence of the human soul. Bez briefly wonders if organised religion was on the right track after all, and this is heaven. She quickly discards the notion as even less unlikely than her original conclusion.

'I'm glad to hear it.' Imbarin raises his fork and takes a bite. Bez, by way of an experiment, does the same. The fork enters her mouth; she tastes sour cherry; she chews, feeling her jaw move; she swallows. The sensations exactly mirror those she would expect, including the sensual pleasure at the initial taste and the feel of food sliding down her gullet. She hates to imagine the kind of processing power required for such faultless emulation.

'Something like this ...' she says slowly. '...even leaving aside being ...' She can't quite say 'dead' and settles on, '... only virtual. It's impossible. All of this is impossible.'

'For humans, yes.'

She looks at him, hard. 'Who are you?'

'You can call me Tarset if you like. Unless you prefer Imbarin, or Arnatt, or ... No, you never met any of the others, did you?'

'The other what?'

'Avatars. Of my consciousness.'

'All right: *what* are you?' Bez hears the quaver in her perfectly reproduced voice.

He takes a sip of wine, then says, 'A very old mind in a very complex machine.'

Bez considers his words. Impossible, yet logical. Certain other facts fall into place. 'You're a Sidhe too, aren't you? A male.'

He raises his eyebrows. 'Very good. I knew you'd work it out.'

Should she reveal how she came to that initially unlikely conclusion? Stupid question: there is no dissembling here. 'I know about the males in the shiftships. Although ... you're not like them.'

'Not mad, you mean?'

'No.'

'That's because I – we – aren't bound into structures that enter shiftspace.'

'No ... because you're bound into a hub station instead! You really *are* Tarset, aren't you?' It's almost as though her dream of the data nexus has come true; she is talking to an individual who holds power and knowledge of that magnitude. Power enough to bring her back from the dead, then recreate reality for her.

'It might be more accurate to say that I *am* the hub-point. One of the hub-points. And we prefer to call ourselves Oberai, not Sidhe.'

'So all of the hubs are ... like you?'

'Oh yes. And I'm not merely at Tarset, you know.'

'Like that's not enough!' Just because what Imbarin – Tarset – said made sense, that didn't mean it was easy to grasp. But just because the implications were hard to grasp, that didn't detract from the wonder of it.

'It *isn't* enough, you know,' he says. 'Being restricted to one location – even an entire space habitat – isn't enough. Would you like me to show you what I mean?'

'Yes. Sweet void, yes!'

So he does.

ACKNOWLEDGEMENTS

Contrary to Bez's worldview, everyone needs support and advice, and mine in writing this book came from the patient and only occasionally sarcastic Tripod writing group, plus beta readers James Cooke, Susan Booth, Neal Williamson, Liz Counihan and Rebecca/Liz Clark. Dave Weddell was, as ever, my pillar and my foil, and Gillian Redfearn a generous editor.